FINCH MERLIN AND THE LOCKED GATEWAY

Harley Merlin 13

BELLA FORREST

Copyright © 2019

Publication place Cyprus 2019

ISBN 978-9925-7621-5-6

ONE

Finch

———————

Being in Ryann's apartment made my heart pound like a kangaroo caught in a spin cycle. Clammy hands, cold sweats, clenched throat—my body gave me all the red flags.

Plus, everywhere I looked, I faced another nightmare... snapshots of Captain Canada with his arm around Ryann, all megawatt smiles, and a couple of obligatory "funny" pictures where they'd stuck out their tongues. Not to mention Ryann's bedroom was *right there*. The sweet scent of vanilla and fake strawberry drifted toward me.

Be cool. Be cool. The Medela serum might've sent the gremlins into a coma, but that hadn't stopped my penchant for inner monologuing.

"Do you want something to drink?" Ryann called from the kitchen. Well, she claimed it was a kitchen. Honestly, it was more of a shoebox with a sink and a toaster.

"Uh... sure. What do you have?" I crossed the living room and perched awkwardly on her cracked leather couch, a remnant of the sixties that didn't look like it had been cleaned since the Beatles were at number one.

"Coke? Coffee? Some Japanese drink I don't know the name of. I think it's got bits of plants in it. Aloe vera or something."

I cleared my throat. "Coffee sounds great."

While she clattered away in her shoebox, I took in my surroundings for the hundredth time. She had another sixties throwback for a coffee table, and a TV mounted on the plain wall. Shelves to either side contained rows upon rows of books, all crammed in to resemble an overstuffed mouth of yellowed teeth. She'd added a few Ryann touches, of course: candles, ornaments, a few prints of Lautrec dancers, and miles of string lights. But she'd only recently moved in, so I guessed the apartment was still metamorphosing into an independent woman's pad.

I'm in Ryann's apartment... I'm actually in Ryann's apartment... I gulped, feeling like a fish out of water. All sense of normal human behavior had flown right out the window, leaving me no idea what to do with my various limbs. Did I cross my legs, uncross them, fold my arms, stretch out like a cat? No clue.

She'd moved out to get some autonomy from our beloved Mr. and Mrs. Smith. There was nothing like parents to cramp one's style, especially with a boyfriend. Plus, given her recent forays into the magical world, she'd wanted to keep the Smiths in relative safety. Living at home meant they could be used as potential targets... again.

Ryann came back with two mugs of steaming coffee, handing one to me. "Don't worry if it tastes a bit... uh... metallic. Apparently, it's just the way the water on this block tastes, but the super said it's completely harmless."

"Comforting." I eyed my mug warily as I set it down. I had no intention of drinking it, even if that made me a rude houseguest. "You sure it's okay for me to be here? I know you want to show off your fancy new digs, but we could've just met at a café, or somewhere in the SDC."

"Why wouldn't it be okay? And who wants to spend six bucks on coffee when you can get one for free?" She chuckled and sipped from her mug of hazardous waste.

I shrugged. "I don't know... is the boyfriend cool with this? I know I've only met the guy a few times, but I sensed he didn't like me much. Wouldn't want to cause any lovers' spats, especially involving the Boston Strangler. He might creep in my window while I'm asleep."

"Finch!" Ryann scolded. "*Adam* wouldn't mind at all. Besides, I'm not expecting him anytime soon, and he'd call before he showed up. Canadian manners at their finest."

Again, Nash's potions had dimmed my gremlin paranoia and accompanying delusions, but it did nothing for good old-fashioned nervousness about a big, buff Canadian coming in and catching me having coffee with his missus. I doubted anyone had a serum or a potion for that. Not even the Atlanteans. Speaking of which...

"So, tell me what Erebus said again," Ryann prompted, as though reading my mind. Man, I hoped she couldn't. I was still thinking about her bedroom, having caught a glimpse of her minimalist setup —grays and creams, with a battered-looking bunny toy sitting on her bed that could have been center stage in a horror movie, one eye falling out of its head and one ear barely hanging on. *Kill me now. Put me out of my misery*, it had seemed to beg me.

"Right. Erebus. Bane of my life." I sighed and pulled out my phone, pulling up the text he'd sent last night. "It says, 'Have no fear, this is not a summons yet. This is merely a forewarning of our next steps. Now that we have the key, we must open the Gateway to Atlantis. But first, we must find it.' That's all he wrote, Erebus being his usual helpful self."

Ryann took another sip of swamp water. "Have you thought any more about breaking away from your deal?"

"Whoa there, one dilemma at a time." I mustered a smile. "And yes, that's pretty much all I can think about, now that I know it can be done. But I'm not a Necromancer, and I don't know where to find Davin, so how about we focus on a problem we *can* solve?"

"Do you remember anything about the gateway on that map you drew? Didn't you take a picture of it?" Thankfully, she switched back to business mode without comment. I didn't feel like getting frustrated about escaping my servitude. Every time I thought about it, and about Davin managing it, I wanted to rip out my brain.

"You can't just take pictures of powerful magical things like that. It's warded against copies being made, as are most creations of that kind. I did try back at the Winchester House, when I had half of it redrawn, and every picture showed a black screen. Oh, I couldn't have just photocopied it either, before you ask," I replied.

She smiled. "Okay, got it, no copies. What does your memory say?"

I paused. "There was something about a Gateway between Life and Death, but Melody ran a check through her mind palace and came up with nada. That could be because it's related to Atlantis, but it could also just be a gap in the Librarian's knowledge."

"Well, fortunately for you, I believe there's no substitute for a bit of ordinary, thorough research." She leaned down and hoisted two massive tote bags onto the coffee table, which buckled under the weight. They were stuffed with books. A stale, old-timey smell wafted off them, reminding me of opening the package of a first-appearance comic.

I gaped at the bags. "Did you take these from the SDC?"

"Where else would I have gotten them?" She pointed to two more bags stowed beside the threadbare armchair across the room. "I took those, too."

"They just let you walk out with that many? O'Halloran must be slipping on his security protocols."

Ryann laughed. "He gave me permission to check them out from the libraries, actually. That's the beauty of working for Miranda Bontemps. I say it's for her research, and I get the all-clear."

"I can't believe you're still working for her after Daggerston's elite shindig," I grumbled, recalling that nasty party. At least I'd had the pleasure of guillotining Davin, even if it hadn't stuck.

"She's a victim of Daggerston's charm offensive. She believes whatever he tells her, including the lies about Davin. Perhaps that makes her guilty by association, but I genuinely don't think she's like Daggerston or Davin. So far, she hasn't given me any reason to believe otherwise," Ryann replied. "We spoke in depth about what happened that night, leaving out you, Garrett, and Saskia."

I snorted. "Let's hope she doesn't come back to bite you in the ass."

"It's on me if it does."

"I said 'she.'"

Ryann nodded. "Yep, and I ignored you." She gestured to the books. "Let's go through what we know, so we can figure out what we don't know."

"Well, Nash's blood can be used as a substitute for extinct ingredients in a spell. The spell will allow Erebus to unlock Atlantis. And... yeah, that's about it." I smiled sweetly.

Nash had been staying at the Winchester House with Melody and Luke, the safest place to be without a djinn curse to protect him from blood hunters. Melody was currently sifting through her mind palace to find any information she might've missed about Atlantis and the Gateway, but other than that, our options had pretty much dried up. And Erebus hadn't been in touch, aside from that text.

Lux hadn't contacted me again either, which I was grateful for despite knowing the reprieve was only temporary. Juggling the whims of two Children of Chaos might have made me spontaneously combust. But I couldn't share the weight of my troubles. Not even with Ryann. Lux would've gutted me like a trout.

"That's really all Erebus gave you to go on?" Ryann frowned.

"Why do you sound surprised? He's not exactly verbose."

She smirked. "Have you been reading the thesaurus again?"

"Hey, a guy's got to sleep. Something about the Vs always sends me off," I retorted.

"So, we don't yet know what the Gateway is or where it might be. That's right, isn't it?"

I nodded. "Yup. We also don't know how it opens, though it involves Nash's blood."

"I suggest we start reading, then." Ryann plucked two books from one of the plump bags and handed one to me. A puff of dust expelled upward when I opened it.

"What makes you think there'll be something in these books, anyway? Especially if Melody hasn't dug anything up." I stared at the mighty tome, dreading the prospect of leafing through it... and the rest of them.

She shrugged. "Melody has gaps in her Librarian knowledge, and maybe one of these has information that can fill that gap. At the very least, there might be a legend or something that we can work from. There's truth in—"

"Stories. Yeah, I know." I hadn't heard anyone say that since the monastery, but it seemed to be making a comeback.

With the occasional slurp as Ryann risked her life for coffee, we sank into companionable silence as she created a mountain of books on the table in preparation for a reading marathon. I skimmed the pages, eyes primed for any mention of Atlantis, absorbing as much as I could. It was difficult with Ryann sitting so close. Her knee kept nudging mine... *very* distracting.

I glanced at her once I was sure she had her nose buried in her book. She looked cute in research mode. All she needed was a pair of glasses slipping down the bridge of her nose, and I'd have gone wild. I still remembered the way she'd looked at me when we'd parted ways at the Winchester House...

Hope is harder to live with than resignation. It seemed my brain had decided to turn into a horoscope, but it had a point. Before, I'd thought there was no chance for anything between us. Then she'd looked at me like that, and now I had to deal with a futile hope. She was an improbable dream, since she was with Adam and she loved him. I just had to look at their pictures, even though it encouraged a little mini-vomit in my mouth, to see how much they cared about each other. He was the man every woman wanted, the man every parent wanted for their daughter.

"Did you find anything?" Ryann's voice broke my thoughts.

"Huh?"

She grinned at me. "You looked like you'd had a eureka moment."

"No... Actually, I was thinking about deal-breaking."

"Oh?" Her eyebrows went up a notch.

"Well, I keep thinking about Davin's amulet." I hadn't been, but it seemed like a good topic to get my mind off the Zodiac Killer. "It got him out of his deal. Yes, he had to die and resurrect himself for it to work, but maybe that's what the amulet does—grants the ability for anyone to resurrect themselves. Davin's a Necromancer, but he shouldn't be able to do that. Maybe it'll work for me."

Ryann's eyebrows lifted even higher. "What are you saying?"

"My only shot at escaping Erebus's service might be that amulet. And, since Davin has it, I guess I need to take it from him." As the words came out, the idea solidified in my mind. He had the answers, which meant he was the only person who could help me out. Willingly or unwillingly. I wasn't above beating it out of him.

Ryann downed a huge mouthful of dysentery. "I don't think that's a good idea, Finch. Going after Davin is a surefire way to get killed. Every time you've fought him, you barely scraped through."

"I killed him a couple times, too." I faked a smile.

"And he bounced right back."

"If I take his amulet, he won't be able to," I reminded her.

"That's a pretty massive 'if.'"

I sighed. "But it's the only—"

My sentence was cut short by a loud knock at the door, which quickly drove a pin into our conversation. It was probably for the best, given how circular the discussion had become. Everyone knew Davin was my only way to escape my deal, but nobody seemed eager for me to go after him. I thought the payoff was worth the risk.

"Pickle?" A familiar voice called through the paper-thin walls, followed by another knock. "Pickle, are you in there?"

"Crap, it's Adam!" Ryann hissed.

I arched a brow at her. "Pickle?"

"Not now, Finch!"

Yeah, this was probably a good time to make myself scarce.

TWO

Finch

This was where my anxiety about getting battered came into play. I would be in a bit of a *pickle* if Ted Bundy found me here. Or would I? Ryann hadn't seemed to think it'd be a big deal, so I didn't understand her—or my—panic. It wasn't as if we'd done anything wrong. We were just sitting here doing a little innocent research. So why were we staring at each other in shock, like we were guilty of something else?

"You need to get out of here," Ryann whispered.

"I thought you said he always called before coming over! What do you want me to do, hide in your closet? Get behind a curtain? Duck under the coffee table and hope for the best? I'd even hide in your fridge, if it wasn't the size of a can of beans."

She rolled her eyes. "Be serious, for once!"

"I'm not sure I'm your main problem." I pointed to the mass of magical books. "He's going to have more to say about all *this* than little old me."

Ryann's eyes bugged. "Crap, you're right!"

"Ryann, you in there?" Adam's voice echoed into the room. "What's taking so long? I might get mugged standing out here."

Ryann stood up, fidgeting. "Hold on, Adam! I need to throw on some clothes. You're early—I just got out of the shower!"

Adam laughed. "If you answer, I promise not to look... well, not much."

Pardon me while I hurl. Obviously, even if she had been showering, this wouldn't be the first time Adam had seen Ryann in the buff. They weren't kids. But that didn't make it any less uncomfortable, since now my head was full of... well, that. And Ryann had turned beet red. Also, her hair wasn't wet, so she'd have to wriggle out of that one. Maybe she'd come up with some excuse about wearing a shower cap. Women used those, right?

"I'm never living this down, am I?" she whispered.

"Not a chance, Pickle." I chuckled, but it sounded hollow to me.

"Help me with this stuff." She gave me a pleading look. "I can't stay naked forever. He might break in, thinking I've slipped and broken my neck or something."

Oh boy... Trying to push away thoughts that would see me at confessional for a week, I scrambled to stuff the books back into their bags. Ryann hurried across the room to hoist the other hefty ones onto her shoulders. I'd managed to haul the first two bags into my arms. They dug in like the world's heaviest shopping bags, but adrenaline gave me a boost of strength as I scampered to the nearest wall. With my charmed chalk, I sketched a door and whispered the *Aperi Si Ostium* spell. The lines fizzed and cracked, forging a doorway to the SDC's infirmary.

"I'm so sorry." Ryann glanced over her shoulder. "I had no idea he'd come by, but I promise I'll catch up with you soon."

"So, you're saying he *would* mind if he found me here?" After all her protestations earlier that it would be fine, it seemed she'd been talking a load of fluff.

Ryann grimaced. "He can be a bit jealous sometimes, though he tries not to show it. I've never had another guy over before. He might get upset if you were here. I really am sorry."

I couldn't help feeling a bit special. I was the first guy she'd invited here, besides her boyfriend.

Yeah, because you're her friend, dumbass. She wanted to help you break your deal and figure out the Gateway, that's all. My brain kicked in with a swift dose of reality. She was trying to be both a good friend and a good girlfriend by throwing me out and keeping Ted Bundy's ego protected. Not that I imagined he had much of an ego, being Canadian and all. Still, it made me wonder if Adam had his weaknesses. Maybe he was human, after all.

"Go!" Ryann hissed, shoving me through the now open doorway. Her two book bags followed me into the infirmary before the door slammed shut behind me.

Rude...

"Finch?" Krieger peered out of his office, wearing a puzzled expression.

"Afternoon, Doc." I dropped my heavy bags.

He frowned. "Did you need something?"

"Ice packs for my arms," I replied.

Jacob materialized beside the good doctor. "Finch—where did you come from?"

"I just got booted out of... never mind." I flexed my forearms to get the blood flowing again. "What are you two up to? Leviathan stuff? Magical detector stuff?" The two of them had grown thick as thieves since Dr. Krieger had officially adopted Jacob. They were always squirreled away in Krieger's office, working on some mystery project or another.

Krieger smiled. "Oh no, the Leviathan business is all finished. Remington took the samples a few days ago, and it looks like it may come to nothing. As for the magical detector, we are still toiling away on that. I'd hoped the secret services would find the old one when they raided Eris Island, but it never turned up. Who knows where it is now? Katherine must have hidden it."

"Sounds like her." I huffed out a sigh. "What was that Leviathan stuff, anyway? You were taking samples, right? I think Leviathan freaked my sister out a bit."

"Yes, that was unfortunate, but he's been refrozen." Krieger looked flustered. "We were looking into his cellular regeneration, but Remington doesn't think it's transferable to the human form. An interesting idea, but not all interesting ideas can be realized."

"Then what are you up to in here?" I squinted with suspicion.

Jacob grinned. "The greatest trick the SDC has ever seen."

"Come again?"

"Halloween is coming up, right? Krieger and I are working on the best spell ever. It's going to scare the bejeezus out of everyone!" Jacob laughed maniacally.

"Don't ruin the surprise," Krieger chided.

"Sorry, I couldn't help it. It's going to be amazing." Jacob beamed with pride. It was sweet to watch the two nerds bonding over their shared love of all things geeky. Like father, like son. I'd have chimed in, but they weren't my brand of nerd. Until they decided to build a working Iron Man suit that I could swipe, I wasn't interested.

I stooped to pick up the bags, wondering how the hell I would carry all four. Then I remembered that I had magic at my beck and call. It'd been a weird afternoon, and apparently being with Ryann made me lose my mind for a minute there. I could've done this from the start. *Idiot.* I sent out four slim tendrils of Telekinesis and picked up the four bags with minimal effort.

"Well, don't you dare spook me, or I'll put dead fish in your mattresses."

"Aww, come on, Finch. You have to be a good sport," Jacob protested.

"Dead fish. I mean it." I flashed him a half-warning, half-amused look.

Jacob pouted. "Promise you won't tell anyone?"

"Sure. As long as you let me know when it's happening, so I can be somewhere else," I replied firmly.

Jacob's eyes brightened. "Deal!"

If only every deal were so easy to negotiate.

"Although, more information would be good, so I'm not accidentally in your pranking crosshairs." I couldn't resist finding out what they were scheming.

Jacob leaned forward out of the door. "You won't say a word if we tell you?"

"Scout's honor," I replied.

"I highly doubt you were ever a scout." Krieger chuckled.

"First, we're rigging drones and dangling those cheap Grim Reaper costumes from them to chase people through the halls. Then, we'll play holograms to scare everyone stupid!" Jacob beamed excitedly.

That sounded like exactly the kind of thing that would set off my gremlins.

I nodded. "Yeah, definitely staying away on Halloween, but you two knock yourselves out. I don't need to see the Grim Reaper any sooner than necessary, and I've had my fill of spooks and specters."

"It's going to be ace!" Jacob relaxed back into the doorframe, satisfied.

"What's with all the books?" Krieger gestured to the floating bags.

I pulled a weary face. "Research."

"Did you find what you were looking for?" He stepped from his office, as if to take a closer look. I moved the bags away to prevent him from seeing the titles.

"What does this face tell you?" I waved my hand over my grim visage. The Vs in the thesaurus really had expanded my vocabulary.

Krieger chuckled, taking the hint. "Well, good luck in your endeavors."

"Same to you. Just remember—"

"Dead fish," Krieger interjected. "We hear you, loud and clear."

"Good. The last thing I need is you two giving me a coronary." I gave a dry smile. "My life is weird and freaky enough."

Lux or Erebus or even friggin' Davin could show up at any moment, and that was terrifying enough for me.

THREE

Ryann

"**R**yann?" Adam knocked on the door again, softer this time. "Is everything okay?"

Finch had vanished through the chalk door, but I needed a moment to catch my breath. If Adam saw me flustered, he'd wonder what on earth was going on.

"All good! Just throwing on a sweater. I still haven't worked out the heating in this place." *What are you saying?!* This was San Diego, not Alaska. I was more likely to sweat buckets than shiver. But I'd said it now. So, I sprinted into my bedroom, yanked a sweater from my closet, and pulled it on.

Crossing to the door and taking a moment to get myself together, I could've smacked myself on the forehead for my stupidity. How could I have forgotten Adam was coming by? I'd had it in my diary and everything, but that diary had gotten somewhat convoluted lately. I had to remember other things—things that weren't written down: the lies I'd had to tell Adam because of magical rules, the dates of important projects I couldn't leave out for anyone to see, and the worrying business with Finch and his mission for Erebus. Mistakes were bound to happen, since I'd been hiding so much from Adam.

With a sharp inhale, I opened the door at last. "Sorry about that."

Adam stood in the hallway, good-looking and sexy as hell, with his sweet smile focused solely on me. I hadn't just forgotten he was coming by—I'd forgotten how much I adored that face. He wore jeans and a gray t-shirt but somehow looked like he'd dressed for a photoshoot. Adam had that effect on pretty much anything he wore.

"I've missed you." He leaned down and kissed me, taking me by surprise. It took a second to remember that I needed to kiss him back, or I'd just be standing there like a mannequin. But it came back to me quickly enough. Kissing him felt as natural as breathing, as sappy as that sounded. As he broke away, he cradled my cheek and lightly brushed his thumb across my skin. It tingled in the best kind of way.

"I've missed you, too." I meant it.

"How come your hair isn't wet? I thought you said you were in the shower." He looked at me, puzzled.

"Oh, it was just a body shower. I couldn't be bothered to wash my hair," I lied.

He smiled wider. "You had me worried for a second. You sure you're not hiding somebody in there? Should I start checking behind the curtains?" He did a jokey charade of peering over my shoulder into the apartment.

My stomach clenched. "No guy, just a bunch of paperwork keeping me company. And now you, obviously. You're the only guy here. Well, you will be, when you come inside."

Why was I freaking out so much? It wasn't like Finch and I had been up to anything sordid. Sifting through books didn't a torrid love affair make. I'm sure, if I explained, Adam wouldn't even mind that much that Finch *had* been here. He was a family friend.

"Good thing I brought takeout to feed that overworked mind of yours, then. I don't know how you do it, working all these hours. I thought I had it bad at the hospital, but you make me look like a part-timer." Adam lifted a brown paper bag with the name of our favorite Thai spot printed on the side. He grinned. "And I wouldn't be much of a lunch date if I didn't actually bring the lunch, would I?"

"My hero." I stood on tiptoe to kiss him again. "Let's eat before it gets cold."

He chuckled. "It may be too late for the spring rolls. They flat-lined while you were putting your sweater on."

"Have no fear, I've got a microwave and I'm not afraid to use it. We'll bring those spring rolls back to life in no time." I settled into a sense of calm as I led him through the apartment. Adam had that effect on me. In fact, he had that effect on most people. It made him the ideal pediatrician; the kids he treated loved him more than I did. Their moms and some of the nurses, too. Good thing I wasn't the jealous type.

My calm died a sudden death when I registered the second mug on the coffee table. *Crap!* I'd been so worried about getting the books out of the way, I'd forgotten about it. Trying to keep up a façade of cool, I put myself between Adam and his view of the coffee table—no easy feat, considering he towered over me.

"Why don't you get plates and silverware from the kitchen?" I suggested. "I'll deal with the papers and stuff I've been working on. You know, NDAs and all that."

He laughed. "Sure."

Once he left, I dove for the mug, only to stand there with no idea where to put it. Rattled, I sprinted for the armchair and stuffed the full mug of coffee behind it. For half a second, I wondered why Finch hadn't drunk any of it, but that was the least of my worries.

Get it together, Ryann! I scolded myself. I was legitimately acting like I *did* have a guy in the curtains. Taking a steadying breath, I made my way back to the couch and sat down. I scanned the room just to be sure I hadn't missed anything else and sighed in relief when I found no further evidence of Finch Merlin ever being here.

Adam returned, sitting beside me. He took the reins, letting me relax while he laid out the plates and started serving. He moved deftly with those healing hands, no movement wasted. The scent of pad thai and jasmine rice made my mouth water, and I realized I hadn't eaten all day. I'd been running on caffeine and little else. And the coffee wasn't good. It dawned on me why Finch's mug was still full. I didn't blame him for avoiding it.

Why am I thinking about him again? Finch had been making his way into my head frequently, and I couldn't understand why. Melody had pointed out that I was, potentially, not being honest with myself. But how could I be honest with myself when I didn't know what my brain was doing? I loved Adam. I really did. So, how could Finch keep creeping into my thoughts?

"You're drooling." Adam gave me a laughing nudge.

"Am I?" I wiped my mouth frantically, almost punching him in the face. "Gah, sorry! I'm all over the place today. Dad would call me butterfingers."

He lifted his hands to my face, steadying me. "You're working too hard. I know this government internship means a lot to you, but you need to take some time for yourself, or you'll burn out before you even make it to becoming president of the United States." He flashed a knowing smile. "Are you even sleeping?"

"Do I look that bad?" I sighed, running a hand through my oh so dry hair. A reminder of the huge fib I'd told about a body shower. I returned my hands to my lap with awkward stiffness. This lying business didn't suit me one bit.

"Don't be silly; you never look bad. You're always beautiful. It's just that you're so busy with work, and I don't want you making yourself sick." He kissed me gently, but I was too distracted to really enjoy it.

I broke away. "It's temporary, while I'm finding my feet in this job. I need to make a good impression."

He thought I worked at the local government office, interning in regional affairs. Given the strict rules about telling humans of the magicals' existence, I had no leeway where that was concerned. I'd wanted to tell him the truth, but I didn't know what the repercussions might be. Bad, I assumed.

"I'd be a hypocrite if I told you to take it easy, but—I miss you. I miss being able to come over because you're not buried in work. I respect that you need to get into ultimate political warrior mode, but that doesn't stop me from missing you every evening we spend apart," he said, draping his arm around the back of the couch. "Though, I guess I'll have to get used to it, if I'm going to be a FMOTUS one day."

I snorted. "A what?"

"First man of the United States. Or would it be 'husband'? I doubt it'd be 'lord,' since we don't have those. Maybe I'd be a FBOTUS—first boyfriend of the United States." He plucked up a spring roll and devoured it whole. "That has a ring to it. A bit naval."

"Or a FDOTUS—first doctor of the United States." I nestled into his broad chest, letting his steady heartbeat calm mine.

"I reckon the senators' heads would explode. They wouldn't know what to make of a female president, and I, for one, can't wait to see it happen." He wrapped his arm around me. "It'd be a good thing to have a doctor on hand when that day comes, so I can piece all the exploded heads back together."

I giggled. "To be honest, I'm not sure politics is really my thing. I like my job, sure, but I'm not sure I want to do it for the rest of my life."

"Are you thinking of going back to law?" We'd talked about this, after I'd dropped out of UCLA to join the SDC. He'd been supportive and wonderful but a touch confused, given how passionate I'd been about becoming a badass lawyer, taking names and chewing gum. But I couldn't explain to him that I'd found something better. Something that made me want to jump out of bed in the morning, even if I'd gone to bed at four a.m. because of drama at the coven. I wanted to share every part of my life with Adam... but rules were rules. Well, unless Finch was involved. Then, I tended to start breaking them.

I shrugged. "I'm not sure. I want to see how this internship goes and whether it leads to anything more inspiring."

I wonder if the heads of the United Covens' leaders would explode if they had a human president. The United Covens had already had a female president, after President Price had been murdered by Katherine. Helena Caldwell had been influenced by Katherine's mental manipulation pills and had been replaced after her death. At least they were more open to the idea of a woman in charge, but a *human* might've been a step too far.

What if I could get magical powers of my own? Maybe then they'd accept me. That had been on my mind a lot recently. Not that I wanted to be their president, but I had a faint, persistent longing to truly be one of the coven, like Harley and Finch and the rest of the Rag Team. A magical in my own right. Being involved in this Erebus stuff had made me realize how vulnerable humans were, and honestly, I envied the magicals. I wanted to be useful to them. I managed well enough without magic, but with powers…

"Earth to Ryann." Adam brushed back my hair. "You alive down there?"

I peeked up. "I was just thinking."

"Work stuff?"

"Yeah…"

"Did you not want me to stop by?" He sounded sad. "I wouldn't have minded if you wanted a rain check."

I twisted to get a better look at him, furrowing my brows. "What makes you say that?"

"I don't know." He glanced away from me. A sure sign that he *did* know.

"Adam… come on."

He sighed. "It just seemed like you forgot I was coming over. I know you're trying to keep on top of everything, so I don't mind, but you looked shocked when you opened the door."

"I'm sorry, Adam. I'm a total scatterbrain." I felt like all I ever did these days was apologize to him for one thing or another, through no fault of his own. He always reacted so sweetly and thoughtfully, saying he didn't mind so I didn't feel bad. But I kept right on messing up: missed coffee dates where he'd sat alone for half an hour, countless rounds of rearranging dates, telling him not to come over so I could spend more time at the SDC. The list went on.

"You just care about your work. It's one of the things I admire most about you." He smiled so wide it broke my heart. "I also admire these beautiful rosy cheeks." He kissed them tenderly. "And this forehead. And this nose. And this chin. And this neck. And these lips." He planted a gentle kiss after every sentence, making me melt.

"How did I get so lucky, huh?" I toyed with the edge of his T-shirt.

He shook his head. "I'm the lucky one."

"Let's agree to disagree."

He kissed me again, letting it linger in the most delicious way. "Actually, since we've both been working like crazy," he said, "what do you say to going away on that tropical weekend we've been talking about?"

He'd been trying to plan a weekend vacation for the last month, and I'd kept postponing.

I grimaced. "I can't, Adam. I don't know when work might need me, so I can't just leave for a weekend. You know what it's like. You get beeped all the time."

"But I also get annual leave," he replied. "This internship has to have *some* vacation days."

"Please, can we not talk about this?" I sensed a storm brewing, and I wanted to hide from it before the lightning struck. "I can't go away with you yet. When things are more settled, I'll have some vacation days. But I need to be in San Diego right now in case they call and need me."

He nodded solemnly. "Well… how about a break outside the city?

Far enough to be a vacation but close enough that you can come back if they call you?"

"I can't."

"You can't go an hour outside the city?" A note of exasperation rippled through his voice.

I placed my palms on his chest. "There's a lot going on, and I don't want to miss it. But soon. I promise, soon we'll go away somewhere."

"Have I done something wrong?" His eyes glimmered like a wounded puppy's.

"What? No, of course not."

"Then why do I feel like you don't want me here?" He lowered his gaze and reached for another spring roll, only to put it back down. It might've been the saddest action I'd ever witnessed, and I was responsible for it.

"Hey. I *do* want you here." I sat up and looked him in the eyes. "I always want you to be here."

He sighed. "I don't want to sound like an asshole, and I hope I don't, but we need to spend time together, Ryann. I can't have a relationship with your voicemail. Sure, you have a sultry voice, and I love the way it goes up at the end of your message, but I prefer your actual voice." He chuckled quietly, but it didn't resonate in his gaze. "I mean, when was the last time we spent the night together? Again, not wanting to sound like a total ass, but I miss you. I really, really do. And, honestly, I feel like I'm losing you. This is how it starts, right? Cancelled dinner dates, forgetting lunch dates, going AWOL for days. I'm not blaming you, and if you're just busy, that's okay. But if you don't want this anymore, you have to put me out of my misery."

What have I done to you? I had this amazing guy right in front of me, who couldn't do more for me if he tried, and he thought he was losing me. And I hadn't been giving him many signs to the contrary. I'd put him at the bottom of my priority list time and time again.

"I'm sorry." I grabbed for his hands. "I don't want you to feel that way. I love you. I *do* want you, and I *do* want to be with you, and you're definitely not going to lose me. I promise. No more cancelled dates, and no more scatterbrained Ryann. I'll do better, I swear."

I wondered if I should tell him the whole truth, then and there. All this lying was driving me insane, and it felt worse knowing that it was driving a wedge between us. I didn't want to lose him, but straddling two worlds had backed me into a corner. I couldn't hide my new life from him forever, now that the magical world had become such a huge part of my existence. But I couldn't explain without breaking a lot of rules. Plus, what if I told him and he took it badly? What if he freaked out and had to have his mind wiped?

And then there's Finch... I needed to keep helping Finch, and that meant more meetings like today. Adam would have to meet him again, and I'd have to explain that I'd been working closely with him. I'd probably have to try and describe our odd friendship, too. Heck, I'd probably have to do that even if I didn't tell Adam about the magical world. I couldn't cast Finch aside, not in his hour of need. But that wouldn't be an easy conversation with Adam.

Finch had been right about his first impression of Adam—my boyfriend didn't like my friend much. Well, it was more that he didn't trust Finch; he thought there was something off about him. If he heard the way Finch called him every serial killer name under the sun, he'd probably form an even worse impression. But maybe it was just because they didn't know each other. Ugh. I wished I could find a way to reconcile all these aspects of my life in one smooth, fell swoop.

"What if you didn't have to worry about dates and things?" Adam asked.

Is he... breaking up with me? "What do you mean?"

"Well, since you're so busy, and I'm so busy, why don't I just move in with you?" He smiled, a hint of mischief in his eyes. "At least we'd see each other more often that way, even if we were just ships passing in the night. We could leave notes on the bathroom mirror. And you'd never miss a date again, because we could have them all right here."

"Are you serious?" I arched a nervous eyebrow.

He shrugged. "Maybe not. I'd probably spend more time out in the hallway, waiting to be let in while you put on a sweater."

"And you'd be searching my curtains for hidden men!" I laughed too hard, my bout of hysterics echoing false. And if I could hear it, he definitely could. I even punched him in the arm, trying to cover my anxiety and shock with a display of manic hilarity.

Adam started to laugh but with way less vigor. In fact, it sounded downright awkward. A flicker of disappointment crossed his face. It made me sick to my stomach, watching him squirm. This clearly wasn't quite the reaction he'd expected. And, honestly, if he'd asked me six months ago, maybe this wouldn't have been the reaction I gave.

FOUR

Finch

Leaving Krieger and his protégé to hatch their Halloween scheme, I left the infirmary with my haul of books. I had no idea where to put them. There hadn't been time to discuss that before Ryann booted me out of her apartment for the sake of Captain Canuck's ego. I figured the best place to store them would be the Alton Waterhouse Room.

In a display of magical prowess, I sent a stream of Mimicry through the Telekinetic strands and matched the book bags to their surroundings, just in case I happened to bump into Miranda Bontemps or O'Halloran, or pretty much anyone who might have some questions about why I was hefting around an entire library. It was the closest thing to an invisibility cloak you could get, outside of fiction.

Fifteen weary minutes later, I arrived outside the Alton Waterhouse Room. Even with the help of magic, these books were friggin' weighty. My muscles were doing a Popeye, and the underarms of my T-shirt had turned unpleasantly damp.

I paused before entering, hearing the sound of voices inside. Curious, I knocked and pushed the door open. "Yello?"

Harley and Wade turned, surprised. "Finch?" My dear old sis spoke first.

"We were just talking about you," Wade added.

"All good things, I hope." I laughed, slightly nervous.

"That depends on whether you think Erebus is a good thing." Wade scraped back his stool and stood, as if I were a fine lady who'd just walked in. Ah, the manners of high society.

I pulled a face. "Nope."

"Why the red face?" Harley came over, wearing a suspicious expression.

"Can't a guy look like a beet for no reason?" I grinned and released the Mimicry hiding the book bags.

"Some light reading?" Wade chuckled as I dumped the books on the ground and heaved an almighty sigh of relief.

"Ryann's idea. She wanted to research Atlantis, see if there were any stories in here that might give us some clue about our next step." I hesitated. "She asked me to put them here for later, you know, so we could sift through them again."

Harley smirked. "You got kicked out, didn't you?"

"Huh?" I feigned ignorance.

"You were supposed to be meeting at her apartment, weren't you?" Harley knelt and picked through the dusty tomes. "What happened? Did Adam show up or something?"

My cheeks burned a tiny bit more. "Something like that. I didn't want to intrude, so I vamoosed. You know, couple time and all that.

Watching folks smooch and canoodle isn't my idea of a fun afternoon. So, just in case you were about to start with the PDA, please don't. I'd hate to empty my stomach on this sacred ground."

Wade and Harley exchanged a conspiratorial look. Man, I hated couples sometimes. Especially the pseudo-telepathic part. *Way to make me feel like a third wheel.*

"Well, your timing couldn't be better." Wade came over to look at the books with his fiancée. I'd never get used to seeing that sparkler on her finger. I imagined it'd be weirder when they added an actual wedding ring.

Ugh, I have to get through a wedding without embarrassing myself or anyone else... If the Macarena came on, it'd be game over. But they hadn't mentioned any plans yet, so maybe it'd be a long engagement.

Harley nodded. "We finished all the smooching and canoodling and were getting down to business."

"What you two do in here is something I never want to hear about!" I protested with mock horror.

"Not that kind of business. We were discussing the Erebus situation," Harley replied with an obligatory eye roll.

Wade nodded, the Tweedle-Dum to her Tweedle-Dee. "We've been thinking of coordinating a task force, but since we don't know Erebus's endgame, it's kind of tricky to make a solid action plan."

"You have that kind of power?" I arched an eyebrow. "Those uniforms must be working for you."

"They do." Harley chuckled. "But it's hard to know where to start when we don't know what we'll have to face."

"Plus, I told you not to," I reminded her. "If Erebus finds out you're messing with his plans—well, you know. Doom, gloom, fire, and brimstone."

Harley lowered her gaze. "I just want to be useful."

"You are useful. But we need to be careful." I softened my tone. She meant well, and I wanted more than anything to give her hope. I almost told her about Lux, just to reassure her that I had some cosmic brawn on my side, but the words wouldn't come. I didn't know if that cosmic help might disappear if I mentioned it to anyone… or if it even *was* help. She'd promised me security, but I had no clue how far that might extend if my tongue flapped. Either way, I knew my previous encounter with Lux wouldn't be the last.

"This would be so much simpler if Erebus just told you more." Harley sighed, absently leafing through the top book. "Doesn't he realize information is helpful? What's his issue with giving you details? It's not as if you've proved to be untrustworthy. In fact, right now I imagine you're all he's got, since he's essentially djinn-less."

"That's just made him shorten the puppet strings, as far as I can tell." I sighed. I envied the djinn their newfound liberation. They'd had the balls to separate from Erebus's power, and it paid off for them with freedom and a new home.

"Do you think he *knows* what the next steps are? What if he's as stumped as we are? What if he's relying on you, Finch, to find answers he can't?" Wade folded his arms across his chest.

I groaned. "Let's hope not."

Just then, the door opened. Raffe and Santana came in, with that nasty little serpent slithering along beside its owner.

"Finch? What are you doing here?" Raffe asked, puzzled.

"Am I not allowed to be here?" I replied, eyeing the snake.

"Of course you are; we just didn't expect to see you. I thought you were at Ryann's today." Santana gave a wry smirk. A second later, Slinky darted for my ankles. I may have shrieked. The look of satisfaction on Santana's face made me want to boot her stupid snake across the room.

I gathered myself. "Does everyone know I was doing research at Ryann's?"

"Looks like it." Harley gave a small smile.

"Why, was it supposed to be a secret?" Santana grinned. Her serpent slid over the floor and hid between her feet, peering out at me with glinting eyes. *Try to nip me again, and I'll turn you into haute couture.* Its tongue flickered, as if it had heard my thoughts.

"No, I just didn't realize everyone had read my diary," I replied.

"Now that I'd like to see. 'Dear Diary, today I had coffee with my unrequited love. Our fingertips touched when we reached for the same book. I know she felt it, too. I wonder if there's any hope for us. Maybe, if I keep giving her puppy-dog eyes, she'll fall head over heels for me.' Is that about right?" Santana looked amused with herself. Shame she was the only one.

I mustered a sarcastic smile. "It's more like, 'Dear Diary, today I had another inane conversation with the forever-irritating Santana. Her snake tried to bite me, so I stole it while she was sleeping, and now I have it locked in a box under my bed. I'm wondering whether to make it into a belt or a wallet. What do you think?'"

"I thought you two were over this." Raffe sighed like a weary schoolteacher separating a duo of warring children for the thousandth time.

"Over what? This is just how we communicate. It's a miracle we made it past grunts and smoke signals." I focused on him, trying to take my mind off the snake. "Anyway, how are the djinn folk? Are they enjoying their new otherworld? I keep wondering if I should just go and live there to escape from Erebus. Do you think they'd accept me?"

Raffe laughed. "I think it's a djinn-only club."

"Well, that's a little exclusionary." I pretended to pout. "But seriously, how are they? I imagine it's been a shock to the system."

"Zalaam has been keeping us updated. His link to them is working again, though it's weaker than before," Raffe explained. "Everything is weaker than before, by all accounts. But they seem happy. They're building things to their tastes, so Tartarus will probably look very different if you ever go back."

"What, no looming darkness and hidden swarms of Purge beasts?" I shuddered at memories of running the gauntlet to reach Erebus's perch atop Mount Sisyphus.

"Nope. I think they're recreating old Arabia, with separate villages for the different kinds of djinn." Raffe smiled.

I made a humph of approval. "Good for them." I might've envied them, but I admired them, too. Their successful rebellion gave me hope.

"How have you been?" Raffe asked.

Harley jumped in. "Have you thought any more about breaking your deal?"

I cast her a withering look. "What else would I think about? Fairies and rainbows? It's literally the only thing in my brain." I picked an invisible speck of dust from my pant leg. "And, right now, the only viable option seems to be Davin. His amulet might be my way out. But that means finding the colossal horseradish and taking it from him."

I felt like I was going in circles. I'd had this conversation once today with Ryann, and judging by the disapproval on everyone's faces, I would have to fight this issue once again.

"That's suicide, or a one-way trip to the infirmary," Harley piped up.

"So is staying in servitude," I pointed out. Facing Davin wasn't anyone's idea of a good time, but it beat sitting back and doing nothing.

"Wouldn't it be easier to find the djinn who helped Davin?" Raffe suggested.

I smiled. "Which would also mean finding Davin, to get that information from him. Either way, I need a one-on-one with the British assclown. I'm inclined to snatch his amulet *and* ask about the djinn, just in case." I paused, sensing the discomfort in the room. "Look, I know it's not ideal, but like it or not, Davin is pretty much the only way to break the deal."

"That's the sort of fighting spirit I never expect from you humans." Kadar emerged, taking me by surprise. "How refreshing, not to see you veer toward cowardice."

I shrugged. "What can I say; the djinn inspired me."

"As they should." Kadar grinned, flashing his fangs. "Stealing the amulet for your own purpose will be the only way to discover if you can use it. If not, you can always strip the flesh from Davin's bones until he gives up the name of the djinn who granted him the amulet. I would be only too glad to assist, should it come to that. I have never tasted British meat before. I imagine it will be quite salty, given its island locale—ready-cured for my delectation and delight."

"You'll have to line up behind Nash, though I'm guessing Nash isn't into human bacon, so maybe he'll leave it to you." I tried not to squirm at the idea of Kadar *actually* devouring human flesh.

"My question is, why hasn't Erebus tried to take Davin's amulet himself?" Santana asked. "He must be pissed that one of his servants got away."

Wade nodded. "I've been thinking the same."

"It may well be that he can't," Kadar replied. "It is djinn magic, and djinn magic cannot be undone by Erebus. Although, it would not prevent Erebus from taking the amulet."

I thought back to my time in Russia visiting the Vasilis family. Erebus had mentioned someone following us, and that he couldn't identify them. And, since Davin kept popping up, he had to be flying under Erebus's radar somehow.

"Could the amulet shield Davin from Erebus's eye?" I looked at Kadar.

He grumbled thoughtfully. "There is no reason why not. Indeed, it would make a lot of sense to add that sort of defense mechanism, considering why Davin wanted the amulet. And djinn magic, as I understand, is the only magic that can hide one from Erebus."

"Well, that explains how Davin keeps running circles around him," I mused aloud. It made me want the amulet even more.

"I'm just going to say it—I agree with Harley. I think it's a dumb idea." Santana petted Slinky's scaly head. *Gross.* "No encounter with Davin ends well, and he's not going to give up that amulet easily. The djinn who created it must be somewhere in Tartarus, right? Why not look there?"

My patience with these naysayers was wearing thin. "How about this? I'll try to find Davin and take plenty of backup when I do. Meanwhile, Kadar, can you pull some strings with the djinn folk— you know, ask around about this djinn?"

"I can't without visiting Tartarus, which I'm not inclined to do for your sake, but I'll ask Zalaam to enquire through the network. It may be that the djinn will answer directly, if he still lives." Kadar's smoke billowed, and a few wisps stung my nostrils.

I smiled, satisfied. "It's a plan." I cast a withering look at Santana. "Does that sit better with your sensitive sensibilities? I think I have that book, actually. One of Austen's finest."

"It's slightly less stupid, if that's what you're asking. I don't care about old-timey novels," she retorted.

"I think you mean 'classic,' you philistine," I countered. "Then it's settled. Now, I need to eat before my stomach devours itself."

Kadar chuckled. "How delectable."

With two potential means to gain freedom—the amulet or the djinn—one of them would work… right?

"In the meantime, we've got to worry about Atlantis." Harley brought me some relief by changing the subject.

"Ah, the big A." Santana clicked her tongue.

"No, that's Davin, and it stands for asshole," I retorted.

She smirked. "Noted."

"We'd just started on Atlantis when you came in. Now, the way to Atlantis is separated into parts, right?" Harley asked, putting down the book she'd been holding. "It started with Erebus getting his human form, though if he'd already been human, maybe that wouldn't have been necessary. So, that's probably an extra step."

"If that's true, the first must've been drawing the map to find Atlantis," I continued on her train of thought. "Part two was the key —Nash's blood. But his blood has to *do* something."

Wade rubbed his chin. "Well, Sanguine blood is usually a spell ingredient, or a replacement ingredient."

"Right, so Nash's blood will play a part in the spell to get Erebus into Atlantis." I glanced at the other two. "Which means part three is an entry spell."

"See, we're already ironing out the kinks." Harley offered a meager smile.

"Yeah, except that's where we draw a blank. What's after the entry spell? What will we find in Atlantis?" I huffed a breath. "Is Erebus already working on the entry spell, or does he expect me to handle that?"

Harley crossed to the workbench and sank onto one of the stools. "Can we make a promise? If you get out of this, we never work with a Child of Chaos ever again. None of them. Not even Gaia."

"Amen to that!" Santana crowed.

"Sounds good to me," I replied, but that prospect was a very long way away.

"Where is Nash, anyway?" Harley asked.

"Winchester House, keeping the spooks company." I shrugged. "And probably doing research or something, though research seems pointless with the tiny all-knowing elf on our team. I tried telling Ryann that, but she got on her high horse. 'There's no substitute for sifting through a mountain of books to find a needle in a stack of needles.'"

Harley chuckled. "She just wants to be thorough."

"Maybe." I leaned against the workbench, suddenly tired. "Anyway, all the research in the world won't give us a better option. For now, I've got no choice but to keep doing the E-man's bidding and move on to the next step."

"The next step he's told you nothing about?" Santana cut in dryly.

"Not nothing. Just next to nothing," I corrected her. "My next mission is to find the Gateway and open it."

Harley sighed and held her head in her hands. "That's pretty freaking vague."

"At least it might be the last stage in the mission." Wade put his hands on Harley's shoulders and squeezed gently. I sensed that he wanted to kiss her but was resisting for my sake.

I nodded. "First, we found Atlantis. Second, we got the key, which suggests some kind of spell is needed. That part may or may not be done by Erebus himself, depending on how much he wants to get his hands dirty. And third, we have to find the Gateway and open it. I mean, that might be stages three *and* four, but we won't know until Erebus gets a bit more chatty."

I shook my head. Without Erebus's input, we were in limbo. He held all the cards.

"Just for the record, I hate that guy," Harley growled under her breath.

I smiled. "Just for the record, so do I."

FIVE

Finch

Ravenous after going in thought circles with the others, I'd swung by the Banquet Hall. Now, stuffed to bursting with the chef's special—a triple-tier Mediterranean sandwich topped with a slathering of sweet mustard—I walked through a chalk door to the Winchester House. In the end, my appetite had disappeared, with everyone's aversion to hunting Davin playing on my mind. But I'd forced the sandwich down regardless. After all, I didn't know how many meals I might have left, so I had to make the most of each.

"The wanderer has returned." Mary Foster appeared through the wall the moment I set foot in the front yard. Not being able to chalk-door right into the mansion had its drawbacks, but at least I could brace myself for the spook patrol.

"Were you watching out for me, Miss Foster?" I teased.

Though her face was perpetually gray, I could've sworn she blushed. "I was merely observing the sunset and happened to see you appear. I certainly was *not* watching out for you. I have other matters with which to occupy myself, you know."

"I'd never suggest otherwise." I offered her a smile.

She visibly relaxed. "Are you searching for Miss Winchester?"

"How did you guess?"

"You are always looking for Miss Winchester," she replied bluntly.

"Touché." I chuckled. "Where can I find the merry little bibliomaniac?"

Mary frowned. "Will I ever become used to your odd idioms?"

"Stranger things have happened."

"Indeed. Well, she is in the first-floor parlor with that handsome sentinel of hers and the fellow with the peculiar silver hair. You may tell the latter, when you see him, that I do not appreciate his hound barking at me." Mary looked affronted, smoothing down the already smooth front of her dress.

I gave a nod. "Of course, Miss Foster."

I made my way up the creaking staircase that led to the house. Glancing over my shoulder, I noticed Mary watching me go, a sad expression on her face. It couldn't be easy for her, existing here. It couldn't be easy for any of the spirits to have to watch the living every day, remembering the life they'd had before the Winchester rifle took it. I wondered if Mary would ever cross over, but she'd been here this long… maybe a half-life was better than no life at all.

Is that what I have? A half-life? This servitude was, at least, keeping me breathing. But it couldn't last. One way or another, I'd stop serving Erebus. I'd either go back to a real life, with the hope of doing all the normal stuff people did, or stop existing altogether. Escape or death, death or escape. Two terrifying options. What if I came close to escape, only for death to catch me? That would be worse than accepting the inevitable outcome of every servant of Erebus, bar one. But I had to try.

On the other side of a long corridor with sickly green wallpaper, I found the parlor and knocked.

"Come in!" Melody called from the other side.

I found her ensconced in an armchair, with Luke standing over her and Nash seated opposite. They looked like they were about to stage an intervention.

"Have you been expecting me?" I joked.

"Not at all, what a pleasant surprise!" Melody chimed. "We didn't think we'd see you until tomorrow. You were supposed to be researching with Ryann, weren't you?"

I rolled my eyes. "Seriously, does everyone know my business?"

Melody looked puzzled. "You texted me to tell me where you were."

"Oh." My cheeks flamed. "Well, then... I'll let you off the hook."

"How did it go?" Luke flashed a knowing smirk.

"I'll be wheezing for a week from all the dust." I crossed to the spare armchair, which was also a sickly green, though darker than the walls. Where had they found all this ugly furniture? "I had to bounce early, due to allergies."

Luke snorted. "Sure you did."

"Be nice." Melody shot him a warning look. "Anyway, why do we have the pleasure of your company?"

"I can't just swing by?" I sank into the chair and unleashed a mighty sigh.

"Of course you can! But I get the feeling this isn't a casual visit, considering everything that's going on." Melody smiled. "I can't wait until all this is over, and you can just swing by whenever you feel like it. Goodness, won't that be strange? A good kind of strange, I mean. It's just... I've never really had friends, and I'd like to know what it's like." She lowered her gaze and fidgeted. "Sorry, that was a bit TMI, wasn't it?"

My heart went out to her. "Not at all. It'd be nice to have a normal life, but I should warn you, you'll be sick of the sight of me when this is over. You'll wish you'd never made friends with me and my folks back at the SDC."

Her eyes brightened. "I could never get sick of any of you!"

"I'll remind you of that when you're on your sixth coffee date of the week." I shot a friendly wink in her direction.

"Why are you here, again?" Luke cut in, clearly not appreciating my excellent winking skills.

"I've made a decision."

Luke narrowed his eyes. "What kind of decision?"

"I'm going to hunt down Davin and take that bastard's amulet from him." I waited for rapturous applause. Instead, Nash gave a discreet nod, which was almost as good.

"About time. I've been waiting for you to come back and say you're ready to find that cretin." Huntress gave a bark of appreciation, and Nash ruffled her fur. "Count me in, as long as I get to settle my own score."

"Naturally," I replied.

Nash nodded to Melody. "Actually, we've already done some of the groundwork for that."

"You have?" I glanced at the Librarian, who jittered with excitement.

"Oh, yes. Nash asked me to search for an obscure tracking spell, one which bypasses some of the defenses Davin seems to have. It's an oldie but a goodie. We've been gathering ingredients while you were away—I hope you don't mind. It was just so we could really get the ball rolling when you came back. You know, if you decided to go ahead with finding Davin. You seemed set on it when you left, so we thought it'd be a good use of our time to get everything in order," she rambled.

"Wow... I... well, I wasn't expecting that." I gaped at them. They'd been a busy bunch of bees.

Nash scratched the spot between Huntress's ears. "Some of the ingredients were harder to come by, it being such an old spell. But we figure we can use my blood instead; it'll replace just about anything that's missing."

I shook my head, amused. "After all the effort it took to get eight measly vials from you, now you're just giving the stuff away?"

Nash remained stony-faced. I couldn't remember the last time he'd cracked a smile. "I've had a change of heart. I've come to realize that I'll never get any peace or normalcy in my life until Davin is dead. I knew that before, when I chose to curse myself. But I should've realized it was only a temporary measure—and one that would've killed me, instead of the person who deserves to die."

He subconsciously brushed his fingertips across the crook of his elbow, where the blood had been drawn. "If we can find a way to keep Erebus away from us and out of the magical world, that's a big win in my book. But that can wait. Davin first."

"So, we're all on the same page?" I glanced at Melody and Luke, who hadn't said a word.

Melody nodded eagerly. "I'm all for it. Anything that can get you out of your deal sounds all right by me. I wish my mind palace could do more, but I keep drawing a blank when it comes to escaping Erebus's service. Whether that's purposeful, and all Children of Chaos evasion tactics have deliberately been blocked, or there really is no other way… I couldn't say. But as long as we have a shot, that must be good, right?"

Bless her. She had more enthusiasm in her little finger than most people had in their entire bodies. Namely, Luke. He looked as stony-faced as Nash, evidently unimpressed that I was, yet again, roping Melody into something a bit dangerous. Melody peered up at him with imploring eyes, likely bracing for the tirade of "Nope. Not a chance. Not gonna happen" about to spill from his mouth. Instead, he rasped a resigned sigh.

"If Melody wants to help, then I guess I'm helping, too," he said.

Aww, come on, admit it—you want to help me. I didn't poke the bear, just in case it made him change his mind. But it felt incredible to be surrounded by folks who were all on my wavelength.

A knock on the door made everyone turn. My jaw hit the deck as Ryann strode in. *What the—? How the—?* She should've been back at her apartment, or at the SDC. Last I checked, she didn't have the magical wizardry to conjure up chalk doors whenever she liked.

"Am I interrupting?" She beamed a million-kilowatt smile. It usually would've turned my insides to mush, but all it did this time was remind me of our awkward last encounter. The highlight being me getting shoved unceremoniously through a chalk door while she covered her tracks for lover-boy.

"Of course not." I managed to smile back. "All good… you know, back home?"

She reddened. "Yep, all fine."

"So, the police finally caught him, did they?" As ever, in a situation I wanted out of, I chose humor. However ill-timed.

"What?" She frowned.

"They finally took the prolific serial killer away in chains?"

"Serial killer?" Melody erupted from her armchair in shock. "What serial killer? Oh my goodness, is there a serial killer at the SDC? I haven't seen anything about it on the news."

Ryann shot me an icy look. "There's no serial killer. Finch is being an idiot. He thinks it's funny to refer to my boyfriend as Ted Bundy, the Zodiac Killer, the Boston Strangler—the list goes on. He had to go back to work. You know, at the hospital, saving kids' lives."

Oof. That one stung. But I probably deserved it. I shuffled my feet awkwardly on the cracked varnish of the parquet floor, like a naughty kid sitting in his dad's chair, and silently urged the sickly green upholstery to swallow me whole.

"Oh." Melody sank back in her chair. Her gaze rested on me for a moment, a glimmer of something passing across her eyes. Was that some kind of Librarian Morse code? Was she trying to tell me something? If she blinked twice, did that mean Ryann had "conflicted emotions?" She turned back to Ryann before I could decipher anything from her stare.

"How did you get here?" I asked Ryann, flipping the subject.

Ryann shook off her apparent annoyance. "Harley opened a door for me. I said I wanted to speak to Melody about my research." She cleared her throat. "I didn't know you'd be here. What were you all talking about before I came in?"

"Davin," Nash said. Simple and to the point. "We're going after him."

"You are?" Ryann turned to me in surprise.

"And we need all hands on deck to prepare the tracking spell. It's not a simple one," Nash continued. "So, it's a good thing you showed up when you did. I know you're not magical, but that shouldn't be too much of a problem."

Ryann looked disappointed for a fleeting moment, as if Nash had said something that hit deep. *Hmmm... I hadn't really thought about her lack of magic that much, aside from her human vulnerability. But that tended to be more about the logistics of protecting her than sneering. Now that she'd seen our world, did she envy it? Being a human among magicals couldn't have been easy. I'd never asked her how that felt.*

"What's the spell?" She perked up, but I could tell Nash's offhand comment still lingered.

"Melody? Would you care to do the honors?" Nash stood and went to a large wooden chest on the far side of the room. Man, they'd really gotten prepared while I'd been munching on my sandwich. It made me feel like I'd been sitting back, twiddling my thumbs. Nash's vendetta had some drive to it, that was for sure.

Melody followed Nash to the chest. Together, they removed a medium-sized wooden box and a smaller wooden box. A veritable babushka doll of boxes. I'd have lost my mind if Melody cracked that smaller box open to reveal a teeny, tiny one.

She set the smallest box down on the coffee table between the puke-green armchairs and opened it up. A vivid blue sapphire, shaped like one of the crystals you'd see above a Sim's head, lay on a velvet cushion. A single silver chain coiled above it.

"Is that a pendulum?" Ryann peered into the box.

Melody grinned at her. "It is! This one is an heirloom from my mother's side of the family. It's extremely old, which is necessary for this particular spell. Imagine if there was no magic on either side of my family. We'd be stumped right now."

That strain flickered across Ryann's face again. This time, I knew what I saw. Day in, day out, she surrounded herself with magicals. It was only natural to want a slice of the action. Nobody wanted to be the odd one out, and this was coming from the guy who'd been the odd one out for most of his life.

"Yeah, that's lucky," Ryann replied softly.

Don't you go asking anyone for magic, Ms. Smith! That never ended well. Katherine had offered it to humans in return for loyalty, and now they were all in Purgatory. Ryann had more sense than that, but still… temptation could sway even the most sensible people.

Nash opened the bigger box, drawing my attention. A roll of parchment, so thin and fragile it looked like it might crumble if someone sneezed, lay tucked to one side. Beside it sat four vials. Two swirled with a thick red substance. I recognized it immediately as Nash's blood. But the other two vials were anyone's guess. One contained a bright purple liquid; the other held a neon orange liquid.

"What's that?" I jabbed a finger at the box.

"The purple liquid is phoenix blood, and the orange is from the pituitary gland of a hellhound," he explained, as if he were listing off items on the cocktail menu. "And in the bag, we've got belladonna, hawthorn, black lotus root, quicksilver, dried gargoyle claw, the crumbled skin of a bridge troll, powdered jade, and powdered black onyx."

I coughed. "All the supermarket essentials."

"What about the paper?" Ryann gestured to it.

"That's the map that'll lead us to Davin." Nash smiled weirdly, and a low growl rasped from Huntress's throat. Whatever thoughts he was having, they weren't sunshine and candy canes.

"No oranges?" I laughed, but it rang false.

Nash looked at me like I was an idiot. "Why would we need oranges?"

"Never mind, sorry. Go on."

"Of course, I already drew some of my own blood in preparation for this," Nash duly went on. "We're missing the healing gland of a Caladrius, so my blood will have to compensate."

I saw their problem. Tobe had a Caladrius in the Bestiary, but he'd have strung me up by my special places if we borrowed it. A Caladrius wouldn't survive the removal of their healing gland.

"How do we do this?" I stood there like a spare part while Melody and Nash arranged the items neatly on the coffee table. The map took center stage, while four gems acted as paperweights—red, green, clear, and blue.

"We mix the ingredients and pour the mixture onto the map. As we chant the spell, we swing the pendulum over the top of the parchment. If it works, it should show us the way." Nash kept it vague, which irked me. I got enough vagueness from Erebus.

Without looking up, Nash took a wooden bowl from the canvas bag and started to blend the ingredients together. He went for the solids and dusty detritus from various critters first, before smushing the mixture into a grim paste with the vials of liquid. The smell was… indescribable. Like the fetid soup at the bottom of a trashcan mixed with pure, unadulterated death, a bit of gangrene, and the end result of a bad curry. My eyes watered as it stung my nostrils, my gag reflex trying to eject my lunch.

Ryann looked pale, though she made a decent show of containing her nausea. Luke had pinched his nose, while Melody and Nash were absolute troopers. Huntress sniffed the air before backing away from the foul scent. I had no idea what Melody had been through that would allow her to endure that stench without batting an eyelid. Nash, I understood a bit better. He could probably gut a rabbit in ten seconds flat.

"All of us need to chant while touching a stone," Nash instructed. "Ryann, watch us. If anything goes south, pull us away from the map. Understood?"

Ryann's mouth tightened. "Understood."

"Everyone, take a spot." Nash went for the red stone. Luke chose blue, and Melody went for clear, which left me with green. I didn't think of myself as the Earth-type Bulbasaur of the magical world. I was more of a Charmander, turning to Fire whenever possible. But I could make an exception, just this once.

I rested my fingertips on the green stone. Luke looked nervous, his gaze fixed on Melody. I took a moment to steal a glance at Ryann, but she didn't look back. She stood firm, with a slight slouch from disappointment. When Nash had mentioned her taking part in this spell, I bet she hadn't anticipated being the watcher in the wings.

"Are we ready?" Nash asked.

"Ready," we chorused. It was sort of true. I had no clue what I was supposed to be ready for.

"Repeat after me." Nash took a breath. "*Audite me. Quaerere mundi. Homo invenire. Afferte huc illum ad nos. Monstra in tabula. Audite me. Hoc faciunt. Et invenies illum. Respice unique. Quaerere mundi. Undique quaerere. Quattuor elementa. Quam quidem protestationem nomen tibi. Et invenies illum.*"

Like good little choirboys and girls, we recited the Latin after him. I noticed Luke mispronounce a word, but I didn't want to point it out to the whole class. As long as he didn't screw up next time, we'd be fine. At least, I hoped. Tracking spells were often child's play, depending on what was being hunted down. I knew that better than most. My sister and the Muppet Babies had used one on me during my Eris days, before my spiritual voyage into becoming a better person. It still bothered me, on occasion, that I hadn't seen it coming—that they'd used something so simple to uncover that I was Katherine's spy in their midst. In the long run, I was glad it'd happened, given everything it led to, but it was a touch embarrassing.

"*Audite me. Quaerere mundi. Homo invenire. Afferte huc illum ad nos. Monstra in tabula. Audite me. Hoc faciunt. Et invenies illum. Respice unique. Quaerere mundi. Undique quaerere. Quattuor elementa. Quam quidem protestationem nomen tibi. Et invenies illum.*" Nash spoke the spell again, and we copied. This time, Luke got it spot on.

Four more times, we regurgitated the Latin. After the fourth, Nash took up the bowl of goop and added his blood to the mix. In a weird twist of alchemy, the entire thing lit up like the Fourth of July, sparks of multicolored light flying out and sizzling on the map below. My heart clenched. This thing could go up in smoke before we found Davin. Luke flinched, too, evidently thinking the same thing.

As the light ebbed, my eyes bulged in awe. Where that nasty pâté of foul mulch had been, there was now half a bowl of pure silver fluid. Threads of luminescence danced over the silver, pulsating faintly.

Nash repeated the spell. Then, in a move that looked like utter madness, he tossed the bowl onto the map. Melody dove in with the pendulum, swinging the blue crystal over the soaked parchment. The silver liquid reacted to it, staying within the parameters of the paper and undulating with the movements of the pendulum. I half expected ghostly faces to appear in the surface, mouths gaping like we'd opened a doorway to Hell.

Nash's chanting grew louder. My voice matched his, not wanting to be left out of the vocal prowess game. Even Luke found his stride, booming Latin like the out-of-tune guy in a high school musical. Melody's voice rang higher than ours, adding a feminine touch to the increasingly terrifying chorus.

Then, just when I thought all the hairs on the back of my neck were standing to attention, faces *did* appear in the churning silver pool.

SIX

Ryann

During my year at the SDC, I'd gotten used to the more peculiar side of the magical world. I'd witnessed Shapeshifting, Elemental magic, transportation spells, and everything in between. But this blew everything I'd seen so far out of the water. Eerie faces pushed through the silvery mass, their mouths open wide as if screaming. It gave me the urge to scream, too.

"What are you doing?" I whispered, struggling to find my voice. Was it okay to speak during a spell like this? I supposed I'd find out if Nash snapped at me to be quiet. Fortunately, he didn't. He kept his eyes focused on the swinging pendulum while he answered.

"I'm tapping into the trace world." His forehead glistened with sweat.

"The what world?" I swallowed hard, trying not to look at those awful faces.

"The trace world." He scrunched his face up. Whatever this spell entailed, it was taking a toll on him. "Every event, no matter how small, imprints onto the fabric of Chaos. With the right magic, we can follow the prints of others who caused an event, no matter how far or near in the past. We're tracing for recent Davin events."

I frowned. "Isn't that Kolduny territory?" I'd been doing my research. I loved research, and learning about all things magical filled me with an immense sense of purpose—the kind I hadn't experienced in a long while, if ever.

"It isn't quite the same," he replied, a drop of sweat falling to the floor.

Out of nowhere, an icy draft blew. The parlor door banged open, and the shutters on the far side of the room clattered against the outer wall. A high-pitched howl followed, piercing my eardrums.

My blood ran cold as objects began to rattle, and the fire in the hearth sputtered out, sending spirals of smoke flooding the room. The strands twisted in the air, moving toward the pendant only to stop short and evaporate when they reached the chanters. Every time Nash repeated the spell, the wind amped up until I could hardly hear myself think, between the deafening chant and howling wind.

A ceramic jug fell from one of the shelves and shattered. Terror spiked in my chest. I instinctively reached for Finch's free hand. He gripped mine back but didn't look up. His eyes shone with silver light, focus unwavering. The others looked the same, and it made for a horrifying scene—four magical zombies with glowing eyeballs, all staring at the ghoulish silver faces pushing outward from a mass of writhing fluid.

What if they break free, whoever they are? My hands were slick with cold sweat, and the rest of me wasn't faring much better. The creepy faces groaned and whispered, making me cling ever tighter to Finch's hand. If I didn't have that to anchor me, I might have keeled over. And I did *not* want to miss this, in case something went wrong while I was out cold.

"These are the echoes of the events I mentioned." Nash provided a brief commentary, but it didn't do much to ease my petrified mind. Especially as his voice sounded detached, like it came from every-where and nowhere all at once, the words not quite matching his lip movements. "They are communicating now... searching for Davin."

The pendulum swung wildly, spinning in circles all across the map. The whispers grew louder, though I couldn't understand a word. It chilled me to the core, like I was witnessing something I shouldn't have been. I knew about spirits and otherworlds, but no amount of research could've prepared me for this.

All of a sudden, the pendulum halted and the whispering silenced. The wind stopped. The jittering objects ceased. In a weird way, the silence felt worse. As if something were coming.

My eyes fixed on the writhing silver. A center-point of bright scarlet bled through the surface and spread until there was no silver left. Only a bleak expanse of red. It looked exactly like blood, viscous and visceral. My heart and stomach lurched as the fluid swirled inward like a miniature whirlpool, spinning into that center-point until most of the liquid had vanished, leaving a single spot of red on the parchment.

"Did we find him?" I whispered.

Nash leaned forward, the silver light fading from his eyes. "Looks like it."

"Where is he?" Finch spoke up, his hand still wrapped around mine.

"You won't believe this." Nash barked a laugh.

"Why?" Finch cocked his head. "If it's somewhere cold again, I'm going to flip this table. My extremities still haven't recovered from Manitoba."

Nash pointed to the spot. "He's in Tijuana."

"Call me a hypocrite, but this isn't the time for jokes, Nash," Finch replied grimly. "Where is he, really?"

"Tijuana." Nash gestured again to the blood spot. This time, Finch bent down for a closer look. I followed, pulled by his hand. Sure enough, the blood spot marked Tijuana, with map lines having emerged through the paper to show Mexico.

"Sneaky son of a gun. Perfect place for him to hide." Finch snorted. "Who'd have thought Davin 'High and Mighty' Doncaster would wind up in this not-so-Wonderland? I can picture him now, downing two-for-one margaritas with a chaser of watered-down tequila. Maybe he's donned a sombrero to get in the party spirit."

I smiled despite myself. After all that terror, Finch's hand, Finch's voice, and Finch's wayward humor were starting to calm me down. Then my smile turned to a frown. I shouldn't have been relying on Finch to comfort me, I should've been relying on Adam. That wasn't Adam's fault, of course. He had no idea the magical world even existed, which was the biggest part of my dilemma. I should've been bowled over with joy when he asked to move in with me. Instead, I'd laughed so hard I almost popped a blood vessel. And I'd sat there, watching the man I loved in pain, because I'd been laughing instead of telling him it was a great idea.

Adam not knowing caused me untold distractions. Like, now I should've been focused on Davin's location and the next step to hunting him down. But Adam had flooded my thoughts. I loved him so much, but the more time I spent away from him, and the more embedded in this world I became, the less I believed that loving him was enough. They said absence made the heart grow fonder, but I no longer believed that.

Maybe if I tell him, all this worry and hesitation will go away. Maybe that's the obstacle here. If he accepted it and was as supportive as he always had been, then I'd be less stressed about all this lying and hiding. It would require magical permission, but I wasn't the only person to ever want to tell a human about this world's existence. There had to be a way.

Finch squeezed my hand. "You okay there? You've gone green around the gills."

"What? Oh… I'll be fine. I wasn't anticipating… well, *that*." Adam disappeared from my mind in a heartbeat. All I felt was Finch's hand, the warmth of his eyes, and the softness of his voice making sure I was okay.

It probably made me a hideous person, but his touch sent my mind into overdrive. I wanted to hug him. I wanted his arms around me, to take away the residual fear. I wanted to bury my face in his chest until it evaporated, the way the silver liquid and the wind had. But I couldn't. My brain was too confused already, and I didn't want to add to it. His touch shouldn't have done this to me. But… maybe there was some truth in the other old saying, that the heart wanted what it wanted.

Does my heart want him? I didn't have the answer. It didn't know what it wanted. Whenever I was near him, it went insane. But then, with some distance, it yearned for Adam again. One thing was sure: I needed to dig my way out of this baffling mess before somebody got their heart broken. I needed to stop being wishy-washy with my emotions and make a choice. Even if that choice was me, and me alone.

"Does this mean we're going to Mexico?" Melody brought some cheer back to the room, thankfully giving me something else to think about.

Nash petted Huntress, who'd come to lick his hand. "I guess so."

"Then let's get going. Wouldn't want to miss happy hour, would we?" Finch grinned, though I detected nervousness in his hand as he gripped mine one last time.

"Once I see Davin ended, it'll always be happy hour." Nash got up with a determined grimace. "Although, hold your horses a sec. We should probably have a plan before we go. He floored us at my cabin. I've got a few knives I've been working on here, but they might not be enough."

I squinted at him. "Valid point."

"You could always use an immobility hex," Melody chimed in. "I can give you the ingredient list and the instructions for making it, and you can pick up the items in Mexico City. It's rife with magic, and there are some powerful alchemists not far from Tijuana."

Nash nodded. "I know one, actually."

"You do?" Finch raised his eyebrows. "Hermit the Frog has mysterious acquaintances? The plot thickens."

Nash chuckled. "There's a lot you don't know about me, Finch. I'm conservative with my words and my anecdotes, unlike you."

"Ouch, low blow," Finch replied.

I had to admit, it felt really damn good to have a solid plan. We were going to immobilize the hell out of Davin, and it was going to be a rare treat to see him vulnerable.

"Then let me write this for you," Melody said. "All you have to do is get close enough to Davin to slip the immobility bag on him. Since you always seem to end up in scraps, that shouldn't be too hard.

Once it's in place, it will work much like Atomic Cuffs, rendering his powers temporarily inert. That should give you enough of a window to interrogate him and search for that amulet." She bristled with nervous excitement and whipped out a glittery pink unicorn notepad with accompanying fluffy-ended pen. Not the sort of thing you'd expect someone to write down a powerful hex with, but hey, whatever worked.

She scribbled the ingredients and the instructions and tore out the page, handing it to Nash. "Remember, if there's one ingredient missing, you can use your blood."

"I will," Nash replied, a satisfied smile on his face. "Now, how about you draw us a chalk door?"

"No problem. Can do!" She sounded a note too cheerful, betraying her inner anxiety. I might not have had magic, but I could hear nervousness in someone's voice.

Luke got up and stood next to her, one hand on her shoulder. A small gesture with a lot of love behind it. The poor guy was besotted with Melody, but there were rules about a Librarian not having relationships. And here I was, with a wonderful boyfriend, doubting myself and the relationship we had. Guilt broiled in my belly.

While Melody drew the doorway, Nash went back to the wooden chest at the back of the room and removed a fabric pouch. He unrolled it to reveal a set of sharp knives before stowing it away in his jacket pocket. The glint of them set my nerves on edge. This had become very real all of a sudden. Finch, Melody, Luke, and Nash were about to go after Davin. The man who'd tied up my family and tortured us to get to my sister.

Finch let go of my hand and dusted himself off. The separation struck me in my chest, so much so that I reached out and grabbed his hand again, pulling him away from the group. I didn't know if I'd get another chance to speak to him, and that thought almost finished me off.

"What's up?" He sounded concerned, and he peered into my eyes as if he could find my secrets there. I hoped he couldn't.

"I... I just wanted to say that... well, I... be careful, okay?" I floundered in the very moment that mattered most. "If things look bad, get out of there. It doesn't matter if you don't have the amulet. You get out of there and come back, and we'll figure out something else."

He chuckled. "Aww, are you worried about little old me?"

"I'm serious, Finch." I took his other hand. "At the first sign of danger, come right home. Don't do anything stupid, and don't do anything heroic. If it looks impossible, escape before anything really bad happens."

His expression changed to one of complete seriousness. "I will."

"Promise me!"

"I promise." Slowly, he lifted my hand up and placed the softest kiss on the back of it. "I'm not dying tonight. Although, if I can't get the amulet, then it might happen one day soon because of Erebus... but not tonight. I promise you."

Tears sprang to my eyes without warning. "I don't want to not speak to you again."

"What?" He gave a half-smile.

"I'm not making any sense. I know I'm not. I just mean... ah, I don't know what I mean. Just come back. I don't want to think about burying you. It was bad enough when we all thought you were dead in Russia. Don't put me through that again. That's what I'm saying."

He kissed my hand again, and I couldn't deny it: my heart fluttered. "I'll come back."

"You'd better, or I'll take all your boxed-up figurines and sell them on eBay for way less than they're worth." I tried some levity, but it fell short with my eyes full of tears and my voice thick with emotion.

"You can threaten all you like, and it still won't be the reason I come back," he said softly.

What? What does that mean? My frazzled brain couldn't make sense of it. Or, maybe it could, and I didn't want to admit what it deciphered.

"Time's a-wasting, Finch!" Nash said loudly from the other side of the room.

Finch slowly let go of my hands. "Duty calls."

I swallowed the lump in my throat as he backed away, his gaze trained on me. His eyes were the last thing I saw before the chalk door slammed shut and the quartet vanished. I'd have to ask Cecily Winchester to help me get home. I'd done that before without any problems. Nevertheless, it would be a long night.

Am I the reason? Is that what he meant? I stood there, alone and confused, not knowing if I'd ever see Finch, or any of them, again. In that moment, it had never sucked more to be human.

SEVEN

Finch

W ho needed gremlins when I had Ryann royally messing with my head? I couldn't stop thinking about the way we'd parted. I could've spouted Shakespeare from the rooftops—the romances, not the tragedies—or curled up in a ball until I figured out what the hell was going on in *her* head. But I had one satisfying takeaway. I'd actually managed to be smooth. So smooth. Buttery smooth. Sean Connery had slithered into my being and made me utter the perfect sentence exactly when I needed it.

You can threaten all you like, and it still won't be the reason I come back. Man, why couldn't I always come up with lines like that? Although, I'd probably end up as a douchebag like Davin, all sleaze and oily charm.

"Finch? Did you hear me?" Nash stared at me from the driver's seat of the banged-up Chevy he'd stolen outside Tijuana. We had all piled in, pupper included, and I'd managed to call shotgun. Luke hadn't seemed to mind, since it meant he could squish up next to

Melody. Well, he would've been able to if Huntress weren't acting as a furry buffer between them.

"Huh?" I hadn't heard him. Not with Ryann on the brain.

"Go into my jacket pocket and get the hex bags. Be careful with the blue one—that's our ticket to stopping Davin this time." Nash muttered something rude under his breath, but the dulcet tones of Metallica drowned out the worst of it.

There were reasons why Nash had wanted to thieve a ride into Tijuana after Melody chalk-doored us just outside the city limits. First, it'd give us a lower profile to enter the city the human way. Second, he'd wanted to swing by an old witchy friend's, as per his vague comment about knowing a powerful alchemist. They'd had some stuff on hand that'd help us slide under Davin's radar and pack a punch with the immobility hex. He'd told us to wait in the car, like he was about to crack a drug ring, and he'd come out with a bag full of goodies: herbs and various grisly bits of creatures to make other hex bags, as well as the immobility one. Apparently, the non-blue hex bags would conceal our Chaos energy. I wasn't convinced that a measly bag of herbs could do that, but who was I to rain on Nash's parade?

"Sorry." I delved into his jacket pocket and removed the four pouches, plus the extra one for Davin's demise. They smelled horrendous. Huntress started to whine when they hit her doggy senses. Sure, they might conceal our Chaos energy, but people would have something to say about the rancid stench. I had to hope Davin's olfactory senses weren't as sharp as his magical ones.

"Will these work?" Melody asked as I passed two pouches to the backseat lovers and gave the immobility bag to Nash. Huntress whimpered at the smell, burying her nose in Melody's lap. "What's in them?"

Nash focused on the road. "They'll work."

"She asked what's in them," Luke prompted.

"And I said they'll work." Nash gripped the steering wheel until his knuckles whitened. "We've got to up our security game. Davin will have all kinds of tricks up his sleeve, and I'm not taking any chances, even with this immobility thing. Especially considering we need to get close to him to make it work. These are powerful hex bags. It's probably best you don't know what's in them."

I snorted. "Great, so we've stolen a car and we're carrying contraband. Good thing we don't need to cross the border on the way back. I don't know about you, but I'm not keen on spending the night in some Mexican clink. I'm the pretty one—they'll eat me alive."

"You think you're the pretty one?" Nash grinned. There was a lot of satisfaction in making the silver fox smile. A tough crowd, but when I got him, it felt good.

"Oh, Nash, you'll be the moms' favorite." I leaned against the window, chuckling to myself. "Do you think he's got feelers out for us? Is that why you went for the hard stuff?"

Nash's humor evaporated. "There's no telling, but since you're with us, I figured it'd be best to cover all bases."

"Me?" I didn't know whether to be curious or offended.

"Davin keeps appearing whenever you're around. That can't be coincidence. Ain't no such thing," Nash replied bluntly. "I'd say he's got a tracking spell on you, but I did a sweep when you came into my cabin. You were clean of hexes. So, it must be something else."

Melody leaned forward and peeped over my seat, Huntress

copying her. "I've been thinking about that, actually, and I think I've hit the obvious conclusion."

"Oh yeah? When did you have this eureka moment?" I twisted my neck to look at her but ended up eye-to-eye with the husky.

"Just now, actually. I've been sifting through my mind palace, and I found something just after we left Nash's friend's house." She smiled excitedly. "The djinn have a network, right? Well, according to my Chaos sources, the servants of Erebus had one, too, back in the days when he had loads of people working for him. It helped them find each other quickly, so they could share information on the missions he had going on. He doesn't do that anymore—make deals with lots and lots of people—so the network sort of dwindled into obsoletion. But it still registers every magical who gets drafted into Erebus's servitude. Which means Davin was on it once, and so are you."

Nash smacked the steering wheel. "And if Davin wanted to know where you were, whenever he wanted, I'd bet my last dollar he's found some way to tap into that network and find your location."

"Will a hex bag be able to cover that?" Luke leaned forward too, so now the two of them were peering down at Nash and me like human backpacks.

Nash clenched his jaw. "It should. It conceals just about everything. If my friend is right, and she's never wrong, it'll block all our signatures from anyone trying to find them. Davin might get a bit suspicious when your servant beeper goes dark, but he hopefully won't know we're coming."

"Son of a nutcracker!" I glared out the window like the glass had called me an asshat. As if being Erebus's servant wasn't bad enough, now Davin was using Erebus's old network to keep tabs on me. Well, at least I finally had an explanation.

"I can look for a more permanent way to block him from finding you," Melody offered. Huntress's breath tickled my ear. "It shouldn't be difficult, as the network is pretty much dead anyway. If it were still in constant use, it'd be harder, but I can find a way to jam your signal for good."

I huffed air through my teeth. "That'd be swell. Otherwise, you may as well pack me off to Tartarus and leave me there. If Davin knows where I am, that makes me a liability. And I'd rather not have to carry around one of these stink-bags for the foreseeable future, either, though at least we've got a temporary fix."

"I'll start searching now," Melody promised, sitting back in her seat. Huntress followed, sprawling across Melody's legs.

"Show a little respect. They're not stink-bags. They're 'saving our ass' bags." Nash shot me a disapproving look.

I smirked. "Ha... ass-bags."

"Maybe the kid should be in the backseat," Luke remarked.

"And stop you from cozying up to Melody? I wouldn't dream of it," I shot back. No way would I let him have the last word. *Ah, he's right... I am the kid.*

"Pack it in, both of you." Nash glared at Luke through the rearview mirror, which prompted him to sit back. "We'll get there soon, and I don't want you two sniping at each other. Focus, for crying out loud." *Okay, Dad.*

I returned my gaze to the window as the streets of Tijuana appeared in full, gaudy Technicolor. The glass vibrated with the bass from the blinding neon bars. It was nighttime, but you'd never have known. Everything was way too bright, like a Willy Wonka factory for merry Americans trying to drown their sorrows in sickly sweet cocktails. The electric bill for this place must've been astronomical.

We kept driving, Nash struggling to avoid the staggering revelers who no longer had any concept of vehicles. And, with alcoholic fishbowls for five dollars, who could blame them? A few totally wasted guys pinballed off the hood of the car, though Nash was moving at a snail's pace.

"Why the hell did Davin pick this place?" I still couldn't wrap my head around a guy like him hanging out in this cheap, hedonistic playground. Being his perpetually upmarket self, I'd have expected Monaco or St. Tropez. *Expensive* and hedonistic, not this place.

"Tijuana is famous for being non-magical," Nash replied, swerving around a gaggle of screeching women. The locals didn't even flinch at the American invasion. They were probably so used to it by now, they figured it was better to sip their un-watered-down tequila in peace. "Davin likes to know when his enemies are coming, and without the hex bags we'd have stood out like sore thumbs. He'd be out of whatever bar he's holed up in before we even got past the bouncers."

"What if he's got a magical detector?" I remembered my worrying chat with Krieger and Jacob. The doc had been right—the magical detector had never turned up. And since Davin had been my mother's right-hand worm once upon a nightmare, maybe she'd gifted it to him.

Nash frowned. "You mean a Sensate?"

"Sure. Or, you know, some device that spots magicals." I also remembered that Nash, Melody, and Luke had no idea what the magical detector was. Melody might have had some knowledge of it in her mind, but I didn't feel like running through the logistics for the other two.

"The hex bags won't do much against a Sensate or a... device of that kind, if one existed." Nash turned down the thrash metal on the radio. "But they'll sure as heck muddle any trace he's got on us, even the servant network one, if that *is* what he's using."

Nash had, once again, proven to be a treasure trove of hidden tips and tricks. I couldn't help but wonder if our war against Katherine might've gone a little smoother if we'd had Nash on our side. Not to mention Melody. Luke probably wouldn't have made much difference, but he'd have been decent cannon fodder.

We drove away from the tacky part of the city into a different kind of nighttime paradise for those in need of escapism. The Chevy rattled past alleyways rammed with people and vibrant clubs that pulsed with Latin heat. Throbbing beats and Spanish guitar filled our car, prompting Nash to turn the radio off altogether. This was the energy of Mexico, vivid and intoxicating—in more ways than one. Santana probably would've turned her nose up, but she didn't hail from these parts. And Tijuana definitely had raw charm, particularly under the clear night's sky. If the electricity had switched off and just let the universe put on its beautiful light show, and that guitar kept playing, I'd have been in my own paradise.

"We're getting closer." Nash had the charmed map spread on the dash before him. The blood spot burned bright red, glowing more intensely as we drove.

"Is this a bad time to say I'm crapping myself?" I formed a nervous smile.

Nash chuckled. "You wouldn't be mortal if you weren't. All this time, I've been waiting for a moment like this, and my guts are throwing me for a loop."

"You didn't drink the water, did you?" I joked.

"You do that a lot, don't you?" Nash side-eyed me.

I side-eyed right back. "Do what?"

"Make jokes when you're nervous."

I shrugged. "Force of habit."

"I notice you do it a lot more when Ryann's around. Something going on there?"

Luke scoffed. "He wishes."

I hadn't expected a therapy session when I'd gotten into this car. "Nope. She has a boyfriend."

"Ah, it's like that, is it?" Nash made an understanding noise. "Let me give you a word of advice, Finch, and you can take it or leave it. I won't be offended. But, unless there's a ring on someone's finger, you've got a chance. Plus, if Ryann felt nothing for you, she wouldn't be around on a Saturday night. So, if I were you, I'd make a move. Otherwise, you'll spend the rest of your life regretting it."

"I keep telling them that," Melody chimed in.

Them? Plural? Had she said something to Ryann, or was she just going on her Empath mind intrusions with Ryann and casting aspersions on my own emotions? Either way, it added to the slice of hope I'd found in the Winchester House.

"Sounds like the voice of experience." I needed to shift the focus off me.

Nash laughed. "That's coming from a twenty-year-old Nash, who left the girl he loved to go and chase monsters overseas with the United Magical Marines. When that kid came back, she was married and happy as anything. I'll never not think about what could've been if I'd had the guts to tell her what I had going on in here." He tapped his chest.

"You were a Marine?" My eyes nearly popped out of my head. He had some rough and ready vibes, sure, but I hadn't pinned him as a military man.

"Back in the day, yeah." Nash nodded. "I had to work out some things in my head, and I figured the best way to do that was to fight for my country. So, maybe things wouldn't have worked out with her, anyway. I was pretty messed up in those days. But going overseas and seeing some awful things—it changes you. Some people for the better, and some people for the worse. I was lucky that it ended up having the former effect on me."

"I'm no soldier, but I know what you mean," I said quietly. The war with Katherine had changed everything about me. Teaming up with my sister, and fighting evil at her side... I'd never be the same person again.

He glanced at me. "Katherine stuff?"

"How did you guess?" I said quietly.

"I know haunted when I see it. You've got the look, soldier or not. I call it the flashback stare." Nash looked back at the road. "So, here's another piece of advice, from an old warrior to a younger one: you'll never change what you've done, but you can change what you're going to do. Your past will always be a part of you, but so's your appendix, and you sure as hell don't need that. Sure, remind yourself it exists from time to time, but don't get hung up on it. You don't have enough life to live to dwell on the bad stuff."

I stared down at my lap. He made it sound simple, but it wasn't. "What if my memories end up giving me appendicitis?"

"Then cut it out, and carry on with your life," he replied. "And tell the damn girl you like her. I know that look, too—and you both had it. Here's my parting word on it. Pining gets you nowhere."

I went to Tijuana, and all I got was this weird life lesson from Sarge over there. But it had gotten the cogs whirring. Not that they weren't already working overtime. If others had picked up on it, could it be true that Ryann felt the same way? Not just some casual musings and a flutter here and there, but actual feelings of "Hey, maybe I want to have something with this guy"?

"Anyway, enough chitchat. We're here." Nash put the car into park. We'd pulled up alongside a shady nightclub with blacked-out windows and a flashing sign with half the letters conked out. It looked like it was meant to say "Tarantino's."

Well, that doesn't bode well. What would we face inside? Ladies in yellow leather wielding katanas? A bunch of dudes with colors for names? Man, I really needed to catch up on the latest Tarantino movies to extend my cultural references. I only had the oldies to amuse myself with. The joint was about as opposite Davin's usual style as it was possible to get. I doubted they even knew how to make a G&T in this dive. If you asked, they'd probably think you were trying to start a fight.

But he was inside somewhere. We'd reached the end of the road.

EIGHT

Ryann

After asking for magical assistance from Cecily Winchester, I decided to call it a night and return to San Diego. A sad excuse for a Saturday night. I had no plans, Adam hadn't texted from the hospital, and my brain simply would not quiet down. I couldn't even enjoy the thrill of stepping through a magical door, which still hadn't lost its novelty for me. I hoped it never would.

The chalk door opened a block from my apartment. That wasn't Cecily's fault; I'd tried to be exact about the location, but apparently it was difficult to pinpoint a chalk door to a precise spot if a person wasn't familiar with the territory. Still, at least she hadn't opened a door on the other side of town. That might've knocked me over the edge into a full-fledged breakdown.

What am I doing? If I closed my eyes, I could picture Finch's steady gaze and feel his firm hand in mine. My heart beat faster at the memory. But that may have had something to do with the ghoulish faces in the silvery liquid and the wind screaming like a banshee through the Winchester House, which wasn't exactly a comforting place at the best of times. Moreover, I'd recently learned from Tobe that banshees were real. This world I'd stepped into got weirder and weirder with every passing day… and I loved it. Maybe that made me a glutton for punishment. Maybe that was why I seemed to be on a one-way train to destroying the relationship of my dreams.

Trudging up the three flights to my apartment, I wrestled my bag for the keys and opened the door. I froze on the threshold. The lights were off, as I'd left them, but a warm, flickering glow illuminated my sorry excuse for a lounge. Candlelight. Soft and romantic. *Antony and the Johnsons* played through my ancient stereo system, which I'd had since I was a teenager. And the album had just settled on my favorite song—"Hope There's Someone." Tears barreled into me out of nowhere. I tended to cry when this song came on, but tonight, it carried a lot more meaning.

Adam appeared in the kitchen doorway, dressed in a smart white shirt and dark jeans. Casual, but it made him look like a million dollars.

"There you are," he said softly. An amazing smell wafted from the kitchen: garlic, onions, roasted pine nuts, and maybe tarragon. I had no words. He'd done all this while I was out chasing after Finch and his troubles. He'd cooked, he'd lit candles, he'd put on my favorite album… and he'd even set up a table and chairs, pushing the sofa forward to make room. The table had a cloth and a glass with a rose inside, the plates and cutlery, and wine glasses were all set out and ready.

"I thought you were at the hospital." I hurried to wipe my tears. *It's just the song… it's just the song.*

He came toward me. "I had some time owed after all the overtime I've been doing, so I thought I'd make the best use of it and cook dinner for you. Your super let me in; I hope you don't mind. You've been working so hard, and we haven't had any quality time, so I decided to surprise you."

"This is... I'm very surprised." I didn't know what else to say. My head said I should be grateful, that I should appreciate all this effort, but my heart said I should be back at the Winchester House, waiting for Finch and the others to come back. It would have made me feel more at ease, at least, to know he was safe the moment he returned. And I could busy myself with the ghosts or ask Cecily about magic. Here in my apartment, I'd be phone-watching until I got the all-clear that he hadn't died. And that did not make a good date.

"It's too much, isn't it?" Adam looked crestfallen. "I thought about texting you to let you know, but I wanted it to be a surprise. I should've remembered you hate surprises. I really hoped you'd like it. Is it the candles? They're clichéd, right?"

I rallied myself. "No, it's not too much. I was just surprised, that's all. It's nice, really."

"Nice? That's the equivalent of saying something is fine. You hate it, don't you?" He stopped in his tracks, leaving a weird distance between us. Not close enough to kiss me but not far enough to be casual. Then again, I'd been all about weird distances lately, especially with him.

What the heck is wrong with me? Look at him! Look at what he's done for me, just because he thought it'd make me happy! Who hadn't dreamt of something like this as a teenage girl, after watching one too many rom coms? Adam was the love interest the protagonist was supposed to live happily ever after with. So why was I fixating on Finch?

Because he might die tonight. Yes, that would definitely do it. And I liked to believe that was all there was to my confused feelings. But… maybe I wasn't being entirely honest with myself.

"It's wonderful, Adam. Honestly, it is. I've had a weird sort of day, and I wasn't expecting this. I thought I'd be spending my night on the sofa, watching true crime with a can of soda and a mostly burnt bowl of microwave popcorn." I was rambling. I could hear it. But I didn't want to see that wounded look on Adam's face anymore; he didn't deserve to be wearing that expression.

Adam's eyes brightened a little. "Well, why don't you sit down, and I'll bring the food out. Then you can tell me about your day— the rest of it, anyway, starting after I left you at lunch."

"Sounds good." I shuffled off my coat as he went back into the kitchen, giving me a momentary reprieve to get my thoughts in some kind of order. The food did smell good, and the atmosphere felt incredible. The perfect kind of romantic. Casual, in my own home, and prepared by a man who could've been plastered on a Hollister store but who had the brains to provide stimulating conversation.

After a stern word with myself, I went to sit at the makeshift table. He'd been so kind and patient with me since I started working at the SDC. Yes, he thought I worked at a government office, but he'd still listened to my stress and anguish, though I'd changed a few names and occupations for the sake of magical rules. After all that, he deserved some quality time. If I kept rebuffing him and pushing him away, his patience would have no choice but to wear thin.

I'll test the waters tonight. I'll find a way to uncover how he'd react to magic.

I tilted my neck until I heard it click, trying to release my residual anxiety. A moment later, Adam reemerged with a pot of creamy, oven-baked risotto that sizzled in the most mouthwatering way. He carried a covered bowl in one hand. Judging by the intoxicating herby smell…

"Did you call my mom for this?" I gazed up at him as he sat across from me.

"I sure did." He grinned. "I know it's your favorite. And, to be honest, it's mine, too. Although, if I'd realized how long it would take to cook, I might've gone for something else. But you're worth it, so here it is."

I smiled, drinking in his face in the candlelight. "It looks delicious. And it *smells* incredible!"

"I hope it lives up to your mom's." He scooped a large spoonful onto my plate but left the sprinkling of parmesan to me. I liked to smother everything in the stuff, to let it melt and really get into my arteries. I didn't even wait before I scooped up the first mouthful and devoured it like a ravenous beast. It tasted amazing, though not quite as good as my mom's. Nothing would ever beat that. It wasn't just the recipe; it was the love and memories my mom put into it that would always make it impossible to recreate.

"Good?" Adam chuckled as I swallowed another mouthful.

"Incredible." The word came out muffled, my mouth stuffed to the brim.

He made a show of wiping sweat from his brow. "Phew."

With the music playing, and the candles glowing, and the amazing food making me feel marginally better about everything, I braced to begin my line of careful questioning. I had to know how he'd take the idea of the magical world, even if I could only speak in hypotheticals. Before I could start, however, Adam came in with questions of his own.

"So, how was your day?" He wiped his mouth with a napkin and poured two glasses of wine.

I sighed wearily. "The kind of crazy that'll need another glass after this," I joked.

"I bought two bottles for precisely that kind of workplace emergency." He smiled as he set the bottle down.

"This guy came into the coffee shop where I was finishing up some paperwork between meetings." The lies came effortlessly. So effortlessly, it made me uneasy. "He started causing a bit of a scene, claiming to be a sorcerer who was going to put a spell on everyone in the café if he didn't get to speak to the manager. I intervened and managed to talk him down until the cops came, but he was babbling some insane things. Things you wouldn't believe, about magic and how everything in this world is imbued with cosmic energy. And how some people have more than others, which allows them to perform magic."

Adam's expression darkened. "Did he hurt you? Are you okay?"

"No, he didn't hurt me. He was just a troubled man who needed someone to talk to," I replied, miffed that Adam had focused on me instead of the subtext, although it was sweet of him to be concerned. "But it got me thinking. What if there was some truth to what he said? Like, what would you think if it turned out that magic was real?"

"I think the poor guy is probably better off in a psych ward where he can get some proper care." Adam sipped his wine. "If he walked into the coffee shop acting like that, then he needs to be somewhere where he's not a danger to himself or anyone else. Delusional disorders are terrible. They make people see and hear things that aren't there and believe things that aren't true. I did a rotation in a psych ward, and I have unending respect for the doctors who choose that profession. Not much scares me, but that ward did."

I hid my frustration. "Forget the medical side for a moment. What if it wasn't a delusion? What if he was telling the truth? What would you think, if you found out magic was real?"

Adam tapped the stem of his glass in thought. "Honestly? I hate to be so clinical, but I don't believe in anything that science can't explain. Magic is impossible. It's the stuff of fairy tales and fiction. For example, I enjoy a zombie show as much as the next person, but do I think zombies can exist? No."

"Okay, but if someone proved that it *did* exist, what would you say? Magic, not zombies," I pressed.

"But it doesn't." He looked puzzled. "Are you sure you're not a bit shaken up by what happened at the coffee shop?"

I took a deep gulp of my wine. "I'm fine, really. It just made me think, that's all. I mean, physicists haven't specifically figured out how the universe came into existence, but they're fairly sure there was a beginning. Don't you believe them?"

"Ah, but there's theoretical science to back that up," he replied. "Therefore, it's something I can get behind."

"What if there was theoretical evidence to back up magic?"

"Is there?" He smiled, amused.

"No, but that's not the point. I'm asking you to entertain the hypothetical, not the theoretical." My patience was wearing a little thin. "Come on, what would you say if someone told you magic was real? No logic, no scientific answers, just whatever your gut tells you."

He squinted. "Where is all this coming from?"

"I don't know. Meeting that guy piqued my interest, I guess. He asked me the same question, but I didn't have time to answer before the cops arrived. It made me curious what you would think."

Adam ate a forkful of his dinner, leaving me hanging for a moment. "Well... if someone were to turn to me tomorrow and claim they could perform magic, I'd probably have a tough time believing it. I'd have to see it to believe it. Even then, I'd want to know the details of how it works... and I'd probably still suggest they see a shrink."

He paused before continuing, as if another thought had come to him. "Plus, no matter how fascinating it might be, it'd worry me. How do you control people like that? What would you do about the murderers and psychopaths? This world would get a lot scarier if those sorts of people had magic at their disposal. And what if they thought they were superior to ordinary humans? Would they try to enslave us? It sounds like the kind of thing that could start a war."

You have no idea. I had to give him props for being so astute. The magical world did have its villains, and one *had* sought to enslave humanity, but there was so much good in it, too. The magical world had made the collective decision to remain secret from ordinary humans to prevent exactly that from happening—all those things Adam had just mentioned. But at least I had him thinking now.

"What if they chose to be secret, to prevent that? And maybe they'd have internal police who helped protect ordinary humans, so no harm ever came to them. Ooh, they might even have a special prison for evil wizards who used their abilities illegally," I carried on, unable to stop now that I had the ball rolling.

Adam sipped his drink. "That would be less worrying, maybe. If they were like us, but with magic, then it'd make sense if they had the same laws and procedures in place that we do. But I can't imagine they would go underground, so to speak, for the sake of ordinary humans. Why would they, when they have all the power? That's not how humanity works. Power always rises to the top, one way or another. It might not be right, but it's true."

"Because they'd know it would start a war, and they'd choose to avoid that at all costs," I said firmly, feeling oddly protective over this world I'd become part of.

"Then they'd be better people than we are." Adam chuckled, devouring another forkful of dinner. I'd been neglecting mine, but this was too important. And we'd reached a turning point.

I inhaled sharply. "Well, what would you say if I told you that it's all true?"

Adam snorted violently, covering his mouth to stop rice from flying everywhere. "Okay, now I know this job is getting to you." He held his stomach while he laughed. "That man in the shop wasn't telling the truth. He needed professional help. I know it's fascinating to think about the possibilities of the universe, but magic isn't real. And if you keep talking like this, I'm going to have to make you go on that vacation and relax, to stop you from going completely insane."

This conversation wouldn't go the way I wanted it to. He'd said it himself—he needed to see it to believe it. Or, at the very least, he needed theoretical science to back it up. So, I did what any exasperated person would do, and laughed.

"I wanted to see if I could get you to bite." The laughter sounded fake, but I kept it coming. "A bit of a joke. Not a very good one, admittedly."

He chuckled. "You had me going there for a second. I thought you'd lost your marbles. Heck, I was about to go into your kitchen and confiscate every form of caffeine you have. Caffeine hallucinations are real, you know."

So is magic... His mockery left a bitter taste in my mouth, but it wasn't his fault. He didn't know what I knew; he hadn't seen what I'd seen. So, maybe my only option to salvage this was to get permission from O'Halloran and prove to Adam that magic was real. Or, maybe, the easier course of action was to leave things as they were... and continue to grow apart. The indecision was giving me more palpitations than any caffeinated beverage could. And my mind still hadn't stopped dwelling on Finch. I must've checked my phone under the table about twenty times, when Adam wasn't looking.

What, so I'm just going to give up? I'd put over a year into this relationship, and I loved him. Plus, I'd never been able to easily call it quits on a relationship. Whenever I thought about parting ways with Adam, I was reminded of how amazing everything had been before I started working full-time at the SDC. I couldn't have been more in love with him. He'd call and my heart would leap at the sight of his name on the screen. Now, I hesitated to answer my phone when his name popped up.

I wanted those butterflies back, but they'd fluttered away and showed no signs of returning. I couldn't reanimate the past any more than I could alter the magical influences that had changed me... but how had everything gotten so screwed up? Why hadn't I been able to hold on to the past and bring it into my future? Why did knowing about magic mean I had to let go of Adam? Maybe because the magical world wasn't the only thing pulling me in a different direction.

These were the facts. I couldn't imagine my life without magic anymore. Continuing to be with Adam without telling him about it would force me to live a double life, and I didn't have the strength to split myself in two. No, I needed to make a decision about all this, and soon. Tell Adam or let him go. Those were my options. So simple, yet so confusing.

This needs a sister's point of view. Only one person could help me if I couldn't help myself. Harley would have the answer. She always did. The only trouble was, what if I didn't like what she had to say?

NINE

Finch

Tarantino's bombarded every sense. Bass thundered through the booze-soaked carpet, making my chest ache with every throb. I could actually feel the music, from the tips of my toes to the roof of my skull. Man, it sucked. I wasn't even sure you could call it music. Maybe I'd turned into an old fogey, thanks to Nash's life lessons, but this just sounded like a lot of noise to me. Techno, I believe the youth called it.

Drunken revelers careened into our *very* sober band from all angles, though Luke proved to be a pro at twisting Melody out of the way of oncoming moonshine zombies. It looked like he had another ability to complement his temperamental Magneton stuff—making drunkards swerve off in the opposite direction with a not so gentle shove. People thronged all around us, dancing like lunatics, their heads hanging low while their arms waggled aimlessly above them. Kind of like those wiggly air monsters in front of sketchy second-hand car dealers.

Did we cross some magical threshold into Ibiza? There were so many glowsticks that my eyes started to see neon when I blinked. Sweaty dudes with glowstick necklaces strewn around their necks hugged each other like they were about to ship out. And equally sweaty girls shrieked to be heard over the pounding beat, screaming about some guy who "wasn't worth it, honey!"

What made it hilarious, despite the reason we were here, was Nash. He was late thirty-something going on eighty-five, and this was not his vibe at all. He ran an anxious hand through his silver hair as a scantily clad young lady sidled up to him, claiming she could do all sorts of things with a cherry stem.

"No thanks," he said gruffly. "And you shouldn't accept drinks from strangers. You don't know what they might put in them."

The woman frowned. "What are you, my dad?"

"Perhaps, if he were here, he'd say the same thing." Nash shook his head as the woman skedaddled, evidently realizing she was wasting her time on Nash.

"Not your scene?" I nudged him in the arm. Secretly, I felt a bit put out that he was getting all the attention.

"What?" he roared back.

"I said, is this not your scene!" I matched his volume, straining my lungs.

Nash puffed out a nervous breath. "It's incredible what people do for entertainment." He dodged another woman wearing what was pretty much a bikini, suggesting she get some water to take the edge off. He got another confused look before the woman sauntered off in search of more willing company. "I need a drink," he grumbled, making his way toward the bar. "And I mean a soft one. We need to stay sharp, Finch. Don't you get dragged into this... hedonism, because I'm not going to pull you out." He do-si-doed another woman, sending her off in the opposite direction without her realizing what had happened. "And I won't confiscate your phone, either. I said you should tell Ryann how you feel, but you don't want to do it three sheets to the wind, let me tell you."

"Hey, I'm not planning to get drunk," I shot back. How much tequila would it have taken to forget Ryann Smith, anyway? A bucket? A truckload?

Nash smirked. "Good. You'd regret it, in hindsight."

We stopped by the bar. Nash flagged down the bartender, who batted spidery fake eyelashes at him. "What'll it be, sugar?" she purred.

"Four lime and sodas, thanks," he replied gruffly.

The bartender frowned but hurried off to make the drinks regardless.

"This is *incredible!*" Melody bounded up to me, swaying to the music. "I've never been to a club before! I've never even been in a bar before! I had no idea this kind of place existed! Who knew? I haven't drunk a single drop, and I don't plan to, but I feel like I'm... buzzing!"

I rolled my eyes. "Really? I couldn't tell you've never partied before."

Melody beamed. "Do I fit in?"

"He's teasing you," Luke interjected, looking as nervous as I'd ever seen him. And I sensed it had nothing to do with Davin. Tending a rowdy little chipmunk like her, flailing her arms and getting into the party spirit, would make anyone anxious, but that got amped up a few notches when said chipmunk happened to be the Librarian. The single most knowledgeable mortal in the known world. How much more thudding bass would it take to start taking out her braincells? Chaos might have to find another vessel before the night was over.

"Oh." Melody stopped dancing and leaned on the bar, visibly dejected.

"You'll have your time to let loose one of these days, but this ain't it." Nash came in as the voice of fatherly comfort. "And don't you listen to any nonsense about not being able to have a life because of who you are. You make your decisions, not Chaos. But don't make your first party experience this dive. You deserve better."

That seemed to cheer her up, and she went back to bopping her head while Nash and I scoured the club for signs of Monsieur Dingleberry.

It didn't take long; he always stood out. I spotted him at a table in the far corner—probably the VIP area, if this place even knew what VIP meant. Since he was sitting there, it was more likely to stand for Very Irritating Prick. The crowd of slinky ladies and dangerous-looking heavies with him only added to the sleaze factor. They weren't the kind of dudes he'd invite to afternoon tea. He'd probably picked them up from local gangs to give him some human protection.

"Aww, would you look at that? Davin brought some friends." I scowled, already itching to swipe his head off his smug shoulders.

"That doesn't surprise me," Nash replied grimly. "Davin always had a habit of paying humans to do his dirty work and getting a bit of cash out of it to pocket for himself. That asshole has fingers in every pie. Tijuana is probably one of the places that funds his operations, though who knows what flavor the pie is."

"It's *Tijuana*, Nash." I gave him a pointed look.

"And? You shouldn't read too much into stereotypes, Finch. He might be dealing in cars, security, or cheap tequila. Anything to keep his money flowing after Katherine's death." Nash kept his gaze fixed on our prey, tapping his fingertips anxiously on the bar top.

How did I not know that? I'd thought I knew every shady facet of Davin's character, but apparently he was even more versatile and cunning, not to mention dangerous, than I'd realized. If he had gangs working for him, then we were swimming in seriously deep doo-doo.

That alone should've made me turn and run, but it was too late for that sort of shirking now. I'd killed him a couple times before. What was once more? Maybe this time, if I managed to swipe his precious amulet, it'd finally stick.

My heart jolted as Davin did a supervillain swivel in his chair. For a moment, I thought his eyes would lock with mine. Hex bags couldn't stop him from seeing what was right in front of him. And, honestly, I couldn't even smell their stench anymore, thanks to the far worse aromas of stale alcohol and human fecundity that ran riot through this place. *Fecundity... great word. Now, focus!* But he didn't see me. Instead, he whispered something to one of his goons. They got up together, with Davin heading for a narrow passageway at the back of the club. The goon disappeared with him, no doubt to act as guard, his steroid-gifted muscles flexing.

"Davin just went down that passage over there." I gestured to the doorway with the massive guard.

"He saw you?" Nash whispered.

I shook my head. "Nope, no 'come to my murder house' eyes. He whispered something to one of his minions and disappeared. But he's on his own, wherever he is. Man, I hope it's not a bathroom. I don't want to have to interrogate him with his pants down."

"Then it's time to move. I've got the immobility hex, so we're all ready." Nash ignored me and turned to Melody and Luke. "You two, go outside and stay in the car. If Davin tries to escape, you be there to hold him up until we get there."

"We'll be the ones screaming, in case you get confused," I added.

"But—" Melody started to protest, but not on Nash's watch.

"We may need cavalry, Melody. And let's not forget who you are. I know I said it shouldn't stop you from making your own choices, but this is too dangerous. Go outside and keep an eye out in case things go south. This isn't taking you out of the equation; it's creating backup in case he makes a run for it." Nash didn't wait for her reply. He strode away from the bar, towing me along.

Together, we made our way past the crowds and slipped down a narrow passageway between the restrooms, adorably labeled *Wenches* and *Studs.* Apparently, the manager hadn't heard about female empowerment. I poked my head around the wall to catch a glimpse of the door Davin had gone through. It stood at the end of the passage, bearing a *Staff Only* sign. The guard leaned against the wall beside it. Ducking back, I let Mimicry bristle through my veins, transforming me from ordinary Finch to hot-as-hell bartender. That wall of muscle and tattoos wasn't magical; he wouldn't know the difference, and no puffed up sted-head could resist a buxom bartender in need of supplies.

"Finch?" Nash gaped.

"This is our way in, trust me." I touched Nash's arm, and he transformed before my eyes into the spitting image of that bikini-clad woman who'd tried to woo him.

He stared down at himself. "What did you do to me?"

"Keep calm. Being a woman for a few minutes won't kill you." Sliding my arm through his, I took the lead, sashaying up to the guard. Everything felt new, with jiggly bits that had never jiggled before. Unsettling but necessary, and Captain Tats seemed to appreciate the sight.

I smiled sweetly. "Excuse me, we need to get through. We've got customers crying out for tequila, and the bar's run dry. It'll be our necks if we don't get a fresh batch up soon."

The goon frowned. "You can't go through yet."

"Please? I can't deal with all those sweaty men yelling at me. Everyone thinks being a bartender is easy, but you have to deal with snapping fingers and a whole bunch of insults hurled at you by drunken idiots. And that *is* the stockroom." I nodded to the door behind him.

"You can't," the guard replied.

I sidled up to him and pushed my newly gained boobs against him. "There's going to be a riot if they don't get their tequila. I'll only be a few minutes, I swear. Please... be the one kind man I meet tonight."

His expression softened. "This won't take long?"

"Not with you out here, sweetheart." I flashed him a flirtatious grin.

"Fine, but make it quick." He smirked, evidently believing his luck was on. "And come over to my table when you get a break. My boss can make this night go a whole lot smoother for you."

I pressed my palms to his chest and kissed him on the cheek, getting an almighty wave of cheap aftershave. "Thank you!"

With the guard all goo-goo eyed, we pushed right on through.

The moment we stepped past the tattooed bouncer, however, Nash turned back and clamped his hands across the guard's eyes. Bright light pulsated into his skull, and when Nash removed his hands, the guy's eyes widened for a second before his face turned completely blank.

"What did you do? I had it covered!" I hissed as the two of us slid past the guard and walked down the rickety stairwell. It clanged, straining under our weight. A foreboding omen. In fairness, the last place I wanted to be when we faced Davin was the dingy basement of a joint like this. If Davin won, the staff would probably leave us for the rats instead of taking the trouble of calling the cops.

"I fazed him," Nash replied quietly.

"Come again?"

"I made him believe he hadn't seen us, since we might need more than a few minutes down here." Nash squinted at me. "Don't they teach you anything in your fancy coven? Fazing is one of the simplest memory spells you can learn."

I squinted right back. "I haven't been in my fancy coven that long, remember? Katherine must've skipped the faze training in favor of something more vicious. Fighting gargoyles, cooking up spells that burn a person from the inside out, that sort of thing."

"Right. I keep forgetting." Nash headed farther into the gloom below, squeezing past stacks of beer barrels and gas canisters. It smelled rotten down here. I had no other word for it. The bubonic plague was likely festering away happily in a corner, ready to take down the entire population of Tijuana. Though they'd probably think it was just the worst hangover ever.

I kept up the Mimicry in the hope of taking Davin by surprise. In these forms, how dangerous could we be? I supposed that depended on how familiar Davin was with stressed-out bartenders.

Nash paused in a semi-open space in the middle of the dingy basement. Something dripped overhead and landed with a thick splash on the dirty floor. A trio of anemic lightbulbs shed their sickly glow on the entire expanse. So, we were pretty much standing in darkness. This felt less and less like a good idea by the second, and in my head everyone's voices screeched, "I told you so!" But at least the music wasn't so bone-shattering down here. Simply a dull, repetitive thud that matched my racing heartbeat.

"What if he chalk-doored away?" I whispered, my head whipping around in case he suddenly emerged from behind an icebox. I couldn't see him anywhere. Then again, I couldn't see much. But we had to be quick to make our preparations before he showed his ugly face.

Nash narrowed his eyes. "He hasn't. He came down here for a reason, and if he'd wanted to leave, he'd have used the front door. That's the beauty of Davin Doncaster—when you know him as well as I do, he's about as predictable as the sun rising in the morning."

"Well then, I hope we get to see another sunrise." I braced for a fight, Chaos at the ready.

Nash darted away, plucking what appeared to be a Sharpie from his pocket. He scratched the tip across the nearest barrels and walls and support beams, sketching rapid symbols. I knew enough about symbology to recognize them as blocking wards.

"A Sharpie? Really?" I raised an eyebrow.

He flashed a grin. "Writes on anything. Best tool in a magical's arsenal."

"Will these wards hold him back?" I doubted it. Then again, Nash had so many tricks and gizmos up his plaid sleeves. Maybe this would work, too.

"It won't hold him back, but it'll block some of the magic he might throw at us, which should give us the chance to get up close and personal. It pays to be one step ahead." Nash popped the cap back on his Sharpie but kept it firmly in his grasp.

"If the Sanguine thing doesn't work out, you'd make a fortune writing inspirational quotes on Instagram." I chuckled anxiously.

Nash frowned. "I don't understand half of what you just said. All I know is, we need to be prepared."

A sharp laugh splintered the darkness, startling both of us. "Be prepared for what, exactly? I don't think the two of you ought to be down here."

I hadn't even heard him step out from wherever he'd been hiding. Like a chameleon who'd camouflaged himself to match the basement's surroundings, he just… emerged. Magic shimmered over him—subtle but definitely there. Yep, he'd used some kind of camouflage spell. Another trick from his hefty arsenal. Every time we met, he ran rings around me. By now, I must've looked like a hundred-year-old redwood.

"Uh… we were just fetching more supplies for the bar," I replied in my newly feminized voice.

"Is that so?" He eyed us from a distance. "Then why don't you take what you need and scarper?"

Nash and I exchanged a look. Time to put on my flirting shoes. "I could ask what you're doing down here, sir. Didn't you see the 'staff only' sign? Or do you like lurking in darkened basements where you can sneak up on an unsuspecting gal like me?"

"I did not miss your sign, but I have some business to attend to." Davin smiled oddly.

"Business? What kind of business?" I sauntered toward him, but he put up his hands to stop me walking any farther. "That is quite far enough."

"But how are you and I, and my friend here, supposed to get to know one another better if we have to keep our distance?" I batted my eyelashes, making sure Nash was beside me. He had the immobility hex bag, after all. "It's not often we see a fella so fancy in this place."

"Ah, now there it is." Davin smoothed down his lapel.

"Where what is?" I giggled with everything I had.

His mouth twisted up into a smirk. "The moment you slipped up, Finch. The barmaids here know who I am and know how I am to be treated. Even the new recruits know that." He glanced at Nash. "And what in heaven's name are you doing with that marker? Are you going to color me into submission?"

Ah, balls...

TEN

Finch

———

"You never learn, do you?" Davin tutted, giving it every ounce of patronization he had.

I immediately dropped the Mimicry to conserve energy for any imminent scrap we might have. Fighting him two-on-one might work, sure, but we didn't need to fight to the death. We just needed to be close enough to put the immobility bag in his pocket or stuff it down his verbose throat. But first, a little chat might throw him off guard.

"We don't want to fight, Davin." I stepped forward, ignoring the singe of Nash's death stare on the back of my neck. "I'm here to talk. Let's not get things twisted, I hate you, but you aren't the biggest fish in need of frying right now. Erebus is the prize swordfish. You're more of a guppy that can be thrown back. And I need you to tell me how you escaped his service."

Davin fell silent. Only to burst into raucous laughter a moment later. Clipped, grating, private schoolboy laughter. "Well, well, well, this *is* unexpected. I presumed you came to have your arse handed to you once more."

"Sadly, I didn't bring my guillotine, so it wouldn't be a fair fight. And you always play dirty." I wouldn't let him have *all* the fun.

"Very amusing, Finch." His face hardened. "I thought you might have lost your sense of humor after a lengthy spell under Erebus's thumb. Perhaps you are hardier than I expected, or merely too dense to realize you are in over your head."

"Ignorance is bliss, right?" I shot back.

He smirked. "Seeing you dead on this vulgar floor would also be bliss."

I made a show of mock horror. "And give up on letting me do all the hard work, so you can swoop in at the last moment? I'm still pissed about those oranges, D. I wanted to make a glass of juice."

"Much good they did me." Davin's expression shifted for a split second, showing genuine frustration. "As for my escape from Erebus, I suppose I can tell you, since it will do you no good. Yes, that may be even more satisfying than seeing you dead."

I leaned against a stack of barrels and cast a glance at Nash, who looked confused. "Go on."

"I am in possession of an amulet designed specifically for my use, created by a djinn and forged in the flames of that djinn's raw Chaos."

"I know the one," I cut in. "The shiny little tool you use to resurrect yourself, right? How else would you manage to skirt the rules of Necromancy?"

Davin snickered. "I've used it every time you have attempted to execute me. How frustrating that must be for you." He stared at me, a creepy darkness bleeding into his eyes. "But if you are here because you think you can use my amulet, I urge you to think again. You cannot use it, because you are not a Necromancer."

"You're forgetting Ephemeras." Nash stepped up, glaring. "Finch can load one with Necromantic power and use that amulet of yours, then wipe that smirk off your face while he's at it."

Davin laughed louder. "This is just too precious. Are you so unwaveringly moronic that you think it would be so easy? An Ephemera wouldn't work. The amulet only recognizes a true Necromancer." He took a step toward me. "Only death can free a servant from a deal with Erebus. You will simply have to face the music and dance... death by your own hand, or death by Erebus's."

No... no... that can't be true. I struggled to hide the pain and disappointment coursing through me. I didn't want him to see that he'd gotten to me. But... I had one hope left.

"Which djinn?" My voice came out as a savage rasp. "Which djinn helped you?"

Davin smoothed a hand through his slick hair. "You will never find him. I made sure of that."

"You double-crossed the djinn who helped you?" Nash looked ready to launch himself at Davin. "You really don't have a single decent bone in your body, do you?"

"I must take care of my investments. And I had to eliminate any witnesses to my evasion of Erebus. When it comes to my life, or someone else's, you should know by now—I will always choose me."

My heart broke. "You killed the djinn who saved you?"

"You do not need the details," Davin replied coolly. "So sorry to be the bearer of bad news. Actually… I'm not. The look on your face will see me through many a tedious evening."

Why don't I believe you? Everything Davin said had to be taken with a gigantic handful of salt. But even if the djinn wasn't dead, I'd stake my life on the fact that Davin had buried him deep, somewhere nobody would ever find him. Which was almost as bad.

A spike of pure anger shot through my chest. "Well then, I have nothing left to lose, do I?" If I couldn't take Davin's amulet and use it to free myself, and he'd done away with the djinn who made the amulet in the first place, then Davin had ceased to be useful. And I'd be damned if I would go to my imminent grave without taking that gargantuan stink-bag with me.

"That doesn't mean I can't still assist you in your endeavor to escape Erebus." Davin threw a curveball I hadn't expected. Slimy, unpredictable ass-wipe. I'd been preparing myself to take him down, then he'd gone and said that.

"Don't listen to him," Nash warned.

"You wouldn't piss on me if I were on fire, Davin. Don't pretend you're interested in helping me." I balled my hands into fists, feeding Chaos to my palms.

"I said I wanted to see you dead, didn't I?" Davin chuckled darkly. "I could always kill you to fulfill that particular desire, then bring you back. That would free you from your deal with Erebus. And I would get a little thrill from it."

Nash came up to me and put his hand on my arm. "I mean it, Finch. Don't listen to a word he says. He will double-cross you, the way he double-crosses everyone. He's got more reason to keep you dead than bring you back."

I understood where Nash was coming from. If I hadn't had the dull thud of techno pounding in my head, maybe I'd have had the sense to think the same way. But Davin made an interesting point. A tantalizing proposal. The kind the devil might offer a guy with nowhere else to turn. And since he'd swiped the hope of the amulet from me and, potentially, the djinn, I really didn't have other options. Sure, he was probably telling some fibs, but a nagging doubt lingered in my head... what if he wasn't? I supposed I could've tried to track down another Necromancer to resurrect me post-death, but Katherine had done away with most of them, and the two who remained had gone deep underground.

Davin straightened his lapels. "If I freed you from Erebus, that would truly rile him up—his most devoted servant betraying him by running away. That would bring me far more satisfaction than turning you into a decaying corpse. It would also mean I would reach Atlantis first."

All my desperate inclinations to accept his offer vanished. Common sense made a comeback. Much as I hated to admit it, Davin and Erebus on the loose in a neck-and-neck race to Atlantis was more dangerous than anything they'd done before. Especially as I had no clue what the deal with Atlantis was. If it related to power, the last thing I wanted was Davin getting more of it to guzzle up like cream soda at a kid's birthday party.

"Finch." Nash gripped my arm tighter.

"I know, I know," I muttered back. This wasn't an easy decision.

"Well?" Davin prompted.

Give me a friggin' minute! I wracked my brain, trying to settle on the right answer.

Eventually, I released a weighty sigh. "It's a no from me, Davin. Better the devil you know, right?"

Davin glowered at me, his expression morphing into a mask of disappointment. "I rarely give you credit for your intellect, Finch, but I thought even you were smarter than that. Truly, I did." He dusted off his fancy suit jacket—a flashy emerald-green number. "If you've chosen this unfortunate path, I suppose we must return to business."

A thread of purple light snaked from his palms, shooting right at us. Nash dove behind a beer barrel and unleashed a blast of Air. Davin twisted out of the way, the magic careening past him and sending a wall of barrels and kegs hurtling toward the back wall.

I followed suit, skidding behind a stack of crates. Peering around it, I lashed out with Telekinesis, fending off the snaking purple tendrils as my own magic headed for Davin. With my other hand, I readied a dose of Fire and hurled a raging torrent at Davin's face. Once again, he ducked away. The torrent hit an air canister, the kind that pumped beer through the taps.

I held my breath and covered my head with my hands. A second later, the canister exploded. Searing flames burst into the basement, knocking Davin forward. He stumbled but didn't fall. Infuriating, considering I would've given anything to see him fall flat on his stupid face.

"Thanks for the warning," Nash hissed.

"I didn't think he'd duck that fast!" I shouted back, my ears ringing.

Davin came back with a vengeance, if slightly singed. With both palms up, he launched a barrage of Telekinesis. It smacked into the crates and the barrels, turning the former to matchsticks and sending the latter clanging against any solid surface they hit.

I ran from my annihilated hiding spot and thundered a wave of Air and Telekinesis back at him, the two threads blending to create a tornado of grabby, destructive energy. The tornado whacked Davin hard, and he arced through the air. He slammed into the ground a short distance away, a labored groan escaping his throat.

"Get down," Nash growled.

I obeyed without question. Nash delved into his jacket of endless magical delights and removed a blade. The handle shone with polished white bone, a glinting ruby embedded in the center. Tiny runes had been carved along the length of the knife. Each one lit up a deep, burning red as Nash clutched the hilt and whispered under his breath. His head snapped back up, his eyes trained on Davin.

The scumbag lurched to his feet. Nash struck. With an elegant overhand that would've made a pitcher weep with joy, he drew back the blade and sent it flying at Davin.

The color drained from Davin's face. He seemed to know what it was, but he could do nothing to stop its deadly trajectory. Like a rabbit in headlights, he faltered. Had he moved a moment sooner, it might've missed him. As luck would have it, he didn't.

The knife thudded into Davin's shoulder. He stared down at it, as though he wasn't quite sure how it had gotten there. My eyes widened as veins of light spiderwebbed out from the entry wound, pulsating through the fabric of his suit. He lifted his gaze back to us, his mouth opening as if to say something. But he never did get the final word.

The ruby in the hilt of Nash's knife brightened to a retina-searing glow, followed shortly by a powerful explosion.

I'd thrown myself to the ground, like Nash told me to. But it didn't matter. The shockwave detonated, barreling into Nash and me and knocking everything else clean out of its way. My eyes squeezed shut as I sailed away from solid ground and smashed into the hard metal surface of a support beam.

Well, this can't be good... And neither could the darkness that came next.

ELEVEN

Finch

E verything hurt. My back felt like a herd of baby elephants had run twelve marathons up and down my spine. Someone had oversqueezed the bellows formerly known as my lungs. And my head thumped as if I were still listening to that techno music upstairs. But I was awake. And, more importantly, alive.

I sat slumped at the bottom of the support beam, something disgusting seeping into the bottom of my pants. At least, I hoped it was seeping in, not out. That blast *had* come as a bit of a shock. The blinding light had disappeared, taking two of the sickly bulbs with it. I squinted into the gloom. Davin must have been in a million fleshy pieces…

A heavy grunt echoed through the basement.

"Nash?" I whispered.

"That wasn't me," Nash's voice hissed back.

Ah, turd-stools…

"Bugger it. Bugger it to hell," Davin cursed somewhere in the shadows. He used some slightly less polite expletives, but they didn't bear repeating. A scuff of shoes on the floor followed his rant. Crates crashed to the ground and metal clanged as he stumbled into kegs and canisters—the ones that hadn't been decimated by Nash's knife. Bottles smashed, sending up the scent of booze.

"We need to get out of here." I fumbled blindly for Nash. The music still pounded from the bar overhead, having shifted gear to drum and bass, which meant it was unlikely anyone had heard the blast. Melody included. So there wasn't going to be any backup on the way.

"That's not my hand, Finch." Nash emerged, and I snatched my hand away. He looked like crap. A big bruise bloomed across his cheek, and blood trickled from his nose. "But you're right, we need to go."

"I'll find you!" Davin snarled. "Once I find my arms, I'll find you!"

I pictured a limbless Davin stumbling through cheap tequila, his fancy suit shredded. *'Tis but a flesh wound!* It made me feel slightly better about having no hope. At least I'd gotten the last laugh, for now.

"I don't feel so good, Finch." Nash stared up at me with unfocused eyes. A moment later, he collapsed, crumbling into a heap. Panic set in. I had two choices: get Nash out of here immediately, or use this moment to immobilize Davin and search him for that amulet. Actually, it was a no-brainer. Nash would've understood and probably would be doing the same in my position.

Thinking fast, I dug through his jacket pockets for the immobility hex bag and high-tailed it over to the spot where Davin's groans came from. A dim glow illuminated his armless body. He writhed in pain, splashing about in a pool of his own blood. Not exactly the imposing image he liked to give off. He looked pretty pathetic, actually.

Crouching down so I didn't dip my knees in Davin's goo, I plonked the hex bag right on his chest. Blue light shivered out, creating thin ropes of energy that bound him there. No putting himself back together just yet. In fact, not ever, if I found this friggin' amulet.

"How's this for a bit of table turning?" I smiled down at him coldly.

He grimaced. "You actually came prepared this time. Between that knife and whatever this is... I'm almost impressed."

"This is where we part ways, Davin. You're dying in Tijuana, and I'm putting that on your damned headstone, so everyone will know you conked it in a dive bar." I leaned forward and started my long-awaited pat-down. Chaos forgive me, I wanted to avoid some of his less savory areas, but knowing him, that's exactly where he'd keep his amulet. At first, I searched calmly. But the more I felt around, finding nothing, that calm gave way to frustration.

"Ooh, that tickles." Davin chuckled grotesquely, blood spattering down his chin.

"Shut it!" I kept searching him but found nothing but a money clip with a wad of notes in it and a pocket watch. I may or may not have pocketed the cash.

"What's the matter? Can't you find what you're looking for?" he taunted.

I glared at him. "Oh, I'm going to find it. You mark my words."

"No, I don't think you are," he wheezed. "Did you think me foolish enough to keep wearing the amulet?"

I paused. "What?"

"That item is too precious to have about my person. I learned that lesson, having almost lost it several times, as you well know." He leered at me, his mouth twisting in pain.

"Where is it, Davin?!" I snarled.

"Somewhere you won't find it." He laughed again, the sound gurgling in the back of his throat. "I learned much from your mother, including how to hide things you do not wish other people to find."

A memory rocketed into my skull. Katherine had hidden the magical detector away in a personal interdimensional bubble, meaning it was attached to her in a way, yet detached so nobody else would be able to get their hands on it. And no one had found that detector yet, so she'd done a hell of a job hiding it.

"What have you done with it?" I grasped him by his sodden lapels.

"It is in a secret bubble of my own creation. One you cannot reach. Only I have access to it, and since you cannot threaten to kill me, as it won't stick, there is nothing you can do that will make me give it up." He grinned with blood-streaked teeth. "Forget about that amulet, Finch. You cannot have it. Ergo, you cannot kill me."

I wished Melody were down here, so she could check him over with some of her Librarian magic, but I didn't know how to call for her. And I didn't know how long this immobility bag would hold. Melody had mentioned it being temporary. But how temporary? What if I brought her down here, and Davin managed to get at least one arm back on in the interim? That would mean putting the Librarian right in Davin's path. Plus, Nash was out cold, wounded by the blast from his knife, and I didn't know how badly he might be hurt.

A choice expletive lingered on my tongue. Grimacing, I reached for the detached arms that lay abandoned on the floor. Anything to give Davin more to do to put himself back together. Swallowing the rising bile, I stuffed them into a plastic bag. These were getting chucked into the nearest garbage heap I could find.

"Take them. It matters little to me," Davin said, eyeing the bag. "The amulet grants me Regen abilities, depending on the circumstances of my 'death.' I will simply grow more arms once this hex wears off."

I thought of Louella Devereaux for a moment, the Regen who'd once been part of our merry band before Katherine ended her. I let her memory spike anger into my heart. Another victim of the games Davin and Katherine had played.

"Actually, I think I feel your surprising little hex wearing off right now." Davin glanced down at his body. Sure enough, the blue threads had started to fade, and his blunt stubs twitched excitedly, as if they might re-sprout arms at any moment.

Crap, crap, crap...

"You absolute son of a naked mole rat!" I seethed.

Davin grinned. "Inventive."

Realizing he'd gotten one step ahead of me, I made the painful decision to get the hell out of dodge before the immobility bag packed it in. Nash needed medical assistance, and I wasn't about to let him die for nothing. Davin had hidden that amulet real good, and I wasn't going to find it today. If ever.

I cursed under my breath and sprinted back to Nash. Wasting no time, I grabbed him and sketched a chalk door on the floor of the basement. We fell through it instantly, tumbling through the air. We landed with a thud outside the bar, thanks to the weird physics of chalk-door drawing, where Luke and Melody waited.

The Chevy door opened, and Melody jumped out, Luke and Huntress leaping after her.

"Finch? Nash? What happened?" she cried. "Huntress was going crazy in the car. I guess I see why, now."

"No time. We need to vamoose. Davin lost his arms, but they're itching to regrow. And that immobility hex has almost worn off. Winchester House, pronto!" I gasped, the landing adding bruises to my bruises.

She nodded and hurried to the wall of the bar, drawing a doorway and whispering the *Aperi Si Ostium* spell. The edges fizzed and crackled with bronze light, a beacon to safe passage.

"Luke, can you lift this grate for me?" I pointed to a sewer grate in front of me.

He frowned. "Why?"

I waved the plastic bag at him. "Arms, Luke! Davin's arms!" I replied, exasperated.

"Oh… right." Luke twisted his wrists, and the sewer grate came loose. I dumped the bag right into the murky, stinking depths, and Luke replaced the heavy circle of rusting metal. Davin may have been bluffing about the Regen properties of his amulet, and I wasn't about to take any chances.

With the arms disposed of, Luke helped us haul the unconscious Nash to his feet and drag him to the door. Man, he weighed a ton. He had to be hiding some serious muscle.

All of us staggered through the entrance hall of the Winchester House while Melody darted back to slam the door shut. If there was one place Davin couldn't reach us, it was here. Yeah, he could hijack the audio systems to his heart's content, but getting inside required more sneaking than he was capable of. The spirits would tear the rest of his limbs off before he set foot through the front door.

I breathed a tentative sigh of relief. "How's that for a Saturday night?"

"This isn't funny, Finch." Melody stooped to check on Nash, who was out cold. "I'm going to get some water for him, and he'll need headache tablets when he wakes up. Luke, can you grab a blanket from upstairs?"

"Of course." Luke cast a grim look at me before he set off. I understood perfectly. I'd put his little love muffin in danger tonight, and that served as a strike against my name. I wondered how many I had by now. It had to be in the double digits.

But Melody was right... it wasn't funny. Nash and I had gotten lucky. And we wouldn't have made it at all if Nash hadn't been armed to the teeth with magic knives. We'd been overconfident about our ability to kill Davin.

Melody departed, Huntress padding after her. The two of them seemed to be getting along like a house on fire. The Familiar and the Librarian—that was the start of a fantasy tale if ever I'd heard one. It surprised me that Huntress wasn't staying with Nash, but perhaps Nash had told her not to from somewhere deep in his unconscious.

Alone with Nash, I sank down and leaned against the wall. I'd hurt a lot more tomorrow, but Melody hadn't bothered to ask if I wanted any headache tablets. They seemed to have forgotten that I wasn't the only one who'd wanted to go after Davin.

"You cannot stay out of trouble, can you?" A strange woman emerged from around the corner. Her skin glowed, making her look partway between human and angel, and her eyes flashed pure, brilliant white. I turned to Nash, but he still lay unconscious.

Lux had returned to haunt me. And what an ironic place for it. But how the hell had she gotten in here? Had she hijacked a ghost? That form didn't look very Casper-like, but maybe she'd given it more solid edges.

"I have been waiting for you," she continued when I didn't reply. Terror crawled up my spine. What did she want this time?

"Have you? You could've just called, and I'd have let you know I was busy." I found enough courage to speak.

She smiled coldly. "Had I known you were going after Davin, I would have stopped you. You are no match for him. You won't be until you find the djinn that made his amulet."

"Yeah, about that… Davin did something to that djinn, so my odds of finding him are pretty much nothing," I retorted. I'd had it up to my eyeballs with these Children of Chaos trying to tell me what was what. "Unless you know he was lying?"

Lux floated closer. "My network of Sylphs do say otherwise."

I knew it! Lying, cheating scumbag!

"Do you know where he is, then?" I pressed.

"Not as yet."

"Then don't come yakking to me about that djinn unless you know, one hundred percent, that he's still around. Because I can't handle another dose of hope souring right now. My gremlins are down, but one more slap in the face, and they might come right on back." I knew it was risky to speak to Lux like this, but I couldn't help it. I was tired of their nonsense.

Lux glowed brighter. "You must be careful with Davin and Erebus, Finch. Neither is trustworthy. This is a prime example.

Davin told you the djinn could not be found because it benefitted him to tell you that. Erebus is the same. He seeks only to satisfy himself. And the pair of ingrates are more like... what is that word you mortals use?"

Of course he lied. I wasn't surprised to hear it.

"Ass-hats? Pains in my ass? I've got plenty of ass-related insults you can use." I tilted my head against the wall, wishing she would just go away. If she had no solid options for me, then she could go right back to her glowing otherworld and stay there.

"No, I was not looking for an insult." Lux chuckled. It made me want to dig into Nash's jacket to see if he had any more of those explosive knives. "Frenemies. Yes, frenemies is the word. They could both turn against you, far worse than they would ever turn against each other, if they saw you as their enemy. You must be more cautious."

I smirked bitterly. "Thanks for the tip."

"I mean it. If you think service to Erebus is bad, you should see what it is like when he decides to use you for target practice instead. As for Davin, he has been manageable thus far because he was tailing Erebus in this Atlantis rigmarole, but he will be far more trouble going forward."

I shook my head. "His arms are missing. That'll delay him for a while."

"Not as long as you would think. He is a powerful Necromancer, used to piecing himself back together," Lux replied. "This entire idea was foolish, even for you."

Something snapped in me. "Then help me find a way out of Erebus's service before it gets me killed! Stop trying to give me some bull-crap advice and put your money where your mouth is! I want out. You claim to want me out. So, *do something!* Prove to me you're not exactly like your pain-in-the-neck husband!"

Lux reeled in alarm, only to return to serene floating. "You are frustrated, I see." She paused. "I will think about it, as there may be a way I can help you. But you will have to give me something in return."

"Another deal? Are you serious? I've got deals spilling from every friggin' orifice, Lux!" This stank to high heaven. I made a deal with Erebus to defeat one dangerous enemy, only for him to transform into my worst nightmare. What would a deal with Lux entail? Whichever way I looked, I wound up staring down the barrel of a cosmic shotgun.

"We can address the details later," Lux said coolly.

"Why would you even want to enter a deal with me? And how come I don't get any of the charity you bragged about, huh?" In that moment, I might've hated her more than I hated Erebus. At least he didn't proclaim to be all shiny and good.

Lux sighed. "Because I need you, Finch. I need you to open the Gateway to Atlantis and continue to do Erebus's bidding. That is an exchange, not a charitable act, so the rules differ."

"Yeah, because you want them to differ. Hypocrite."

"Watch your tone, Finch!" she growled. "Once you succeed in opening the Gateway, we can address breaking your service with my husband. And what it will require in return."

I shook my head and slammed my fists into the floor. "Are you off your rocker, Lux? And no, I won't watch my tone, because I'm on the edge of a nervous breakdown here. Why would you want me to open the Gateway when you seemed majorly pissed about Erebus going to Atlantis? What am I missing, huh?"

"A fair point." She softened her tone and bobbed agitatedly above the floor. "I want to see how far my husband will go in this endeavor, and if he continues in a manner I do not care for, I will trap him in the center of the earth. I can only do that if he reaches Atlantis."

"Excuse me?" My jaw dropped. "You want to... trap him?"

"If he displeases me, yes." She tossed her glowing hair.

That one took me by surprise. Their marriage must've been hell these past millennia. Erebus deserved what was coming to him. Maybe this would be my way out.

But what'll the price be? Not small, I'd bet. And Lux had already said she wouldn't tell me until the job of opening the Gateway was done.

"And if Erebus doesn't 'displease' you—whatever that means— will you stand by your promise to help me? Or will that go swishing right down the toilet?" She'd better stick to her word. She owed me that much.

Lux twisted her hand with a dramatic flourish. "I will stand by my promise."

"Then... we'll talk later."

"Excellent." She grinned, a gesture that set my nerves on edge. "Until then, stay as far from Davin as possible. Those two may hate each other now, but you never know how the wheel will turn. Before you realize it, Davin may end up switching focus and targeting you more viciously than before."

I smiled sarcastically. "Noted."

"I will see you again, Finch, soon enough." She lifted her palms. "I have my eye on you. Now, more than ever. My husband might have lost his network, but I have not. And my Sylphs are more prolific than his djinn ever were."

Is everything a competition between you two? If that was meant to comfort me, it hadn't worked. And if it was meant to freak me out, then she'd hit the mark. It made everything far worse, in fact. I'd started getting used to the idea that Erebus couldn't watch me, and now I had Lux and her fairies to deal with.

"Goodbye, Finch." Glowing energy rippled from her fingertips, enveloping her. And when the light faded, she was gone.

Just in the nick of time. Luke thundered down the stairs, Melody entered from the side hallway, and Nash groaned beside me. The lumberjack had awoken.

TWELVE

Finch

"Rise and shine, sweet cheeks." I helped Nash sit up. Huntress bounded over to him and began licking his face frantically. "Do you two want a room?"

Nash laughed stiffly. "That was a close call back there. Thanks for getting me out."

"Well, I wasn't going to just leave you, was I?" I tugged the collar of my shirt. Lux's visit had shaken me, but they couldn't see that. "What was that knife, anyway? A heads-up would've been nice."

"A special blade I've been experimenting with. I wasn't quite finished testing it, but I'd say it did a pretty good job of getting Davin off our case. At least I knocked a couple limbs off him. That'll have to do for now." His brow furrowed. Maybe he'd hoped the knife would finish Davin off for good.

"You'll get him next time," I promised. "By the way... I may have left you for a minute to use the immobility hex on him. But I didn't find what I was looking for. He's hidden it away somewhere it can't be reached."

Nash's expression darkened. "Where?"

"A personal interdimensional bubble. Same kind my mother used to use," I replied bitterly.

Nash sighed. "Well, you did the right thing in trying. It's what I would've done."

"I hoped you'd say that." I lowered my gaze, still fuming that Davin had fooled me.

"Is everyone okay?" Melody handed a glass of water to Nash, who took it gratefully and downed the pair of pills she gave him. She passed two to me, as well, which made me feel a little more loved.

I nodded. "I've got Muhammad Ali going ten rounds in my skull, but I'll live."

"Same," Nash agreed.

Mary Foster floated through the far wall but didn't come any closer. She folded her spectral arms across her chest, giving me a stern look. *What did I do?* She tossed her head back and waved her hands, playing a game of charades. And she wasn't very good at it. But I understood. Lux. She'd seen me talking to the Child of Chaos and clearly knew I wasn't being entirely honest with the others.

I ignored her and focused on the living. "So, Davin lives another day."

"You tried your best." Melody crouched on the ground and patted Huntress's head. The husky butted her hand appreciatively, trying to get a scratch in the right spot. "It might not have turned out the way we all wanted, but it was worth a shot. What did Davin say? Anything helpful?"

"Nada. Oh, except that I have no hope of breaking this deal with Erebus, since the amulet won't work on me, and even if he's lying about that, he's got the amulet hidden so far up his magical caboose that I'll never retrieve it. And the djinn who made it is AWOL, if not dead. I mean, I'm fairly sure he's not dead, but Davin probably hid that sucker away real good." I held my head in my hands. My gaze flitted to Mary for a second, who pointed to her nose and started to pull her finger away from her face.

Is she... calling me Pinocchio? How did she even know who that was? The nerve! I mean, she was right, but still.

"What?" Melody looked crestfallen.

"Are you serious?" Luke frowned, the closest to concern he could manage with his limited range of facial expressions.

I nodded. "Yep. Short of making a deal with another Child of Chaos, I'm screwed." I gave a sharp laugh so they'd think I was joking, and it seemed to work. It made Mary stop with the Pinocchio performance, anyway.

"Can you imagine?" Luke scoffed. "Finch Merlin, with all the Children of Chaos fighting over him. It'd be like using a bunch of credit cards to pay off debt. You use one to pay the other what you owe, but then you owe that one, and so on and so forth. *Then* you'd be royally screwed. At least you've only got one to deal with. I'm sure you'll find some other way."

Nash made a grunt of agreement. "Like you said, Davin was probably lying anyway, to put you off the scent. He wouldn't risk killing the djinn who saved him. What if he needed more djinn juice for his precious amulet? Nah, he's probably got him tucked away somewhere secret. You just have to find him—the djinn, I mean."

"Gee, I hadn't thought about just finding him." I made a face.

"Sorry." Nash patted me on the back, almost dislodging my voice box.

I shot him a stare. "I'm not Huntress, you know."

"Even humans need a stroke now and then," he replied with half a grin.

My gaze flitted back to Mary, who'd given up the charades. She beckoned me with a ghostly hand, like a harbinger of doom, and drifted silently through the wall. Clearly, she wanted me to follow. As if I was meant to know where the hell she went. And it didn't do anyone any good to keep a ghoulie waiting, not if I liked using the restroom in peace.

"I need to go wash about twenty tons of tequila off me. It's sticking in all the wrong places, and I think something nasty got in my pants." I hauled myself to my feet.

Melody wrinkled her nose. "I thought that was the hex bags."

"Sadly not." Having made my excuses, I headed down the hallway in pursuit of a ghost.

"Miss Foster?" I whispered, my eyes darting back and forth as I stood around in a random corridor. "Miss Foster, where are you?"

She poked her head out of the wall, and I jumped. "You were supposed to come to the library."

"How was I supposed to know that?" I clasped a hand to my chest, hoping my heart would recover from all the surprises tonight. Ryann being the hard hitter. I didn't know why, but I'd kind of expected her to be here when we got back. Perhaps Ted Bundy had called her away. Speaking of which, I probably needed to send a text to let her know we were all still breathing. But that could wait until after I'd chatted with the spookmeister general.

"I pretended to open a book. Did you not see?" She emerged from the wall and hovered in the corridor before me.

"Nope, must have missed that one, between all your Pinocchio-ing." I arched a savage eyebrow at her. "Thanks for that, by the way. Kind of distracting when I'm trying to talk to people."

Mary bobbed anxiously. "But you were telling them untruths, Mr. Merlin."

"Was I? I don't remember lying."

She sighed. "You may not have lied outright, but you maintained falsehoods by omission."

"And you say I'm hard to understand." I offered her a friendly smile.

"I saw you speak with that glowing creature. Why did you not mention it to Miss Winchester and the others? Should they not know that a powerful being infiltrated this mansion? It is not easy to evade the security measures placed upon this house, yet she drifted in and out with nary an alert. I would not have known she was here, had I not been nearby."

I leaned against the wall to take the weight off my weary legs. "That 'being' is insanely strong. I doubt *any* security measures could keep her out. I mean, I might've thought they could, if I hadn't seen her waltz in."

But could the house keep Erebus out, now that he's gone to the human side? I might not have much hope about the amulet and the djinn, but I had a short list of places I could run to if it came to it. Tartarus was one of them, and this house was the second, if push came to shove. Well, if this place *could* keep him out in his shiny meatsuit, that is.

"Oh, I am aware of that, Mr. Merlin. I sensed her power the moment I saw her. I have never experienced anything like it. I immediately knew her to be a Child of Chaos, for such magic is ancient and much too complicated to be suppressed by the spells upon this mansion. Why, if I still possessed real hair, it would be standing on end at this very moment." She shuddered. It had to be bad, if a spook was spooked.

"Then you can probably see why I can't say anything to the others. Lux doesn't want me to, and I can't defy her. Not if I want to keep my head all snug on my neck," I explained.

Mary wrung her hands. "But you should not keep anything from those you hold dear. You should never put your friendships in jeopardy, and they care for you so very much. I may not know the minutiae of your acquaintance with that Child of Chaos, but I would not see you risk all on a secret like this. You ought to inform them, immediately."

"I'd be risking everything if I *did* tell them," I replied, feeling drained. "So, please, for my sake and the sake of our friendship, don't tell them yourself. It's to protect them, I promise."

Mary drifted down the corridor for a moment before returning. "I would not break our confidence, Mr. Merlin. It is your duty to inform them of what you are contending with. I only wish to tell you that I think you must, but I will not breathe a word of it."

Lucky for me, you can't breathe at all... I wished I could've blamed the gremlins for that biting thought, but it was all me. Lux had tugged my last nerve, and it showed.

"Look, I know you mean well, but Melody and everyone else would be in danger if they found out I was in cahoots with Lux. It might even get them killed. In some ways, she's worse than Erebus. She pretends to care about magicals, but I get the feeling she's only really concerned with what they can do for her. Erebus is upfront about the fact that he doesn't give a crap. She's… I don't know. Sneakier, maybe."

Mary got right in my face, sending a chill through me. "But why is she meddling with you in the first place? You have made no deal with her, from what you told me. Your servitude rests solely with Erebus."

I wafted a hand. "They're having some marital drama, and little old me is wedged between them, stuck in a tug-of-war. I can deal with that, mostly, but I don't want my friends getting involved."

My, my, aren't I the hypocrite? Harley had done the exact same thing during Operation Murder Mama, trying to keep secrets from me and the rest of the Muppet Babies. And that had almost gotten her killed. Plus, I hadn't let her get away with it. I'd followed like a bloodhound, knowing precisely the trouble she'd get into if she attempted to fly solo. But I was trying to avoid getting killed, right? Didn't that make it better? No clue.

Maybe Mary was right. Maybe I needed to find a way to tell Luke, Melody, and Nash about Lux. Not to mention Harley and Wonderboy. But how? And when? Seriously, how could I do something like that without Lux or Erebus finding out? I didn't need to be reminded of Lux's parting warning. She had eyes on me.

Before I could wreck my head dwelling on it, the air suddenly thickened, like a storm rolling in. A second later, the lights flickered wildly, and an icy wind swept through the hallway, clawing at my cheeks. Not comforting in a house like this, which was already an eleven on the creep scale. Mary seemed to agree. She jolted backward, her hands clasped to her mouth.

"Mary? What's happening?"

Mary just shook her head. "A great darkness is upon us. I must go." Before I could urge her not to, she vanished through the wall.

A great darkness? Oh, you have got to be kidding me!

I sprinted back through the corridor and skidded to a halt in the entrance hall, but Melody, Nash, the loyal hound, and Huntress weren't there anymore. Panicking now, I ran through the house, calling their names, trying to be heard above the racket of crazy wind.

"Melody? Luke? Nash?" I yelled, bounding up a staircase.

"Finch!" Melody's scream pierced the air. I scanned the landing, noticing the door to the grand salon lay open in a corridor full of closed doors.

"Melody?!"

"Finch!" she shouted again. This time, I had no doubt she was beyond that open door.

Steeling myself, I barreled inside. My heart stopped at the sight ahead. Melody, Nash, and Luke stood on one side of the room, their faces mirroring my horror. Huntress had her head down and hackles up, her lips pulled back to reveal her sharp teeth, though Nash held her back.

We had a visitor.

Erebus stood on the opposite side of the room, as eerily human as I'd last seen him. But he showed his full Child of Chaos venom as wisps of pure Darkness slithered out of him, the way smoke billowed from Kadar. The air crackled with electricity, the lights flashing in response.

So much for him not getting in...

"I'm sorry, Finch. He forced us to let him in. He tricked one of the ghosts into telling us my mom was outside, and she was hurt. Then... he made us let him in. I'm so sorry!" Melody gasped, tears streaming down her face. Whatever Erebus had threatened them with had hit home. Melody clung tightly to Luke, who had his arm wrapped protectively around her shoulders.

"Nice of you to join us," Erebus purred, his dark eyes glinting.

"I'd have found you faster if you'd texted."

His face twisted into a snarl. "You did not reply."

"Huh?" I fumbled for my phone, only to find the screen shattered. It must've gotten damaged in the fight with Davin. I'd thought it was a bit odd that Ryann hadn't messaged, and now I knew why. She was probably freaking out somewhere, thinking I'd kicked the bucket. "My phone broke. So, how about you chill for a sec. I wasn't ignoring you. I didn't know my phone was busted."

"Nevertheless, you made me go out of my way to track you down. You know how I despise being distracted from my work." Erebus lifted his palms, and I braced for retribution. All because of a broken phone. "Let this be a lesson to you. If you ignore me again, or seek to try my patience, I will always come after you."

He twisted his hand, expelling a tornado of black mist. I squeezed my eyes shut, anticipating the worst. Unbearable pain, burning lungs, me on my knees, the whole nine yards. But none of that came. Confused, I opened my eyes. And immediately wished I hadn't.

Ryann appeared from within the black mist. Her head whipped around in terror, her hands flying to cover herself. She stood there in nothing but a delicate lace top—a camisole, I remembered them being called—and matching silk shorts. Her hair was strewn all over the place, like a bird's nest.

In retaliation for not replying to him, Erebus had literally snatched Ryann out of her bed.

THIRTEEN

Ryann

———————

How? What? Huh? I stood shivering in the grand salon of the Winchester House, with Erebus leering at me. My hands hurried to cover myself, since I appeared to have been swiped from my bed in nothing but pajamas. And since I'd tried to make an effort with Adam, those pajamas weren't exactly rated PG.

"What the heck is going on?" My voice trembled. Dazed confusion muffled my sleepy brain, shot through with a sharp bolt of terror.

A creeping cold had woken me, but I hadn't seen anything amiss. Not immediately. Maybe there'd been a shadow out of place, but my bleary eyes hadn't registered it. Then I'd heard that laugh, icy and cruel, before I was snatched from my cozy covers and dragged here. I remembered the smell of fire and the feeling of being… disintegrated and put back together again. That was the only way I could describe it. A portal of some kind, I guessed, from my limited magical knowledge. Adam had been sleeping beside me, for Pete's sake! He hadn't woken, but when he did, he'd wonder where I went.

"You were needed." Erebus brushed his fingernails against his lapels. "Finch did not reply to my messages, so I must ensure he has not lost his loyalty. I had to bring you here, to remind him what he is fighting for, lest he seek to evade me again."

Finch stared in abject horror. "I didn't try to evade you! My. Phone. Broke!"

So that's why he didn't reply. I must have sent him at least ten messages and received nothing in response. Had it not been for the copious amount of wine I'd drunk to get through dinner with Adam, I'd never have managed to fall asleep with all that worry weighing on my shoulders. Truth be told, I was probably still tipsy. I severely regretted drinking at all. It made this whole scenario that much more petrifying. It was like being drunk in the street and seeing the reds and blues flashing, immediately striking paranoia into your heart.

"What do you mean, remind him what he's fighting for?" The words slipped out before I could stop them.

Erebus snickered. "Oh, I think you know. I think everyone knows by now. You mortals and your complex love interests." His expression altered to one of contemplation. "Though… perhaps we cosmic beings are not so different. At least you do not tear stars apart when you argue. The universe would have died a long time ago if you mortals' squabbles manifested those same effects."

Complex love interests? My heart thundered. What did he know? Could he read my emotions, the way Melody could? Did he know my conflicted feelings about Adam and Finch? I hadn't been looking at Finch that much, had I? Oh, no…

"Why are you here?" Melody murmured, evidently as freaked out as me. Though at least she wasn't standing there in a camisole and silky shorts.

"I am here to give you all your next mission. Interesting, isn't it, how helpful you've all become, when only one of you is actually bound to me? I suppose Kenzie was, temporarily, but I mean in the broader sense. A job shared is a job halved. And your loyalty to Finch is so valuable. Why, it's almost like getting five for the price of one." He sneered. "Your next mission is to find the Gateway to Atlantis so that Finch may open it for me."

Finch stepped toward me, hesitating when Erebus put himself between us. "Are you going to tell us how to do that, this time?"

"Yes, actually." Erebus edged forward, prompting Finch to step back. "It is time to proceed with the spell to open Atlantis. A trio of pieces is required to make it work. The first step was your expert map-making, the second was fetching Sanguine blood from an Atlantean line, and the last... well, that is locating the actual Gateway. Satisfied?" Erebus smirked.

"Why does it always come in threes?" Finch asked. "And no, not exactly satisfied. First, you dragged Ryann all this way just to show you've still got some oomph, without letting her stop for a coat or a change of clothes, or stopping to think there might be a reason I hadn't replied. Seriously, losing the djinn has made you paranoid, Erebus. Unlike them, I *can't* leave you. Kindly remember that in the future, instead of flying off the handle and kidnapping people. And second, you could've told me it was all one spell sooner, instead of leaving us to wrack our brains. But hey, at least you're improving."

Don't poke the bear, Finch. I appreciated him defending me, in a manner of speaking, but I didn't want him to do that at the expense of a magical slap across the face... or worse. But, weirdly, Erebus didn't look at all annoyed. Instead, he seemed sort of resigned. No, maybe that wasn't the right word. He almost looked like he agreed with what Finch had said. A momentary expression that soon passed into a shrug.

"She needed to be here anyway, so I saved you the hassle of repeating all this information," he said. "Now, back to what is important, instead of your mortal gripes. The Gateway acts as a connector between this world and the interdimensional pocket where Atlantis is hidden. The Atlanteans created it to be complex, long before they sank it beneath the ocean so that no one would find their city."

"Complex how?" Nash spoke up. Huntress sat beside him, her fangs bared. She and I had similar feelings about Erebus, from the looks of it.

"Through a series of moving islands. An ever-shifting entry, one that permits few to enter the city," he explained.

Finch paled. "Don't you dare say what I think you're going to say."

What does he think Erebus is about to say? I often forgot how much Finch knew about the magical world from his days in the cult. He had a wider understanding than any of us realized, sometimes. Even Harley underestimated him on occasion. And he certainly knew Erebus better than any of us.

Erebus paused for dramatic effect. "The only island with that capability which is still present in this world after the submergence of Atlantis is Eris Island. Back then, it was not called Eris Island and had been seized by enemies of Atlantis. Your ancestor, Drake Shipton, inherited it long after that, after it had passed down through claimants and purchase after purchase. And now, as you know, it is under a spell of your mother's making."

"I told you not to say it." Finch sighed. He ran an anxious hand through his strawberry-blond hair, looking like he wished he could be anywhere else.

I could tell the mere mention of that island brought back awful memories for Finch. He'd lived there during his formative years and called it home. Only to infiltrate it with Harley after developing a healthy hatred for the place and the woman who reigned over it. He had two golden apple tattoos as proof of the torment he'd endured there, twice over. No wonder he looked stunned. Of all the islands in all the world, he no doubt wondered why it had to be that one. The place where he'd been put on the wrong path, never knowing his sister would alter his future course.

I'm so glad she did. I tried to catch his eye, but his gaze had fixed firmly on Erebus. He'd completed mission after mission for that Child of Chaos, and I sensed this might be the worst one yet.

"Katherine didn't know it could be a Gateway, though, right?" Finch asked.

"No, fortunately." Erebus smiled. "But she did leave Eris Island on a fixed trajectory. It is your job to find it and take it off its trajectory, before moving the island to the location marked on that delicious map you made for me. By way of another spell, of course—one that shifts islands from one place to another. Only then may we use the Sanguine blood spell to open the Gateway and make the connection to Atlantis."

Move an ISLAND? That seemed like a major ask, even from Erebus. I knew Eris Island had moved locations before, after Harley and Finch's infiltration. It had been in Dry Tortugas then and had emerged off the coast of Hawaii after Katherine had realized it wasn't safe to stay in a known spot. Not with her son and my adopted sister after her head.

Finch eyed Erebus coldly. "And you know how we can find it and exactly what that island-moving spell is, right? I mean, you've practically vomited up information this time—let's keep a good thing going, huh?"

Erebus chuckled. "Why would I, when you can do the hard parts for me? That is why I have brought you all together, because every single soul in this room will be required for this task." His gaze sharpened on Melody. "You must delve into your Librarian knowledge, Melody Winchester, to find the spell to override Katherine's and move Eris Island. Finch, Luke, and Nash, you will be needed to perform the magic itself, with my assistance, of course."

Melody paled. "You... know what I am?"

I remembered Finch telling me about Librarians being able to fly under the radar of Children of Chaos, and he certainly hadn't known what she was when we were in Kenzie's apartment. Or maybe he had, and he just hadn't let on.

"What do you take me for? An ignorant human? Of course I know what you are. You were gifted by Chaos, and we Children sense any new power that comes into the world." Erebus puffed out his chest, evidently affronted. "Though I did not sense you immediately upon our first meeting, the news filtered through. If you recall, until recently, I had spies everywhere. You must be more cautious about what you say."

Melody's cheeks turned scarlet. "Perhaps you shouldn't listen to people's private conversations!"

"What sort of Child of Chaos would I be if I didn't?" He gave a casual shrug. "We all do it, and I wouldn't want to be the only one with any decency."

Luke put his hand on Melody's shoulder to stop her from stepping forward. It was probably a good idea. Melody might've been the Librarian, but even that didn't give her carte blanche to say whatever she wanted to a Child of Chaos. And judging by the conflicted look on her face, she knew that, too. Fortunately, before things got nasty, Finch defused the situation.

"You still haven't told us what Ryann has to do with this. Why drag her here in the middle of the night if you don't have a role for her? She's human. She can't help, so leave her out of it!"

Ouch. Why did people feel the need to keep reminding me of my lack of magic? Although, in Finch's case, the initial offense wore off fast. He had a legitimate reason for it—to keep me out of harm's way. More specifically, out of Erebus's way. He'd already proven once tonight that he had no qualms about using me to get to Finch, so of course Finch would try to prevent that from happening again.

He cares. He's saying it because he cares. Unlike other people, it hadn't come from obliviousness or ignorance. It came from affection. One that I still wasn't ready to face. But it gave me a warming sensation nonetheless, the same kind I'd felt hours ago when I'd thought I might lose him. When he'd held my hands and said those sweet things and looked at me until the moment the chalk door closed.

Erebus leveled Finch with a hard stare. "Ryann is here to keep your mind where it ought to be. If she is around and under my watchful eye, you will do anything to keep her safe. You will obey every order I give you without hesitation. *That* is why she is here."

Finch's hands balled into fists. It irked me to know I was nothing more than leverage to this big, bad Child of Chaos. And it saddened me to know Finch would suffer because... well, because of the way he potentially felt about me, or the way Erebus perceived he felt. I wasn't about to put words in his mouth; it didn't seem fair. But Erebus didn't play fair.

What was more, Finch had never expected anything in return for keeping me safe. Aside from referring to Adam as a million serial killers, he'd never been anything but respectful of my relationship and hadn't sought to undermine it. I was the one who was destroying it. Why? Because... I had a few feelings of my own. Ones that wouldn't relent, even though I had the world's best boyfriend.

Even now, I'd been torn from my human refuge and tossed into magical danger with Finch, yet I would rather have been here, camisole and all, than back home in bed with Adam.

FOURTEEN

Finch

I wanted to batter Erebus six ways to Sunday. The only thing I could take comfort in was how his meatsuit had weakened him. He'd had to threaten Melody et al. to even enter this house, and Lux had just waltzed in as she pleased. That would've stung his fragile masculinity, if he'd known. Which seemed to be as present as ever, judging by the way he was leering at Ryann in that rather eye-grabbing camisole. I was determined to be a gentleman and not look.

At least he was being a bit chattier. I couldn't remember the last time he'd coughed up so much information. Maybe he'd really been in the dark this whole time and hadn't wanted to admit it. The blind leading the blind.

Nash scratched between Huntress's ears. "You've given us some intel about how to get into Atlantis, but what is it you want there, huh? It's been underwater for ages. The water will have destroyed most of the artifacts by now. If you're after a book, forget it."

Erebus peacocked a little and began pacing forward. "There is something in Atlantis I have always desired. The rarest of jewels. Something I have tried many times to obtain in the past."

"But you failed, right?" Nash asked.

"Not 'failed.'" Erebus shot him eye-daggers. "I would say I made certain missteps which prevented my success."

Nash smirked. "That's just a flowery way of saying you failed."

"What jewel?" Melody chimed in, tapping the side of her head. "I might have information about it up here. Not that I'm eager to help you, but since you already know what I am, I guess there's no use hiding it from you."

"This sort of jewel cannot be found in any archive. It is much too rare." Erebus looked, dare I say, *nervous.* "This time around, I am so close to obtaining this ardent desire. Closer than ever before, because I had the wisdom to draw from the lessons I learned during previous attempts."

Nash shook his head. "Nope, you're closer than ever before because you have a magical slave with some power of his own. You must've been slapping yourself silly when he offered up an exchange in return for Katherine pushing up daisies."

Aww, Sarge is standing up for me... It warmed my bitter old heart. Of all of us, he had the freest rein to say whatever the hell he liked to Erebus. If the blood vials I'd already handed over didn't work for whatever reason, the E-man would need more. It was a gory blanket of bubble wrap that kept Nash relatively safe. Plus, he wasn't in my predicament. He didn't have a long list of people Erebus could threaten to get him to do his bidding.

"As I said, I had the wisdom to learn from past mistakes," Erebus hissed. "I had weak servants before Finch. He has proven his worth and was certainly worth the cost of ending a would-be Child. Do you think that was easy? Do you think it was just an amble through the park for me to kill her?"

"No harder than picking your toenails, pal." Nash held his ground like a pro.

"Some places on the body are exceedingly hard to reach." Erebus's lips lifted in a dangerous grimace. "I have come to learn that, in my human form. So many places where dust and dirt can collect. It is truly vile."

Nash stroked Huntress's fur to calm her down. "If you hate this body so much, why don't you give it up?"

"I did not say I hated it. There are benefits to this form. Atlantis, for one." Erebus pressed a hand to his heart. "I can almost smell victory. I can almost taste it on the tip of this human tongue. I have to give credit where it is due: you humans have a remarkable sensory system. Why, seeing Ryann here, dressed as she is, is most—"

"And that's where you learn the human art of thinking before you speak," I interrupted. I didn't want to hear what he had to say about Ryann in relation to his human sensory system. I didn't have the money in my bank account to pay for that level of therapy.

Erebus cackled. "You already have one rival. I suppose you don't need another."

He was winding me up, but I wasn't going to bite. "How about we get back to business? How do we crack Eris Island? It's still in Hawaii, right? You've got to know that much, in that bulbous head of yours. And if you think I have insider knowledge because I spent a few years there, you've got it twisted. I don't know how to undo Katherine's spells, and I don't know *all* the places that island can go. Funny enough, she never taught me that."

"I will aid you in breaking the spell, as I have mentioned, but I cannot find its location. All I know is that it is no longer in its last known location, nor any of the locations prior to that—it was stolen by cultists and has moved on," he explained.

"How can it not be in its last location? The United Covens Secret Service impounded it after Katherine died." I narrowed my eyes at him. How did he know cultists had stolen the island?

"You shouldn't believe everything you are fed by your mortal higher-ups." Erebus smirked. "The Secret Service *planned* to go to Eris Island and sweep it for anything valuable after removing all the cultists. The first stage went fine, and all the cultists were taken straight to Purgatory. However, when they organized a second task-force and headed out to the coordinates in Hawaii, the island wasn't there anymore."

"How could you know that?"

"My djinn network overheard some cultists discussing it, though those ingrates have also moved on." He sighed. "The theory is the Security Services missed a cultist somewhere, and that someone pushed the self-preservation protocol button before the taskforce returned. It vanished, and the government has not found it since, though they claim they have it in their possession to maintain appearances. It would not improve the UCA's reputation if everyone found out they'd lost an island."

"Makes sense." I wracked my brain for any Eris Island knowledge I might have missed and remembered a morsel of intel. "If that did happen, and someone put the island into self-preservation mode, that means it's stuck on a cycle. It'll keep moving every few days or so, popping up in approved places which have been logged into the system. The cultists might know at least one of those locations, so we'll have to hope it's headed there soon."

"It won't be in any of the island's former locations, though. I should warn you of that." Erebus was finally giving me more than a breadcrumb. "My djinn gave me a list of former sites, prior to their mass betrayal. They garnered it from the same list you gave your government, and I have checked each one for any signs of recent disturbance, but there have been none. It is blocked from my sight by Katherine's magic. No doubt a protective protocol to ensure we did not discover what she was up to before she launched her plan to become one of us. As such, once you have located the current position of Eris Island, you must break the wards on the monoliths," he replied coldly.

I frowned. "Those big-ass stones shaped like you all?"

"*Monoliths* is the preferred term." Erebus's dark eyes glinted.

"They *block* you from seeing the island?" I'd thought they were decorative. A bygone remnant of someone else's DIY nightmare, before Mother Dearest implemented her queen bee aesthetic and made everything look like the hexagons in a hive.

Erebus rolled his eyes. "Unfortunately, yes. Once you have broken the wards, you must light a signal." He slipped a hand into his suit jacket, making me anxious about what he might pull out. "This is how you light said signal." He retrieved a blue flare-like stick and handed it to me. A bit anticlimactic.

"Seriously? This?" I eyed it slowly, just to let him know how pathetic I found it.

"It may not look like much, but this is an ancient Egyptian signaling device used by magicals to call upon Children of Chaos back when we were permitted to walk this mortal realm more freely."

"You mean, without having to trick innocent folks into bringing you to the Fountain of Youth so you could get your mitts on a human body?"

He ignored me. "It was not easy to come by, but I had one remaining after one of my former servants... fetched it for me, at great cost to himself."

He died. Just say it. He died getting this puny stick for you.

"This one is engraved with hieroglyphs, including my ancient Egyptian name, so it will summon me specifically." Erebus gazed at the flare with worrying fondness.

"Come again? You have an ancient Egyptian name? What is it— like, Terry or something? Gavin? Geoff?" I had to try and bring some levity to the situation. Humor was my only weapon.

Erebus pouted. "No, it is Kek."

Yeah, well, I'll Kek your ass one of these days.

"Kek? I know that name. It means darkness, doesn't it?" Melody went into nerd mode. "Although... in historical literature, weren't you paired with the goddess Kauket? Yes, I'm fairly sure that's right. You would've been part of the Ogdoad."

"Octo-dad?" I frowned.

"No, Ogdoad. It consisted of four pairs of Ancient Egyptian deities—four male gods paired with their female counterparts." She paused. "Kek and Kauket represented, in some ways, night and day. Kek was known as the 'raiser up of the night' and Kauket was the 'raiser up of the day.' So, Lux must have been Kauket back then?"

Erebus grimaced. "She and I have been beside each other for longer than I care to remember."

"Cheers to the happy couple." I pretended to toast, winning a scowl from the Prince of Darkness. I could've gone further, but Lux still weighed on my mind, and I didn't want my face to give me away. You know, since I knew Lux wanted to trap the hubster in the center of the friggin' earth.

"But Katherine couldn't have put those wards there." Melody tapped her chin in thought. "I haven't been to the island, so I've never seen them, but my sources suggest that those monoliths predate Katherine. And even Drake Shipton."

Erebus shifted uneasily. "That is true. Perhaps you are a little too well informed." He sighed. "They were implemented when the island was first seized from the Atlanteans. Gaia had a penchant for the Atlanteans, and their enemies didn't want the Children of Chaos involving themselves. We had more liberties back then, you see— smiting and such."

"Wait... Gaia was in league with the Atlanteans?" Nash interjected.

"Not that it did them much good, if the stories are true," Luke added, with a note of surprising intellect. For a brawny dumbass, he had his moments.

Melody nodded. "I believe that was around the time the Children of Chaos were cast into their otherworlds because they had taken to choosing favorites. Chaos itself didn't like that sense of superiority among the races of magicals, so it punished them."

"Damned if we do, damned if we don't." Erebus scowled. "However, Katherine, or indeed, Drake, must have found a way to use the monoliths for their own endeavors, to keep us out. Ancient magic, but easy to learn if you know where to look. And we all know what a voracious reader your mother was, Finch."

My mother, the proverbial book maggot. She was always lifting something or other out of this book and that book pilfered from all across the globe, from every race that had ever existed. She'd probably have had a book on Neanderthal magic, if one existed.

"It provided the perfect hideaway for her, given her desire to take the place of a Child of Chaos," Erebus went on. "And I cannot enter until the wards are removed. So, remove them."

So, that gives me three places I can run if it looks like my head's gonna roll: Tartarus, Eris Island, and... I realized the Winchester House had to be taken off the list, since Erebus was standing right here. Sure, he'd had to be let in like a naughty dog, but he'd still weaseled his way through the protections. A real shame. Out of the three potential places, this would've been my top pick. I mean, I wouldn't have said no to spending the rest of my days on a tropical island, sugary drink in hand with a bevy of tiny umbrellas and fake fruit, but Eris Island didn't fit the bill. Too many terrible memories.

"Remove them? That's it?" My tone firmed up.

"What more needs to be said? It is better to be succinct, I find." Erebus flashed a grin.

I wasn't impressed. "There's a difference between succinct and vague."

"And that is my problem... how?" He checked his wrist, though he wasn't wearing a watch. "My, my, is that the time? I should be going." He lifted his hands in preparation.

Oh no you don't, buddy!

"What's so important that you need to rush off when you've literally just told us we have to do everything for you? What's keeping you from—oh, I don't know—actually *helping?* This is your 'ardent desire.' Show that you give a crap!"

Melody shot me a worried look. "Don't push him, Finch. Remember what I said last time."

That he's a Child of Chaos? Yeah, I remember. Frankly, I didn't care right now. Not enough to bow down and lick his boots, anyway. I was too tired for that. And I didn't like the taste.

"Truth time, Erebus." I stood firm.

Erebus smiled. Not a good sign. "Actually, there is much of importance you don't know about. As you continue to mention, I don't tell you everything. But perhaps a little more wouldn't go amiss, given your obvious stress. I am busy putting various things together. First of all, finding a means to get Davin out of our way, once and for all."

It should've comforted me. But then I just *had* to go and remember my conversation with Lux. She'd told me about the complicated bromance between Davin and Erebus. So, how serious could Erebus really be about destroying Davin? Maybe he enjoyed the challenge more than he hated the enemy, so to speak. Also, if Erebus was genuinely focused on destroying Davin, then he must be after the djinn who'd made the amulet. Said enigmatic djinn being the only way to end Davin's loophole immortality, now that he'd hidden his amulet away where nobody could find it.

"Now I really must go." Erebus didn't wait for me to call him out again. He twisted his hands faster than a Bhangra dancer and disappeared in a burst of black smoke.

As I stared at the space where he'd been, an idea exploded in the weary mush of my noggin. Melody and Luke looked at me in shock while Ryann shivered and tried to look anywhere else. Nash kept it casual, patting Huntress on the head.

Tell them... Mary Foster's guilt-tripping haunted me.

I took a breath and caught a memory of *Muppet Babies Go to San Jose.* "I think we need to do something about Davin, and Erebus, too."

"Like what?" Nash's antennae were pricked for Davin destruction.

"First, we need the cavalry."

FIFTEEN

Finch

Our group returned to the SDC through my favorite mode of transport. Chalk doors all around. Harley had been itching to get involved in this Erebus malarkey since she first found out about it, so she'd like this. All it had taken was a quick text, and she'd gathered the ranks.

That was how we found ourselves in the Alton Waterhouse Room, sitting around the main workbench like executives at a boardroom meeting. I had my firing finger at the ready, and Erebus and Davin were the employees in the running to be axed.

Melody had lent Ryann one of her fluffy jackets and a pair of Luke's jogging pants. An odd sartorial mix—halfway between a skinned pink wombat and a gym bunny—but I still thought she looked cute. She always did.

"To break down this long list of folks for you, in case you missed any of the Original Muppets—this is Raffe, Santana, Harley, Wade,

Tatyana, Dylan, Garrett, and Astrid." I gestured around the table. "And before you ask, yeah, they're all couples. Sickening, right?"

Melody smiled shyly. "I think it's nice."

"Pfft. You would." I rolled my eyes and did the honors for the newbies. "Everyone, this is Melody, Luke, Nash, and Huntress. Not couples, though you'd never know with the lumberjack and his dog."

Nash narrowed his eyes at me. "Huntress is my Familiar. She's no ordinary dog."

"That doesn't mean you can go around breaking laws." I flashed a grin, trying to keep it Finch even if I wasn't feeling up to my usual comedic excellence.

"A Familiar?" Santana went all gooey-eyed, no doubt picturing herself soul-bound to her nasty little snake.

Nash nodded. "Ignore Finch."

"Oh, I always do." Santana cast me a butter-wouldn't-melt smile.

"Nice to meet you all." Dylan draped his arm around Tatyana's shoulders. "It's good to finally meet the folks we've been hearing about. But I have to ask, what's with the late-night call? I was dead to the world when Taty booted me out of bed."

"You can catch up on your beauty sleep later," I replied. "I got you all together because we're going to mess with Erebus and his precious status quo, and Davin, too."

Harley leaned forward. "What's the plan, bro?"

"First, there are a few things you need to know." Giving them the *Rocky* training montage, I told them everything that had been going on with Erebus: Atlantis and his search for that "rare jewel," the three parts to opening that baby up like an Easter egg, and his latest demand that we a) find Eris Island and b) find some way to break the Child-proof lock so he could actually enter the island and hoist it off to… wherever. Antarctica, probably, since that was Atlantis's location on the map which had very nearly cost me my sanity.

"Eris Island? Are you kidding me?" Harley threw her head back in exasperation. "Why there, of all places?"

I chuckled dryly. "My exact question, but before we get to that crap-storm, there's more. This is what we do next, if you're all game. Erebus wants to stop Davin, which means he must be looking for the djinn who made Davin's amulet. Funny enough, I'm after the same thing. Davin spouted a load of bull about how he got rid of that djinn, but everything Davin says has to be taken with a bucketload of salt. Which is where you come in, unless you want to be singing 'Ding Dong the Finch is Dead' at my funeral."

Harley flinched. "Don't say that."

"Sorry. Gallows humor." I offered her a reassuring smile. "Anyway, we need to find that djinn first, wherever he is. That might give us the upper hand, because that flamey devil must know more about Erebus than we do. And Davin, for that matter. If Erebus gets him first, it's bye, bye, Beetlejuice."

"Of course we'll help," Wade chimed in.

I tilted my head at him. "Well, I knew you would. If you didn't, Harley would have your ass for breakfast."

"Did someone say ass for breakfast?" Kadar emerged, giving his bodily smoke the full billow to show how much the idea pleased him.

"Not literally, man! Doesn't Raffe ever feed you? All you talk about is munching on human bits and pieces. Anyone would think you're half starved." I hadn't expected the djinn to come out so soon. "And if you so much as nibble on my sister or future brother-in-law, I'll take a bite of you and see how you like it."

Kadar chuckled. "I don't think you'd like the taste. I'm much too spicy for you."

"Does that mean you're on board? This whole thing kind of needs you, if it's going to work." I swallowed the desperation in my voice. We were at last-chance saloon, and the owner had just rung the bell for final orders.

"I will help track down this djinn, and enlist my father, as well. It's always nice to beg favors off family. You know they won't ask for anything in return," he replied sarcastically. "But I've grown used to having you around, Finch. It would be a shame to lose you. I wouldn't shed a tear or anything, but your absence would feel strange."

That might be the nicest thing a djinn has ever said to me.

"In case it's not obvious, we have to do this without Erebus finding out," I went on. "I won't blame any of you if you don't want to get involved. Hell, I've spent enough time trying to keep you all out of it. But I can't do this on my own. I know that now, especially with this task. So… I'm asking for help."

"You can count on us." Tatyana leaned against Dylan. A subtle movement that made me wonder if she was thinking about what she'd do if Dylan were in my situation. There was nothing like imminent death to bring people closer, even if it wasn't *their* death.

"We're here for you." Garrett pulled Astrid closer.

She nodded. "Anything you need, you've got us."

"I agree with Kadar." Santana offered an olive branch. "Who would I have my daily crap-slinging matches with if you weren't here? I don't want to have to train a replacement."

"Touching." I pretended to clasp my heart. "But thank you. Oh, and Harley, before you start shouting from the rooftops that you're coming to Eris Island with me, that isn't happening. I need you here, taking care of djinn business."

She pursed her lips. "I guess there's no point arguing."

"Thanks, sis. I don't exactly have the energy to go ten rounds of back-and-forth with you." I hissed a small sigh of relief. She was the one I'd been most worried about. When it came to my problems, she liked to be on the front lines. And, honestly, I liked having her at my side when things got rough, but knowing she was here, getting everything up and running, would settle my wayward mind more than worrying about her on the island.

"Are we going to search for this djinn, too?" Melody asked, also leaning closer into Luke. That broke my heart. It showed she cared, and his bittersweet smile showed he felt it. But what could they do? Oh, these star-crossed lovers. It never ended well. Remington and Odette were testament to that.

I shook my head. "No. We're going to stock up on whatever we can get our hands on and try to find this island."

"Don't you know where it might be?" Santana eyed me. "You spent enough time there."

"I don't know *all* the places it can move." I sighed. "And Erebus said he checked all its previous locations already. So, I'm as stumped as everyone else."

"I can help with hex bags and magical objects." Ryann raised a hand, though she'd been avoiding my gaze ever since Erebus's little midnight flirt with her. "Miranda has a plethora of rare herbs and things tucked away in her private library, and I've got the key."

"Not sure whether that's comforting or worrying," I replied, wishing she'd just look at me. "But, for now, it's useful, so I can shelve my concern until later."

Nash raised his head. "I'll come with you to sift through the herbs and stuff, Ryann. I know what we might need."

Don't you dare talk to her about how I feel, or you can kiss your Davin vengeance goodbye. I shot Nash a look I hoped conveyed the threat. He grinned, clearly getting my drift.

"And there's no way you're going to Eris Island without staying in touch." Astrid peered at me over her specs. "I'll fetch some earpieces for you all, so we have an open line of communication. Your last trip to Eris Island had us all panicking. This time we're coming with you, even if it's just through your ears."

I smirked. "Also not sure whether that's comforting or worrying."

"I'll throw in some emergency buttons, too, in case you get in trouble," Astrid added with a firm nod.

"But once you've gotten everything together for hex bags and whatnot, you're going to stay with us, right?" Harley gave her foster sister a pointed look. I hated to be the bearer of bad news.

"She can't," I said hesitantly. "Erebus wants her with us because he thinks it'll keep me on the straight and narrow. I tried explaining to him that I had enough threats to motivate me for a lifetime. But he wasn't having it, stubborn old bat."

Harley's face hardened. "If I've said it once, I've said it a thousand times. I never should have let that smarmy bastard strike a deal with you. Who does he think he is, pulling innocent humans into all this?"

Careful with the human talk. I glanced at Ryann, but if she'd heard Harley, she didn't show it. She was deep in conversation with Nash, the two of them discussing herbs and items as if picking out their favorite things from a catalogue. Man, that really showed my age. Catalogues. Who used those anymore?

"And if I've said it once, I've said it a thousand times. You'd be right where I am if you'd done it instead. And I'd have had my head on a pike a long time ago for trying to get in Erebus's way." I felt her frustration, but there wasn't much we could do about it.

"I hope you have a plan to find Eris Island, because Melody isn't going anywhere unless I hear about it first." Luke shattered the tension between darling sis and me.

"Luke!" Melody protested, but he folded his arms across his chest. Apparently, that meant he wouldn't be taking any BS.

"I know you want to help, Melody, but everywhere Finch goes, trouble follows. I want to at least know his plan; otherwise, we're heading straight back to San Jose to do something safe. Like play Monopoly. I don't care if Erebus insisted we be involved. He doesn't hold any deal over us. If I don't like what I hear, we're going home." Luke furrowed his brow, evidently uncomfortable playing the bad guy. But I got it. I'd have teased him for wanting to protect Melody so vehemently if I'd been a bit sharper. But Erebus and Lux and Davin had dulled my edges.

I held up my hands. "My next stop is my least favorite place in this world, right after Eris Island. Or maybe just under my mother's womb. It depends on what mood you catch me in."

"Can you try and answer me seriously?" Luke shot back.

"Okay, okay, sorry for being hilarious. I thought it might be more fun to make it into a guessing game, but Captain Killjoy apparently disagrees." I paused. "My next stop is Purgatory."

In the depth of silence, some people say, "You could have heard a pin drop." Instead, I heard about a dozen jaws drop.

"Are you insane?" Harley rasped.

"Not as much, since Nash gave me some anti-gremlin juice," I replied. "And I'm not a wanted man anymore, so it's not like they'll clamp me in chains and drag me off for a cold shower. Oh, the showtunes I used to sing in that place. I used to get rapturous applause. Or maybe they were screams—hard to tell through those thick walls."

Wade leapt to his lover's defense. "That seems foolish, Finch, even if you're not a wanted man. You put away a lot of the people in there. You'll cause absolute mayhem."

"Come on, guys, give me some credit. I'm the master of discretion," I protested. "Anyway, it needs to happen, so you can all click your jaws back into place. Madre never told me every place the island could go, but I did see a few old locations in a book once. One of Drake's endless, self-indulgent journals about how great he was. Seriously, he's got a whole shelf in his library, gathering dust. He had no flair for narrative."

"You're about to run off on a tangent, Finch," Garrett said with half a smile.

"Right, sorry. We need to go to Purgatory because we have to get some intel on the island's most recent whereabouts. And the only folks who'll know anything about where it might be are the artists formerly known as cultists. Hence... Purgatory. You know I'm serious because I used the word 'hence.'"

"Yet you managed to sound anything but serious," Santana jibed.

"What can I say? It's a talent I've been blessed with," I retorted. No way would she get the last word, olive branch or not.

"Hang on a sec." Dylan raised a hand. "I thought the Secret Service had the island impounded after Katherine got skewered. Shouldn't you be going to the UCA instead of Purgatory?"

I rolled my eyes. "The Secret Security Services lied about that to save face. They missed a cultist, and that little rodent set the self-preservation protocol off, meaning the island abandoned ship before the Security Services could go back to claim it."

Astrid flushed with embarrassment. "How do you know that?"

"I keep my ear to the grindstone, if that's the right phrase."

"It's not, and it still doesn't explain how you know that... uh... well, how you know what happened." Astrid shifted awkwardly on her stool.

I looked to her. "Erebus may have mentioned the inconvenient truth. Although, it's convenient in this case. I'd rather visit Purgatory every day for the rest of my life, which may be quite short, than speak with the UCA about gaining access to anything Katherine-related. They've probably got her used tissues on lockdown."

Astrid put her hands on the table like she'd been caught stealing. "Ah... of course. Erebus."

"Did you know about this?" Raffe had taken Kadar's place. He stared at Harley and Wade—Mr. and Mrs. Secret Agent.

"We may have," Wade answered sheepishly.

"Oof, and after all the hassle you gave me about lying?" I tsked. I couldn't resist.

Wade cast me a withering look. "*We* had to sign an NDA."

"*I* had to sign a deal that might very well kill me and hurt the people I love. Your point?" I raised a haughty eyebrow to match his, though mine was less manicured. "Anyway, that's why we're heading to Purgatory. One of the cultists there must know something about the island or can at least lead us to someone who does."

"In the meantime, even if you can compile a short list of locations that haven't been checked yet, that'll narrow our odds of finding it at the right time," Astrid replied.

"Okay, so OG Muppet Babies, you're going on djinn watch. New

Muppet Babies, you're coming with me. Oh, and Astrid?" She squinted, probably worried about what I was going to say. "Could you rustle up a tasty official document for me and my team, so we don't get into a pickle when we get to Purgatory?"

She sighed. "I suppose that would be best. I'll handle it. Although, Harley, you might need to sign it. It'll save me from forging a signature."

"No problem," Harley replied with a concerned glance at me.

"A superb pass from Kepler-Waterhouse to Merlin! Now that that's settled, Ryann, Nash, you two go shop around in Miranda's pantry, and don't get caught. In the meantime, I've got one more thing to pick up, so Melody and Luke, you hang tight until I get back." I scraped back my stool and made for the door, only for my sister to call after me.

"Where are you going?"

"I need some vessels," I replied cryptically. Not from any need to lie, just to keep things interesting.

She frowned. "Vessels?"

"Oh yes." I strode out without another word, headed for the Bestiary.

SIXTEEN

Finch

A fter indulging in my best ninja moves to get in and out of the Bestiary unseen, though Tobe had caught me in the act and let me carry on anyway, I met the others back at the Alton Waterhouse Room with my Mason jars in tow—tucked neatly in a rucksack I'd picked up from my room. Black smoke swirled inside them.

Unfortunately, that made me the group packhorse. After all, Nash could only fit so many hex bags in his snazzy jacket. Laden down with hex bags, a handful of defensive amulets, and a few random items—a pendulum, a golden pen-looking thing, a cluster of pellets that would explode in a haze of colored smoke, and a few other miscellaneous swipings—we made the trek back through the SDC to the Assembly Hall. Chalk doors wouldn't cut the proverbial mustard here, not without setting off every alarm. No, this "official" visit required an official entry.

Ryann, Nash, Luke, Melody, Huntress, and I bid farewell to the others, leaving them to their djinn-ward journey. I presumed Ryann had sent word to Adam that she was okay, considering her phone wasn't ringing off the hook, but that wasn't too high on my list of priorities. Instead, I hoped Davin had lied about the amulet-crafting djinn being dispensed with. Otherwise, they'd be on a wild goose chase. And I *really* wanted to get one over on Erebus. His djinn had abandoned him. I planned to follow suit.

Clutching my official capacity document, rustled up by Astrid and courteously signed by my dear sis, the new Muppet Babies stepped through the Assembly Hall mirror into Purgatory with me. Honestly, I'd been so busy thinking about how to get this show on the road that I hadn't considered the repercussions it might have on me, to be in Purgatory again.

The memories hit like a tidal wave to the skull. All that steel and glass, looking like every gentrified area of town but way less appealing. Dark eyes glinted behind the panes, blending two horrors into one—this place and Erebus. I had to swallow my anxiety and fear as I walked up to the warden's station.

"What's your business?" the Kevlar-clad man behind the counter asked. His name badge read *Officer Wiley*.

Where's Roadrunner, Mr. Coyote?

At least Officer Mallenberg wasn't here anymore, after sipping Mama's Kool-Aid. He'd died in the Battle of Elysium. But I didn't know if the other officers were here—the ones who'd made my life a living hell back then. Although, maybe I'd deserved it. Did that make it worse? Probably. A stark reminder of the nasty little worm I'd been, squished under Katherine's thumb.

His companion, another gruff-looking fella who'd spent too much time pumping iron, looked up at the clock on the wall. "Do you know what time it is?"

"We've got urgent business with Emily Ryder." We'd made the decision to go big or go home, so we aimed for one of Katherine's finest. Even I felt a flicker of uncertainty about speaking with her. She'd been a prime example of a cult drone, and she'd lost her brother because of us. Well, because of Harley and the others. She might've been behind glass now, but that didn't make the prospect of facing her any less scary.

Then again, if anyone knew the location cycle Eris Island was on, it was Katherine's former archive monkey. When she'd first arrived with her brother, they'd been given the task of organizing all Katherine's gathered information, old and new. They'd constantly had their noses buried in my mother's documents before they became field agents.

"What urgent business? We didn't get no memo that someone would be coming." Officer Wiley scowled, the default expression of the guys who worked here. "We always get a memo if someone's coming to see a high-security prisoner."

I shoved Astrid's document in his face. "It's all on here."

Wiley scanned the sheet. "Hmm... fine." He noticed Huntress padding along beside Nash. "What's with the dog?"

"Emotional support animal. My friend here was a victim of the cult; he's had her ever since, for anxiety reasons." I jumped in before Nash could say a word about Familiars.

"Fair enough." He gestured to the other officer. "Renholm, will you take these folks to see Emily Ryder?"

"Can't you do it?" Renholm complained.

"I did the last two rounds because you wanted to watch them *Jeopardy* reruns. So, no, I won't do it." I sensed Wiley and Renholm didn't like each other much, but their names would've made a great cop drama.

Renholm sighed. "Fine. But put some coffee on while I'm gone. I could probably do with some pins to hold my eyes open, too, in case the coffee doesn't work."

"Sooner you get going, sooner you can come back." Wiley dismissed him with a hand wave. Their bickering would've been amusing had my state of mind not been in an immediate and drastic decline. This place smelled of despair. I'd forgotten the stench—clinical, somehow, sweat mixed with metal.

As Renholm led us through the cavernous entrance hall, I peered at the cells overhead. Levels upon levels of glass boxes, framed with steel. Big steel doors held the captives inside. In fact, now that I saw it through an old-timer's eyes, it reminded me of the Bestiary. A human Bestiary for badly behaved creatures—the worst of the worst. And I didn't want to be here.

"Are you okay?" Melody whispered. "You've gone all... puce."

"Puce?" I frowned down at her.

"You know, feverish-looking. Red cheeks. Well, mostly red cheeks—the rest of your face has turned white, and you look all sweaty and strange," she replied. "Do you feel sick? Do you need a minute?"

Ryann edged closer to me. "She's right. You don't look good."

Luke gave me a sharp nudge. "Probably reliving his criminal days."

"Not far off, actually." I sighed. I wished I could jab him back.

"This is your appendix, Finch." Nash lowered his voice. "It's reminding you it exists, but you don't need it."

As far as analogies went, that one still didn't sit right. And it definitely didn't help. Purgatory was giving me sensory overload, underscored by the pounding of fists against glass. The prisoners always did that when visitors came. I'd never taken part, and the sound had sort of faded into nothingness back then, but I heard every thud now. I searched for my old cell overhead, but I'd been kept in the secure section. Somewhere above the network of metal walkways that crisscrossed the different levels.

We got into the elevator and whizzed to the very top. My stomach lurched as it stopped abruptly, but it had nothing to do with the ride up. These were my old stomping grounds.

The doors hissed open. If I turned left, I'd see my old cell. *Don't look at my appendix, don't look at my appendix, don't look at my appendix.* It took every ounce of willpower I had not to. Instead, I stared dead ahead like a psychopath and followed Officer Renholm to a cell at the very end of a long suspended walkway. The drop-down still freaked me out. One false step and there'd be Finch smush all over the polished floor a million levels below. That was why the officers wore magnetic boots up here, so they'd never accidentally slip and die. Sensible, really.

"Who *is* Emily Ryder?" Luke whispered behind me.

"You've never heard of the Ryder twins? Murdering maniacs? Katherine's little pets, until Harley and the others took down Emily's brother?" I replied in a hushed tone.

Luke shrugged.

"Even I've heard of them, and I've been in the Canadian wilderness for years. Read a paper or watch the news once in a while," Nash muttered under his breath.

"Is she as bad as everyone says?" Ryann stayed behind me but kept close.

I took a nervous breath. "Worse."

We stopped in front of the farthest cell. Through the glass, a young woman sat behind a desk. Naturally, it'd been nailed down, like every piece of furniture in this hellhole. Weirdly, though, Emily wasn't chained at all. No Atomic Cuffs, no Hannibal Lecter face-mask and straitjacket, no restraints whatsoever. Though I knew there'd be a serious magical barrier keeping her in, and us out. It'd been the same with me.

"How's she doing today?" I asked Renholm. "Anything we should be worried about?"

Renholm snorted. "With this one? Nah. If it weren't for her rap sheet, you'd wonder why she was here. Wouldn't say boo to a goose."

"Emily Ryder?" I asked, boggled. "We're talking about the same one here, right?"

"She's been on a 'spiritual journey.'" He air-quoted the last two words. "Seems to have done her some good." He used a gigantic set of keys to open up what I used to call the sewer grate, revealing a barred gap in the center of the door so outsiders could talk to insiders.

"Emily Ryder? *The* Emily Ryder?" I couldn't believe it.

Renholm stowed his keys away. "Everyone says that. Anyway, I'll be over here if you need me. Knock yourself out." He wandered away to speak with another officer, leaving us to it.

"I thought she was pure evil." Ryann glanced at me. It was the most eye contact I'd had with her since the Winchester House visit tonight. Progress.

"Yeah, so did I." I moved up to the grate. "Emily?"

She looked up, surprised, and a faraway smile turned up the corners of her lips. "Finch? My goodness, is that you?"

"Uh… yeah." I'd crossed paths with her a few times in my Eris days, but she'd never been like this. All floaty and weird. She'd been hard as nails back then.

"She knows you?" Ryann hissed.

"I was pretty famous in my Eris days. Unfortunately, for all the wrong reasons." I winced at the memory of the awful things I'd done. Yet another reason why Ryann was probably better off with Captain Canuck. He'd likely never hurt so much as a fly in all his life.

Emily got up and crossed to the grate, grasping the bars. "You look well, Finch. How long has it been?"

"A few years," I replied.

"Has it really? How time passes." She gave a soft, disarming chuckle. "And who are your friends? I don't recognize any of you. You aren't... anyone I hurt, are you?" Sadness glittered in her eyes.

Ryann shook her head, her eyes steely. "No. We're friends of Finch."

"Well, then you're very welcome. I was always fond of you." She gazed at me. "Actually, I've thought about you quite a lot while I've been locked up here, though I had no idea you were free. I have to say, I'm glad you managed to leave these cells. I often hoped you'd find a better way in life. You suffered more than most under your mother's hand."

"Sorry, did they give you some kind of lobotomy when they put you in here?" I had trouble believing this was the same woman who'd killed masses of people without batting an eyelid.

She laughed. "I understand your surprise, but a lot has changed since we last met. You must know that better than anyone, if you're back out in the world. *I* have changed a lot since we last met, and I can see that you have, too." That sadness came back. "We were all pawns in your mother's game, and when she died, it was as though her hold over me disappeared as well. I had to look at myself and think long and hard about the things I did. I came to terms with them as best I could. That was the only way to find peace."

"But you killed a whole bunch of people." Nash stepped up beside me.

"I did." She nodded slowly. "And I have forced myself to picture every single one of their faces and send an individual apology into the ether in the hopes they might hear. I know what I've done, and I despise the person I was. But that's why I'm here, in Purgatory, to atone for those sins. And yet, I'm alive and they're not, and that is hard to come to terms with. I must spend every day here with a willing heart, as penance for my actions, because I can't restore what I took."

"What about Emmett? What would he have made of all this?" I wanted to test the waters, to see if I could get the real her to spring out.

She sighed. "I can't speak for him, and he can't speak for himself, so I don't know. But I have to live for myself and my sins and the people whose lives I ended. That's all I can do now. If I could change things, I would, but there's no use in wishful thinking."

"Do you miss him?" Melody peered at Emily.

"Every day. We were twins. When he died, it was as if a part of me did, too. Half of me, in fact. But I can't change that, either. I can mourn him, and mourn the innocents we killed in Katherine's name, and hope that one day, I may be forgiven. And that I have repented enough for the both of us, so we can be reunited. But that won't be my decision." Emily lowered her gaze, her eyes twitching as though trying to hold back tears.

If this really was the new and improved Emily, she'd done a

serious 180. She seemed genuine. Maybe I was being fooled, but it didn't feel like it. Something had happened to her after Katherine's death. Clearly, her time in Purgatory had given her a brutal perspective on the things she'd done. I'd seen reformed prisoners before. And man, she must've had major demons rattling around that brain of hers. Demons she'd chosen to face, instead of continuing on as she was.

"But it's not all bad," she continued. "After losing my brother, after harming so many, and especially after Katherine died… learning to deal with it all, and to repent for my sins, has made me feel oddly free. I now answer only to myself and the souls of the departed."

"You can change, just like that?" Luke looked as dumbfounded as I felt.

Ryann frowned, suspicious. "Nobody changes to that extent at the drop of a hat."

"It hasn't been a quick or easy transition, but it had to happen." Emily looked back up. "I owed them all that much."

Melody leaned closer, only for Luke to yank her back. "And you're okay with spending the rest of your life here, even though you've changed?"

"I am. This is my punishment. I deserve this," Emily replied quietly. "I'm sorry to ask, but was there a reason you came to see me? I'm happy to talk with you all, but it seems strange that you would appear so late at night just to discuss my metamorphosis."

Hold onto your hats…

"We hoped you might help us with something," I explained.

Her brow furrowed. "Oh? It's not cult business, is it? I don't do that anymore."

"I don't do that anymore, either," I assured her. "This should hopefully help people instead of hurting them." *Namely, me.*

"Then… go on. I'll see what I can do." She waited patiently for me to continue.

"We need to know where Eris Island might be right now. Someone set off the security protocols, so now it's bouncing around like a broken pinball, and we need to find it. Do you have any idea where it could be?" My heart leapt into my throat, hopped up on anticipation.

She paused in thought. "I can't help with recent locations, considering my imprisonment, but I can tell you of a place I know where cult members still gather. Though I'm not in that world anymore, I listen to the whispers that pass through this prison. The remaining cultists might be able to give you more information. Or it may lead you to the island's location. I can't say for sure, but there must be a reason they continue to gather in such an odd place."

"What place?" I pressed.

"Kennebunkport, Maine." She met my gaze and I saw nothing evil in her. But that name…

"That's made up, right?" Luke cut in, reading my mind.

She smiled. "It sounds strange, I know, but Drake Shipton liked strangely named places. And if someone set off the security protocols, it'll follow the course he charted many years ago. Katherine never changed the cycle the security protocols were set to. Not while I was in her archives, anyway."

"So, we have to go to Stephen King country?" I shuddered at the potential irony.

"After the crackdown on the cult, many rogue members sought refuge in New England. It's easier to hide away in the small towns there. And most have gathered in Kennebunkport. Some have been captured since and brought here, but nobody is allowed to visit them, without exception. They're the ones whose whispers I listen to, usually in the canteen or during my hour of exercise," Emily explained. "If you can find them, you'll have a better chance of finding out all the locations where Eris Island has been this past year."

"But you've got no idea where the island might be now?" Melody asked.

"Also, how would any of the cultists know where it is, if they aren't actually on the island and nobody else is, either? The Security Services got rid of everyone." Ryann came in with that useful addition.

I raised a finger. "One person evaded them."

Emily gripped the bars tighter. "Precisely. You'll have to find the one who triggered the emergency protocols. They won't be on the island anymore. Those protocols would've booted them off once they'd been set in motion, as part of the self-preservation aspect. However, they'll have a device that shows the island's location—a key of sorts, which starts the cycle but allows the one who implemented it to keep track. The cycle follows a constant pattern, and they will know where it is in that pattern. If that makes sense."

"Weirdly, yeah." Luke gave a thoughtful nod.

"And, if my sources are right, they will surely be in Kennebunkport. It's the only safe haven left for rogue members. I dislike the fact that they continue to live free without paying for their part in Katherine's evil, but it may help you in this instance." She loosened her grip on the bars, as though it'd taken a lot to say that.

"A safe haven for rogue cultists? Sounds like a nightmare to me, and I've had my fair share of those tonight." Ryann took a shaky breath. I wanted to offer her some comfort, but I didn't feel too hot, either. Being here, talking to Emily, hearing my own feelings echoed back in terms of finding redemption… didn't make for a comfortable situation. I had to clench all my muscles to stop them from jittering.

Emily stepped away from the grate. "If you go there, please be careful. Don't alert anyone's suspicions, or you may not make it out alive. I would hate to have your deaths on my conscience, in addition to those already residing there."

Not helping, Emily. I almost screamed in shock when fingers closed around my hand. Staring down, I realized Ryann had taken my hand in hers, evidently noticing I was having a difficult time. This time, she hadn't grabbed my hand to seek comfort. She'd grabbed it to comfort *me.*

"We can do this. You don't need to be nervous." She gazed into my eyes. "We've come this far and faced worse odds. Let's find this island. Let's finish this and hope the others can give you your life back while we're at it. You asked for help. You got it. Because we're not losing you, Finch. *I'm* not losing you. Not now, not ever."

A fresh surge of courage and determination flowed through me, and all because her hand held mine. If this wasn't love, then I didn't know what was.

SEVENTEEN

Ryann

I wasn't sure what came over me. I'd noticed Finch in distress and I'd taken his hand, simple as that. I'd done it almost without realizing. A subconscious desire to help him, the way he'd helped me when faces were swimming in the silvery liquid. And now, I couldn't let go. He didn't seem to want me to, either.

"The only problem is," Emily continued, giving me something else to focus on, "the group only gathers once a week in Kennebunkport, in a local pub. It seems to be a meeting to discuss acts of Eris and find out whether any Secret Service agents are on their trail, though the meetings appear to be declining in frequency."

"How do you know that, if you've only heard whisperings?" I interjected. We needed certainties, not rumors. I never went into anything half-cocked, especially not something as dangerous as this.

"I have heard it over and over. My change of heart isn't common knowledge with them yet, so they have no qualms about talking around me. It is mentioned so frequently, I believe it is more than mere hearsay," she explained.

It seemed surreal, but I sensed good energy coming from Emily Ryder. She spoke with an honest face, if such a thing existed. I wished I'd known her in the past, so I'd have something to compare this to. That might've given me a better grasp on just how truthful this woman was being. Then again, I'd probably have been on her hit list back then. If what Finch and the others had said about her was anything to go by, that list had been miles long.

"I suppose that makes sense," I said, eyeing her closely in case she happened to slip.

Nash frowned. "So, that one day a week is our only chance to find these rogue cultists before we have to wait another week?"

"Exactly," Emily confirmed. "And I believe they are using hexes to hide the fact that they're magicals, which means discovering which patrons are cultists and which are ordinary Maine residents will be tricky."

I had Harley living with me for years, and I couldn't tell the difference. Magicals weren't always easy to pull out of a lineup, unless they were hurling elements from their hands. So, she had a good point.

"How come you haven't told the authorities about this?" I still needed to know that she was what she appeared to be. And I couldn't swallow the nagging doubt that, had she really turned the other cheek, reporting these meetings to the authorities would surely have been her first port of call.

She paled. "I may be seeking redemption, but I can't redeem myself if I am dead. If anyone were to discover that I told you this, I would be done for."

After what Kenneth Willow had tried to do to Finch in this place, I could buy her fear.

"So, what day is their meeting?" I asked.

"Friday. They use the nightlife to their advantage." Emily paced slowly in front of her cell door.

"Friday?" Finch groaned. "Why couldn't Monday be party day in Kennewhatsit? It's probably Sunday morning by now, which means we have to wait five days." With so much on the line, I shared his frustration. But if it had to be Friday, then it had to be Friday.

Emily paused in her pacing. "You could try and speak to them individually, but that would prove even more complicated. They are in hiding. The moment a magical wanders into town knocking on doors, they'll be on guard. But, if they are all together gathered at their meeting and you can mask your own magical qualities, they'll be less likely to flee."

"Why are you helping us?" Luke's voice was laced with suspicion. "No offense, but after everything you did, how can we trust you?"

Melody tapped Luke gently on the shoulder. "I can sense her emotions, Luke. Her heart is at peace. There's a lot of turmoil in her mind—but not turmoil that would make her untrustworthy. She's working through grief and guilt, but she's being honest with us. I don't feel any deceit whatsoever."

"You're an Empath?" Emily sighed as though relieved. "I am glad of that, because I know better than anyone that I can speak the truth until I'm blue in the face, and everyone will still doubt it. Everyone thinks it's an act, but it's not. I am not who I was then. Having so much time alone, knowing you will never be free again, forces you to face things you wouldn't normally have the chance to. Purgatory is my penance, and I have seized this opportunity to repent. Here, speaking to you, I can at least try to mend some of what I've broken. Even if it's only in a small way."

My phone went off, and the ringer echoed through the prison. I hurried to pull it from my pocket, letting go of Finch's hand in the process. He stared down at his palm, as if something had vanished without him realizing. But I couldn't let the phone keep ringing. Officer Renholm was already squinting at us.

Adam's name flashed on the screen. *Not now... not now!* I declined the call and breathed a small sigh of relief. How could I deal with him now, when we were trying to get important information? Unfortunately, he was persistent. The phone rang again, and I declined again. When the third ring came in, I started to wonder if it might be an emergency. Usually, he'd have gotten the message after two cancelled calls. Reluctantly, I swiped the answer button and lifted the phone to my ear.

"Adam?"

"I don't know where you went last night, but I need to talk to you." He sounded anxious. "As soon as possible. I'm talking in the next hour."

"Adam, I'm b—"

"Don't tell me you're busy. Please, don't. I need to see you. I need to talk to you now."

My stomach lurched. "Has something happened?"

"It's an emergency," he replied simply. "We have to meet now."

I glanced at the others, conscious of their eyes on me. "Can't you tell me what's up?"

"No. I need to tell you face-to-face. This isn't something I can say over the phone."

I turned away from Emily's cell, cupping the phone as if that'd give me some kind of privacy. "Well... you'll have to give me at least an hour to get there. I got called into work last night, and I didn't want to wake you, but it'll take me some time to get back. Where do you want to meet? Back at my apartment?" I didn't say "our" apartment or "the" apartment. A small thing, but it felt weighted somehow.

"No, not your apartment. Meet me at Clover Coffee. You know the one," he said. "Can you get there by eight?"

I tried to do the mental math. "I should be able to, yes."

We'd made a habit of going to Clover Coffee back when we first started dating because it was between my parents' house and the hospital where Adam had done his first-year internship. It was a cozy spot north of San Diego with nitro coffee that could have kept a narcoleptic awake. But his desperation worried me. Why was he so intent on getting me to meet with him? If it really was an emergency, he'd have given me the details over the phone.

What if Erebus got to him? It seemed unlikely, since Erebus wasn't the discreet type. Case in point, he'd dragged me out of my bed because Finch hadn't responded to a text. But stranger things had happened. And maybe he'd figured out Finch was up to something on the sly and wanted to play the same game.

"Okay, I'll be there by eight." I sighed, already terrified of what he might want to tell me. I'd immediately gone for the worst-case, Child-of-Chaos scenario, but what if it was something more... human? What if he planned to break up with me? What if my disappearance last night had been the last straw?

"I'll be waiting," he replied. "I love you."

That doesn't sound like what a guy about to break up with me would say... But it could've been a test.

"Yeah… me, too." With the others staring at me, I couldn't say the words back. And I felt like utter crap for it. He hung up, and I put the phone away.

"What's going on?" Finch jumped straight in.

"I need to go and meet Adam," I replied.

Finch furrowed his brow. "Now?"

I nodded.

"Doesn't he know you're busy?" Nash asked.

"He says it's an emergency." I shifted awkwardly, aware that we'd left Emily hanging. "He thinks I work in a government office, so he doesn't know that this is also an emergency."

"He doesn't know what you do? Or that you're here with us?" Nash cast a strange look at Finch before turning back to me.

I shook my head. "I can't tell him. Coven rules."

"Right, coven rules." Nash's lips straightened into a grim line. "Another reason I'm glad I don't have to deal with them anymore. Covens are more hassle than they're worth."

"But… we need you." Finch lowered his gaze. "If you go AWOL, Erebus will wonder where you are. You're supposed to be my shackles, remember? Keeping me on the straight and narrow."

"I have to go. He sounded really troubled." I didn't want to leave this mission for the sake of my rapidly unraveling human life. But I couldn't abandon Adam, either. If he needed me, I had to make an effort and go to him.

"What if this *is* Erebus, trying to draw you away from us?" Melody chimed in, agitated.

"I thought about that, but I don't know why he'd go to that extent. If he wanted to keep *me* on the straight and narrow, why wouldn't he have just snatched Adam the same way he snatched me and dangled that over my head? Locked him away or something—that seems more like his style," I rambled, trying to make sense of my thoughts by saying them aloud.

Nash gave me a sympathetic glance. "I'll come with you, just in case this is Erebus trying something new."

"No, I'll go with you," Finch cut in. "I'm not letting you wander right into a trap if Erebus is getting all psychological warfare on our asses."

Oh yes, because that'd go down great if you came with me to meet Adam. He meant well, but sometimes Finch couldn't see the forest for the trees, or the logic from his protective streak.

"You can't, Finch." Nash came to my aid. After all, I had no idea how to dissuade Finch from tagging along when he was in body-guard mode. He was the Luke to my Melody... in more ways than one.

"Who says I can't?" Finch shot back. "If Erebus *is* there, he'll think we're obeying. You know, because Ryann will still be with me."

"And if it's *not* Erebus, you'll make things insanely awkward for Ryann here. She's been through enough over the last twenty-four hours. Let me go instead. That way, we're covering all bases. If it's Erebus, then Ryann is still with one of us. If it's just Adam wanting to talk because it really is an emergency, then there'll be no awkwardness. He doesn't know me the way he knows you." Nash gave Finch another pointed look that I didn't understand. Had they been talking about me?

Finch pulled a face that screamed unwillingness. "I'm not going to win this one, am I?"

"Not tonight, pal," Nash replied. "Do the right thing. You know it makes more sense."

"I presume the fleabag will be with you?" Finch huffed out a breath.

"She isn't a fleabag, but yes. Where I go, she goes." Nash's eyes narrowed at the insult, but he let it slide. Another worrying sign they'd had words about me. He was clearly taking it easy on Finch for some reason.

"I can go alone, you know," I offered.

Nash chuckled sharply. "Not tonight, Ryann."

"And what do we do in the meantime? Twiddle our thumbs? Wait to hear that Erebus has dressed Adam in a monkey outfit and made him clash cymbals?" Finch clearly didn't like the turn this had taken. Neither did I. I'd have stayed with them if I could have, but I needed to see what was wrong with Adam. He'd never acted like that before. Guilt and fear churned in my stomach. It would almost be better if he wanted to talk to me about normal stuff, because if he was in magical trouble… then it was all my fault.

"You go and get some rest, and we'll regroup tomorrow—actual tomorrow, not a few hours from now. Ryann needs to get some sleep, too, once she's met with Adam. After that, we get everything prepped and ready for our trip to Maine. We'll need hex bags and any other magical artillery we can throw at the cultists, in case things go south. We'll get everything ready for the next step, too, as soon as we've spoken to the cultists and gotten that damned location." Nash had taken the authority role, likely to relieve the burden from Finch. He'd been through enough this year to warrant a decent sleep.

"At least you'll be protected," Finch said softly, looking at me. "Nash is a sly dog with some nifty tricks up those waterproof jacket sleeves. I wish it were me, but I suppose he's an acceptable substitute."

Nash laughed. "High praise."

"If anything happens to her, though, I'll—" Finch started a tirade, but Nash stopped him short.

"Yeah, yeah, you'll do a bunch of vengeful things to me. I've heard it all before. I used to be hunted, remember? But nothing will happen to her. Huntress and I will make sure of it." Nash turned his attention to me. "I won't even need to go inside with you. You can take Huntress, make up some excuse about looking after a colleague's dog, and she'll relay everything to me."

Finch sighed. "See what I mean about nifty tricks? Telepathy with a pooch. Who'd have thunk it?"

"That sounds like a good idea," I replied. They wouldn't let me go alone, but at least I'd have a shred of autonomy going into this meeting with Adam. And it probably was sensible to have some magical security with me, in case it did turn out to be one of Erebus's games. Even if I hated to admit I needed magical help. Being surrounded by magicals had never made me feel so powerful and so vulnerable at the same time.

"Ah… I see now." Melody clasped her hands together, a sad smile on her face.

I frowned at her. "What do you see?"

"Well, it's quite obvious from the way your emotions are behaving that—" Her eyes widened. "Uh, never mind. I have to learn to be quiet in situations like this. I can't keep saying the first thing that pops into my head. Right?" She nudged Luke for moral support.

"You're doing great, Melody." He smiled down at her as if she were the center of his universe.

For the first time, I genuinely wanted her to tell me what I was feeling, because I sure as heck couldn't sift through all this by myself. But my private emotions might never be secret around Melody again if I gave her permission to reveal all. So, I did the same as her and kept quiet.

Besides, I didn't need an Empath to tell me that Finch cared about me... likely more than he should. And that I cared about him... likely more than *I* should. We were stuck in an odd limbo, where he was waiting for me to make a choice. To choose him.

My hand itched to hold his again, but I didn't dare reach out. That would only have muddied the waters even more, and I had this awful feeling they were about to drown me.

EIGHTEEN

Finch

"It's good that I didn't go with her, right?" I tapped my fingernails on the table in the Winchester House kitchen, and it sounded like a thousand tiny drummers mocking my heartbeat. I'd had ants in my pants since we'd returned twenty minutes ago. I just couldn't sit still. Up and down like a friggin' yo-yo, thinking about Ryann's meeting with Adam. It wasn't even happening yet, but the anxiety… seriously, it was worse than anything the gremlins could've lobbed at me.

If you guys were awake, you'd be having a field day. My Nash Juice worked wonders. So, why did I find myself missing the voices in my head? Maybe I'd grown so used to them, it was a bit *too* quiet upstairs.

"Yes, for the millionth time." Luke scraped his mug along the table surface. Right now, he might as well have put his nails to a chalkboard.

"What he means is, it's better this way," Melody added softly.

"You wouldn't want to start any awkwardness with Adam, and Ryann would be on edge if you were there. She's always distracted when you're around, and she needs to focus on whatever Adam has to say. Meanwhile, we have to hope it's not—"

"Errol. Call him Errol," I interjected. "I'm sick of his name."

She smiled. "Okay. Meanwhile, we have to hope Errol isn't responsible for that phone call. It doesn't fit his usual MO, but there's always a chance he'll surprise us."

"Plus, I'd be pretty miserable company if I'd gone with her." Purgatory had left me drained. All the shower showtunes in the world couldn't have made up for the despair I'd experienced in that place. More so when I was actually behind bars, of course, but that little trip had done a number on me.

I hated to give any sort of props to Emily, considering the awful things she'd done, but I didn't know how she did it. How could she sit back and accept a lifetime in that glass cube? How could she just nod and say, "This is my world now"? It'd driven me to the brink of insanity when I'd been in her position. Knowing you'd never see real sunlight again, just the fake glow of the exercise yard, or feel rain on your face, or swear at a passing pigeon that pooped on your new shirt... no thanks. I never wanted to go back to Purgatory, ever again.

"And Nash is with her, so if you're freaking out about her being safe, you shouldn't be. Nash is the best option," Luke continued. I almost turned around and called him out, burning to ask what he'd have done if Melody had been the one going off to some covert meeting. Captain Beefcake would've flipped his lid if anyone else had insisted on going in his place.

Melody clutched her mug of cocoa. "And if he needs help, he'll call. We can be there in the blink of an eye, I promise."

"Besides, if… Errol has eyes on us, then we can't be seen running around on human nonsense, not when we have an important task ahead. Well, important to him." Luke hit me with a sharp gaze. "Errol worried about you disappearing off the face of the earth after your broken phone incident, so he's probably more focused on you than Ryann. His resources are limited, with his djinn network gone. So, if you stay away from other vulnerable humans like Adam, that'll serve everyone better."

I gaped at him. "Congratulations, you've finally learned how to string more than one sentence together. That might be the most I've ever heard you say in one sitting."

"Very funny," Luke replied.

"Actually, you make a valid point. With Errol's djinn network gone, is there another way he could be keeping an eye on us? I wouldn't put anything past him, right now. The kid is desperados." I took a sip of my drink. Coffee, though Melody had insisted on decaf. Which defied the entire point of coffee. But hey, placebo effect and all that jazz.

Melody paused. "I couldn't say for certain, but we can't be too careful. He may have enlisted the help of some spirits or something to make sure we're where we're supposed to be. I haven't heard any chatter, and I haven't seen any ghosts around this part of the house, but you never know. It's best to simply believe we're being watched at all times, so we don't accidentally slip up."

"And he might show up unannounced." Luke sat back in his chair. "If he appeared to find us all gone, or found us here and you gone, he'd immediately go on the offensive."

"Did you add a spoonful of common sense to that cocoa?" I arched an eyebrow at him.

"I'm not an idiot, Finch. I'm selective about when I speak. You should learn that skill; it'd do you a *lot* of favors," he shot back.

Or zero favors... I was being selective about what I said to Ryann, and that hadn't exactly brought me rainbows and happiness. Nope, right now, it was all anxiety and a dash of envy. She'd held my hand, she'd given me "the look," and I had no clue if it meant a single thing. I pulled out my phone and set it on the table, just in case she sent a text.

Melody chuckled. "Why don't *you* send *her* a message? She's not a mind-reader."

"I wasn't…" I trailed off. Lying to Melody seemed pointless, when my feelings for Ryann had already been laid bare repeatedly by pretty much everyone. Erebus, in particular. Man, he loved pointing it out. I guessed the poor guy had to get his kicks somehow, now that he couldn't whoosh around in his otherworld pretending to be king of the castle.

"You should talk to her about how you feel, Finch. Avoiding it will only stretch the tension between you. We can all feel it." Melody offered me a kind smile. "And you should probably discuss it before it's too late, whether because of Adam swooping in with a ring or all this Atlantis business."

"Me dying when it's all over, you mean?" I took a furious gulp of my coffee.

"Your friends would go to the ends of the earth to stop that from happening, but it ought to give you a kick in the butt. If you thought you had limited time on this rock, wouldn't you want to do and say everything you could before it came to an end? Even if it doesn't end up ending, if that makes sense?" Melody shuffled back in her chair. The sound of a dripping tap provided the soundtrack for my interrogation.

I sighed. "Or maybe it just makes it harder for the people left behind when you die. Why make it worse by spewing out a bunch of feelings?"

"Because living life should be about regretting the things you did, rather than the things you didn't do. You should be fulfilled knowing there are no loose ends. Again, I reiterate, even if death doesn't come for decades and decades, which I hope it doesn't, act like you *are* on a ticking clock and tell her how you feel!" Melody squealed. "I can't bear sensing her emotions, and seeing how smitten you are, and watching the two of you do nothing. She needs a prompt, that's all. Sometimes, that's all we ladies need—a sign that we'll be safe and secure after we make a difficult decision. You know, that someone will be there to catch us."

Luke gazed longingly at her. No doubt he had found some hope for himself in her words. But what sign could he give her? He'd been even more obvious, in my humble opinion, than I'd been. Yet she continued to appear completely oblivious. He'd have to arrange a parade or get a Child of Chaos to pull some strings and make the stars spell out how he felt. Even then, Melody would likely miss it.

She made some painfully good points, though. Ones I didn't want to face. If Adley had told me everything she'd wanted to say before she died, would it have made her death any easier to handle? No... it would have broken me completely. And maybe she'd have shared some harsh truths I wouldn't have wanted to hear. I couldn't shake the fear that Ryann might be the same—that she'd say things I didn't want to hear. That she wouldn't choose me.

"I can't put her in that position, Melody." My shoulders sagged. "I don't want to tell her everything just to offload my emotional baggage. That's not fair to her. Talk about awkwardness central."

"But I know... argh, I can't say. Just trust me when I say you have to let her know." Melody toyed with the handle of her mug. "You love her. You have to take risks for love. There's a reason books and poems talk about it as if it's the most valuable thing a person can possess. If you let it slip through your fingers, you'll break both your hearts."

Luke lurched to catch his mug just before it toppled from the table. He'd been pushing it along the surface, his focus entirely on Melody and her words. I knew a fellow lovestruck fool when I saw one, and Luke had it bad for Melody. Worse than I'd previously thought. Judging by the gooey glint in his eyes, this wasn't a passing fancy or some kind of Stockholm syndrome. His feelings for Melody were serious.

Her words had hit us both hard. I mean, she was right. What did I have to lose? If she didn't choose me, we could scrape our way back to friendship, right? And I kept thinking it'd be a chubby old no. But what if it was a yes? What if she saw me as her safety net, the same way she'd reached for me when the trace spell scared her? What if she *did* just need a prompt to let her know I was here, standing by?

I need to tell her. If I had limited time left on this earth, I needed to say all the unspoken things that lingered between us.

NINETEEN

Ryann

Showered and dressed in normal clothes to try and invigorate some humanity back into my weary self, I headed to Clover Coffee with Nash. A painfully bright morning had somehow risen between my kidnapping and all the activities since—from organizing the pursuit of Davin's errant djinn to visiting Purgatory for the first time and everything in between.

Purgatory itself had been somewhat unsettling. I'd heard about it from Harley, but I'd never been before. It made sense that the worst of magical kind would have to be locked up somewhere, but Purgatory had both petrified me and taken my breath away. Perhaps it was the legal eagle in me, taking interest in this kind of thing. I wasn't sure. Powerful people resided behind the plate glass in that structure. Powerful, dangerous people—people who made human serial killers look like amateurs. People who could explode other people with a flick of their wrist. I'd been terrified enough from what I'd heard about Emily Ryder, but she'd turned out to be a gentle dove.

"All good?" Nash pulled me from my thoughts.

I nodded. "Just looking forward to the coffee."

"You aren't worried about what Adam will say? If he said it was an emergency, it must be bad, right?"

I inhaled sharply. "If I think about that too much, I might walk away." I grimaced. "Does that make me a horrible person?"

"Not at all. It's fight or flight, and sometimes it's better to choose flight." Nash looked up at the sky. "And, since you don't know what he wants to say, and it might be Erebus's doing, you've got every right to feel apprehensive."

Huntress padded along beside us. We'd taken the non-magical route to north San Diego, since we'd ended up with more time to spare than I'd anticipated. I wondered if Nash had the right idea—perhaps we'd all be better off just keeping pets instead of diving into relationships. A dog would never make me feel nervous or guilty or confused. Animals were simple. And who needed the other stuff, when you had a fluffy creature to cuddle?

I froze on the sidewalk. "We're almost there. It's around that corner."

"Do you remember the plan?" Nash's matter-of-fact manner brought me some comfort.

I nodded stiffly. "I go in with Huntress and tell Adam I'm looking after a colleague's dog. If we leave the café, we're going to 'run into you,' and I'll introduce you as the colleague whose dog I'm taking care of. Any danger, I signal Huntress. You'll be out here, waiting."

"You've got this, Ryann." He reminded me of my dad, in a way. Firm and reassuring.

"Wish me luck," I murmured.

He chuckled. "You don't need it."

Unconvinced, I took a breath and headed up the street. The moment I turned the corner, I saw Clover Coffee in all its glory. An unassuming little coffee shop with a swinging black sign and floor-to-ceiling windows that revealed the customers inside. The scent of coffee drifted out the door as a young woman, about my age, left with a to-go cup.

I bet you're not dealing with psychopathic cosmic beings. Sometimes I envied the ordinary folks simply going about their daily business. The nine-to-five, with nobody snatching them from their beds in the middle of the night. Maybe they had some romantic difficulties of their own, sure, but they must be easier to handle without all the extra magical layers on top. But ordinary, human-world Ryann was gone. I couldn't have gone back to that life, not now. Who opened an incredible box and wanted to close it again?

Well, Pandora, for one.

I pushed through the main door and was hit with that incredible smell of coffee again, but ten times as strong, mingling with the buttery, sweet aroma of fresh pastries. My stomach growled. I hadn't eaten since last night's gourmet dinner, which didn't sound so odd until I remembered that I'd been up all night and my body needed compensation for the additional waking hours.

Glancing across the half-full room, I spotted Adam immediately. He sat in our usual corner by the window with two coffees on the table. I'd have bet all the money I had that it was a hazelnut latte—my favorite. A *pain au chocolat* rested on a plate in front of the empty seat, too. He'd thought of everything, as usual. My heart jarred at the sight. The perfect guy sat in our spot, in our favorite café, having ordering everything I liked. Only, what if he wasn't my perfect guy anymore? I'd changed, and he hadn't changed with me. Not his fault, obviously, but the fact remained.

What if fate brought Harley into my life so I could meet Finch? Stop it! Stop it! Now wasn't the time for that train of thought. No, I was definitely getting off those tracks before I spoke to Adam.

"Ryann!" He waved. Weirdly, he didn't seem panicked at all. He seemed his usual, laid-back self.

"I got here as quickly as I could." I hurried to the table, Huntress in tow. Fortunately, this café happened to be dog friendly. "What happened? You sounded worried on the phone."

He eyed Huntress. "Did you get a dog?"

"No, no, she's my colleague's dog. We were in meetings all night and my colleague needed someone to walk her, so I said I would. I'd already agreed when you called, and I didn't think you'd mind." I sank into the vacant chair and took a long sip of what was, indeed, a hazelnut latte. Meanwhile, Huntress got to work on licking her paws.

Adam scratched between her ears. "Why would I mind? I love dogs. I've been bugging you about getting one for months, but you said I'd never be home to feed it and walk it, so we had to wait until we had our own place."

"Right." My cheeks burned. How could I have forgotten? No wonder he'd been so upset when I'd laughed about moving in together. It wasn't as if we hadn't discussed it. Just like everything else when it came to him, I'd put it on a back shelf in my mind. "Anyway, what's going on? You had me freaked out. Is someone hurt?"

"I've made a decision I hope you're going to like," he replied, his tone anxious.

"Huh? I thought it was an emergency."

He looked sheepish. "I knew you'd stay at work if I told you the truth. Totally uncool of me, I know, but I needed to get you here this morning. And that was the only way I knew how, with you vanishing in the night like that. I'm sorry I scared you. I shouldn't have stooped to that level, but..." He trailed off. I heard the words he'd wanted to say hovering in the air: "But you left me no choice."

"Then why am I here?" I took another long sip of coffee.

"Grab the coffee and pastry. We've got somewhere to be." He grinned as he stood. The next moment, he took my elbow, giving me only a moment to grab my things, before leading me from the coffee shop. Huntress followed obediently, without the need for a leash or anything.

I spotted Nash on the street as we walked and gave a subtle shake of my head. He gave a subtle nod back, understanding that I wasn't in any clear and present danger... as yet. He turned away and pretended to read a newspaper as we passed, though I noticed him glance at us as we continued on.

We walked a short way up the street to a snazzy apartment block I'd always commented on when we passed by. Each apartment had a balcony that overlooked the city, with potted plants and smart outdoor furniture, depending on the tenant's taste. Leading to the doors, the building had an expanse of greenery, with palm trees and benches, a manicured lawn, and even a small fishpond with kitsch statuettes of gnomes and toadstools and frogs. Blooming flowers swayed in the breeze, content in their border beds, while birds chirped in the branches overhead. And, around the back, it had residential gardens that would've put most parks to shame. A paradise in San Diego.

"What are we doing here?" I glanced over my shoulder, expecting some kind of danger. Huntress brushed up against my leg, her eyes darting around. Both of us were on guard.

"You'll see," he replied, pulling me through the main entrance and into the elevator. The concierge cast a disapproving eye at Huntress but said nothing. I didn't know what I'd have done if they'd asked me to leave her outside.

The elevator pinged, and the doors slid open. He didn't answer my questions; he simply dragged me along the corridor until he came to a halt in front of one of the doors. There, he took out two sets of keys.

"Adam. Did something happen?" I was frustrated now.

He smiled so wide I almost forgot my annoyance. "Oh yes, something happened."

"What?"

"I had a revelation." He slotted one of the keys into the lock and swung open the door. It revealed a beautiful two-bedroom apartment, the doors standing open. I ambled inside, utterly baffled. The place had airy, high ceilings and hardwood floors, with neutral-toned walls and soft lighting. It certainly put my puny apartment to shame.

I peered through every doorway, as if they might lead to unknown realms. Each room was more beautiful than the last. The spacious master bedroom had a chic en suite bathroom decorated in dark grays, with stone floors and a rainforest shower. The second bedroom would've made a great study, given the large windows that let in the morning glow.

Farther down the hall, I found the apartment's pièce de résistance—a huge lounge with plush gray sofas and fluffy white rugs, which ran directly to an open-plan kitchen. It had a breakfast island with a pale granite top and brass light fixtures that looked like they'd come straight out of the 1920s, in the best way possible. Everything was sleek and expensive looking, from the lamps and tables to the freaking door handles. No IKEA here. It was absolutely mind-blowing.

I could picture making coffee on the fancy espresso machine and drinking it on the sprawling terrace, which looked out directly over the residential gardens. Maybe, in the evenings, I'd sit out there and watch the sunset. Or perhaps I'd go to my study to leaf through paperwork, with music playing through the Bluetooth speakers that ran through the apartment. Ooh, or what about a long soak in the huge clawfoot tub in the main bathroom, with all the bubble bath a girl could need? Chillier nights spent curled up on those comfy-looking sofas, watching television or reading a good book under a blanket? Perfection.

"Do you like it?" Adam hovered nervously nearby.

"Like it? Are you kidding? This place is amazing!" I blurted.

He grinned. "I'm glad, because… I want you to move in here, with me." He took the second set of keys and pressed them into my palm. "With you so busy all the time, and being in your own place, I realized how much I love you and miss you when I'm not with you or waking up next to you. I thought it over after we spoke the other day, and this is definitely the best way for us to spend more time together."

The fantasy evaporated. Faced with reality, and the cold, hard keys in my hand, I didn't know what to say. Part of me wanted to scream the biggest yes from that incredible terrace, but the other part… yearned for magic and madness, for the other world I'd entered into. This place was amazing in every way, but living with Adam would only mean more lies and secrets. And I couldn't juggle that. I'd proven I couldn't.

Unless... Unless I told him the whole truth now, before this went any further in either direction: away from him or toward him.

I looked at Huntress, who had her blue eyes fixed on me. She whined softly—a sad whimper. I didn't need to be soul-tied to her to understand what the sound meant. She'd likely relayed the information to Nash, and this was his response, combined with hers. They clearly didn't think moving in with Adam was a good idea.

"Help me out," I murmured to the dog.

Adam frowned. "Me?"

"No, I was talking to... never mind." The world started to spin.

"Who?" Adam pressed.

"Uh... I was just asking for some... um... spiritual guidance. This is a big decision." I was making a mess of this.

"Spiritual guidance?" He sounded concerned, like I was away with the fairies.

"Just, you know, a sign or something." *Just keep your mouth shut!*

His face scrunched up. "You need a sign?"

I wished the ground would swallow me up.

To make it ten times worse, Nash sprinted in at that very moment. *This wasn't the plan!* I'd given him the nod to say everything was okay. Had Huntress thought I needed someone to get me out of this and passed the message on? It looked like it.

"There you are, Ryann!" Nash said brightly. "I tried to catch you in the elevator, but the doors closed before I could slip through."

"Who are you?" Adam looked deeply confused.

"This is my colleague, Nash," I replied, wishing I had magic to disappear.

Nash reached out to shake Adam's hand. Polite Canadian that he was, Adam hesitantly accepted. "I just got a call from the office," Nash went on. "Finch wants us back, so we should probably get going."

You didn't just say that. The ultimate face-palm moment.

"Finch?" Adam glanced between us, his voice tense. "Why would Finch be calling you back to the office? Are you working with him?"

"Remember I told you we'd been outsourcing, and he happened to come in to work on a project?" I kept it vague in hopes it'd make some sense in Adam's brain.

Adam's eyes narrowed. "No, I don't remember you saying that. And I would have, if it had something to do with Finch." He glared at Nash. "What's going on, Ryann?"

Crap, crap, crap, crap!

"Nothing's going on. I honestly thought I told you Finch came in for a project." I fumbled through my reply, noting the way Adam's expression had changed. He looked... not angry, not jealous, just hurt. I realized he was probably playing through a million scenarios —all my late nights and long workdays, all the missed dates and unanswered calls. It didn't look good on my part, because it wasn't. I'd been treating this man so badly, but I didn't know what else to do. Either way, I would hurt him. I couldn't *not* hurt him. The realization settled over me, bringing unhelpful tears to my eyes.

"I asked you about work last night, and you didn't mention him." Adam toyed with his set of keys, no doubt wondering what the heck he'd been thinking, bringing me here.

"I haven't been working with him much. Only now and then,

when the project needs it. Nash is the one who's been working with him." My voice had gone up an octave. A sure sign of guilt.

Adam shook his head. "Why wouldn't you tell me Harley's brother works at the same office? I ask you about your colleagues, and you always say something vague. In fact, I hardly know anything about where you work or what you do, even though I ask all the time. Seriously, Ryann, what's going on? Because my head is going to some dark places right now. Are you in the CIA or something?"

Before I could reply, another figure entered the beautiful lounge. And my heart almost stopped.

"Good morning. Not interrupting, am I?" I'd have known that British accent a mile off, even if I hadn't been looking at his smarmy face. A reminder of the time he took me and my family hostage.

"Davin," I hissed.

"Who?" Adam looked like his head might explode.

Davin smirked. "Foolish of you to wander about in such small numbers."

Adam's eyes bugged. "Who is this guy?"

"A past acquaintance of Miss Smith here." Davin stepped forward and lifted his hands.

"Get behind me." Nash put himself between me and Davin, but Davin just laughed.

"My, my, how many admirers do you have, Miss Smith?" Purple tendrils snaked around his fingers. "Finch won't be able to resist rescuing his damsel in distress…"

An eruption of purple-tinged black haze enveloped us all before I could say a word in retaliation. We'd been so worried about Erebus, we hadn't stopped to consider the others watching our every move. And now, Davin had us exactly where he wanted us.

TWENTY

Ryann

My cells tore apart at the seams, only to be slammed back together again. An indescribable sensation, like having pins and needles all over your body, prickling through every vein and limb and inch of skin. For a moment, I thought we'd portaled somewhere. I'd experienced a similar sensation when Erebus kidnapped me. But this had a more dangerous edge to it—as if my cells might not come back together this time.

The purple-tinged haze faded, but we were still in the plush apartment. My feet were rooted to the ground, yet I felt somehow distant, as though I were having an out-of-body experience. My head whipped around frantically, searching for Adam. He lay on the ground, curled in pain, his face contorted.

"Adam!" I yelled. Nash was also in the throes of some deadly spell. Huntress crouched in front of him, baring her fangs and acting as a defensive wall between her soul-partner and Davin.

"Poor fellow." Davin cackled, his palms still up. "Would you like to see his heart break, Ryann? Not in the figurative sense?"

"NO!" I screamed, trying to run forward to help Adam. But whatever that mist had done, it held me fast. I floated, hovering in the air as though I were shackled to the atmosphere itself.

"Pardon? I didn't quite hear you." Davin edged nearer. "Oh, and if you think your screams will alert the neighbors, think again. That mist created a bubble. You could scream until your lungs burst, and no one would hear."

He twisted his hands sharply, and Adam soared. His head crashed hard into the ceiling, and his body went rigid, a vein straining his temple, his forehead slicked with sweat. I saw him fighting Davin's hex, his muscles popping in an alarming way, as if they really might burst wide open. But what could a human do against someone like Davin?

"Davin, please!" I howled, but he ignored me. His hands twisted again, and Adam careened through the terrace doors. The balcony railing stopped him, but it served as a potent warning. A moment later, Davin hauled Adam back inside and began throwing him around the room like a rag doll, slamming him into every wall before sending him back through those doors. Again, the railing stopped him. Davin was taunting me, and it was working.

"Davin, STOP!" I shouted. He brought Adam to an abrupt halt, leaving him floating in the air, same as me. "Please stop. Don't hurt him. He's not part of this. He doesn't even like Finch. Please, please don't hurt him. Let him go."

Davin walked toward me, peering up at my hovering figure. "And why would I do a thing like that? He may not like Finch, which I can respect, but he cares a great deal about you. Which means you'll behave and do as I ask if I keep him on a tight leash."

He grasped Adam again and moved him slowly across the room. Adam's face contorted in a mask of horror, but the spell that held him had also silenced him. Once more, Davin manipulated him out the terrace doors, lifting him higher this time. My heart lurched as Adam dangled precariously over the lip of the balcony. We may only have been on the second floor, but a fall like that could kill him or leave him seriously injured. I couldn't let that happen.

"I'll give you whatever you want!" I gasped, panicked. "I'll do whatever you want, as long as you leave him alone. Please stop it. Let him go. Wipe his mind if you have to, but let him go!"

"You would like that, wouldn't you?" Davin glanced back at me. "If I were to wipe his mind of you, for example, you would be free to partake in a dalliance with Finch. And before you ask how I know about that, I have been watching. That would be the perfect solution for you, wouldn't it? You could pretend to be noble and muster some crocodile tears when poor Adam stared blankly through you—when it would really give you free rein to do as you pleased. My, my, I knew women could be cold, but that is downright Antarctic."

"That's not true!" I protested, straining against the invisible chains that held me. "I care about him. Don't hurt him! Please, I'll do anything."

Out of the corner of my eye, I noticed Nash unfurling from the painful spell. A hex bag glowed faintly in his palm. Somehow, it'd managed to break him free of the curse. I just needed to keep Davin talking while Nash went on the attack. Huntress was already primed and waiting for the order, her teeth gnashing. Fortunately, if there was one thing Davin loved above all else, it was talking about himself.

"Whatever you want, I'll do it," I went on. "Name it. As long as you let Adam go, I'll do whatever you ask."

Davin snickered. "A tempting proposal. I wonder, would you be even more fraught if Finch were here in Adam's place? I very much look forward to finding out."

"You won't kill Finch, though, will you?" I switched tactics. "You need him. He's the one who's been leading you through the stages of reaching Atlantis. You need him to keep going, or you won't get to the end of the road. That's right, isn't it?"

Davin wandered behind my would-be sofa, trailing his fingertips over the fabric. "Very astute, Miss Smith. But it is better to have a terrier you can control than a beast who does as they please. I will use him to hunt down what I seek, ensuring that he becomes a double agent—working for me and pretending to work for Erebus. And after my business concludes, I will finally have the delicious victory of killing him. And it will be so very slow."

Nash leapt forward, dagger in hand, aiming for Davin's neck. My eyes widened as I watched the scene play out in slow motion. Nash had nearly touched Davin's skin when Davin ducked and twisted, moving with startling agility. Tendrils of violet shot out of his palms and wrapped around Nash, squeezing tight, the strands slithering under his skin. Nash cried out in pain, his veins pulsating with purple light that, worryingly, turned black.

Huntress launched herself at Davin, her jaws open. She managed to clamp them around Davin's arm and hung on with all her might. Horrified, Davin flung her back and forth.

"Get off me, you furry bitch!" He grasped the scruff of her neck, his free hand trying to send tendrils of purple darkness into her. But it didn't work. Her husky shell appeared to be impervious to his magic. I could hardly watch as Davin resorted to brute force. He pincered her jaws with his fingers, pressing so hard she let out a sharp whine. But still she hung on. And for a moment, Davin dropped the magic that held Adam and me, his focus entirely on Huntress. After all, he couldn't keep it all up—the bubble, the hovering, and the painful curse he'd thrown at Nash.

Adam crashed to the ground and landed in a heap. I rushed to his side, using every ounce of strength I had to help him up. His bloodshot eyes peered at me, his busted lip trembling slightly. Through his arm, I felt his entire body shake. Even the toughest human would've had a hard time with this, and shock was taking over.

"It's true… it's all true," he rasped, a spatter of blood raining onto his chin. "Everything you said about magic… you meant it. You weren't joking. You were… trying to make me understand, weren't you?"

I nodded. "I'll explain later, but we have to get you out of here." I slung his arm around my shoulders and looked for the best exit. The path to the main door stood open, with Huntress and Davin brawling in the lounge. Huntress had released Davin and scampered back, preparing to lunge again. I went for it, pulling Adam along.

We'd barely gone five steps when I heard a canine yelp. Huntress hit the wall just in front of us and collapsed to the ground. She didn't get up, though I saw the rise and fall of her chest. Evidently, sometimes Davin's magic could hurt her, but other times it couldn't. By the looks of it, it seemed to be a proximity thing. If she was close, it did nothing. But if she was farther away, it did.

"And where do you think you're going?" Davin's voice cut through me like one of Nash's knives.

"I'm getting Adam out of here. Then I'll do whatever you want." I spoke firmly. Davin was like a shark; he could smell fear in the water, even the smallest drop.

He slid between us and the door. "Apologies, but I need everyone where I can see them." His arm was bleeding where Huntress had bitten him, but he didn't pay it any attention. No doubt he'd patch himself up later. "This is abject defiance, Miss Smith. I do so hate that."

"I'm not defying you!" The panic came out strong.

"Nevertheless." Davin's Telekinesis wrenched Adam away from me and flung him back through the terrace doors, leaving him dangling over the balcony. My heart plummeted. One false move, and Adam could end up in the hospital. Or the morgue.

I stared at Davin. "Why didn't you just kidnap me? Finch would've come after me, like you said. And nobody else would've gotten involved. You could have sent Nash and Adam and Huntress away—they'd have passed the message on faster, advancing your endgame of having Finch as your pet. So, why do this?"

He leered at me. "I enjoy the tantalizing pleasure of bending people to my will. It is far more satisfying to know you'll come with me willingly than to simply kidnap you. How coarse that would be. It reminds me of Erebus."

I looked back at Adam, whose eyes were filled with tears and fear. "Let him go, Davin."

"As you wish." He began to lower Adam over the railing.

"No!" I screamed. "I mean, let him walk free. Keep Nash and Huntress if you have to, but please let him walk away."

Davin rolled his eyes. "Tut, tut, Miss Smith. You aren't listening, are you?"

"Please." A pathetic whisper hissed from my throat.

My head snapped up as the muffled sound of the door handle rattled through the hallway, and a Latina woman entered the apartment. *No, no, no! Get out of here while you have the chance!* Davin wouldn't hesitate to pull more innocents into his game of torture, even those who had nothing to do with me.

"No cleaning is required today," Davin said, his tone snarky, jumping to stereotypes. "I suggest you leave before I decide to keep you merely for the fun of it."

"You would be hard pressed to," the Latina woman replied. Her palms rose, and her body transformed to pure, radiant light. I had to cover my eyes before the glare seared my retinas.

Who are you?

"Not again." Davin's mouth turned down in a grimace. His hands snapped to his sides, and Adam tumbled from the sky, disappearing over the edge of the balcony.

"NO!" I howled, my voice ragged with despair.

Everything happened in a weird mix of speed and slow motion. One moment, Davin was standing there, facing the strange woman. The next, he'd darted across the apartment and out onto the terrace, leaping across to the next balcony. I raced after him, finding some strength in my legs. When it came down to fight or flight, I'd chosen fight.

I skidded to a stop on the terracotta tiles in time to see Davin sketch a chalk door and disappear inside, the door slamming behind him. I hadn't managed to glimpse the place he'd gone, but that was the least of my worries. I sprinted for the railing as a whoosh of energy soared past my shoulder. A burst of light detonated below, blocking the gardens from sight. From the epicenter, a figure rose at lightning speed.

Adam yelped and flailed as he flew back to the balcony, then landed gently on the tiles. The moment his feet hit solid ground, his knees buckled, and he sank to the floor.

I whipped around to face the Latina woman, whose glow had ebbed. "Who are you?"

She smiled. "Greetings, Ryann Smith. My name is Lux."

"As in—"

"Yes, the very same," she replied. "Child of Chaos, Ruler of the Light."

Holy crap... If she hadn't just saved Adam's life, I'd have run in the opposite direction.

TWENTY-ONE

Ryann

—————

"It was all true. I can't... I can't believe it was all true." Adam's voice drew my attention away from the shining Child. He stared up at me as if I were a stranger. "You told me everything, and I... didn't listen. You wanted me to understand, and I didn't. It wasn't a joke. How can it not be a joke?"

I steeled myself. This was what I'd wanted, wasn't it? The truth, out in the open. No more lies, or hiding, in an attempt to salvage our relationship. But, judging by the way he looked at me, we may well have been past the point of no return.

"I wanted to see how you'd react," I admitted.

"How I'd react?" His eyes widened, his words stilted. "How did you think I'd react?!"

"I... I don't know."

He used the terrace furniture to lift himself. His body shook. "What are you, Ryann? Are you one of them? Have you done something to me, to get me to... I don't know, not see things, or... You mentioned wiping my mind. Have you done that to me, when I got too close to the truth?"

"What? No!" I gasped. Terror had warped Adam's mind, making him see me in a different light. I saw doubt in his eyes. A horrible, horrible doubt that I wasn't who he thought I was.

"Then why didn't you tell me everything was real? Why did you wrap it up in hypotheticals and make a joke out of it? Because, I'm telling you right now, none of that was funny for me." He gulped loudly, running a hand through his hair. "How do I know you're not just hiding what you are? You've been hiding so much from me. Working with Finch, this magic stuff, and who knows what else."

I shook my head vehemently and walked toward him. He stepped back immediately. "I'm not a magical, Adam. But... I do have a magical family."

Lux stood by, watching with interest. No doubt this was entertaining for her, watching the inner workings of troubled human relationships. I'd worried she'd be annoyed at the delay, but she seemed to be enjoying herself enough to wait.

"The Smiths are magical?" Adam leaned against the balcony for support.

"No, not them. Harley is a magical, and so is Finch." I knew I'd get in trouble for telling him, but after what he'd endured, he deserved to know the truth. "I only found out about the magical world a year ago, when that man, Davin, kidnapped me and my parents. He wanted to trap us, luring Harley to rescue us. It worked, but he has a way of surviving pretty much everything. He deals in Necromancy—resurrection and that kind of thing."

Adam paled. "I feel sick."

"Put your head between your legs and take deep breaths," Lux interjected. "I find that works for most humans."

"I'm guessing you're a magic person, too?" Adam could barely lift his head. To be honest, I was surprised he hadn't passed out altogether after the abuse Davin had just put him through. He'd always been strong. Perhaps stronger than I'd ever realized.

Lux chuckled. "Oh no, I am far more."

"Lux is…" I paused, wishing I could ease him into this more gently. "She's basically a goddess, but we call her a Child of Chaos. Chaos being the thing that fuels magicals… uh, though it's also present in humans; we just get less, so we don't get to do the magic part. It's the world's energy, so to speak. It flows through everything." I stumbled through my explanation, struggling with the enormity of it.

"I'm really going to be sick." Adam shivered as he gripped the terrace furniture tighter, his knuckles whitening. "This isn't… this is impossible, Ryann! This can't be happening."

"It is happening, and it will become easier to stomach in time." Lux walked over to him and reached out, about to touch his shoulder. He yanked his body away so sharply, he'd likely gotten whiplash.

"No offense, Miss Child of Chaos, but I'd prefer you didn't touch me," Adam murmured, looking very green.

Lux nodded. "As you wish."

"Why does that guy want to punish you?" Adam lifted his gaze to me. Tears welled in his thread-veined eyes. An aftereffect of Davin's painful curse. He was having a hard time with this; I didn't need to be an Empath to know that. He was scared and overwhelmed, and who wouldn't be? I'd had a freak-out here and there when I first learned about the magical world, even though we'd discovered its existence in eerily similar ways.

"Because of Finch. They have a long and nasty past, and Finch recently did something to really piss Davin off, so this was his attempt at revenge." I turned to Lux and made an awkward bow. "Which he'd probably have pulled off if it weren't for you, Lux. Thank you for saving us."

Lux curtseyed in response. "I must take care of those who matter. I am the Child of Light, after all. It is my duty to bring hope in the darkness, and Davin is entirely a creature of darkness."

"Magic is real… goddesses are real… I can't get my head around this." Adam closed his eyes and breathed deep. "What else is real? Dragons and fairies?"

"Yes, actually, though the number of dragons has diminished in recent years. A true shame, but hunters are eager to retrieve their skins and sell them at exorbitant prices, just to make all manner of clothing and accessories." Lux sighed sadly. "Fairies are as pernicious and abundant as ever, though. Vicious little things."

Adam sank down and brought his knees to his chin. "This isn't happening. I'm in your apartment, having a terrible dream. That's all this is. None of this is real."

"I'm sorry, Adam." I went to him and crouched at his side. "I'm sorry I didn't properly tell you before, but I hope you can see why I had to keep it from you. I wanted you to be safe. Plus, there are covens, like I told you, and they have strict rules about humans knowing of the magical world."

"So, you're magically gagged or something?" Adam held his head in his hands. "No, this isn't right, Ryann. If there are powerful beings like that Davin guy in this world, who can swing people about the room like freaking rag dolls, then someone needs to know it. I need to call the Air Force or alert the Pentagon that we've got a global threat on our hands. This is ridiculous! This is so dangerous… that magical beings live among us and we had no idea! How many ordinary humans die every year because of these magicals, huh? Can you tell me that?"

My cheeks burned and my stomach clenched. "Some."

"Some?!" he barked. "Some is too many, Ryann! I want you out of this madness. You can't honestly be okay with this! I don't know how, but I'll protect you. I don't know what they've done to you, or what they've fed you to make you so cool and calm about this, but we'll find a way to reverse it. We can go to the cops with this! No, the FBI, or the NSA, or even the CIA! They need to know before more humans wind up tossed off balconies!"

The disappointment that struck my heart was unlike anything I'd ever experienced. I'd handled his dismissal of the magical world when he hadn't known the reality, but now he did… and he still didn't get it.

"They're not dangerous, Adam. *Davin* is dangerous. He's like…I don't know, the Ted Bundy of the non-magical world—an anomaly in everyday life." I couldn't believe I'd just used Ted Bundy as an example, after every time Finch had called Adam that. "The rest are good people. You know Harley. Do you think she's dangerous?"

Adam threw back his head in exasperation. "Right now, I don't know. I feel like I don't know anything anymore. But what I do know is that magicals can't just live in secret, without the ordinary world knowing. That's not right. It's sneaky and sly, and it goes against national safety. Heck, against global safety! Ted Bundy wasn't wandering around shooting purple magic out of his hands or resurrecting himself! Can you imagine how many women he'd have killed if he was magical? One 'anomaly' of theirs is way worse than one of ours could ever be. It's like saying, 'Well, there's only one nuke, so we should be fine.' I can't believe you're standing there defending this! What have they done to you? I want to know, so I can take it away."

Take it away? Nobody will take this world from me. Nobody.

"You said you'd be fascinated if magic were real. You said it'd be interesting. Where did all that go?" A bitter note edged into my voice, but maybe I was being too hard on him. He'd almost died a moment ago, which was bound to make him less open to the idea of magic. He'd witnessed the bad before I could introduce him to the good, and first impressions counted for a lot.

Adam hugged his knees tighter. "That was before I knew it *was* real."

Everything I'd built with Adam was crumbling beneath us both. Once upon a time, I'd thought our foundations were rock solid, only to find out they'd been constructed on the sands of change. I could've supported those walls if he'd understood and wanted to change with me, but seeing him now confirmed the stark truth: he'd never understand the magical world, and if he couldn't understand it, then how could he support my decision to live and work in it? It'd be a perpetual wedge between us.

"Oh dear. And I thought I had romantic troubles," Lux murmured, clearly somewhat amused by my unraveling personal life.

"Is this funny to you?" Adam snapped, clearly on the edge of a nervous breakdown. "I don't care what sort of goddess you are, you have no right to laugh at me."

Lux's eyes narrowed. "Be careful, boy. My understanding only stretches so far."

"He doesn't know what he's saying," I said, eager to protect Adam from any retribution Lux might hand out for being insulted.

"Do you see what I mean?" Adam turned to me in despair. "I'm not seeing any of that good magic you mentioned."

"Nash and Huntress are good." I gestured to the two figures on the floor, still out cold but breathing. "You'd like them if you got to know them. You'd like most of the magical people I know. Lux, can you heal them? Show Adam what good Chaos can do."

Lux sighed. "I suppose I could summon one of my Sylphs to attend them." She opened her arms and lifted her head. A moment later, a strange being appeared at her side, translucent like a ghost but seemingly made of the air itself. It flowed liquidly, as though suspended in water, with two gossamer wings at its back and a childlike face that looked so sweet it almost made me cry.

Lux gestured, and it swept toward Nash and Huntress, setting to work on them. Streams of white light worked their way from the Sylph's small hands, feeding into the two downed figures. I glanced at Adam, hoping he'd be impressed, but he wasn't.

Adam grimaced. "That only proves my point. It's not natural! What even is that thing?"

"That *thing* is a Sylph. A creature of Air," Lux retorted. "Gifted with healing abilities, courtesy of me."

"This is too much, Ryann." Adam shuddered. "If they have this enormous, unchecked power, and all these creatures running around, then I don't want to know them. They should be monitored. They should have security personnel watching them, day in and day out, to make sure they can't accidentally, or intentionally, hurt anyone." He staggered to his feet again. "I need to leave. I don't want to be here, thinking about this. And the moment I'm out of this building, I'm calling the cops, or *someone*, on this Child of Chaos, and I'm going to blow the whistle on this secret world you've been hiding."

Lux snorted. "As if they would be able to do anything to me. I would disintegrate their guns before they could even pull the trigger."

"Do you hear her?" Adam clenched his jaw. "There's no way you can be all right with this. I know you, Ryann. They've messed with your head. They've used their glowing stuff and manipulated your mind."

"No, they haven't." I stood my ground. "They wanted to wipe my mind, but I insisted on remembering, and they *respected* that. And I've been working with the covens to improve human-magical relations ever since because I *didn't* think it was right that they could go around wiping minds and making non-magicals forget everything."

Adam recoiled. "Are you telling me you're... into this whole magical thing?"

"I wouldn't change it for the world. I wouldn't give up all this knowledge. The magical world is an amazing place, and you would see that if you could just forget your fear for a second," I urged.

His jaw dropped. "Then I never knew you at all. The Ryann I know wouldn't stand for this. She'd be on the phone with the freaking White House, making sure justice prevailed."

The Ryann you knew doesn't exist anymore. What I had with Adam would never work. This apartment, this life, this fantasy... was precisely that. A fantasy, one that belonged to someone else. I wanted adventure and danger and a life more extraordinary than paying my dues at a law firm. But he would never get that. He didn't see magic the way I saw it.

"And what do you think the non-magicals would do to the magicals if they found out?" I heaved a miserable sigh. "It'd be the start of World War III. That's why they stay secret, why they have so many rules surrounding non-magicals. If you think that wouldn't happen, then it's willful ignorance."

"Then this is a ticking timebomb that I don't want any part of." Adam stepped forward. "But that won't stop me from taking this as high as I can, to see some sense of fairness and transparency restored."

He brushed past me and headed for the main door. Panic seized me in a vise. Adam was about to leave, but I couldn't let him walk out of here, not if he intended to bring down the magical world. I wasn't sure anyone would believe him, but I didn't want him labeled a lunatic, either. Given all my arguments against mind-wiping, I knew this went against everything I believed in, but Adam had become a danger to an entire people. So, perhaps I could make one painful exception. One person's mind to save millions from a war of persecution.

"Lux, help me!" I hissed. She was my only option. Nash was dead to the world while the Sylph continued to heal him. Huntress had stirred and now lay in Nash's lap, licking his hands. But it did no good. Nash didn't wake up.

Lux observed her fingernails, feigning nonchalance. "Help with what?"

"Help me stop him." My heart ached at the prospect, but he'd left me no choice.

"I can if you truly want me to, but only if you agree to grant me a favor later. Only then will I resolve this problem for you," she replied.

I knew deals with Children of Chaos wouldn't lead anywhere good. Finch was living proof of that. And he might be dead proof soon, which only emphasized the fact that deals with the likes of Lux never ended well. It broke my heart every time I thought about Finch's future. I couldn't handle the thought of him being gone, and it made me want to slam Lux into a wall until she vowed to change Erebus's plans.

I wished Finch were here. It might've made everything ten times worse, but at least he could've held my hand and let me know everything would be okay. Although, he'd have told me never to agree to a deal like this. But what else could I do? I had my back against the wall, and Adam—sweet Adam—had put me there. And who knew, maybe Lux meant well. She was the Child of Light. Maybe she was here to be my light.

I'm sorry...

"Fine. I accept. Adam can't remember any of this. He'll cause untold mayhem, and I don't want that for him. I don't want it for any of us," I pleaded.

"Excellent." Lux twisted her hands, and Adam skidded back into the room, dragged by an invisible force. He strained and flailed, utterly confused, but he couldn't escape Lux's clutches any more than he'd been able to escape Davin's.

"Let me go!" he begged, his eyes wide with fear. I couldn't watch. My heart broke all over again. This wasn't how I'd thought this day would go.

"Calm down," Lux purred. Adam instantly fell silent. "This won't hurt, I promise." She cupped her hands to his face and leaned in, pressing her lips to his. Something I'd never do again. Even with his mind wiped, I knew it was over. And it hurt like nothing else. A sharp stab to the heart that I knew wouldn't feel bearable for some time.

Light erupted from within him, snaking down his limbs and up his throat, glowing brighter at his mouth where his lips connected with hers. It should've been uncomfortable to see another woman kiss Adam, and it was, but for more than the usual reasons. It also represented everything I'd fought against since I'd joined the SDC. Mind-wiping.

A moment later, Lux pulled away. Adam stumbled forward, his eyes closed. The kiss had knocked him out. Lux caught him, holding him with her impressive strength, and lay him on the ground beside Nash. With a nod from Lux, the Sylph who'd healed Nash and Huntress swept forward, doing the same thing to Adam. Light enveloped him, and when the Sylph drew away again, there were no cuts or bruises in sight.

"Is it done?" I breathed.

Lux smiled at me as she straightened. "It is done, Ryann. He won't remember anything of this incident when he wakes, and my Sylph has ensured he feels no pain. What you do about the rest of your troubles is entirely up to you." She pulled a tube of bright red lipstick from her vessel's pocket and swiped it across her lips. I'd heard enough about Erebus taking over Finch's body in Elysium to understand what the Latina woman was to Lux. "Now I must go. I will collect my favor another day."

Speechless, I watched her leave. Part of me wanted to chase her and demand to know what she would ask of me, but the larger part of me just wanted to make sure Adam was okay. Just because we'd come to the end of the line didn't mean I'd stopped caring. He would've been the perfect husband to the old me. The perfect partner to share this apartment and a normal life with. But normal had vanished from my life, and I couldn't pretend to be someone else anymore. It was too damn hard, and it wasn't fair to Adam, either. He deserved the world, like Harley and Finch and the Rag Team had given me this world. And, looking like he did and being the man he was, it wouldn't be long before someone came along who could give him the normalcy and happiness he longed for. But she wasn't me.

I knelt beside Adam and shook him gently. "Adam? Adam, can you hear me?"

He groaned.

"Adam?"

His eyes blinked open. "Ryann?"

"I'm here."

He peered around at the apartment in confusion. "Oh… I showed you the apartment already?"

"You did." I managed a smile, though my insides were in pieces.

Nash woke with a groan. "What the hell happened? Did that son of a—"

"There was a gas leak, remember?" I cut in quickly before he could say anything damning. Adam had forgotten about Davin and all that unpleasantness, and I wanted it to stay that way.

Nash frowned, then his eyebrows shot up. "Ah, right, that must be why my head's pounding like a jackhammer." Huntress whined and nuzzled his chin. "Hey there, little one. Did I scare you?"

"A gas leak?" Adam asked, squinting as if trying to remember.

I nodded. "I went to the bathroom to check out the shower, and when I came back, you were both passed out. That's why the terrace doors are open. I ran straight to them, to get some fresh air before the gas got to me."

"Is this the… uh… Actually, who are you?" Adam gestured to Nash, evidently not remembering that the latter had come into the room.

"A neighbor," Nash said quickly.

"Yeah, a neighbor. He came by to introduce himself, and… uh…" I stumbled over the lie, not knowing what to say next.

"I saw you passed out on the floor and rushed to check on you. That's when I must've got caught in the gas leak, too." Nash came in with the right words. More lies, but necessary ones.

I put out my hand to help Adam stand. "Now, come on, we should get out of here. I don't want you both keeling over again."

And I didn't want Davin coming back, either.

On our way out of the building, Adam showed no signs of remembering anything. He didn't even recall blacking out, but he took my word for it. Guilt churned in my stomach. It made me happy to see him back to his usual self, with none of the fear and doubt and pain in his eyes, but that happiness came with the price of knowing I'd just stuck the last nail in our coffin. I'd gone against my moral code to wipe his mind so he could move on with his life without trying to bring down the magical world. The right reasons, maybe, but I knew he and I were done.

"If we got knocked out by a gas leak, we should probably all swing by the hospital to get checked out," he said matter-of-factly.

"I'm sorry that happened. I'll talk to the super about it and make sure it's fixed."

"That slimy son of a banshee," Nash grumbled.

"No, the super's a nice guy. He'll have repairmen over by this afternoon and get this fixed in no time. I asked him a ton of questions earlier, and he seemed like the good kind," Adam protested. "Now, let's hail a cab to the emergency room."

I shook my head. "I feel fine, and the neighbor seems to be okay. But if you don't, you should definitely go and see one of your doctor pals to get checked out."

"You might feel fine now, but gas is dangerous. It can cause problems later on, without you realizing," Adam replied, looking worried. "The building should be evacuated."

"I'll see to that, don't worry. They'll react to a report quicker if it's a resident telling them there's a leak." Nash intervened. "No offence. You're not quite a resident yet, so it's better if I do it."

Adam nodded slowly. "Right. Yes, that'd be good."

"As for me, I'm so sorry, but I need to get going," I said. Nash had an excuse to leave, but I needed one, too. The perfect one came to me, though Adam wouldn't like it. "I've got a mega important meeting in an hour. But I promise I'll get checked out afterward, Adam, if I feel weird. I can't miss this meeting."

Adam furrowed his brow. "Your health is more important than your job."

"Honestly, at the first sign of anything wrong, I'll go to the emergency room. But I've been working for months on this pitch, and I need to be there." I gave him my best firm-but-fair voice.

He sighed. "I guess you didn't pass out, so you must not have inhaled as much as we did." He looked over at Nash. "But you should definitely see a doctor."

"I will, after all this reporting I'm going to do," Nash replied.

"Now, what about the apartment? Did you like it? I don't remember." Adam looked puzzled. "But if you do, then I can make an offer today, and we'll move in as soon as the gas leak is fixed. This can be our new home; you just have to say the word. Sure, it didn't give the greatest first impression, but this place has so much potential." He lowered his gaze, quivering with emotion. "I love you, Ryann. I want to make a home together."

Nash cleared his throat. "I'm going to walk Huntress inside and make sure everyone's evacuated, then take a walk to clear our lungs. It was nice meeting you."

He knew where this was going, and so did I. If only I could've run away so easily.

"What do you say?" Adam prompted, once Nash was far enough from us. He smiled with so much boyish excitement that I wanted to slap myself silly. But this needed to be done. He'd found out the truth, and he'd wanted to call in everyone from the local police to the CIA to annihilate the magical world. I couldn't make this work, but it hurt to give up on something I'd put so much time and effort into creating. It stank of failure. But sticking with it would've been worse.

I took the second set of keys and grasped his hand, folding them into his palm. "I can't, Adam."

"What?" He stared at me in complete surprise.

"I love you; I don't want you to think I don't. I care about you so much, and that's why I have to say no, because we're not the same people we were a year ago. I'm not making you happy anymore. I'm hurting you, and that kills me. I'm canceling dates and I'm always busy, and you deserve more." I paused, my heart heavy. "There's a reason we've been drifting apart, and it's nobody's fault, but living in the same apartment won't solve our problems."

Tears glittered in Adam's eyes. "But... we've only been having problems because we're so busy. Please don't do this. We can make it work, Ryann. Come on, this is you and me. We have to make it work."

"We tried," I said softly. "It's not fair to you, and it's not fair to me. We need to end this before we wind up resenting each other. I never want to hate you, but if we keep going the way we have been and start living together, it'll only result in more misery for both of us. It's not going to be easy, but we owe it to each other to part on good terms."

He shuffled his feet, looking so vulnerable my throat clenched. "Why are you doing this? Is it because there's someone else? Did I do something? Please, Ryann, tell me how to fix this."

Tears brimmed in my eyes. One blink and they started to trickle down my cheeks. "I'm sorry, Adam. I'm so sorry, but I've... I've made up my mind." I reached out for his hand. "It's not you. It's nothing you've done or haven't done. You've been incredible, and I'll miss you like crazy. But our lives are too different. I'm not who I was when we met. I'm so sorry. I'm so, so sorry."

Adam said nothing. He simply stared at me, his eyes wet. What else could he say? What else could I say?

Forgive me...

TWENTY-TWO

Finch

W e were meant to take the day to rest. But sleep wouldn't have come unless I'd been smacked in the head with a bulldozer. To make it worse, I'd lain awake in a strange room that smelled like an antiques roadshow, with ghosts chattering at all hours about total nonsense. Even under those circumstances, I'd thought only about Ryann.

I'd expected us to all get together the same afternoon, but a curt text had trashed that idea. Weirdly, it hadn't come from Ryann. Nash was the harbinger of my heart's future coronary.

Ryann's fine. No Erebus. We'll get together tomorrow. Winchester place, grand salon, noon. This is my number, in case that wasn't obvious. —Nash

It might've been borderline stalkerish, but I'd headed out a couple times to stand on the landing and see if she'd come back. Once, I thought I heard the front door open and close, but when I'd gone to investigate, there'd been no one there. Likely a spook or a gust of wind, giving me added creeps.

But the day passed and so did the night, with zero sign of Ryann. She must've come back at some point, given Erebus's threat, but it seemed she wasn't in a talkative mood. I hadn't seen Nash, either. He probably didn't want to face the barrage of questions I'd have slammed him with if we'd crossed paths. Even at meals, which Cecily and Richard had prepared, the errant duo had been absent.

What could've happened to make her want to hide away? Maybe Ryann had argued with Captain Canuck and there was trouble in paradise.

Agitated and exhausted, I dressed and headed for the grand salon. The moment I stepped into the room, the mood soured. Or the mood had already been on its way to curdling, and my presence had tipped it over the edge. Leaning back in her chair, Ryann sat glaring at the far wall. Yep, something was definitely up with her.

"Morning, Ryann," I chirped.

I got a grunt in response, a clear signal she wasn't up for any conversation. It must've been a bad argument.

Nash stood by the door, drinking coffee. I made a beeline for him, since he'd snagged my place in the front row of whatever had happened yesterday. Huntress peered up at me with her icy eyes, and I could've sworn they held a warning.

"What's up with Ryann?" I whispered, all furtive-like.

Nash sipped his coffee. "Can't tell you, pal."

"Are you kidding me?" I gaped at him.

"I'm sworn to silence, and I keep my promises." He offered an apologetic look. "But I can tell you that we met our old friend yesterday. Didn't take that slippery eel long to put himself back together again."

"Davin was there?" I must've looked like a moron, with my jaw hanging so low. "And you didn't think to call in the friggin' backup? What the hell, man?"

"I *was* the backup," Nash retorted. "Not that it mattered. He knew we wouldn't be watching for him, thinking he was still licking his wounds somewhere."

My stomach twisted. "How did he find you? What happened? Tell me everything, or I'll make you wear that coffee."

Nash stroked Huntress's fur. "He got desperate because my hex bag is blocking your signal. I guess he followed us. I don't know for sure. But we made it out alive, and Adam got glamorized, so he doesn't remember anything. He probably wishes he... never mind." He clammed up quick as Ryann pushed herself from her chair and walked toward us.

"Adam got what?" I fumbled for something to say. Ryann's glower had me all hot under the collar, but not in the nice sense. I didn't like seeing her this way. And though I was eager to know what made her feel like this, it wasn't my place to pry. Don't get me wrong, I'd have interrogated Nash to within an inch of his plaid if Ryann hadn't walked over, but she had, so I'd keep quiet.

"Glamorized. Mind-wiped. Whichever term you prefer," Nash answered.

Ryann sighed heavily. "Lux did it."

"Excuse me?" I choked out. *Oh, for the love of Chaos...*

"Lux showed up out of nowhere and saved our asses, sending Davin running for cover," Ryann went on. "Adam freaked out, so she wiped his mind. Before you call me a hypocrite, don't. I hate that it came to that."

I raised my hands in mock surrender. "I would never."

My usual humor technique wasn't enough to cope. And frankly, being told that Lux had shown up to the party and saved them scared the hell out of me. Children of Chaos didn't do anything for free, despite Lux's claims of magnanimity. Was this supposed to be a persuasion tactic, to get me to see that a deal with her was a good thing? She saved Ryann, so I should scratch her back? I swallowed the urge to tell them about my own shenanigans with Lux. Ryann didn't look like she needed anything more to worry about. So, I had to put on a stellar performance.

"Lux saved you?" I gasped. It came out perfect. "Was she all floaty and liquid, in her true form?"

Ryann shook her head. "She'd taken a human host."

"She can do that?" Another perfect pretense of shock.

"Apparently," Nash chimed in.

"But how did she find you?" That part I didn't know, though I guessed it had something to do with her Sylph network.

Nash shrugged. "Damned if I know, but she did, and I'm glad. Otherwise, we'd be trapped under Davin's spell and you'd be wandering into his snare."

I've put her in danger again. And I couldn't even pretend to be surprised. I'd known something like this would happen the moment Ryann got involved with all the map-making stuff. If it hadn't been for Lux... no, I didn't feel like dragging myself through that emotional hedge. Lux had evidently saved the day.

I felt eyes burn the back of my head. Turning, I saw Melody across the room, watching me closely. Being a Mimic and a Shapeshifter had some major perks. Transforming into Tom Hardy whenever I needed a confidence boost and remaining blissfully unaffected by the privacy-thwarting abilities of an Empath. If she'd been able to read me, I'd have had to spew my guts about Lux and everything that mess entailed.

"I'm sorry." I turned back to Ryann. "I'm sorry he followed you, and that he put you in that position. If it'd occurred to me that he might come after you, I'd never have let you go without proper backup. I'm talking bigger numbers, full ammunition, the works."

She fixed her gaze on the floor. "We lived, and that's what matters."

"But why would Lux get involved?" Melody stepped forward, and Luke mirrored her. "It's not like a Child of Chaos to intervene without a reason. Even then, they aren't really supposed to, and using a human host must've taken a great deal of effort. I've never heard of a Child doing that before. Plus, since you aren't a magical, Ryann, you couldn't have accidentally summoned her. This doesn't make any sense."

"And her timing is odd," Luke added. "We've got a big mission ahead of us. Do you think Lux knows what Erebus is after in Atlantis, and that she sent Davin running to stop him from getting in her way? That would explain why she protected the two of you, as well."

More like she doesn't want to stop Erebus because she wants to lock him in the center of the earth. I held my tongue. This particular secret would probably drive me mad before all this was said and done. It was massive, truly massive. And I couldn't utter a whisper.

"We should focus on the mission." Ryann lifted her head high. "I don't want to talk about yesterday. And it's not like we've got a lot of time to get ready for Maine. It's Monday, and we need to infiltrate the cultists on Friday. There's too much to do without the added stress of these freaking Children of Chaos, and speculating about why they do what they do, on top of it."

I gazed at her until she met my eyes. "You might not want to talk about it, and that's your right, but Davin crossed a line yesterday. He targeted you to get to me." My blood boiled just thinking about it. "We need to find that djinn and kill this Necromancer son of a toad already!"

Ryann's expression softened the tiniest fraction. "The others are working on that. Let's not start crossing wires and losing focus."

"Hard not to, when he tracked you down and almost hurt you," I retorted.

"Well, he didn't hurt me. So get your head back in the game." Her tone hardened again. "Melody found a list of pubs in Kennebunkport, and we need to scout them all before Friday. See if anyone knows anything about a gathering, but discreetly. Forget Davin. Leave him to Harley—she'll find a way to tie a noose around that bastard's neck. One he won't be able to wriggle his way out of."

I clenched my fists and fought to let go of my rage. "What, so we're going to Maine today?"

"No time like the present," Nash replied. "We can chalk-door outside of town, with our hex bags concealing our magic. From there, we find this pub. And when Friday comes—"

"We stake it out and set the stage for an Eris Cult capture," Ryann finished his sentence.

Nash turned to Melody. "Melody? I hate to keep asking, but could you do the honors? I know it's not far, but I'd rather not traipse outside first. We don't know who might be watching."

The group dispersed, somewhat deliberately, leaving me alone with Ryann. I'd done my best not to pry, but she was right here, and she looked so sad and bitter. What was I meant to do, stand there like a statue and say nothing?

"Are you okay?" I asked softly. "I don't need to know what happened, but if there's anything I can do to help, just say the word."

She looked at me, and tears glinted in her eyes. "No, there's nothing you can do. It'll be okay, eventually."

Is this the time to give her the prompt Melody was going on about? I reached out to take Ryann's hand, but she drew away as if I'd lit a candle under her palm. *Okay, guess not.*

"Well, like I said, say the word and I'll be here." I put my hands awkwardly behind my back, the way old men did when they walked.

"Doorway's ready!" Melody called, providing a much-needed break of the tension stretching between Ryann and me.

TWENTY-THREE

Finch

Over the next week of zipping back and forth between the Winchester House and the mysterious backwater town of Kennebunkport, we finally located the bar where the rogue cultists would gather on Friday. The Bloated Porpoise. Nasty name for nasty folks, though the human patrons seemed suitably New England nice. They had no idea what sort of criminals they had drinking with them.

Kennebunkport itself was a sleepy fishing town on the East Coast, with fresh seafood and creepy homes on the sparser stretches of bay, like Walkers Point, that looked somewhere between colonial and haunted house. The main area of town, however, was like a Scandi, chocolate-box, Christmassy wonderland, instilled with an eerie despondency only when the tide went out. But when it came back in... man, what a beauty.

Truth be told, I liked it a lot. That mix of beauty with a touch of spooky from a stilted red church-looking building, and the stark rocky promontories that jutted out in the distance, gave me some major fall feels. I'd found that a sense of wonder and intrigue often came with seaside towns, where the foundations were built on drowned spirits and fireside folklore. But we weren't here to admire the scenery. We were here for information. And, since Erebus, Lux, and Davin hadn't turned up to harass us, I figured they had their own fish to fry. I'd managed to get my hands on a new phone and had kept Erebus up to date with what we were doing. Weirdly, he hadn't seemed to mind the short delay. I guessed he was just pleased we were on track.

While pairs of us had gone on a bar crawl to find the cultists' hangout spot, the others gathered an arsenal of magical goodies in case things turned vicious. We carried anti-magical hex bags on us at all times, but we needed more. Not only for the cultists, but for Eris Island.

Early evening on Friday, with the sun close to setting, we arrived at the bar and pulled into a parking lot across the street. We'd acquired a car to keep a low profile, chalk-dooring just outside the town limits and driving in each time. Nash, Huntress, Melody, and Luke got out, per our plan. They would lay traps and scope out the place before I came barreling in. Since Ryann was human, she'd been benched. But we had to bring her along for Erebus reasons, so she'd become the victim of Nash's huge rucksack, filled with magical supplies. I noticed the tiny hex bag attached to Huntress's K-9 vest and smiled despite myself. We had our very own dog unit.

"How's it going there, pack mule?" I decided to break the tense silence with a little teasing.

"Not funny. This thing weighs a ton." She huffed a sigh. In four whole days, she still hadn't told me what went down at the coffee shop, but she'd thawed a little. No more glaring at unfortunate walls. And she'd been pretty useful on our trips to Maine. In fact, she'd been the one to talk the proprietor into telling us about the rogue gathering, though he'd thought it was a meeting for Dungeons and Dragons enthusiasts. I'd had to hold onto a snort when I heard that one.

"Nash knows how to pack a bag, that's for sure."

Ryann looked out the window. "What's he doing, anyway?"

"Nash? He's placing hex bags and drawing sigils to set up a perimeter and stop certain spells from being cast. With so many humans around, we don't want to have to call in a huge cleanup operation. It's probably another reason the cultists chose this place, knowing the authorities wouldn't risk blowing magical-kind wide open."

"Does that make us rogue agents, then?" Ryann fumbled with the edge of her sweater, evidently uncomfortable.

"In a way, but we'll try not to make too much of a mess." I flashed her a winning smile, but she wasn't looking at me. "That's why it's good to have Melody. When the time comes, she'll use one of her transformation spells to put up a powerful time-lapse trapped in an interdimensional bubble. Complicated stuff, more complex than a normal time-lapse, as it has to come in at a precise moment, but that's what the Librarian does."

I peered through the window and spotted Luke and Melody sitting at a bus stop opposite the bar. The only ride they'd be catching, if all went well, was an all-expenses-paid trip to Eris Island. Land of my nightmares.

Ryann nodded absently. "Cool."

Cool? That's it? Who'd snatched my Ryann away and replaced her with this morose creature? I wanted a word with them. *Ah, screw it.* If I didn't ask now, I never would. And we had serious time to kill before the magical revelry began.

"What's up, Ryann? I know you don't want to talk about it, but maybe it'll help. You haven't been yourself these past few days." I dangled the carrot in the hopes of a bite. "Is Adam okay? Is it the emergency? Was it bad?"

She sighed. "Adam is fine, and the emergency... well, that's between the two of us. Doctor-patient confidentiality and all that."

Okay, not going to get anything Adam-related out of her... "What about Lux? Did she say anything when she saved you?" Really, I wanted to know if Lux had said anything about *me*. Ryann had been acting weird around me. She'd chosen to pair up with Melody on our previous recon visits, avoiding me every chance she got.

"Just something about bringing light in the darkness, and that she'd been watching Davin's behavior, but that was it." Ryann turned her gaze outward. A sure sign she wasn't telling me everything. But I wasn't exactly being forthcoming, either.

It frustrated the hell out of me that she wasn't being more open about the Lux business. Adam, I could understand. I wasn't exactly an objective spectator. But Lux *must* have had an endgame in mind when she rescued Ryann from Davin. The whole thing worried me.

"You can't trust her, Ryann." I stared into my lap. "You can't trust Lux or any Child of Chaos. They're only ever out for themselves, even if they say otherwise. They're selfish and crazy powerful. If you enter a deal with them, they'll get you into more trouble."

"I know," she said simply.

You know? What does that mean? My mind raced with every awful possibility.

"Incoming." Ryann gestured to the car window, bringing our conversation to an abrupt halt. I followed her hand and saw people starting to gather outside the bar. Man, they stood out like a bunch of sore thumbs. Enough to fill two hands, with there being around ten or so. Now I understood why the proprietor had presumed they were D&D enthusiasts. All that black clothing, those crazy hair-styles, and the various weird accessories spelled outcast... or magical. How they'd ever blended in was beyond me.

I recognized a few: Wilhelm Snebbles, Marianna von Erschwin, Jemima Smart, and Lorelai Fishwick, among others. They'd never been in my mother's upper echelons, but maybe that was why they'd made it out alive.

I hadn't expected the sight of them to hit me so hard. It was like Purgatory all over again. I'd lived with these people, worked with these people, ordered them around because I was the son of their goddess and what I said went. They'd been expendable, and I hadn't batted an eyelid sending them on dangerous missions. I struggled to believe I'd ever been that... evil. There was no other word for it. I'd been a human shell filled with darkness and blind obedience to my mother, and so had they. But I'd managed to break free, and they hadn't. They'd clung to darkness long after my mother had turned to dust.

Does that make me a better person than they are? Emily had pounded home the truth—redemption didn't erase the past. Nash had a different perspective, but it was like reading a thousand positive reviews and only remembering the one negative. I had done terrible, terrible things that haunted me, even now. My gremlins may have quieted down, but the memories hadn't. I'd sent these people into combat, time and time again. I'd made them steal and lie and kill in Katherine's name. It made me sick to my stomach to think about the monster I'd been.

"Finch?" Ryann put her hand on my shoulder.

I flinched. "Sorry."

"Are you all right?" She peered at me.

"I'm fine." I sucked in a breath. "A few familiar faces, that's all."

"You're not part of that world anymore." She gripped my shoulder tighter.

Maybe not, but I was. I swallowed my rising emotions. We didn't have time for them; I could wallow in self-pity later. Conscious of Ryann's hand still on my shoulder, I watched the cultists enter the Bloated Porpoise.

Nash emerged from the far side of the building, still visible in the fading light, and peered around it like a burglar in a comedy. He gave us a slow nod—the sign we'd been waiting for. Luke and Melody stood, their eyes fixed on the front door. Nash slipped through first while Ryann and I exited the car and waited for the next sign.

My gaze darted to our compadres up the street. Melody had her eyes closed and hands up, her mouth moving as she conjured the time-lapse bubble. A streak of glittering light slithered across the road and slid smoothly over the building. It thrummed for a moment, then glowed brighter before the shimmer ebbed. Our protective shields were up, and we had the corresponding hex bags to let us inside. No human would be able to enter. In fact, they'd walk straight past the bar as if it didn't exist, the bubble leaving a temporary gap in their memories.

The sound of glass shattering splintered the heavy silence. Roars erupted. Loud thuds followed, along with erratic shouts. I heard swear words so shocking I'd never heard them in real life before, and they echoed back in vulgar force.

"Showtime." I sighed. Instinctively, I took Ryann's hand and led her across the road, keeping her behind me. She was safer with us than left on the sidelines where someone could pick her off. But we didn't go through the main entrance. Only an idiot would do that. I pulled her down a side alley, swamped by the Bog of Eternal Stench. Aka, the dumpsters. It reminded me of my industrial park meetings with Erebus, but he could stuff it for now. After all, we were risking our necks for him.

I came to a stop halfway down the alley and stepped back against the wall beside us. Ryann was breathing heavily, though it'd only been a short run. She was nervous; I could feel it in her clammy hands. But I wasn't about to let go of her for the sake of some sweat.

"What if they overwhelm him?" Ryann whispered as the clatter of pure violence continued in the pub.

"That's why we have the rucksack full of goodies, remember?" I wished that filled me with confidence.

Melody and Luke sprinted toward us, Melody whipping out a golden orb. It looked like an Ephemera, but apparently it held an old-timey version of a time-lapse. One that'd draw all the magic away from the pub and create a concentrated bubble exactly where we wanted it, powered by the shield Melody had already created. A lesson in recycling.

She placed it on the ground and cupped her hands over it, whispering a spell under her breath. It glowed blue and began spitting sparks. Clearly, the engines needed to warm up a bit before the power kicked in. Which worked in our favor, since Nash hadn't come out yet.

In a stroke of perfect timing, a door crashed open. The shouts grew louder, followed by the thud of boots as people ran in our direction. Nash hared around the corner first, the cultists in hot pursuit. Wisps of multicolored light flashed on the ground—hexes hurled at Nash.

Melody waited until the very last moment before she jumped away from the artifact. Nash barreled past her, and the artifact ignited. A fierce blue light exploded outward, swallowing the alley.

I hoped this would work. They had the numbers, but we had the element of surprise.

"Let's light this baby up." I twisted my hands and got some Fire burning, sending a torrent over their heads to block the exit. A wall of flames surged upward. The cultists halted suddenly, their heads whipping around like a bunch of confused owls. The penny had dropped. They were trapped in our sneaky little ambush.

"Who are you?" Their leader, Wilhelm Snebbles, stepped forward. He would've made Quasimodo look like a beauty queen, with his greasy, thinning hair and beady eyes that looked like two raisins stuffed in dough.

I met him in the middle of the alley, keeping a safe distance. The alley shadows hid my face, but I decided to Shapeshift, just in case. I chose Gerald Daggerston as my muse, given his ties to Davin. Even in this fake form, I could smell the dollar bills. "We just want to talk."

"Secret Service? Government agents?" he guessed wildly.

"Neither. Like I said, we just want to talk." I let sparks fly from my hands to let him know I meant business.

"Who are you?" he repeated.

Okay, time for the big guns. This guy hadn't recognized Daggerston, and neither had the others, so this wouldn't help me as much as I'd hoped. But maybe they'd react differently to Katherine's son, in the flesh. I sent up a small ball of Fire like fireworks and discarded my Daggerston disguise, revealing my true face. A gasp of shock traveled through my audience.

"Is that... Finch Shipton?" one of the cultists whispered.

"Did you miss me?" I mustered a grin.

Snebbles glowered. "What do you want, traitor?" *Not off to a great start, here.*

"We want to know where Eris Island is. One of you was the last to leave. You set the security protocols in motion, and you know where we can find it. So, who's got the coordinates?"

A few of the cultists ran toward my wall of flames, only to stagger back from the heat. A few others looked to the opposite end of the alleyway, evidently weighing their chance of breaking through Melody, Nash, Huntress, and Luke.

"Even if you managed to get through the fire, you won't be able to leave the time-lapse until I disable it," Melody announced, her voice so strong it brought a proud tear to my eye.

Lorelai Fishwick, a stunningly beautiful woman with no empathy whatsoever, smirked. "You think you have *us* trapped?"

Huh? Why weren't they calling out for their brown pants? They should've been terrified... but they weren't. Even Snebbles seemed uncharacteristically calm, and he wobbled and jittered all over the place at the smallest inconvenience.

Horror struck me as tiny blue cracks began threading across the bubble, snaking back toward the artifact that had created it. The moment the cracks hit the golden orb, the whole thing glitched. The bubble shivered for a moment before it fizzled completely.

My head whipped around. As the blue light vanished, it revealed a figure standing behind the fearsome quartet at my back. One last hex bag burned in his hand, spitting wisps of multicolored smoke.

TWENTY-FOUR

Ryann

As the time-lapse bubble started to fail, I dove behind the nearest dumpster. I'd learned enough about self-preservation from Harley and the Rag Team to know when things were going south. Hearing Finch gasp, I took the risk of peering through a gap between the huge metal monstrosities and spotted Davin. He'd come for us again. I ducked and crouched in the darkness, my nostrils overwhelmed by the disgusting smell seeping from the garbage. But I didn't dare move.

"D-Davin?" A strange voice rasped. The big guy, I guessed.

"I suggest you make yourselves scarce," Davin replied, with his usual annoying confidence. "Aside from my favorite seven: Snebbles, de Montfort, Hernandez, von Erschwin, Smart, Durance, and Fishwick."

"Y-yes. Of course. Right away." I heard the scuff of boots as the majority of cultists made a run for it. Having a decent view of the end of the alleyway, I watched them sprint back the way they'd come. The fire wall had sputtered out. Oddly, the running cultists didn't keep going. Instead, they disappeared back inside the bar, leaving Davin to his revenge. Clearly, he scared the crap out of all magicals, not just those he had a vendetta against.

"That's better, isn't it?" Davin walked up to the wall and sketched a pattern of some kind. A charm, presumably to keep the cultists from returning to bother him. "It's nice to have some privacy in poignant moments like these, with only the crème de la crème in attendance." He nodded to the handful of cultists remaining, prompting them to smirk.

"You never do see me coming," Davin went on. "Or perhaps you think yourselves above my retribution, because you have some cosmic 'protection'? But Children of Chaos can't come and save your behinds every time, can they?"

"Come on, of course you were going to come back and annoy us." Finch went on the offensive, and my heartrate accelerated. *Don't bait him, Finch!* "I just thought you'd have the common sense to do it once we'd completed our task. You know, since you're about as desperate to get to Atlantis as Erebus is."

A leggy blonde cultist with some obvious attitude draped her arm over Davin's shoulder, only to be brusquely shoved away. *Hah!* She recovered quickly and focused her sass on Finch instead. "Don't you get it? Davin doesn't need you anymore, worm. We've been working for Davin for a long time now, and we're here to take him to Eris Island. So, the four of you and your dog will be dying now."

It looked like Davin had gotten to Eris Island first, but it wasn't too late. They thought they only had four people and Huntress to deal with. They didn't know I was hiding behind the dumpsters, listening. I needed to find a way to help them, fast, but I wasn't sure how. Could I summon Lux? *No... not a magical, remember?* Even if I had been, I'd have had no clue how to summon Children of Chaos.

Mayhem erupted, with Davin taking the lead. Purple tendrils shot from his hands and twisted toward my friends. But it looked as though they'd learned a few things since their last encounter with Davin. Nash spun his rucksack to the front and delved inside, hurling hex bags at the attackers. One of the bags exploded in Davin's face, prompting him to stagger into the blonde. She tried to catch him, but the two of them crashed to the ground in a tangle of limbs.

"You wretched little pilchards!" Davin bellowed, scrambling to his feet.

"Finch, cover me!" Melody shouted.

He did so, twirling his hands wildly as he conjured a shield of Air to protect Melody. She darted forward, and Finch used one hand to muster up a blend of Fire and Telekinesis, aiming the thrumming strands at the big guy's face. Snebbles, I recalled. Melody snatched up the golden orb that had created the short-lived time-lapse.

On the front line, Luke raised his palms. The filling in my back tooth tugged strangely, and that wasn't the only thing affected. Any metal in the vicinity responded to Luke's call, nails and trash cans and shards of scrap steel flying toward him. Fortunately, the dumpsters protecting my hiding place only vibrated and stayed where they were, while he wasted no time launching the artillery at the cultists, who struggled to duck away from the jagged missiles in time.

A few nails thunked into the cultists, and one particularly nasty shard of steel lodged in the other woman's shoulder. I had no clue what her name was, but she had a short blonde buzzcut and the kind of jawline you'd see on a linebacker. She howled with pain.

"Get them!" Davin shouted over her.

Huntress arched through the air, her blue eyes fixed on Davin's throat. His hand rose, and a shield slid over him. Huntress crashed into it with a whine, shaking her head as she landed on the filthy ground.

Don't die, don't die, don't die... please don't die! I repeated the mantra as the fight amped up. Davin sent a fresh batch of purple tendrils at Finch and the others, the edges hungry for contact. Behind him, the cultists rallied, even those pierced by metal. With their combined force of Elemental energies and a few abilities I didn't recognize, they leveled the playing field.

Air surged toward my friends, and slithering vines crept up from the cracked earth, trying to snag their ankles. A crackle of electricity sparked from the woman with the buzzcut, and her fork of lightning narrowly missed Melody as she hurried back behind allied lines.

"You won't win!" Buzzcut shrieked, sending another fork of lightning toward Nash. He spun away just in time, the electricity hitting the ground with a hiss and a plume of smoke.

Davin's purple tendrils reached Finch, and his face contorted in a mask of pain. Nash retaliated by launching a red hex bag at Davin. This time, Davin didn't even flinch. He kept right on with his tendrils, pumping more magic into Finch's skin.

"I've got you!" Melody shouted, holding the golden orb in her palms. Her mouth moved rapidly as she whispered something.

A moment later, the orb lit more vibrantly than ever. Melody chucked it into the center of the alleyway, where it landed with a clink. The cultists looked at it in confusion. The light inside the orb built until, in an enormous expulsion of energy, it sent a violent shockwave through the alleyway.

The cultists toppled like dominoes, and even Davin sailed backward with the force of all that raw energy. Unfortunately, it had the same effect on my friends and the dumpsters protecting me. The hulking metal slammed into me, knocking the wind from my lungs and crushing me against the wall. On instinct, I pushed back to give myself room to breathe, and the dumpster skidded slightly forward.

I'd have taken the ghoulish faces in the silvery liquid over this any day. At least then I'd have known it could be stopped at any moment. But this... I didn't know how it would end. What if Davin and his cultists really did kill them this time? And what if I was next?

Finch, Nash, Melody, and Luke got back up, Luke helping Melody to her feet. Air, Telekinesis, Fire, hex bags galore, and any metal remaining in the bar's vicinity tore through the atmosphere, making the most of the brief opportunity.

I need to help... I need to do something. My mind raced, but all it could focus on was what that clingy woman had said. I kept trying to push past it, but the conversation kept replaying.

They're here to take Davin to Eris Island. They said they didn't need Finch's unwilling help anymore.

The cultist wouldn't have said that if Eris Island weren't nearby. Davin didn't need Finch, and we didn't need the cult members! We just needed to get rid of them, which was arguably the hard part.

Finch ran forward and paused beside the dumpsters, lashing out with a burning torrent of Fire. He glanced back. "The bag... help us!"

Huh? He disappeared again before I could ask any questions. But he'd sounded panicked, and that was good enough for me. Wriggling the rucksack off my shoulders, I unzipped it and peered in. Cluttering the bottom of the bag were a cluster of small Mason jars. I definitely hadn't put them there. *Finch!* Well, they had to be there for a reason, and they looked important. Making the choice to go for them instead of our other supplies, I removed each jar and spread them on the ground in front of me. Black smoke swirled inside.

That could only mean one thing. Monsters from the Bestiary. Finch must have had a plan when he'd packed these. And I trusted that guy more than anyone else in this world right now. Even if he had slipped them into my bag without my say-so.

I poked my head around the dumpsters, and my heart lurched. Davin had Finch in a vise of purple tendrils. Black veins spiderwebbed across Finch's visible skin, and his mouth opened in agony as he fell to his knees. An execution position, and Davin held the axe.

Melody staggered weakly, her eyes blinking as if she were struggling to stay conscious. Luke grabbed her and held her up, taking a blow to the back as he put his arms around her. Nash had run out of hex bags and turned to knife-throwing to make up for the magical deficit, while Huntress had retreated, licking her bleeding paw clean.

I knew enough about seeing smoke in Mason jars to know there could be something inside to help my friends. I grabbed the first two jars and squeezed my eyes shut as I slammed them against the hard ground with all the force I could muster. They shattered on impact. I didn't wait for the smoke to transform. I grabbed the next two, and the two after that, and smashed them all.

The cultists stood directly ahead of me, and all their heads snapped around at the sound. The big guy stood closest. He froze, his eyes widening with horror as the black smoke swirled and swelled, growing limbs and solidifying into a Purge beast. Six, actually.

Oh my days... A smirk lifted the corners of my lips. Finch had brought gargoyles.

TWENTY-FIVE

Finch

How do you like them apples, you slick blobfish? I stared up at Davin through pain-blurred eyes as the gargoyles emerged. Ryann had done it. She'd set my secret weapon loose. I'd taken the critters from the Bestiary on my SDC detour. Sadly, not without Tobe noticing, which was the way I'd planned. But he'd been oddly chill about my borrowing them. When it came to Merlins and gargoyles, he knew better than to ask too many questions.

I'd swiped six because I didn't like odd numbers. And Harley's absolute fave was among them.

"What have you done?" Davin reeled back in alarm as Murray bowled for his legs.

"What's the matter?" I asked through gritted teeth. "Don't like it when the tables turn?"

Davin dodged the beast, releasing his hold on me.

I couldn't have left Murray behind. He wasn't just Harley's favorite; he was Davin's, too. Ah, here came the delicious memory of

Murray nibbling away at Davin like there was no tomorrow, back in that dingy motel where he'd kept the Smiths. This was payback. And man, it was sweet.

"Gargoyles! Attack!" I'd always wanted to say that… in the right setting, of course. We'd just forget me unleashing a horde of them on the SDC. I'd had enough bad memories tonight, and I wanted to enjoy this. Just like dear old Madre, I had the ability to control these suckers. Although, it had only been fully released post-Suppressor-snappage, along with the rest of my abilities. Harley could control all monsters—always showing me up—but gargoyles would do for now. The Shipton bloodline still ran in my veins, and we'd had an affinity for gargoyles since the first Shipton magical had been created.

Murray took flight and divebombed Davin's face. I'd have sworn blind the British ass-wipe shrieked like a tiny girl. He scampered backward as Murray climbed into the air again. This time, Murray skimmed his shoulder with a claw, and the ass-wipe *definitely* screamed.

"Gargoyles! Obey!" I yelled. The other five glanced at me and licked their oily fangs. "Attack the cultists!"

They seemed to nod, then rose on their leathery wings. As they circled and chose their targets, the cultists freaked out. Davin wasn't setting the best example, ducking and diving away from Murray as if the devil himself were after him. The gargoyles plummeted down-ward, and ear-throbbing screams and cries filled the air as the fight spun rapidly in our favor.

My flappy bastards were in their element, their claws tearing into the rogues. Jaws gnashed and talons scraped, and the cultists had nowhere to go. At one end of the alley, Nash, Huntress, Luke, and Melody blocked their exit. At the other, a ravenous Murray flitted between scaring the crap out of Davin and stopping any escapees.

"Stop coming after me!" Davin shouted, frantically searching for a way out. I noticed he had charmed chalk in his hand. *Oh, no you don't...*

"Murray! Get Davin! Don't let him draw that doorway!" I hollered to my main man.

Murray wheeled in the air and folded his wings, hurtling at Davin full pelt. Davin turned just in time to get smacked in the face with a leathery missile. I smiled through the dull ache Davin's spell had left pulsating through my insides. Nothing made a near-death experience feel better than a last-minute rescue by a bunch of frisky gargoyles. And Murray clearly remembered our friend from across the pond.

With his slimy black tongue, Murray licked Davin from navel to chin, leaving a trail of goop up the length of his fancy shirt. Next, he drew back the loose flaps of skin from his mouth and bared his fangs. His version of a grin. His head lunged, and sharp teeth sank into Davin's neck, blood spurting until Murray may as well have been showering in the stuff. It wouldn't kill the royal pain in my ass, but it was satisfying to watch Davin wriggle and writhe as Murray had his wicked way.

"Bite me again, and I will turn you into gargoyle soup!" Davin hissed. It only encouraged Murray to bite him harder.

"Finch!"

I followed the sound of Ryann's voice. Somehow, in the mayhem, she'd gotten onto the roof of the bar.

"How did you—never mind. What are you doing up there?" I was glad she was out of harm's way. And that I had a moment to catch my breath and speak to her. The gargoyles had the cultists on the ropes. In fact, the others were just watching the cultists get shredded by my secret allies. Melody buried her face in Luke's chest. I got it. Watching creatures clamp down so hard on a person's chest that they actually exploded could be a little much for most people.

"Eris Island is nearby!" she shouted back. "The cultists met Davin here, at this exact time, so it must be close. It makes perfect logical sense. We don't need the cultists anymore!"

Holy crap... She was right. Davin didn't crawl out from under his rock for just any D&D meeting. The island had to be close. With that in mind, it was time to change strategy. I looked at the others. Luke and Nash were focusing their magical efforts against Davin, who still had Murray in his face, among other things. A three-point attack. All the while, Luke held Melody to his chest.

As for Huntress, she'd gotten into the gargoyle spirit. Launching through the air, she tore into every cultist she came across, dragging them across the ground with the help of her new winged pals. They had things covered, which meant I could join Ryann and give her a hand. She'd already smashed it, literally, with the Mason jars. But this next step required a magic touch.

I darted across the alley and up the nearest wall like a regular parkour enthusiast. An incidental staircase of bricks led to the roof, and I took them two at a time to reach Ryann.

"How do we find it?" Ryann asked, looking at the distant horizon. The ocean lay eerily still, with just a few waves catching the moonlight. It might've been romantic, except for the blood and guts splattering the ground below. I peered down to check on things, and I was glad I looked when I did.

Murray ripped out Davin's throat at the exact moment a shard of steel pierced his chest. Davin's eyes met mine, blood oozing down his chin and mixing with the gargoyle slick that covered him. He opened his mouth as if to say something... and fell still. Murray had ended the dick-bag. Sure, he'd rise again like a B-movie zombie, but I'd never get tired of watching him die. Morbid, yes, but he deserved it. And maybe he wouldn't rise again, if we found that pesky amulet.

Using the spell Erebus had taught me for finding interdimensional bubbles, I cast my magical net outward, toward Davin. No bronze sparks drifted back. Evidently, the interdimensional bubble Davin was using was on some alternate plane that this spell couldn't reach. I'd suspected as much, in fairness, but desperation had made me... well, desperate. Frustrated, I looked to Melody.

"Can you search him for the amulet? I know I gave him a pat down in Tijuana, but this calls for a magical onceover! And the spell I'd normally use to find interdimensional bubbles isn't working!" I called to her. She may not have liked the gore, but she was the only one with the oomph to delve that deep into Davin's magical hideaways.

She nodded and rushed over, kneeling at what remained of Davin's side. I mean, I was surprised the amulet hadn't fallen out of his pocket or... you know, his intestines or something. She moved her hands over his body, bronze light flowing from her palms and into him, her eyes closed in concentration. Her expression quickly changed to one of frustration as she searched him twice more.

"I can't find it," she said, her eyes snapping open.

"Search beyond him. He said he had it hidden in a bubble, as I mentioned, so it has to be there somewhere."

She shook her head. "I can't access a personal interdimensional bubble, Finch. No one can, aside from the person who made it.

There's no information on that in my brain. Just a bunch of… well, nothing."

"Come on, you've got to have something in there you can use. A different, souped-up tapping into bubbles spell, or something?" I said desperately. I could feel this second opportunity slipping through my fingers.

"Even if I could search my mind palace for a spell like that, it would take days, maybe weeks. Davin would be back on his feet before I could even start." She peered up at me apologetically. "He's taken major precautions to protect that thing."

I clenched my jaw. "So, you're saying we don't have time for this?"

"No, I don't think so."

"Then… we have to leave him behind." *Again.* It didn't make sense to lug him along to the island, and I had no idea how we *would* lug him along with us. He'd fall apart into sludgy pieces with so much of him missing. After all, that would only give him a faster path to the place he wanted to go, if he regenerated right there on Eris Island. He'd definitely amped up his game. Though, I had to wonder if he'd been lying about that Regen stuff he'd spouted off in Tijuana. A memory came into my head, of him being ripped to shreds in Marie Laveau's church. He'd recovered from that. So, maybe he hadn't been fibbing. Either way, I had to do something to slow him down, without massively slowing *us* down.

A small smile crept onto my face. "But we can take some precautions."

"We can?" Melody looked puzzled.

"Oh yes." I turned to her. "I need you to transform him into something else. I don't know, make his limbs flap off to the far corners of the world, or turn him into stone. Anything. Just make it as hard as possible for him to come crawling back from the dead."

Her eyes widened. "Now that I *can* do."

She set to work, feeding multicolored strands of Chaos into what remained of Davin's body. One of his arms took flight and winged into the distance, while another turned to soil in front of my eyes, mingling with the dirt and grime of the alleyway. His head got the stone treatment, becoming what Davin had likely always wanted—a statue. Only this one wasn't going to be erected anywhere good. In fact, Luke picked it up and heaved it over the back wall of the alleyway, where it landed with a splash in the water below. Meanwhile, Melody transformed a leg into a snake, which slithered off into the darkness, and his other leg into a suitably cartoonish turkey leg, which Murray immediately gulped down. The only thing she left as it was, was his mangled torso, which Murray's jaws had already turned to mulch.

Try coming back from that, you squelching ball of goo.

"Will that be enough?" Melody looked green around the gills.

I sighed. "Let's hope so."

As for the rest of the cultists... well, let's just say it was total carnage in that alleyway. Not a single one so much as stirred, and the gargoyles had set to munching, devouring their hard-won gains with slapping chops. That wasn't easy to watch, so I didn't. The cultists had aligned with Davin, that was true, but having seen Emily's 180, I'd realized anyone was capable of rehabilitation. And now these cultists would never have the chance. They'd be gobbled up and pooped out. That wasn't a good way to go in anyone's book.

Leaving the gargoyles to feast, the others joined us on the rooftop. Nash had to carry Huntress, who'd dyed her pure white fur a macabre shade of pink. A lot like Melody's jacket, actually. But everyone made it in the end. All we had to do was ignore the crunch of bones getting chewed and focus on this damned island. Or island of the damned, depending on who you asked.

"What's the plan?" Nash asked, catching his breath.

"The island is here somewhere; otherwise, Davin wouldn't be." I relayed Ryann's logic. "And Davin isn't the only one with some tricks up his sleeve." I rolled up my sleeve to reveal my twin Apples of Discord. After my heart-to-heart with Harley, during which she'd told me she didn't view them as negative anymore—more as a bond between us—I didn't hate them so much. And they still had some juice in the tank. They burned as I held my arm out to the ocean, the sting worsening when I pointed dead ahead.

Melody unfurled from Luke's burly chest and looked outward. "Do you see that?"

"See what?" All I saw was water.

"There's a glimmer over there." Melody jabbed her finger at a spot directly below the moon. "Yes... it's definitely a glimmer of something."

Hope, my friend... hope. I aimed my arm in the direction she was pointing and winced as a jolt of white heat shot through me. I didn't know if my burning apple was psychosomatic, but my subconscious seemed to be reacting like crazy.

It turned out quite a few things had changed since Erebus broke my Dempsey Suppressor and unleashed full Finch on the world. Including my ability to sense my mother's residual energy.

"Give me a sec, I want to try something." Bringing my palms up, I focused my energy into them. I used the same spell Erebus had taught me for sensing interdimensional bubbles, which I'd just attempted to use on Davin's personal bubble. A nifty trick I'd used to pursue Nash, though he hadn't been at the abandoned airplane Erebus had told me about.

Powering the bubble spell along a strand of Telekinesis to reach farther, I sent my Chaos out over the ocean. At first, I felt nothing. No pushback whatsoever. Determined, I fed more and more Telekinesis into the strand, forcing it to its limits.

"Are you sure you know what you're doing?" Nash arched an eyebrow.

"I'm working here!" I shot back. I pushed even more Telekinesis across the ocean until I no longer knew how much distance I'd crossed.

Where the moonlight struck the water, night having fully set in sometime between darting into the alley and leaving the cultists in visceral heaps, sparks appeared. Bronze flakes drifting down toward the tiny waves. The interdimensional bubble of Eris Island revealed itself for a fleeting moment before my strength gave way and I had to release the Telekinesis. But it was enough. I knew what it meant.

Melody gasped in awe. "You found it."

"See? Told you I've still got a few tricks up my sleeves." I grinned, more relieved than anything else. Eris Island really was out there, within our reach.

"But how do we get there?" Luke came in as the voice of pessimism. "Do we steal a boat? Nash already has car theft on his record. Why not add piracy?"

"He'd make a good pirate," Melody chirped.

Nash chuckled. "You think I could pull off an eyepatch and a wooden leg? I'm not sure Huntress would be too happy about turning into a parrot, though."

Huntress gave a low growl of agreement.

"We don't need to steal anything," I interjected. "We've already got mighty steeds awaiting. Well, once they've finished dinner, anyway." I stole a look at the alleyway and immediately regretted it. *The Walking Dead* could've taken a few tips from the disembodied array below.

"Excuse me?" Luke looked horrified.

I smiled. "Oh, I think you heard me."

Those bronze flakes had showed the way to Eris Island, and my friendly neighborhood gargoyles were going to get us in. They were creatures of raw Chaos, and if I knew anything about interdimensional bubbles, there was always a way to trick the system. The island's Bestiary would recognize the gargoyles as validated critters, and we'd ride that leathery wave straight to the center of my former nightmares.

TWENTY-SIX

Finch

———

"I'm not getting on one of those things." Luke shook his head. He looked into the alley and grimaced. "They'll eat us in midair."

I smiled. "They won't, I promise. First, because they're probably stuffed by now, and second, they're like big, ugly pussycats when it comes to me."

Murray flapped up as if summoned, landing with a scrape of claws on the rooftop. I couldn't resist looking down to see the state Davin's lingering torso was in. It wasn't pretty. His insides were now his outsides, and he'd never wear that sleek suit again.

"I'm not sure about this," Melody said. "They might be big enough, but... I'm with Luke on this one. What if they flip around and munch us?"

"Watch." I stepped up to the edge of the rooftop and closed my eyes, allowing a sense of calm to wash over me. Energy flowed into my chest, ready to be expelled.

"Gargoyles! Obey me!" The energy spiraled down my arms and

thrummed outward. The gargoyles below lifted their heads from their grisly dinner and took flight. A moment later, they hovered before us, awaiting instruction.

"Turn three circles," I commanded. And they obeyed, twisting around like airborne pups at training school. "Now, fly as high as you can, and come back."

They shot up like bottle rockets, with Murray joining the aerial display. I followed their trajectory until I couldn't see them anymore, their dark skin blending with the night sky. I heard their return, though. An unsettling beat, like a storm battering a sail. They landed on the rooftop. Melody skittered backward, with Luke taking a few more stoic steps away from them. Ryann remained where she was, but her shaky hands revealed her fear. Only Nash and Huntress seemed unperturbed by my pretties. *Nope... too Katherine.*

"See?" I observed the group. "They obey me. It's about the only good thing that came out of the Shipton blood. I may not have my sister's superhuman monster-wrangling skills—you know, since nobody beats my sister at anything—but I can get these little beauties to do what I ask."

"Are you sure they won't bite?" Melody edged closer.

"Not unless I tell them to." I watched her approach the nearest gargoyle, a female by the oh so ironic name of Belle. Nothing beautiful about her, unfortunately. She looked like she'd been smacked in the face with a frying pan. The gargoyle tilted her head curiously. "Be nice, Belle."

The gargoyle made a squelching sound in the back of her throat, halfway between a coo and a growl.

"Her name's Belle?" Melody's eyes widened. "I've read a lot about these creatures, but I never knew they could be… tranquil. They're always described as vicious garbage cans of the air who'll eat just about anything. I suppose that's true, but they're not what I expected. And I'm grateful they saved us back there."

Belle padded nearer to Melody and dipped her head. Tentatively, Melody extended her hand and let Belle nuzzle her palm. A sweet moment, if slightly gross, especially when Melody pulled her hand away and strands of stringy mucus followed it. But Melody seemed delighted, which was all that mattered.

"She's gorgeous." Melody sighed, and Belle trilled, pleased with the compliment.

"Then you can ride her," I replied. Whether Belle could sense Melody's Librarian juju or not, the gargoyle had taken a liking to her soon-to-be jockey. "I'll ride Murray."

"Which one's Murray?" Nash looked over the beasties as if surveying the meat section of a supermarket. Murray gnashed his jaws in reply. "Right, got it. The one who crunched Davin. Nice choice."

Murray licked some of Davin off his lips, just to hammer home the grim point.

"Luke, you can have Larry." I gestured to the most placid gargoyle.

"Why do they have old guy names?" Luke frowned, clearly still unconvinced about our mode of transport.

I shrugged. "Tobe's choice, and since he's kind of an old man— well, an old part-lion, part-eagle, part-who-knows-what—I guess it's what he likes."

"Nash, you can have Joker." I pointed to the gargoyle gnawing at his talons. The creature looked up and licked his lips, his eyes staring off in two different directions. He gurgled, spewing up a ball of… I didn't even want to say. The remnants of the poor cultist he'd gunned for. He'd always reminded me of the crazy one in *Gremlins*, but I was fairly certain Nash could handle the challenge.

"What about Huntress? We won't both fit," Nash said, staring Joker down.

"I thought she could ride Bingo. She's the smallest one, and she's got a calmer temperament than most." I nodded to the runt of the litter, who stood away from the main group. "All Huntress has to do is cling on, and Bingo will do the rest."

Huntress snorted. For a husky, she had a very clear way of getting her feelings across. And she didn't seem to like the idea one bit.

"You'll be okay," Nash said soothingly. Huntress turned up her snout, but I knew she'd do it.

Ryann shifted awkwardly, not looking the gargoyles in the eye. "What about me?"

I saved the best for last. "You can ride Selma." Selma and Murray were mates, but she didn't need to know that. That could be my private secret.

Unfortunately, the grisly duo had other ideas. They took the opportunity to start licking each other in the most grotesque way imaginable, big black tongues smearing each other's faces. That wasn't what I envisioned for Ryann and me, but… hey, I'd take anything over sullen silence.

"Uh… do they all do that?" Ryann looked horrified.

I swallowed the embarrassed lump in my throat. "No… she's… um, well, she's Murray's partner."

Melody gasped. "Yes! I'd completely forgotten that. Gargoyles are like penguins and swans, aren't they? They mate for life once they've found the right one. They make such a sweet pair!"

Ryann stared at me, a bittersweet look. "Selma? Why do I know that name?"

"Tobe named her after his Purger, one of the most powerful magicals in the world. He names quite a few beasts after her, to keep her memory alive, but he's fondest of this one." I walked up to the gargoyle in question, and she bumped me with her slimy snout. "Isn't that right, Selma?"

Selma bumped me again, gurgling.

"That's heartbreaking." Melody's eyes went anime wide. "Poor Tobe. He must miss her so much. I suppose it's only natural to miss the one who gave you life—with a few exceptions." She glanced at me awkwardly. "But he must have adored Selma. From what I know, she died a long time ago, which means he's been on his own for most of his thousand-plus years. The fact that he still thinks about her... oh, it's so touching. Poor, poor Tobe."

Ryann kept staring at me. "And they're mated for life? Murray and Selma?"

"They are." I nodded, trying to keep the embarrassed redness out of my cheeks.

"How do we even ride these things?" Nash saved us from unbearable tension. "It's not like they've got saddles."

"Allow me to illuminate the situation." I strode up to Murray, breaking apart the sickening tonguing. "Murray, crouch."

He did, and I clambered onto his back. Honestly, I was improvising as I went, but it felt like the right way to go about it. I tucked my knees behind Murray's wings and held onto two bony prongs that protruded from his shoulders. Surprisingly, I slotted nicely onto his back. Who needed a saddle when you had spiny nobs sticking into your... never mind. This would work; that was all that mattered.

The others stepped up to their mighty steeds with a mixture of reluctance and excitement, varying by person. Ryann had visibly softened toward her gargoyle. It gave me a slight bristle of hope. Finding out they were a mated pair who chose only one partner for the rest of their lives had switched her perspective in the space of a minute or two. *Pfft, how desperate can you be, finding "signs" in slobbering gargoyles?*

"Crouch down and let them get on your backs," I commanded. "Guys, make sure you tuck your knees in and grip the bony prongs on their shoulders tightly. That's the only way to hang on."

The others mounted as I'd instructed. Nash had clearly ridden horses in his lifetime, because he got on like it wasn't anything to call home about. Luke managed pretty smoothly. A shame, as I'd been looking forward to teasing him about his lack of finesse. Melody held on with white knuckles, her body trembling with excitement. Huntress had dug her claws into her gargoyle, the two of them growling at one another in a way that seemed almost friendly. And Ryann scratched Selma's skull, the gargoyle smacking her foot against the rooftop like a regular Thumper.

"Gargoyles, keep them safe. Don't let them fall," I ordered. Selma had precious cargo to carry. And I didn't want anyone ending up sick.

The wind rushed through my hair as we soared skyward. Murray's muscles moved to the beat of his wings. It was like riding a massive, sloppy bicycle who might take a bite out of a passing stranger. It felt exhilarating. Adrenaline coursed through my veins, making me want to throw up my arms as if I were on a rollercoaster. Murray dipped low over the ocean. If I'd dared to reach down, I could've touched the dark waves.

I glanced back over my shoulder to check that nobody had dropped out of the sky. A perfect formation flew behind me that would've put geese to shame. I should've been scared out of my mind, knowing where we were headed, but there was no room for fear with this kind of thrill shivering through me.

Selma raced to catch up to Murray, and the two gargoyles began nudging each other playfully and shifting places, Murray sweeping beneath Selma and her arching over the top. They could've been an allegory for me and Ryann, only Selma looked like she'd been run over by a lawnmower. Ryann had never looked more radiant, illuminated by the moonlight, her hair whipping back from her face.

"Are you doing this on purpose?" Nash broke the idyllic moment. He gripped tight to Joker's back, but the gargoyle hadn't received his name for no reason. Joker kept bombing down, then pulling up inches from the water's surface. With Nash holding on for dear life.

I chuckled. "Nope, that's just Joker."

"You're the joker, putting me on this thing," he grumbled.

"We're not far now." I nodded to the place where I'd seen the bronze flakes fall. Any minute, we'd come up against the protective shield. I hoped my theory was right. "Would you rather I'd put Huntress on him?"

Nash grumbled. Huntress, on the other hand, was having the time of her doggy life. She stood proudly on her gargoyle's back, the wind rustling her fur, claws gripping that leathery skin. Her tongue lolled from her mouth. This beat any car window, hands down. And it was impressive to watch, considering she wasn't strapped on or anything.

"Try that spell again," Melody urged, grinning ear to ear.

I nodded and clenched Murray's bulk between my thighs as I lifted my palms. Light shimmered outward and stretched on a strand of Telekinesis over the empty ocean. No more than a hundred yards ahead, the strand hit something. Bronze flakes followed, drifting down like metallic snow. The island's shield rippled.

"Can we get in?" Luke's voice trembled slightly.

"The gargoyles won't have a problem, and if we duck down, we should be able to trick the system," I yelled back.

"Are you sure about that?" Nash chimed in, as Joker climbed back up after a hair-raising drop.

I hesitated. "Honestly? It's a guess at best." The others fell silent. "Hey, if it doesn't work, at least it'll be a soft landing."

"A wet landing, you mean," Nash corrected.

"What I'm saying is, no one's going to die." I looked ahead to the fading sparks. The gargoyles showed no sign of slowing. That was good. We needed momentum to get through the protective outer layer. "Everyone, lie flat against your beasties!"

I watched to make sure they obeyed. They flattened themselves against the stinking skin of the creatures until I could barely see them anymore, even Huntress, who clung tight with her claws. I did the same, minus the claws. My heart leapt into my throat. It'd sting like a bastard if we slammed into that outer shield. But no guts, no glory, right?

My eyes squeezed shut as I gripped the bony prongs tighter.

Come on, come on... give us a win!

A crackle like static electricity sparked across my skin, and the air suddenly changed. No more cool Maine breeze drifting through the trees and smelling of fall. Instead, humid heat washed over my face. My eyes shot open. Eris Island sat below, a whole world hidden from sight. I spotted the old hive huts that'd been the hub of the place and a few of the imposing statues we would have to un-hex. Yep, we definitely weren't in Kansas anymore. Or, you know, Maine.

I punched the air. "Take that, Katherine, you crusty old hag!" Her old defenses weren't infallible, after all. Victory surged through me, better than adrenaline. I'd finally pulled off something great, with a smattering of planning and an educated guess. I glanced at Ryann. None of this would've been possible if she hadn't figured out the Island-Davin equation.

You absolute beauty...

"Gargoyles, land in that clearing!" I gestured to the building where Harley and I had spent our time awaiting Eris's trials. The place where we'd formed our lasting bond. The one good memory in this hellhole.

The critters obeyed, making way for the shack. With a jarring thud, Murray landed, the others following suit. Once the seatbelt signs were off, I slipped off Murray's back and took a deep breath of that sickly, syrupy air. An entire ecosystem was set apart from what-ever was going on outside its walls.

Melody and Luke high-fived while Nash crouched to ruffle Huntress's fur. That left Ryann and me. I hadn't expected anything, so it came as a shock when she rushed up to me and threw her arms around my neck. My hands slid around her waist on instinct, pulling her closer. She buried her face in my shoulder, and my heart damn near detonated. I smelled that sweet vanilla and sugary strawberry, and everything else slipped away.

"We did it," she whispered.

"All because of you," I whispered back.

Over her shoulder, I watched Murray and Selma nuzzle each other, before the tongues came out and got all gross. They reminded me of two oversized, featherless, utterly deformed lovebirds. And there'd never been a more beautiful sight.

Joker seemed to have developed a bit of a thing for Nash, too. He nipped at Nash's arm, trying to steal his attention away from Huntress, only to receive a shove backward. Undeterred, Joker went in for another nip, forcing Nash to put one arm around the hulking beast and give him some love, too. The gargoyle liked Nash, but he played rough. It could've very well led to an accidental amputation.

But we were here. We'd made it. After so many setbacks, it finally felt like we were close to a win. Even if that win would work in Erebus's favor.

TWENTY-SEVEN

Finch

This island reeked of past trauma. Every corner held the story of another episode where I'd been smushed under my mother's thumb. But the hut centered me. I thought of my bathroom talks with Harley, the first time anyone had reached out and let me know I could be more. That I could be better. I owed this life to my sister. If I'd stayed on my mother's side or bowed to her offer of resurrecting Adley if I rejoined her... it didn't bear thinking about. I'd be behind plate glass, or worse—staring at the reflection of a demon with no hope of redemption.

But we had a moment now to catch our breath. Melody tended Luke's injuries, using the Mary Poppins rucksack Nash had brought. I noticed the way she focused on him, so engrossed in her duties that she missed the longing stare he gave her in return. It hurt, and I was only a spectator. *Poor guy... poor her...* Librarians couldn't love freely. Chaos friggin' rules.

"How does it feel to be back?" Ryann drew my attention away.

She sat on the grass with me kneeling at her side. I was supposed to be checking her over, making sure she was okay. You know, since she'd only just revealed, after some noticeable wincing, that she'd almost gotten squashed to death by a dumpster. Not what anyone wanted on their headstone. And not what I ever wanted for Ryann. The whole reason I'd started watching Luke and Melody in the first place was to distract myself from the bare skin of Ryann's stomach and ribcage… which I was meant to be observing with a purely medical eye.

"Horrible." I offered a smile. If I concentrated, I could still feel her in my arms and sense the tickle of her breath on my neck when she'd whispered. My throat clenched.

"At least we won't stay long." Ryann put her hand on mine.

I forced myself to stay calm. "I hope not, but who knows with Erebus. He might like it here and make it a vacation spot for his human self."

"Speaking of this human self, how am I looking?" She gazed into my eyes. "I'm aching all over from that dumpster nearly squishing me."

Divine. Angelic. Ethereal. The most beautiful woman I've ever seen. Take your pick. "I think you'll live."

"That gargoyle ability is very cool, by the way." She grinned, eyeing Selma, who was still tongue-bathing her mate.

"I'm just relieved they got us past the shield." I smiled at the grisly duo. They'd seen more action in the last five minutes than I'd seen in a long time. "Though it's always nice to have Murray around. He and Harley have an adorable love-hate relationship, but I dig that ugly mug."

"I remember." Ryann chuckled. "Davin probably has nightmares about him, though I wonder if Murray ever gets sick of the taste of Necromancer. This is the second time he's chewed him up, right?"

I nodded. "Oh yes."

"Good." A steely glint came into Ryann's eyes.

"As for getting sick of the taste, Murray will eat just about anything." I laughed, pleased I'd gotten to see Davin die again. I wondered how I'd feel when I actually managed to stop that sleazy toilet brush from resurrecting himself. Man, I hoped that day would come soon. His popping up at every opportunity was giving me major anxiety.

Nash untangled himself from Joker's bitey affection. "Everyone good?"

A grunting chorus of yeses echoed back.

"Then how about we get on with cracking these monoliths?"

Huntress barked agreement as Nash delved into his rucksack of wonders. He removed a few potions he'd mixed in preparation, with Melody's Librarian help and the handy substitution of his blood in any of the spell-breaking hexes. They were, if Nash was right, like lockpicks for these statues and their curses. They wouldn't undo the spells completely, but they'd... lubricate the process a touch. I'd picked enough locks in my day to know how useful that could be.

"Sounds like a plan." I got up, reluctant to leave Ryann's side. But I couldn't look clingy, now, could I? I put out my hand to help her up, and she took it without hesitation. I almost kept holding on once we were standing, but I didn't want to get into the creep zone. So, I let her go.

As a group, we trekked around the island. My memory of the place hadn't faded. I knew where every one of those stone suckers stood, though I'd never understood their purpose. Or why they looked so old. It made sense now. They'd been here before Katherine was even born. They'd been built before Drake Shipton came into being, by the Atlanteans' enemies. I felt a slight twist of irony, considering that they'd be used to connect the Gateway to Atlantis itself.

Funny enough, I couldn't picture what the Atlanteans might've looked like. My comedic mind wanted to believe they'd been underwater fish people, with mermaid tails and gills—the whole nine yards. But if Nash was anything to go by, as a direct descendant of two escaped Atlantean bloodlines, they'd look the same as the rest of us. Very human, very boring... no gills.

I stopped at the first monolith, a big-bosomed slab of rock that no longer had much of a face. I noticed a few carved symbols in the rock. After smearing away years of dirt and moss, more revealed themselves. I'd seen similar ones before—Katherine had used them to spy on newcomers and build her defenses in case anyone turned out to be a traitor.

"Hand me some of that stuff you made." I gestured to Nash. He gave me a test tube of scarlet liquid, which sloshed in the glass.

I trickled a few drops over each symbol and handed the tube back. We needed to be stingy with the stuff to make it last through all the monoliths on this island. If memory served, there were twelve. Some likenesses had been taken directly from Child of Chaos mythos, while others were plucked from other legends and ancient religions. I guessed this one was meant to be Gaia, considering the deformed stone babies she clutched and the worn-down globe that hovered before her ample chest.

"What are they?" Ryann stared at the symbols. Not the boobs. She was too classy for that.

"Protective wards," I replied. Getting through twelve of these bad boys would take a toll on me, that was for sure.

"Can you undo them?" Melody chimed in.

I nodded. "With a bit of room, yeah."

The ladies, Nash, and Luke stepped back to give me space. I'd said that so they'd think I knew what I was doing, which was only half true. I had a vague knowledge of this kind of spell, but I had no idea what might happen when I broke the wards. Explosions, dangerous booby traps—pardon the pun—or even total island self-destruction. I hoped for something less life-threatening, but you could never be too careful on Eris Island.

After a steadying breath, I placed my palms flat against Gaia's shapely calves. My head barely reached her knees, so it had to be the calves. I closed my eyes and sent a surge of Chaos into the first symbol. It pushed back immediately, a tangible shove that sent me staggering.

Undeterred, I went right back to the statue and anchored my feet to the ground with two twisting strands of Telekinesis.

"Are you okay?" Ryann called.

I nodded. "Yep, just getting a feel for this beauty."

I focused on the symbol. My Chaos slithered into the stone, seeping into the carved edges of the marking. This time, when it pushed back, I stayed put. With powerful exertion, I pummeled more Chaos into it, using the finer threads to unpick the protective ward. With a bit of jiggery-pokery, the first parts came undone. The rest followed quickly, after which the ward broke altogether, with a blast that ruffled my hair a bit. But no evil aftermath. That spelled good news for the rest.

I moved at my own pace, unpicking each protective ward. It

didn't take long to get back into the rhythm of undoing powerful magic. Katherine had trained me well. Another attribute I owed to her but didn't want to credit her for. Her lessons had been tougher than anything I'd ever endured, and I'd survived because of my own skill and determination, not her harsh teaching.

Finally, the last ward came loose. A splintering crack shot through the air like a revolver going off. I ran for cover, shouting a warning. Nash hit the deck, Melody dove behind a rock, Ryann scrambled into some bushes, Huntress ducked behind Nash, and Luke... ah, bless his heart. He hid behind a tree that would've had trouble covering his forearm, let alone the rest of him.

I managed to get behind some abandoned building materials just in time to watch the monolith crumble to dust. It went with a whimper, not a bang, tumbling to the ground in a heap of formless rubble. The Divine Boobage had fallen, and I could only be grateful that Gaia couldn't hear my thoughts.

"You did it." Nash poked his head up.

I emerged from my hiding place. "Yeah... only eleven more to go." I already felt tired, and my T-shirt was sticking to all the uncomfortable places. But I could rest when I was dead. Or on a tropical vacation. Whichever came first.

Moving on from Gaia, we made our way around the island. It had an eerie quality to it that hadn't been there before. Sure, it'd had an uneasy undercurrent with Katherine ruling the roost, but this was different. The island lay empty and neglected. Nature had reclaimed most of it, the manmade parts falling into dereliction.

You can derelict my ass, Katherine. Her empire had truly fallen. Eris Island had been her castle, and now the throne sat vacant. The roofs of a few huts had caved in, their integrity thwarted by overgrown vines that flourished in this humid heat. The walkways were shrouded in greenery and strange plants that made Melody pause to investigate.

"I've never heard of these growing outside the deepest depths of the Amazon," she cooed, almost getting her fingers bitten off by peeved flesh-eating blooms.

After a few hours, and half my body weight in sweat, the last monolith crumbled. A godlike entity I didn't recognize, wearing a crown of spikes. He held a spear in one hand and some kind of winged creature in the other. I could have slept for a week, but this was only stage one of our next step. We still had to light that flare to bring Erebus running. Man, I would rather have scooped gargoyle crap for a month than face that moron again. Speaking of which, the gargoyles had grown bored of watching my struggle. They'd taken to flying around the island, happy to be free for a while.

"Who wants to do the honors?" I sagged onto the ground and lay flat on the grass, staring into the cosmos. The stars had come out in force. I'd forgotten how beautiful the universe could be when I wasn't thinking about Children of Chaos.

Is there someone else like me out there, going through hell? I envisioned an alien lying on bright purple grass, sweating diamonds or something, staring up at a similar display of pure nature.

"The flare, you mean?" Nash replied.

I sat up. "What else?"

"I hate to say it, but I think you have to do it." Nash offered an apologetic look. "You're his servant; you have to summon him."

Melody grimaced. "He's right."

I huffed a sigh and got to my feet. Nash had crouched to rummage through his rucksack for the fabled flare. He handed the anticlimactic stick over, as if we were lackluster partners in a relay race.

I turned the flare over in my hand. Except for the symbols etched along the length, it looked like any old flare. Rolling my eyes, I touched my fingertips to the long fuse and urged Fire down them. The wick ignited. Fear struck me as the flare vibrated in my hand. I flung it away from me just in time.

An explosion burst and climbed high in the night sky. Instead of vivid light that would bring rescuers and hope, it released a dark pulse of raw black shadow that engulfed the stars and moon overhead. And sent a shiver right through me. I'd been enjoying the universe in all its vibrant glory. Of course Erebus had to go and ruin that, too.

Everyone stood frozen as a column of smoke spiraled down, hurtling toward the island. A plume of roiling fog drifted over the clearing where the last monolith had collapsed. From within, Erebus rose, playing up to the special effects the flare had gifted him. He would've played background music if he could've.

Erebus smiled and opened his arms. "Here you all are. I didn't think it possible to welcome the sight of mere mortals, but it gives me a certain thrill to see that you've accomplished this task."

"You keep your thrills to yourself," I muttered.

"With the unexpected delay, I thought you might be trying to buy yourself time. It looks as though I underestimated the magnetic pull this place must have on you." He chuckled darkly. "Congratulations. You have pleased me."

Oh, goody...

"What can I say, your missions are never easy." I gestured to the rubble pile. "Cracking these wards took a good few hours. What time is it, anyway?"

"Time we continued with my journey," Erebus replied smugly. "I am glad you have not lost your affinity for spell-breaking. I suppose it helped that these particular wards were placed here by your ancestor, Drake Shipton, so you would already have had an advantage. Why else would I have been so ecstatic that *you* ended up as my servant?" *Drake Shipton?* I'd thought these wards predated him.

"I've never seen you ecstatic about anything, especially when it comes to me," I shot back.

He snickered. "This is an exception."

"Anyway, I thought the enemies of Atlantis put the wards here." My timelines were getting all mixed up.

"No, the monoliths were erected by the enemies of Atlantis to pay homage to their gods and goddesses. Mere monuments to show their loyalty. But it was Drake Shipton who installed the wards to keep us Children of Chaos firmly out, using our images to indulge a sense of irony, I imagine." His face hardened, a flicker of something passing across his black eyes. Clearly, Erebus and Drake had some kind of history I didn't know about. Again, not a surprise, considering the old prune had put the idea of becoming a Child into Katherine's head in the first place.

"Are you saying Drake Shipton knew about Atlantis?" Melody stared at him, wide-eyed.

Erebus shrugged. "It is hard to say for certain, as he shrouded this island in secrecy. But why go to the trouble of keeping us out if he didn't have some dastardly plan in mind? He also thwarted an attempt of mine at coming here, but that is by the by."

Just how many times have you tried this? The mind boggled. Though it really didn't surprise me that Drake had been as much of a double-crosser as my mother.

"I know you already told me Katherine didn't know about Atlantis. But do you think you might've been wrong? This place was shrouded from you, after all." I waxed curious.

He shook off his dark expression. "I highly doubt it. She merely continued to uphold the wards because he told her to."

"How many times have you tried to enter Atlantis?" Nash asked what I didn't dare to.

"That is none of your business." Erebus smiled with satisfaction. "But this time will be my long-sought success. I cannot fail now."

TWENTY-EIGHT

Ryann

I didn't know too much about Drake Shipton. Finch had never been very forthcoming about his family history, aside from the obvious devil in the family tree. But I wondered… what if there was information about Erebus and Atlantis on this island?

I vaguely remembered Finch mentioning that Drake had written super-dull journals, which resided in his library on this very island. What if those journals weren't all dull? What if they had something in them that he'd missed out of boredom, the first time around? I wanted to take Finch aside to suggest my thoughts to him, but I couldn't with Erebus here.

"Now that you have dealt with the monoliths, we must move quickly." Erebus cut through my thinking. "You must learn to counteract Katherine's grip on this island and implement a moving spell of your own. You have until the full moon rises tomorrow."

Finch frowned. "You're not going to portal off again, are you? I almost busted a blood vessel trying to get you here."

Erebus chuckled. "I will remain to assist. As this is so important, it would be imprudent of me to leave you to your own devices." He glanced at Nash. "You will do nicely as my assistant. The rest of you, progress with your own research. Finch, since you know this island better than anyone, I shall expect results."

I noticed the gargoyles perched in the trees surrounding the clearing, their weight bending the branches they'd landed on. They looked on with a mixture of fear and curiosity, but they had the sense to stay away from the Child of Chaos. If only we were so fortunate as to have that option.

"Me?" Nash gestured at his chest.

Erebus nodded. "Did I stutter?"

"Why?" Nash evidently didn't want to go with the Child of Chaos.

"Because I do not trust your power, so I prefer to have you near. Also, that delicious blood in your veins is extremely useful, so it makes you the perfect choice," Erebus replied, leaving no room for negotiation. "I may happen upon some spells that require ingredient substitution. It is better to have the cow beside you than to have to search an island as large as this one to acquire that proverbial milk."

Nash narrowed his eyes. "I'm not a cow, Erebus. You can't just tap me whenever you need something."

"Oh? That's funny, because I presumed you were only here because of your blood's efficacy. If you no longer wish to be useful, I am certain arrangements can be made for your removal. At the very least, I have no need for the dog." Erebus bristled. "Perhaps I should punish her for your reluctance?"

Nash froze. "No... I'll come with you. You leave Huntress out of it."

"Mortals are so easy to manipulate." Erebus grinned to himself. "But I'm glad you made the quick and painless decision. You humans have such an affinity for animals. Even I might have hesitated a moment before harming a canine, and I do so hate to have doubts."

Nash bent and whispered to the husky. She whined in reply before nuzzling Nash's face and padding slowly to Melody. Clearly, Nash had told her to head for safety. Erebus threw threats around like candy, but it was better to be cautious than risk losing a loved one. I knew that firsthand. I doubted I'd ever forget standing in the Winchester House in nothing but pajamas.

"We don't need to do any research." Melody patted Huntress's head, a fierce glint in her eyes. "I've been fishing through my Chaos knowledge since I found out why we were coming here, and I have the spell we need to counteract Katherine's magical system."

Erebus looked slightly surprised. "I suppose you would, wouldn't you? You have information that not even we Children have been blessed with. Our father, Chaos, always did like to keep a few secrets from us."

That's probably sensible parenting. Keep the kids away from the medicine cabinet and the plug sockets...

"What does it entail?" Erebus demanded, his voice tinged with tangible excitement. An entire cosmos swirled in his black eyes. It hadn't been there before, and it was weirdly hypnotic.

"It's similar to unraveling the protective wards on the statues," Melody replied, her tone still cold. "We have to unlock the spell covering this place. To do that, we go to the northern, southern, eastern, and western points of the island, but we have to be exact. Nash, do you have a compass with you?"

He nodded, stealing a worried look at Erebus. "I brought one for each of us."

That bag had everything in it. I suddenly felt grateful to have Nash here. He provided the organization and forward thinking we desperately needed. His blood had paved the way, but he was still helping us out.

"Perfect." Melody smiled.

"Is Chaos not good enough for you?" Erebus peered at the Librarian.

"We need to minimize our magical footprint in case it affects the spell. So, we'll have to rely on non-magical means for now," Melody shot back before turning a softer eye on Nash. "Do you have all the ingredients I asked you to pack?"

He pulled out several small cardboard boxes and scowled up at Erebus. "Do you have those vials you conned from me?"

"Correction. Finch conned them from you." Erebus grinned and took the tin box out from... actually, I had no idea where he'd hidden it. But he handed it to Nash regardless. Nash set the tin box beside the other boxes and moved aside for Melody.

She set to work, removing four leather bags. Hex bags. Or what would become hex bags when she put the ingredients inside. I'd seen enough of them to know what they looked like now. Finch still wore his to prevent Davin from tracking him, though the smell had worn off. Even if he stank to high heaven, it wouldn't have kept me away. He'd become my comfort blanket—all I had, since I'd left Adam.

I wonder where you are right now... I was almost entirely focused on the mission, but a few Adam thoughts slipped through. He'd been so sad when we parted ways. That kicked-puppy face was hard to forget. No matter how necessary the break had been.

Melody made small piles of ingredients inside each bag—from vivid herbs and dried petals, to what looked like dust. She put a few drops of various neon liquids into the piles, rehydrating the dusty stuff, before adding a healthy dose of Nash's blood. With that done, she tied each one shut with strange string—strands of a tree branch with very little give to them. But she managed, like the professional she was, until the bags were complete.

"You think hex bags will solve this?" Erebus scoffed.

Melody imitated his scoff. "They're more than ordinary hex bags. These hold a kill-all spell, which we need to undo the spells on this island. They won't actually kill anyone, of course—that's not what I mean by kill-all. It's like... an antibiotic for the bacteria Katherine instilled here. It will wipe the slate clean, giving us the chance to instill a moving spell of our own."

"Won't that reveal the island?" Luke asked, his tone worried.

Melody shook her head. "I'm not explaining this very well. The Chaos in these bags will remove Katherine's magic and replace it with a generic bubble that belongs to no one. Sort of like the ones used on covens. It doesn't respond to one person alone, if that makes sense."

"That makes sense," Luke confirmed.

Erebus clicked his tongue. "Impressive, Librarian. My, am I pleased you decided to befriend my best servant. He'd have run around this island like a headless chicken. He'd likely find the solution moments before moonrise, purely to aggravate me."

"How's that for gratitude?" Finch retorted in a low voice.

Poor guy... He'd done everything for Erebus and got no credit.

"Each bag must be taken to the most precise cardinal points. There can be no mistakes." Melody's voice held a slight tremor.

"That's where the compasses come in. And as the full moon rises tomorrow night, we will set the bags on fire. That will release the old magic of Katherine's spell on this island, so we can implement the new moving spell afterward."

"*An American Werewolf in London*, anyone?" Finch smirked.

"Huh?" I responded.

He sighed. "Never mind. Let's just say it's got something to do with a bad moon on the rise."

"There's nothing bad about this," Erebus chimed in. "This is success, Finch. Surely you can smell it. We are almost there!"

You *are almost there. But we all know what happens to Finch when this ends.* I prayed Harley and the others were well on their way to finding that djinn, so we could save Finch from this mess before he faced the death that befell all Erebus's servants. I didn't want to live in this magical world without him. That might have sounded dramatic, but it was the simple truth. My new existence wouldn't make sense without him.

"And what happens to me when this ends?" Finch asked coldly. Evidently, he couldn't bite his tongue anymore. "Do I get my freedom, like you promised? You let Kenzie go once she'd fulfilled her mission for you. You're going to do the same for me, right?" Erebus didn't know what Finch had found out about the rest of his "long-term" servants and their contractual deaths. I supposed Finch wanted Erebus to look him in the eyes and give him the courtesy of telling him the truth. Or lie, so he could fuel his fires of resentment to melting point. And the rest of ours, too.

Erebus faltered. "As we have discussed, you will get what you desire the most when your contract with me has come to its conclusion."

"But this is the last stage, isn't it?" Finch pressed. Everyone held their breath. Me included. "So, my freedom must be coming up, served piping hot? No?"

"You will have reached the final stage when I say you have reached it," Erebus said simply. "It is still some way off."

Of course it is. Why wasn't I surprised to hear that? The truth was, Finch had made himself invaluable to Erebus. That Child of Chaos would extend this mission for as long as he wanted to, and as long as he needed to, using the vague terms of engagement as a loophole to keep getting Finch to do his bidding. Until the moment he finally failed, and Erebus could off him, the same way he'd offed everyone else, aside from Davin. It made me sick to my stomach. How could *anyone* survive that kind of continual servitude? By the sheer law of averages, each one would wind up dead, one way or another.

But not you, Finch. Not you. He can't have your life. We weren't going to let him.

"As for Kenzie, she and I had a short-term deal," Erebus continued, evidently feeling he needed to clarify. Or rub salt in Finch's wound. "A one-task affair, which does not, in any way, reflect the situation you are in. I would not even class that kind of exchange as servitude, merely a favor for the benefit of two parties. I aided her, she aided me, and that was the end of that."

Finch glowered, his hands balled into fists. "So, what you're saying is, you don't owe me anything?"

"You will not ruin this moment for me with the 'woe is me' performance, Finch. Not when I am so close to triumph. We can discuss this again when we have come to the right point, in which your mission has come to an end. As I said, that is still some way off, so I suggest you perk yourself up and focus on what comes next."

"Looks like you won't need me after all, Erebus." Nash came in to relieve the gathering tension. And, in turn, barely hid his relief that he wouldn't have Erebus traipsing after him. "Huntress and I will head east."

"An excellent example of someone who is entirely focused on the task at hand." Erebus smiled, though it swiftly turned into a frown. "Hmm… I suppose I will not be needing you, Nash, but if something goes awry with the eastern bag, I will know who to blame. And I *will* make good on punishing your precious Familiar for any errors."

"There won't be any," Nash retorted.

"Then I will take the north." Erebus puffed out his chest, undoubtedly feeling very important now that he actually had a task of his own.

Melody cast a glance over her shoulder. "Luke and I will go west."

"Which leaves the south for me and you." I gazed at Finch, giving him no chance to refuse. He nodded slowly.

"That works for me, though I've never been much of a Southern boy." He smiled, and my heart did the strangest thing. It clenched, but not in a bad way. No, it clenched in the way it had when I first met Adam, a lifetime ago.

Wisps of smoke rose from Erebus's body, apparently to hold our attention. "Stick to your mission and heed the same warning I gave Nash. This spell must not fail, under any circumstances. I will not wait for another full moon. There is no time for mistakes."

Ah, so that's why he had no problem with the first delay. Given his track record, I'd thought it odd that he hadn't harassed Finch more, to find the rogue cultists sooner. Now it made sense. The timeline had fit his plans, so he'd had no reason to pester Finch more than usual. But he'd definitely have a tantrum if we missed the mark on this spell.

Erebus strode north, only for Nash to call him back.

"Aren't you forgetting something?"

Erebus tilted his head. "What?"

Nash tossed him a compass. "No Chaos, remember? I guess that'll probably be tricky for you, but give it a try—unless you want to risk the spell failing. It wouldn't look too good if the north bag failed, would it?"

"I bet you enjoyed that, didn't you?" Erebus caught the compass.

"It wouldn't be polite for me to say." Nash clearly had enjoyed bringing Erebus down a peg. "Do you know how to use that?"

Erebus sniffed. "I may not have possessed a human body for long, but compasses have been around for two thousand years. Of course I know how to use one."

Finch and Nash exchanged a skeptical look.

"How?" Finch jumped on the bullying-Erebus train.

"Fine. I don't know." Erebus squirmed a bit, which I had to admit was satisfying to watch.

"You hold it and follow the arrow north. When it hits the *N*, you'll know you're there," Finch replied. He didn't bother to conceal his smirk.

Erebus stared at the object. "Sounds rather simple when you put it like that." He stalked off to avoid more ribbing. All those years of cosmic power, and he had to be taught how to use a compass. Tragic.

With the boss gone, the rest of us split into our groups. Luke and Melody headed west, with Belle and Larry flapping behind them. I wondered if Finch had sent silent instructions to the creatures, to protect Luke and Melody. Honestly, I wasn't completely sure how the control over creatures worked, but it was impressive to watch. How many humans could say they'd ridden a gargoyle?

Nash and Huntress went east, with Joker and Bingo padding after them, making a whole bevy of squelching sounds. Joker kept licking the back of Nash's head at every opportunity, but Nash didn't let it bother him. After years developing a bond with Huntress, I supposed he was accustomed to animal affection. Even if Joker was a million times more terrifying than Huntress, with a much bigger, sloppier tongue. Already, the back of Nash's silver hair had gone crispy, like he'd overdone the gel.

"Are you controlling them, or do they like us now?" I asked Finch, once we were alone.

He laughed. "A bit of both. In Nash's case, I think he's got a new admirer." His expression turned serious. "But the Bestiary here has been unguarded since Katherine's death, so there might be stray critters around the island. I don't want anyone getting munched on. So, I had a few stern words with my gargoyle pals."

"I didn't hear any." I wanted to understand.

"I can do it silently, when I have the proximity and time to send the message across. And I didn't want to freak Luke out by making a big, loud command. He's a sensitive soul." Finch had a mischievous twinkle in his eyes. I adored that twinkle, though it'd been a while since I'd seen it.

I hesitated, thinking of Drake Shipton. "Can we—"

He lifted his hand. "Do you hear that?"

"Hear what?" I listened for a noise but only heard sounds I would expect: an island breeze rustling the leaves, birdsong, waves colliding with the shore.

He fidgeted uncomfortably. "I want to give Harley a call to see how things are coming along on her end." He took out his phone and scrolled to Harley's name. The call didn't go through—when he pulled the phone away, he showed me the screen. No bars. "Son of a nutcracker!"

"No signal?"

He stuffed the phone back in his pocket. "That smoky-ass mother of a gremlin cut off communications. Hell, he probably jammed them the moment he landed."

I put a hand on his shoulder. "You know Harley. She'll have everything under control. She won't let you die. None of us will."

"Weird, because I started hearing the 'Imperial March' the moment Erebus answered that friggin' flare. Or is it the 'Death March'? I can never remember which is which." He ran a nervous hand through his hair.

"You won't die, Finch." My tone hardened. "I might have a way to get some insurance to prevent it. At the very least, it could give us more information about what Erebus is up to, so you can get a step ahead."

I meant it. Finch wasn't dying on my watch. Sparks of romance aside, he was one of us. Erebus couldn't have him. End of story. I didn't care what stunts we had to pull—Erebus would have another escaped servant to deal with soon, if it was the last thing I did.

He cocked his head. "What information?"

"We don't have to worry about lighting these bags until the full moon rises tomorrow, right?"

"Right."

"So, we have some time to look through Drake Shipton's journals. You mentioned them before and said he had a bunch in his library." I brushed my thumb across the curve where his shoulder met his neck. I couldn't stop myself. "I've been thinking. What if they weren't full of boring diatribe? What if they were coded—in language so dull that anyone reading wouldn't think twice about the entries?"

Finch's eyes brightened. He lunged forward and scooped me into his arms, swinging me around the way I'd only seen happen in cheesy rom coms. Maybe those movies were onto something, because I sure felt lighter.

"This is why I love you, Ryann Smith!" he cried. "Best brain in the business!"

My stomach fluttered. *You... love me?*

TWENTY-NINE

Ryann

I let Finch lead the way, still reeling from his unexpected hug…
and words. I struggled to even look at him without getting
flushed and awkward. But focusing on Drake Shipton's journals
went some way toward distracting me. Now certainly wasn't the
time to start seeing Finch in a more confusing light.

Besides, the island ensured I had sights and sounds to divert me.
Among the wild undergrowth and pockets of dense forest, creatures
howled and leaves rustled, providing us with a deeply unsettling
walk to the library. I noticed buildings and overgrown walkways,
the former shaped like honeycomb hexagons. Remnants of the lives
that had inhabited this place lay scattered, with a shattered mug
commemorating the very moment the security magicals had come
to take the cultists away. Broken-down doors and smashed windows
revealed the force it had taken to make those criminals obey.

Peering through the cracked window of what had once been a
canteen, I saw plates still on the tables, exactly where they'd been

when the cultists were arrested, the rotten food long since stolen by maggots and probably the beasts that had escaped the island's private Bestiary. Some of the hexagonal buildings had beds with rumpled, moldy sheets inside, twisted as if someone had leapt from bed in a hurry. Which they likely had.

"It's a ghost town," I murmured.

Finch nodded grimly. "Worse than that. It's a death island."

I shuddered as an alien scream pierced the air and stepped closer to Finch's side. He didn't seem to mind, and I felt his arm brush against mine.

Concentrate, Ryann! We walked one of the vine-strangled catwalks that crisscrossed Eris Island, leading from one part of the former compound to another. The rusting metal, warped by the island's personal weather system, squealed under our weight as we picked our way over the tangled reclamation of Mother Nature. I gripped the railing, though it wouldn't have done much good if the whole thing collapsed. Finch took my hand, as if reading my mind.

"You'll be fine, Ryann," he said softly. "You're with me. I'll Air the bejeezus out of you if you fall."

I chuckled nervously. "I thought you weren't supposed to use Chaos until tomorrow night."

He flashed me a conspiratorial grin. "Nah, that was Melody making stuff up on the fly to keep Erebus in line. I'd say she had the brightest mind in this bubble, if I weren't standing next to you."

"I'm no Librarian."

His eyes glittered with sudden feeling—a bittersweet joy. "No... you aren't."

What's that supposed to mean? I had a kneejerk reaction to people pointing out my lack of magic, but this didn't feel like it was meant as an insult, or even a remark about my limitations. I thought of Luke and Melody and hoped I understood Finch's sentiment. If I *were* a Librarian, there'd be no chance of any relationship between us. But I wasn't. So, what did that mean for us? I guessed that was up to me, once we'd finished this mission.

I'm a massive jerk, aren't I? All that fluttery excitement vanished as though someone had netted those beautiful butterflies and demolished them. I'd only just broken things off with Adam—the man who, once upon a time, I'd planned my entire future with. How could I even contemplate starting something new with Finch? That broke every moral code I had. And it certainly didn't make me look, or feel, good.

"Penny for 'em." Finch nudged me.

"Huh?"

"Penny for your thoughts."

I shook my head. "Atlantis stuff."

"You sure about that?" His voice was thick with unspoken emotion.

I gulped. "One hundred percent sure. Now, what do you think about the journals?"

"I think you're onto something, but it may not be in those journals." He looked disappointed. "Still, that doesn't mean there aren't Drake Shipton secrets spread across this island. If he wrote something about Erebus and Atlantis, we'll find it."

I wished I could tell him what I truly wanted to say. That I cared about him… that I had these confusing feelings for him, and that I… oh goodness, I didn't know. Or maybe I just didn't dare think it, in case that would make it a reality. Could I really tell him I wanted to see where these feelings might lead?

He kept pulling me in like a veritable black hole, and I couldn't fight against that influence anymore. It would tear me apart. So I was stuck in a difficult dichotomy. I longed to blurt it all out and get it off my chest, but the thought of Adam and all that lingering guilt silenced me.

So, I kept my head down and let Finch walk beside me, his hand in mine, until we reached a monumental structure of stone and chrome. Another hexagon. Katherine must've liked those. From an architectural perspective, they provided the greatest structural strength. Maybe that was why she'd chosen to build everything this way, though this hexagon was built horizontally on the ground, instead of like an upright hive pocket, and reminded me an awful lot of an old fortress.

"What is this place?" I gaped at the rising walls.

"The Hexagon." Finch smirked. "Katherine's answer to the Pentagon, with one more side. She always had to be extra, my mother."

The main door swung half off its hinges, giving us smooth entry into the building. Lucky, as I didn't know how much energy Finch had left. Everything about the Hexagon made me want to run away. I couldn't put my finger on why, but it sent a shiver of dread through me, as if I sensed every soul who'd walked these halls. Including those who hadn't survived their Eris experience.

To add to my fears, the temperature plummeted the moment we entered, despite the humid climate outside. And, with only dim emergency lighting to illuminate our path, my forehead was slicked with petrified sweat before we'd even moved a few yards. I gripped Finch's hand tighter as he calmly strode on. He'd lived here for so many years, he probably knew the layout like the back of the very hand that held mine. He might've found his way in pitch darkness.

"You're okay," he told me. "There's nothing here that can hurt you anymore."

"What about the loose Purge beasts?"

He gave my hand a squeeze. "Okay, so there's *one* thing that can hurt you, but that's what Selma and Murray are for."

I'd almost forgotten our leathery bodyguards, who'd flapped over our heads all the way from the last clearing. They padded into the building, the wet slap and nerve-wracking scrape of their clawed feet setting my teeth on edge. I had to remind myself that they were the good guys—just two ugly creatures in love. But, in the bleak glow of the Hexagon's corridors, it was hard to forget the image of Murray chewing Davin, and near impossible to believe he wouldn't seize a dinner opportunity.

Finch has them under control. He won't let anything happen to me. I repeated the mantra over and over as we made our way down the extensive labyrinth of shadowed hallways. At every turn, Murray stuck his head out first to check for other beasts. I heard rattles in the air ducts and the sound of something skittering across the floor, but no creature reared its head.

"Here we are." Finch halted outside an imposing blast door with *The Drake Shipton Library* written above it. The door had been tampered with; it lay partially open. Another lucky break that gave us access to the underbelly of Katherine's fallen empire. The trouble was, my mind kept thinking: *It can't be this easy. Nothing ever is, in the magical world.*

We slipped through the narrow gap, and I expected the electricity to start up again and the blast door to crush us to death. But it didn't. Although, the gap wasn't quite wide enough for the gargoyles. I comforted myself with the knowledge that if the gargoyles couldn't fit, then nothing bigger than them could, either.

Finch took us straight to the shelves where Drake's journals sat, gathering dust. "These are the ones." He brushed his fingertip across the spines. "The world's dullest collection of daily endeavors."

"How many are there?" The journals all looked the same—thick, navy, leather-bound tomes which seemed to stretch down the whole aisle.

He shrugged. "Too many."

I plucked the first one from the shelf, and a tiny monster flew out. A winged, fanged fairy with big bug eyes that glowed red in the gloom. It flew right at my face, and I screamed at the top of my lungs. Murray and Selma threw themselves at the blast door, creating a bang so loud that another scream tore out of my throat.

Finch grabbed me and hurled a ball of Fire at the fairy. It shrieked at him in distaste before fluttering off to hide behind another book.

"All good?" He pulled away but kept his hands on my arms.

I swallowed. "I might have a heart attack, but... yeah, I'm good."

"Nothing to worry about. It was just a tooth fairy. The Purge beast equivalent of a really annoying rat chewing at your wires." He smiled and held me tighter.

"A... tooth fairy?" I gaped at him.

"Not the kind you want to stick a tooth under your pillow for, but they share the same name," he replied. "I feel sorry for the nice kind, lobbed in the same category with those bitey bastards. They hail from South America and creep into bedrooms to steal human teeth for their fairy kingdoms. They'll tug them right out of your mouth."

I felt sick. "Not really helping me here, Finch."

"Sorry." He offered an apologetic glance. "As long as you keep your mouth closed, they won't be a problem."

I pursed my lips shut and turned to the book in my hands. "We should start reading. It might be a long night."

"A bit of light bedtime reading. You'll just have to smack me if I fall asleep." He took the second book in the row and sank to the floor as he flipped it open. I copied him, our backs flat against the towering bookshelf.

As we settled into companionable silence, I became ever more conscious of his proximity. I'd never been like this when we sat on the sofa in my apartment together doing research. But it felt different with so much at stake. And there was an air of secrecy that added to the excitement of the situation. An anxious excitement that filled me with anticipation. As if he could turn and kiss me at any moment. He didn't, but my mind went wild, regardless.

Tell me how you feel, and I'll tell you... It felt so very backward for someone like me, but I needed him to make the first move. After what I'd just put my heart through, ending things with Adam, I didn't think I could handle rejection. And since Finch hadn't flat-out told me how he felt, some doubt remained. What if I'd gotten the wrong end of the romance stick? What if I had all these feelings, stronger than anything I'd ever experienced, and he felt nothing?

I fell into the drab world of Drake Shipton to take my mind off Finch and Adam. The more I read, the more I doubted my idea about it being code. Or, if it was code, then I had no clue how to decipher it. Alan Turing, I was not.

The journals held some interesting tidbits about the Shipton family, though, which made for slightly more invigorating reading. I found out about Drake's wife, Iphigenia, who'd died under mysterious circumstances. Drake alluded to it being an alchemical accident, though where the evil branch of the Shipton line was concerned, I wasn't sure accidents existed. I didn't include Finch or his aunt, Hester, in that classification. Or the others, really—the ones Katherine had killed for the sake of that cruel hex she'd put on Hiram Merlin. No, Katherine and Drake had been a crazy branch of their own.

I took to skimming until the journals touched on Katherine and Hester's birth. He spoke of the fortune the twins were destined to bring, but how he felt more drawn to the smaller one—Katherine. He mentioned feeling the power in her as he held her, conjuring a sinking sense of dramatic irony in me. If Drake hadn't singled Katherine out from the moment he first held her, would she always have been destined to do evil? Or could she have been a different person, given the chance? She'd been smart and strong, with a sharp sense of who she was. The kind of woman who could've gone either way.

I reached the last page of the journal and was about to put it back with the others when a tiny symbol in the right-hand corner caught my eye.

"What's this?" I pointed to the symbol.

Finch frowned at it for a moment before his eyes widened. "A protective spell. The kind meant to keep things hidden." The frown returned. "But, if it's what I think it is, we'd need some kind of lens to see what it's hiding."

"What about the Eye of Erebus?" Finch had taken to wearing the pendant at all times, though the juice that powered it had run dry. He'd told me what it did at the monastery, revealing the "captured" Blanche to be Mr. Abara.

Finch pulled the pendant from under his shirt and stared at it. "Holy crap."

"What?" I leaned into him.

"Erebus said this needed rare ingredients to make it work, right?"

I nodded. "I think I remember him saying that, yes."

"How about *this* for rare ingredients." He delved into his pocket and removed a vial of Nash's blood.

"Where did you get that?" I eyed him suspiciously. As far as I knew, all Nash's vials had gone into the tin box.

"I saved a few for a rainy day." His smile widened. "This seems like as good a time as any to call in those chips. I may be mixing metaphors, but hey—if this gets us some information, that gets me off the hook, right?"

I sighed. "I suppose."

"That's what I like to hear." He twisted the two halves of the pendant open to reveal the dead eye inside—the one that'd been plucked from Hephaestus's head, offered to Erebus in exchange for the love of Aphrodite. There was so much wrong with that scenario, but I couldn't exactly cuss out any of the parties involved. Not if I valued having a tongue in my mouth to cuss them out with.

I looked away as he opened the vial and tipped a small stream of blood directly onto the eyeball. For a few minutes, nothing happened. Then, the entire eyeball blinked and glowed with a soft, bronze light. Unperturbed, Finch swung the pendant over the symbol in the corner of the journal. The glow shifted to red, then green, before settling on a vibrant, deep red. Words began to appear in the air, hovering before us.

Blood of his blood. Open the secrets.

"The secrets I get. But blood of his blood?" I glanced at Finch. "Any idea what that means?"

Finch stared down at his arm. "I think so. Man, am I glad I got my tetanus shot." Without warning, he dragged his forearm against a nail sticking out of the bookshelf behind us. A trickle of blood welled in the cut. He swiped it with his finger before smearing the viscous liquid across the tiny symbol on the journal's back cover.

The etching turned jet black. As if someone had set fire to it, the symbol sank into the journal, and the surface peeled back in a rush of curling leather, revealing a fresh page. All my qualms evaporated as I leaned in, eager for a look at the hidden writing. It looked like a diary entry, like the rest of the journal, only it was written in the same ashy black the symbol had transformed into—as if it had been burned into the back page instead of written.

"Drake Shipton, you sly sucker," Finch remarked.

My eyes scanned the page, my heart racing.

I feel I have uncovered something truly important and escaped something truly awful. A matter that may have stolen my freedom from me. I had the good fortune to receive a warning from a concerned spectator, which prevented me from making a dire mistake. Some may call it divine intervention, but I know better. These Children seek to destroy and protect, though it is difficult to decipher which has which intention.

I came too close to the truth; I am certain of it. And Erebus sought to stifle the progression of my knowledge by entrapping me in his deal. I was very fortunate indeed that another stopped me from taking such a step. I did not understand what the outcome would have been, had I accepted untold power in exchange for indefinite servitude. But now I understand why Erebus sought to imprison me in that crafty manner. I'd learned more than he wished me to.

He seeks Atlantis. He seeks its lost treasures for himself. He spoke of a rare jewel—I can only imagine what gifts such a jewel could give. If a Child of Chaos seeks it, it must be worthwhile. I have the common sense not to pursue it, which is why I must hide this entry, though I will leave the trail open should a descendant attempt to discover more, and avoid mistakes using my advice. Although, I do not know that it can end well. One thing I do know for certain is that he will do everything within his power to achieve it. He will stop at nothing to prevent those who would thwart him or take it first. That is the sort of Chaos I will not deign to dabble in. Yes, I had a blessed escape, for which I thank Lux.

My heart lurched. Lux *and* Erebus in one journal entry? It seemed Erebus had tried to entangle Drake Shipton in a deal, but Lux had stopped him from accepting. Circumstances had been different for Finch. If Lux had stopped his deal, Katherine would've reached the lofty heights of a Child of Chaos. Still, it struck me as strange to read that Drake had almost been one of Erebus's servants.

Boy, trouble just ran in this family, didn't it?

THIRTY

Finch

The hidden journal entry left me hollow. So, Lux had gotten her bad self involved in other Shipton nonsense back then, too? She'd stopped Drake from making a deal with Erebus, which begged some interesting questions. What would've happened if he *had* entered that deal? Would he have found a way to escape the death sentence?

I understood why she hadn't stopped me from going into Erebus's service—there'd been too much at stake. But maybe she was trying to remedy that now. You know, with *another* deal. Never out of the goodness of her heart.

I left Ryann so she could read the entry a few more times, though it hadn't given us the insurance policy I'd hoped for. There was no leverage I could use against Erebus, just the same old, same old. Erebus was gunning for a rare jewel, and who knew what it would do? The prospects didn't leave me feeling optimistic.

Scanning through the other books Katherine had left alongside her beloved prune's journals, I stopped to tear out some pages. Sacrilege, yes, but I didn't give a hoot about destroying my mother's things. She'd ripped me up and spat me out, so it only seemed fair. And she had some useful bits and pieces in this here library: a spell that could grant an extra minute of life, a spell that provided a powerful forcefield, a few notes about the island's Bestiary and how it powered everything. The last could've proven useful—a manual of sorts.

I shoved the tidbits into my rucksack. A bit of my former kleptomania was showing through. I mean, you never knew what you might need until you needed it, especially if I got separated from the munchkin of all knowledge, Melody. Nash had reminded me of that, with his seemingly bottomless bag of ingredients and artifacts.

Where would I be now if I'd stayed on this island? What if I'd never gone to the SDC? I wasn't that dumb, desperate kid anymore, so it was hard to get perspective. But I still retained a few flickers of my former self, with the stealing and the constant need to seek validation from the people surrounding me. Plus, the ill-timed bouts of comedic genius. They'd all been defense mechanisms, once upon a time, before becoming an ingrained part of my personality.

Does it matter, in the end? This Finch wouldn't last much longer, with this massive mess I'd entangled myself in. My freedom depended on my sister finding one very lost djinn. Not the best odds, but maybe I'd had worse? Any race with my sister in the running had a chance of success.

I walked down a random library aisle and froze dead in my tracks. A figure drifted across the far edge of the room and vanished into shadows... A ghost, in every sense of the word. A woman I'd thought about often, especially this past year, after losing her to

Katherine's evil. A cruel end for the sweetest woman—my first true love, who'd died because she'd stupidly loved me back.

Adley...?

My legs took on a life of their own, sprinting down the aisle. I saw her again, solemnly turning down another aisle. My mouth opened to call her, but she disappeared again, sinking into the darkness.

Am I going insane? Are you really here?

She'd died. I'd heard it straight from Harley. I'd seen the coroner's report once I'd gotten out of Purgatory. It couldn't be her... could it?

My mind descended into utter confusion, flitting between what my eyes had seen and how this could possibly be happening. Had Davin pieced together the chewed-up bits of himself so quickly and come to stab me in the heart? Or was one of the cultists still lingering here, using Shapeshifting to trick me into believing Adley haunted this place? Her body had been taken to her home coven, and her spirit had gone with it. It wasn't possible for her to be here!

I chased after the sad specter. I had to know. I had to speak to her —*then* I'd know if this was really Adley. The figure reappeared with her back to me. I hurtled toward her, my hand outstretched. My fingertips had almost touched her shoulder when she disintegrated into a haze of sparkling white.

I scanned the library frantically, trying to find her again. A cold breeze drifted over my skin, setting my hairs on end.

Following that ghostly compass, I skidded around the corner. She'd reappeared at the far end of the passage, and I ran with everything I had. My heart almost blew straight out of my chest as another face erupted behind her spectral features, and Adley disappeared once more to reveal another woman.

"Finch?" Ryann's brows furrowed in concern. "Are you okay? You look like you've seen a ghost."

I clutched at my ribs. "You don't say."

"What's wrong?" She came closer.

"No... no, I'm fine. Being here... is bringing back all kinds of things I was pretty sure I'd buried in therapy," I replied, catching my breath.

She hesitated. "Where did you go?"

"Following a trail." I glanced over Ryann's shoulder, looking for Adley.

"Well, I couldn't find anything else in Drake's notes. But this jewel might be your way out of the deal if Harley can't find the djinn." Ryann smiled nervously at me. "If you can get your hands on it first, then you can use it as a bargaining chip. He's gone to all this effort—it must mean a lot to him. Maybe enough to free you, in exchange?"

I couldn't think straight. Ryann had my heart now, sure, but Adley... she'd had it first, and I'd hurt her so much. Our love had been a poisoned chalice that ultimately took her life. I had to make amends for that. Even if I could go back and fix everything from those days—treat her better, actually invest in her, and friggin' listen when she had something to say —I hadn't been this version of me then. That Finch had been a clueless idiot, but this one wanted to apologize, if nothing else. One moment to tell her how much she'd meant to me and how I would've saved her if I could have. How that agonizing loss had changed me forever and gotten through this thick skull in a way that nothing else managed to do.

"Are you sure you're okay?" Ryann put her hand on my arm.

I swallowed hard. "No, not really. Like I said, this place is doing a number on my noggin."

"I'm sorry Erebus made you come here." Ryann lowered her gaze. "It can't be easy."

"It's not easy for any of us," I replied quietly. She had her own problems, though the two of us were carefully avoiding our respective issues.

Ryann sighed. "You and I need to start trusting each other more. It's hard to be honest with each other, and I know you find it harder than most to open up, but... we're friends. We care about each other. We should say what's on our minds."

No, no, no... This wasn't the moment I'd envisioned having a romantic heart-to-heart. With Adley appearing literally out of nowhere, my mind wasn't exactly primed to say the right things. And I really, really didn't want to mess this up. I only had one shot to open my heart to her for the first time. And considering my track record, she'd have plenty of reasons to back right off.

"The reason I've been acting a bit weird is because... Adam and I broke up." Ryann lifted her gaze, her eyes glinting with sadness.

My eyes widened. "You broke up?"

"It needed to happen." She wrung her hands nervously. "I'm not the person I was when I met him."

"That had to be... uh... tough." I fumbled for the right thing to say, stifling the urge to make a terrible joke. Growth, right?

She nodded. "It hurt like hell, and ending things made me feel like the worst person in the world, but... I had to let him go. It wasn't fair anymore. I kept neglecting him, and he didn't understand why. I could've gone on lying and hiding and making us both miserable, but that felt wrong."

"You wanted different things?" I prompted. *Like... me, maybe?* I crossed every extremity, though this wasn't the right time to get my hopes up. Being a rebound would suck.

"Yes, we did." She looked surprised. Maybe she'd been expecting jokey Finch, too. "In a nutshell, I couldn't give up the magical world for an ordinary existence."

"That's a hell of a nutshell," I replied. "But, if it's okay, can I ask what made it happen? Did he do something? It wasn't, like… um… a ring, was it?"

Pain tightened her features. "That might've been easier."

"Then what was it? If you want to tell me," I hastened to add.

She sighed quietly. "He found out about magic, thanks to Davin trying to trap me for bait. And his reaction… well, it wasn't what I'd hoped for. I realized that things would never work between us."

"He knows about magicals?!" Thoughts of red tape and O'Halloran exploded into my mind. The paperwork on this would be huge.

"Not exactly."

I arched an eyebrow. "But I thought you said—"

"I asked to have his mind wiped, so he couldn't destroy everything the magicals have built," she interjected. "I chose my side when I did that. I realized where I belonged, and that's here. With the Rag Team, with the SDC… and with you."

I tried to speak, failed, and cleared my throat. "With me?"

It hit me all at once, like a supercharge to the brain. Ryann and Adam weren't together anymore. That meant she was free… free to be badly romanced by me. I was no Casanova, but I had my charms.

And if she was telling me this, there had to be a reason. Everyone had told her I adored the ground she walked on, though I'd tried to shrug it off. Sometimes, however, I thought I'd seen hints, moments and looks, that suggested she'd known it was true.

Ryann smiled anxiously. "Yes, with you… and everyone else."

Now or never, Finch!

"I know this is probably a terrible time to say this, and I'm sorry if it's too soon, but… I'm glad you picked our side. I'm glad because… uh… I care about you. In fact, it's pretty common knowledge that I'm crazy about you. You've heard it from everyone, except this horse's mouth." I took a breath. "But I'm saying it now. I like you, Ryann. Like, not in a friend way… well, also in a friend way, but I meant in an 'I *like* you' way. Does that make sense?" I really should've practiced this.

She shifted awkwardly, making me think I'd gone and blown it. "That makes sense."

"Good. Okay. Right." More words wouldn't come. I'd told her how I felt. And now I didn't know what to do.

"I like you, too."

My heart damn near burst. "Pardon?"

"I like you, too." She chuckled. "It took a while to understand that my heart wasn't racing because of the dangerous situations. It was racing because you were there, and I'd started to develop feelings for you. I was so confused."

"Because of Adam?" I found my voice again.

"He'd seemed like the perfect guy for me, but he was the perfect guy for a person who didn't exist anymore," she explained. "The me I've become wants you, and cares about you, more than I should. I don't want to let that slip through my fingers, when I don't even know if you'll be breathing tomorrow. So, I'm being honest with myself for once."

"I don't want to let that slip through my fingers, either." I couldn't believe it. Everything we'd been dancing around was out in the open. "And I care about you, exactly as much as I should. I knew I was in trouble the moment I met you."

Her smile widened. "That explains why you barely talked to me those first few meetings."

"Yeah, it was rough. But if you want someone who's always smooth, always knows what to say, I'm not your guy." I gave her an out, just in case.

"I don't want that," she replied. "But… can I ask something?"

I nodded. "Anything."

"What was bothering you before? Is it the island? Or something I said? I know I haven't been acting like myself, but at least now you know why."

I gulped, my hands sweating. This was the last thing I wanted to talk about after what we'd just discussed. "I'd just seen Adley de la Barthe."

"Adley? Where?" Ryann gasped. Harley had filled her in on my past love, so I knew the name meant something to her.

"Drifting between the aisles, but she's gone now." It took everything I had to keep talking. "The timing is so strange, because I loved her as much as I could, but I never gave her what she deserved."

"I know that feeling." Ryann gazed out of a window toward the ocean. "But I'm sure you tried your best."

I shook my head and shoved my hands in my pockets. "I really didn't. My heart wasn't capable of it back then. Katherine had shrunk it down to a walnut."

"Adley was the catalyst for who you've become, wasn't she? Or did I get my stories twisted?" She rubbed the side of her temple, as if it would bring forth the right memory.

"No, you didn't. When I heard she'd been murdered by Katherine, I finally understood how much I'd loved her, and it hurt so much to know I'd never see her again. It held a mirror up to my face and forced me to examine my choices and decide if I liked them. I didn't, for the record."

"You must have really loved her, to throw everything away and start your life over for her." A mixture of emotions moved across her face: a flicker of jealousy, a note of sadness, and a glimmer of hope. I had to make her understand that, though I'd loved Adley, she wasn't the one in my heart now.

"Honestly, after losing her, I thought I'd never be able to feel the same about anyone," I went on. "I never thought my walnut heart could find room for someone else, let alone love them properly... until I met you. And I couldn't be around you without stammering like an idiot, as you said."

She pushed a strand of hair behind her ear. "Now that I know why you were stammering, it's cute. Not idiotic."

"Oh, it was idiotic, I know. I wanted to smack myself every time I opened my mouth. But, in a way, it was a defense mechanism. If you thought I was a clown, I'd never have to be serious with you or put my heart on the line again." I paused. "It's different now."

"You want to be serious with me?" she asked thickly, as though it scared her.

"When you're ready, I'd like that. But... I have to be honest." I looked down at my shoes, scuffing the floor with my toe. "I'm starting to feel like the ghosts of my past are coming back to remind me of an important lesson, while reigniting all my guilt and misery for good measure."

She frowned. "What do you mean?"

"I'm not explaining very well, but seeing Adley makes me think I'm not supposed to have a happy ending, even though I… feel this way about you. This is the moment in the movie when the audience is screaming at you to run away from me—away from danger."

"You're not a danger to me, Finch. How could you be, when you make me feel like this?" Ryann took my hands. "Nobody is screaming, and I'm not running. Not from you, ever. I've fought my battles to be able to tell you this, and I haven't come this far for nothing. I don't care if you think you're some kind of jinx, because you're not —you're my lucky charm."

Don't say something in a stereotyped Irish accent! Don't you do it!

"Then you must be my saving grace," I said instead, mustering my courage in case I lost Ryann before we'd even started anything. "And who needs a happy ending when we can have a moment like this? This is enough."

Ryann shook her head. "Not quite."

She moved closer, releasing my hands and pressing her palms to my chest. She cast me a long, lingering look that let me know what would happen next. A glance at my lips cemented the unspoken thought. I just had to lean in and kiss her. How hard could that be? Steeling myself, I lifted my hand to her face. I was moments from grazing that sweet mouth when Murray and Selma clattered through the blast door, sending Ryann and me flying apart as if a bomb had detonated between us.

"Hold that thought?" Ryann laughed nervously as Murray and Selma growled.

I smiled back, despite wanting to turn those two creatures into a pair of leather jackets. "With everything I've got."

"We should keep searching for the southern point and get this hex bag in place." She glanced around her, visibly nervous about stray ghosts, or maybe tooth fairies that might flap out and steal her molars to use as bricks.

So close... But possibility remained in the air—a rain check, not a change of heart, and I wouldn't let go of that for anything. Ghosts, tooth fairies, and Erebus be damned.

THIRTY-ONE

Finch

I'd never been much of a geographer; compasses were tricky little weasels. They'd confidently show south, then some magnetic flutter would send the needle off target. And there was a whole lot of south to cover on this island. I'd have used some magic, since we'd only told Erebus we couldn't use Chaos to stop *him* from using it, but I had no compass-esque spells in my inventory. So, we had to rely on this stupid thing.

We walked together through the creepy forest, ignoring the rustles in the undergrowth and the glints of eyes in the branches, until we reached the southern beach. The moonlight illuminated it, an ethereal hideaway. As annoyed as I might've been with Murray and Selma, I was grateful that their snapping jaws would save our asses if any loose beasties jumped out and attacked. The gargoyles were keeping their distance, sensing my irritation at the interruption of what would've been an earth-shattering moment for me.

The beach was more of a cove, really. An inlet where boats occasionally departed on nearby missions, or to collect supplies from terrified mainland folks who knew better than to ask questions. I remembered this place as one of my few sanctuaries, when Eris life became too much—calming me with the soft hiss of water lapping the sand and the quiet embrace of the cliffs surrounding it.

"This seems to be it," Ryann said, observing the compass. "The needle isn't moving."

"What if the bag gets washed away?" The point that the needle insisted on was smack in the middle of the small beach, literally an inch or two above the tideline.

Ryann frowned. "Can you protect it somehow?"

"Maybe." I delved into my rucksack for the forcefield spell I'd nabbed from Mother Dearest's library. It hadn't specified whether it could be used for objects as well as people. And it didn't require much in the way of ingredients. It called for the blood of the spell-maker and a drop of phoenix tears. We didn't have the latter, but we still had Nash's all-purpose life juice.

"What's that?" Ryann nodded to the torn page in my hand.

"Some pilfered spell from Katherine's library. It's not like anyone else is using it." I grinned and crouched on the sand, dragging my finger through the cold granules. Drawing a pentagram had been Katherine's version of finger-painting for children, though my instructions had come through Mrs. Anker back then. A pentagram may have been the first thing I'd ever drawn, albeit badly.

With the pentagram in place, I placed the leather bag in the very center. We had a few hours until the sun came up and plenty of time before the next moonrise, but after walking across this island for so long, Erebus might've been right about me cutting it close. Still, everything was in place. Now I just needed to protect this puppy from the tide.

"You might want to turn away for this." I pulled my Esprit from my pocket and transformed it into a blade.

Ryann's mouth widened in a startled *O*. "What are you going to do?"

"Draw some blood. Nothing too gory."

"Oh… you know, you should lead with that, instead of telling me to turn away while you pull a knife out of your pocket. That's usually the start of a true-crime documentary." She smiled, but a hint of sadness crossed her features. I decided to name it the "Adam Look." I'd called him a serial killer so many times, but I bet he'd never whipped out a knife in Ryann's company.

"Sorry." I drew the blade along my forearm, just below one of my golden apples. Ryann made a point of not turning away, which made me smile. Blood welled immediately, and I let it trickle down my skin, until a few drops fell to the sand.

Moving around the pentagram, I made sure all the points had at least one scarlet mark before I moved on to Nash's vial. Adding a drop of his blood to each of the five points, per Katherine's spell, I closed the vial and slipped it back into my pocket.

"Is it ready?" Ryann asked in a hushed tone.

I nodded. "Prepare to be Latined."

"I love this part." She glanced at me, a hint of envy in her eyes.

I raised my palms and recited from my mother's torn page. "*Ad protegere intus. Defendere muros. Ingressum permittere. Vulnerable defendere. Partum a clypeus. Ad protegere intus.*"

I repeated the words five times. The moment I finished that final round, the drops of blood lit up like the Fourth of July. A fizzing line circled the pentagram, hissing in the sand as the forcefield went up. A shimmering dome surged over the top, enveloping everything in its protective defenses: pentagram, hex bag, and a poor hermit crab that'd gotten caught midway through a scuttle.

"Can I try something?" Ryann stepped forward, pulling a bottle of water from her bag.

I shrugged. "Knock yourself out."

She tossed half the contents at the forcefield, only for the drops to ricochet and hit the sand with a series of wet thuds. It made me feel a lot better about leaving the leather bag out here with the unruly tides. Well, not unruly, actually—they were like clockwork—but I didn't know the schedule.

"It works." She grinned as she stowed her bottle away.

"Turns out my mother was useful sometimes." Bitterness dripped from my words. Part of me wanted to traipse right on back to the library and burn the damn thing, but common sense resisted. There was a slim chance we could return this island to the security magicals after Erebus finished with it. And the wealth of information in that library was worth preserving.

"Should we go back to find the others? We've got a lot of time to kill before moonrise tomorrow." Ryann faced the cliff, where steps had been carved directly into the rock.

"Probably, before they send a gargoyle after us." I calmed myself down just by looking at her.

"Yeah, where did those two go?"

"Murray and Selma?" I chuckled. "They're probably off doing something disgusting in the trees. Licking each other silly."

Ryann's cheeks turned red. "Ah… right."

Leaving the protected leather bag behind, we climbed the stone steps away from the cove. We paused for breath at the top, all flushed and gooey-eyed. I wanted to take her in my arms and pick up where we'd left off, but I didn't know if that was allowed. Were we in that stage yet? Were we in *any* stage yet?

This spilling-my-guts thing had given me a shove from the awkward tree, but I was hitting every branch on the way down. I didn't even know how to walk next to her—was I supposed to match her step, or was that creepy? Did I pull away if we accidentally grazed hands? Man, romance could be exhausting.

"Actually, I could do with a rest, if that's okay." Ryann sat down on the clifftop and leaned against a boulder. "And if the others worry, at least they'll know where to find us."

"Oh… yeah, of course. Fair warning, though: I might have to take down that protection spell pretty fast if Erebus comes along, since we told him we couldn't use additional Chaos. Or we'll have to tag team some smoke and mirrors stuff to hide it from him." I hesitated, but the dark circles under her eyes strengthened my resolve.

"I'll put up the best diversion you've ever seen." She chuckled wearily and tilted her head up to the night's sky. I sat beside her, giving her enough space to seem chivalrous.

Staring out at the ocean, we stayed for a while in a comfortable, yet charged, silence, bristling with the romantic potential we'd narrowly missed out on making reality. All because of a pair of loved-up slobberers who'd sniffed something they didn't like. The kiss, or a lurking Purge beast? I still wasn't sure.

Somehow, before I knew it, sleep had claimed me, though I didn't remember it happening. One moment, I'd been chattering about the smell of my hex bag and how she might want to keep her distance—

the usual flirtation expertise of one Finch Merlin. The next, it'd been lights out.

I woke to sunlight streaming through the interdimensional bubble. It took a few seconds to remember where I was, and a few more to remember how I'd come to be lying next to a boulder with Ryann in my arms. She looked peaceful, sleeping. No guttural snores or drool dribbling out of her mouth. Not that I'd have cared. She could've been a hideous sleeper, and I still would've thought she looked like an angel.

Unwilling to disturb her, I looked for Murray and Selma. But the tree line behind us remained empty of gargoyles. They'd gone AWOL while we'd snoozed, by the looks of it. They weren't off the hook for that, but the morning had risen quiet and sunny and beautiful, and nothing could've ruined that. Except waking up to Davin standing over me, taking pictures. But he'd still be putting himself back together, like a slimy, bloody jigsaw puzzle. The thought made me smile.

"Finch?" Ryann blinked awake.

"Morning, sleepyhead." I hugged her closer, not wanting the moment to end.

"What the—?" She sat up slowly and looked around. "When did we fall asleep?"

I shrugged. "No clue."

"Where are the others? How long did we sleep?" A flicker of panic crossed her face.

"Again, no clue, but I'm sure they're around somewhere. They didn't come looking for us in the night, so everything's probably fine." I held onto her for reassurance. "But we should get back to the center before Erebus freaks out about me slacking."

"In a minute." She turned her gaze to me, a half-smile tugging the corners of her lips. "I was having the most amazing dream, and I wouldn't mind finding out if it's just as good in real life."

My jaw dropped. "Was... I in the dream? Or am I the replacement for Henry Cavill?"

"It was all you." She leaned into me, and I tucked a strand of her hair behind her ear. I'd seen guys do that in movies, and it usually turned out well for them. My breath hitched as she edged closer, moments away from our first kiss.

I could literally feel the heat of her breath on my face when a movement over her shoulder caught my eye. Adley stood on the other side of the clearing, under the shadow of a tree branch. Her eyes were big and sad, her hand pressed to her heart as if it hurt.

I leapt up and ran to her, leaving Ryann behind. I didn't want to, but I owed it to Adley, and she kept slipping from my grasp every time I got close. But no sooner had I drawn near than she vanished, taking those sad, heartbreaking eyes with her.

Stop running away! I stooped and clutched my knees, feeling suddenly shaky. Adley had gone... if she'd even been here in the first place. For the first time since that initial sip of Medela, I wondered if I might be losing my mind all over again. Maybe Nash's potion wasn't working anymore. Maybe it'd had a shelf life, and I'd been so confident in its ability to keep the gremlins at bay that I hadn't anticipated my brain overcoming the medicine. What if it was like an overused antibiotic, and my brain had built up immunity?

An unexpected hand on my shoulder made me whip around. And, Chaos help me, I thought I'd see Adley there. Instead, Ryann looked up at me with worried eyes.

"Did you see her again?"

I nodded slowly. "She was right here… then she disappeared. I'm losing it, Ryann."

"You think you're having delusions again?" She sounded skeptical.

I gave an exasperated sigh. "Did you see her?"

"No," Ryann replied hesitantly.

"Then, yeah, it seems likely that I'm seeing things that aren't there." I wanted to delve into my head and rip out the goop. Anything to stop me from heading down a slippery slope to Nutcase Town, population me. I'd broken free of that place. I didn't want to go back.

"Not necessarily. There are a million potential reasons you saw her but I didn't. For one, you're looking for her. Until we know for sure it's a delusion, we should consider other possibilities. Besides, why would the delusions come back now? I know this island has a lot of bad memories for you, but Nash's potions didn't fail you in Purgatory, remember? That stuff is strong. Believe in it, okay? You aren't going crazy."

I hope you're right. Or did I? Would a delusion be so bad, compared to the alternative—that Adley was still here, trapped alone and grieving on this island? I wasn't sure which was worse.

"Where did it all go wrong for us, huh?" I asked as I recovered my breath.

She side-eyed me. "Who says it's gone wrong? I'd say we're moving in the right direction."

"This isn't the way people start… something, though. It's not exactly romance and flowers and chocolates." I wanted us to be normal, but then, I'd never been normal. Why would this be any different?

She smiled shyly. "Those first weeks with Adam, I'd never known anything like it. I had to be near him all the time. I had to hear his voice, see his picture, and get those amazing butterflies. You said you never thought you'd feel the same way about someone after Adley. I was the same. Then you came along, and now I feel things I've *never* felt before, even with Adam. Who needs chocolates and flowers? I don't."

"You're feeling things you've never felt before?" I looked at her in astonishment. Little old me had managed to get under her skin.

She nodded. "With him, it started out great, and then everything changed after Davin and Harley. My world changed. I suppose I thought he would, too, but he stayed exactly as he was. And I began to love this world, and everyone in it, more than I loved him."

"Chaos has a way of reeling folks in," I agreed.

"But it was only when I began to see you differently that the threads started coming undone."

"Oh... sorry." Guilt churned my stomach.

"No, that's not what I mean. You didn't cause my breakup with Adam, but hearing Melody and other people tell me you felt the same way helped me make my choice. I choose this world, and you, because you get it. You would never ask me to give this up, no matter how much danger you thought I was in. And that means everything to me."

"I come with a truckload of baggage," I replied quietly.

"Don't we all?"

I chuckled tightly. "See, I never understood what I had with Adley until it was too late. She gave everything to our relationship, and I lied and abandoned her. I got her locked up for protecting me.

That was all she ever did—try to keep me safe and rescue me from the life I was living."

"Déjà vu." Ryann offered an encouraging smile. "Only, I'm trying to rescue you from Erebus's service."

"Funny, isn't it, that it took my mother killing her for me to see what was there all along? That she'd been right about Katherine, that I should've left long ago." We'd gotten into some wallowing, and I had to stop it from dragging me down.

"You were under your mother's influence," Ryann said softly.

"And how long can I use that excuse?" I shook my head. "It's not enough. It's not an apology for all the wrongs I did to Adley. It's like Emily said—no amount of redemption will ever bring back the ones we hurt. All I want to do is give Adley her life back, away from me, where she'll be safe."

"I know you do." Ryann slipped her hand into mine. "But if she were really here and could see you now, she'd be so proud of the person you've become. It's awful how it happened, but you are who you are because of her. And when you see her again, in this life or the next, you can tell her that. And apologize. But your past doesn't mean you don't deserve happiness, or what would be the point in trying to improve and make amends?"

I stopped to look at her properly, the way I should've with Adley. "I don't know where this is going, you and me, but I won't ever make those mistakes again. If this is what I hope it is, then I will cherish you from this day until my last. You will never be second place in my heart or my thoughts."

"I wouldn't let you put me in second place." She grinned.

"I mean it, Ryann." A lump formed in my throat.

Her smile turned sad. "Then let's have our future, because nobody, not even Erebus, will take you away from me."

That hit me with a sharp dose of reality, because there was one person I'd forgotten when pouring my heart out to Ryann. Not Erebus. Not Adley. But Harley, who was hard at work trying to save my pert buttocks. What would she make of all this?

"Now, come on. We should get back to the others." Ryann took my hand and walked, giving me no choice but to follow.

We'd barely gone a few steps when a glistening figure in the near distance made me freeze. For a second, I was convinced Adley had reappeared. But my legs didn't experience the same kneejerk reaction to run as before. *Odd...* I understood why a moment later, as the figure drew closer. Nope, not Adley... but someone I *really* didn't want to see.

"I see something has changed between you two," Lux purred. She rippled with light, her vaguely human-shaped edges swirling inward.

"What are you doing here?" I narrowed my eyes at her. If Erebus caught her wafting around, we'd have a cosmic feud on our hands.

"After you kindly removed the wards, it wasn't difficult." She smiled. At least, I thought she did—in her Child of Chaos form, it was hard to tell. "It is good to see you again, Finch. It has been some time since our last encounter, but I am pleased to see that you are proceeding well in your task. You must continue what you are doing, so that we may all achieve our goal of reaching Atlantis."

Ryann gasped. "*You're* after Atlantis, too?"

"For my own purposes, yes," she replied.

"Wait a second." Ryann glanced between me and the Child of

Chaos. "You've met Lux before? You didn't say anything when I told you she saved us."

Ah... I'd reached the last branch of the awkward tree, and it hit me right in the nuts. *Way to go, Lux.* Apparently, human-Child confidentiality didn't exist.

"Uh... yeah, we've kind of met before." Understatement of the century.

Ryann shifted nervously. "Just how many of them *are* you working with?"

"I wouldn't say I'm working with Lux; she's just swung by a couple times." I wished the ground would grow jaws and munch me up, so I didn't have to deal with this.

"And you didn't think to mention that?" Ryann's brows shot up, her face confused.

"I instructed him not to," Lux cut in, rescuing me. "And he knows better than to cross a Child such as me, despite my benevolence."

Ryann squirmed. "Right... well, that's a pretty good reason, I guess."

"Now, I suppose we ought to get to the reason I have visited you." She wasn't looking at me, and my heart went into overdrive, thumping wildly. She had fixed her shining gaze on Ryann. "In order for a Child to reach Atlantis, as you know, a different body is required. A human body."

Why are you looking at her? Why are you looking at her?!

With a flourish, she withdrew a coin-shaped object—old and rusting, a half-eroded face on the center. "This will bind me to a willing human," she continued. "Unlike my husband, I do not use unnecessary force, nor do I go about burying sacred sites for my own benefit. Such a fool. He has never learned."

"And who do you plan to possess, Lux?" My voice hardened.

Lux ignored me, still staring at Ryann. "This binding is brief, ranging from hours to a few days, but this coin allows me to depart and reenter the willing human whenever I need to, until no power is left in the coin."

"Why a h-human body?" Ryann stammered. With good reason. Lux chatting about needing a human vessel and staring intently at Ryann had *me* freaking out. Not that I could do anything about it. Child of Chaos always trumped magical.

"It is necessary in order to cross the threshold into Atlantis; otherwise, the forcefield surrounding that ancient city will reject me. Similar to the wards placed upon this island but not nearly so specific—as long as I appear human, I may pass through," she explained. "My husband acquired his human form for the same purpose."

Well, that explains that. I'd wondered about it ever since we'd left the Fountain of Youth. Obviously, I'd realized it was the first part in getting to Atlantis, but I'd never had the facts laid bare with such wonderful simplicity. How hard would that have been for Erebus to say, huh? But I didn't like where this was headed.

"You're not possessing her, Lux." The words rasped from my throat, my hands balling into fists.

"That is not up to you, Finch. Not everything involves you, though I understand why you would think it does. And, since you are bound to my husband, you are not a viable option. Though, no offense intended, I prefer a feminine form to make my earthly visits." Lux shot me a dark stare. Ironic, considering she was the Empress of Light.

"You want to possess me?" Ryann squeaked.

"Must we call it that? I would rather refer to it as temporarily cohabiting your body." Lux glowed brighter, no doubt to show her power and frighten Ryann into submission.

"That doesn't make it better." Ryann gulped audibly, and I stepped between her and Lux.

"No way, Lux. Choose someone else." I couldn't bear the thought of Ryann going through what I had in Elysium. Being a backseat driver to your own body wasn't fun.

Lux turned back to Ryann. "You recall the deal you made with me, don't you? An exchange—I wiped that poor boy's mind, and you agreed to return the favor when the time came. I hope you are not the sort who breaks deals, as that never ends well. Rules must be upheld, Ryann. Your refusal will bring consequences."

It was my turn to be shocked by secret revelations. "Deal? You didn't mention a deal!"

Ryann paled. "I... had to."

"Are you friggin' serious? Has all this misery with Erebus not taught you anything about making deals with Children of mother-fudging Chaos?!" I dug my nails into my palms to stop myself from going off like a rocket. "You don't do it, Ryann! You just don't do it, not unless the whole damned world is at stake! Even then, at least hesitate. Adam would've been easy to mind-wipe if you'd called in the cavalry. We were waiting for your call, if anything went south. I can't believe this. What the hell were you thinking?!"

Tears brimmed in Ryann's eyes, and I immediately felt like a giant asshole. "It's like I told you—Adam freaked about the magical thing, and he wanted to bring down this world. What I didn't tell you was that he threatened to take it as high as he needed to. I panicked. I knew that if he left the apartment, he might blow the magical world wide open, and I couldn't let him do that. Lux made me the offer, and I... had to take it." She paused. "I should've told you, but I knew you'd be furious. It sounds stupid, even now, but I had no choice. I wanted to protect the people I cared about. You understand that, don't you?"

I sighed, totally shaken. "Of course I understand. That's been my mantra for the past year, but nobody took the least bit of notice! You should've taken a page from Harley's book, and your own book, for that matter, and found another way."

"There wasn't time," Ryann said quietly.

"I know, but—" I turned and cupped her face in my hands, deciding to be bold. But Lux chose that exact moment to mount her high horse.

"I hate to break this up, but there is no time now, either. Ryann made a deal with me, and she must uphold it. I am certain you would not care to see her suffer any ill effects of breaking her bargain."

I'm going to curse you out if you don't pipe down! Terror shivered through me. The worst kind... helpless terror. I couldn't intervene. Lux knew that; Ryann knew that; I knew that. Deals were deals. Hell, mine was proving damn near impossible to get out of, so what hope did Ryann have? But I hated it, right down to my core.

"You said you'd tell me the terms." Ryann's voice sounded stronger.

"I have." Lux tossed the coin before Ryann could say another word. Ryann's hand shot out to catch it, and the coin rested in her palm. Then it sank beneath her skin. Her face contorted in pain as the metal embedded itself in her flesh. I wrapped my arms around her, as if sheer willpower could fend off Lux.

"What's happening?" Ryann stared at me with panicked eyes. "I don't… feel so good."

"Hey, you just keep looking at me, okay? Just keep looking at me." I didn't know what else to do or say. I looked over my shoulder in time to see Lux spiral up in a stream of pure energy. I pulled Ryann into the tightest hug. She clung to me, and I felt her face scrunch up as a gasp of pain escaped her throat.

Next thing I knew, her body stiffened and her hands fell from my back. She lifted her head and looked me dead in the eyes. Instead of Ryann's beautiful blues, two pools of vivid white light shone back, and an icy smile rested on the lips I'd almost kissed.

"You can release me now," Lux said coldly. "I do not like to be touched by mortal hands. Years of human worship have left a rather unpleasant mark, and I should hate to have to forcibly remove you from this… rather awkward embrace."

Lux had taken over.

THIRTY-TWO

Finch

I glared at Lux, so furious I could've burst a blood vessel. "Why did you make a deal with her? She's human, Lux. What happened to all that BS about helping humans? You're just helping yourself because you can't keep a leash on your husband."

Lux hit me with another dark stare. Weird, through Ryann's eyes —the kind of look I used to get when I lashed out with Ted Bundy quips. "Need I remind you that it is not a good idea to irk me, Finch? I believe in aiding humanity when I can, but this is personal. One must pursue one's own path, even if that necessitates utilizing the occasional human vessel."

One can take a running leap into a woodchipper...

"You saved her just to use her," I shot back. "Everything you claim to be—shining light, the opposite end of the spectrum from Erebus —is a lie. Gaia would never do this."

"Gaia is soft. I am not. But I am not without kindness or under-standing. I will take good care of this form until I release her," Lux replied tersely. "As I mentioned, I chose her because I require a compliant human to cross into Atlantis. Note the word 'compliant.' I did not force anyone into anything."

"I bet that's what Hitler said, too." Venom dripped from my words. If she hadn't been in Ryann's body, I'd have done something stupid.

Lux rolled her eyes. "You are obviously upset, but there is no need for insults. Ryann asked a favor, and I granted it. That made her the perfect choice. She gained from it, and so have I. This is temporary. You will have all the sweet moments you desire when I am finished."

"Yeah, you say whatever makes you feel better." I fumed quietly, wishing the gargoyles would come back and tear Lux a new one. Once she was out of Ryann's body, of course.

Ryann-Lux's face hardened. "There was another reason I selected Ryann."

"Ah, now you're reaching the honesty part. Come on, what is it? Did you want to show Erebus up by proving it could be done without ruining the Fountain of Youth?"

She smirked. "No, though that is a side benefit. I needed to make sure you continued your part of the deal with my husband. You must be on the brink of panic, as you evidently have little faith in my ability to protect you from Erebus. I had to ensure you did not do something foolish. I will do all I can to get you out of your deal, when the time comes. But you must not interfere. You must continue to pretend to be a loyal servant."

"You think burying Erebus in the center of the earth will stop him from dragging me down with him? You're crazy, Lux." I shook my head in despair, wedged between a Lux-shaped rock and an Erebus-shaped hard place.

"I *will* help you, but if you continue to whine, I may feel less inclined to keep you breathing when all is said and done." Lux waited for my reply, and I forced my lips shut. Nothing good would come out of them now, and I didn't want to piss her off to the point of losing her assistance. I might need it if Harley's mission failed.

Plus, I had the slight satisfaction of knowing I had another pot on the stove, one which Lux knew nothing about. Katherine's words rang in my head: "I have backups for my backups." Evil or not, she'd had some good advice.

"What's he done to turn you nuclear, huh?" I peered at her curiously.

Lux chuckled. "It is not what he has done but what he hopes to do. I must see for myself how far he will go. If he pleases me, he lives. If he doesn't, he can expect a long few millennia sweating his Chaos away in the center of the earth. My terms for you are not dissimilar."

"Have you ever tried marriage counseling? The two of you could save yourselves, and the rest of us, a lot of hassle if you just sat down and talked it out." I folded my arms and looked over the ocean beyond the island. The sun still shone, and the water sparkled, but I couldn't enjoy it anymore.

Lux sighed. "Erebus does not like to talk."

"Are you kidding? I can't get him to shut up, if it's about himself."

"That's precisely the point," Lux replied with a note of sadness. Their problems seemed oddly human and reminded me of Adam and Ryann's relationship. They'd drifted apart somewhere along the way and were never able to put the pieces back together. By the looks of it, Lux and Erebus were in the same boat. But Lux was the Adam in this scenario—still clinging to something that had already died.

"Anyway, we are getting off topic." Lux rallied. "Either you do my bidding, or I hurt Ryann. It really is that simple."

"And you know what I have to say to that?" I leveled my gaze at her. The face I loved, worn by a goddess I hated.

She arched an eyebrow. "And what might that be?"

"You're more like him than you think."

The last hours before the moon rose stretched in awkward silence. Ryann-Lux and I perched on the cliff overlooking the leather bag. I'd suggested some games to pass the time, but she'd vetoed instantly. I guessed she needed more time to get comfortable inhabiting Ryann's character and couldn't be distracted with I-Spy or charades.

"What does he want from Atlantis, anyway?" I prodded a bit, to see if she'd give me any more details about this rare jewel.

Lux side-eyed me. "That is for me to know, and you ought to remain quiet on the matter. It does not concern mere mortals."

Uh, it kind of does, when I'm the one building all these bridges for Erebus to get it... But I knew better than to argue with uppity pseudo-deities. She'd probably turn me into a lizard or "accidentally" break Ryann's arm to get me to shut up.

Leaves rustled in the woodland behind us, the imposing trees standing sentinel over the cove. I turned, expecting to see my two favorite gargoyles galloping out of the shadows. Instead, Erebus emerged, as if he'd appeared from the darkness itself.

Oh, crap... Lux looked entirely like Ryann, now that her glowing eyes had faded to Ryann's usual blue. But would the ruse fool Erebus?

"Play along," Lux hissed. "He won't be able to sense me in this vessel, and you had best not give me away. Otherwise—"

"I know," I interrupted.

Erebus approached, looking very stressed for a lazy Child of Chaos.

"There you are!" he barked. "You were supposed to return to the center of the island. How did I know you would be the one to cause me unnecessary strain, Finch? Sometimes I think you enjoy annoying me, to see how far I can be pushed."

I blinked innocently. "I assumed we were meant to protect our bags until the moon rose. Wouldn't want an animal running off with it."

"Hmm..." Erebus eyed me, barely noticing Ryann. "I suppose it saved you an additional journey here, though I can't say the same for myself. I do not appreciate chasing after my servants."

"Maybe you should give me a bell, so you always know where I am." I immediately regretted the joke, in case he actually decided to run with it. Honestly, I was just trying to buy myself some time. All this had happened so quickly, and control appeared to be slipping through my fingers like water.

Lux may have warned me not to give her away, but right now, Lux could shove it where the sun didn't shine. She wasn't the only one you didn't want to piss off, which these Children seemed to have forgotten. I wasn't all happy little elf and starshine, either. And

I was done making boots for this shoemaker, who showed no appreciation whatsoever.

"Yeah, it must be *sooooo* hard, walking everywhere in your human body. Good for the glutes, though." I had no idea what I was doing. "I bet spiraling down onto this island took a lot out of you, huh? How are you doing with all those limitations, anyway? It must suck being weak, after millennia of being the toughest guy on the block. Well, I guess you got what you asked for."

If I can get him angry, maybe it'll force Lux to reveal herself. She still needed me. She couldn't let Erebus pound me to dust and ruin her plans. But she'd have to use magic if he tried it, and then he'd know she wasn't who she appeared to be. Not exactly foolproof, but it was the best scheme I had. Plus, he had a vested interest in not harming Ryann. He still needed me. And, if I blew Lux's cover, I'd have leverage to get Erebus to keep Ryann safe, whatever might happen next.

"What did you say to me?" Erebus's smoke billowed from his human body.

"It must suck that you need a human body to get into Atlantis, right? You have all this cosmic juice, and you can't even get across the threshold to a drowned city. It's… well, it's frankly embarrassing." I kept up the insults, knowing I was pushing some dangerous buttons. I had to admit, I was enjoying myself a little. "What is this rare jewel you're after, anyway? Does it give you more power? Seems a bit greedy, if you ask me. How much power do you need, when you're locked up most of the time in your otherworld? Oh wait… you don't have an otherworld anymore, do you? Another limitation, courtesy of your fancy meat suit."

"You dare to speak to me this way? I'll show you how much

power I still possess, and I guarantee I have more in my little finger than you do within your entire measly person!" Erebus hurled black magic at me. Smoky strands tore from his palms like tentacles and pummeled my chest. Blinding pain tore through my veins, my cells jangling. I'd been through Erebus's pain spells before, but this felt different. Like something important was being torn from my insides.

White tendrils snaked from my skin and lifted into the air, creating a spectral version of me. I stared up at the ghost, horrified. Well, I should've been horrified, but I couldn't actually feel anything. Just an ache where my soul had been. Everything echoed back... hollow, like shouting into the void.

Well, I got him angry... But Lux hadn't moved a muscle. Damn. After thousands of years bound to each other, maybe she knew something I didn't. And I'd paid the price for trying to get a step ahead of her.

This hurt beyond ordinary pain. Having your soul torn away couldn't be described. But it was like a microscopic gnome had crept under my skin and unpicked all the minute fastenings that tied my soul to my body, each tiny pinprick forming one gigantic throb of agony, combined with the wrenching void of losing the most precious part of yourself. The intangible who-knew-what that made us who we were.

"I do not know what game you're playing, Finch, but I am not to be toyed with. I am under an exorbitant amount of stress, and I'm sure you do not want me to snap!" Erebus shoved my soul back in my body like a careless airport worker chucking baggage into the hold, disregarding the *Fragile* stickers. It took my breath away, leaving me doubled over and panting as all those unpicked soul threads fastened back into place.

"That wasn't… you snapping?" I wheezed.

"No." He lowered his hands. "You are lucky I still require you, or I'd have sent your soul directly to the afterlife. I expect you shortly at the island's Bestiary."

My gaze lifted in confusion. "The Bestiary? Why?"

"Melody informed me that we do not yet have enough power to charge the moving spell. Which she somehow neglected to mention beforehand." He puffed out an exasperated sigh. "So, we must gather more power, and we do not have long. The full moon is coming, and the bags must be set aflame. Those Purge beasts will be the answer to our deficit in strength."

Erebus turned on his heel and strode off without another word, though I noticed him get whacked in the face by a low-hanging branch as he stormed away. Had I not been reeling from having my soul temporarily removed, I'd have snorted. Oh, to be that branch.

As soon as he disappeared, Lux turned to me with a smug grin. "I told you not to try anything foolish."

"I was trying to keep his focus off you," I lied. "You're welcome, by the way."

"Whatever you say." Lux walked to the edge of the cliff. "You had better light that pouch. The moon is, indeed, rising."

Ignoring her from sheer frustration, I headed back down the stone steps cut into the cliff and made for the protected leather pouch.

The tide had come in, and the water gingerly touched the defensive bubble only to be diverted by the forcefield, like a magnet bending tap water in third-grade science class. Gritting my teeth against the cold, I waded through the shallows up to my ankles. My hands delved into the bubble, and I conjured a ball of Fire. As the creator of this forcefield, I could reach in and out.

I waited until the moon had fully risen and cast a silver glow on the ocean before I shot a few bursts of Fire at the bag. It ignited instantly. I watched the flames for a few more moments to make sure the whole thing had been engulfed. Satisfied that Erebus wouldn't have anything else to complain about, I left the bag to do its thing.

"That is a rather neat trick, Finch. Where did you learn that?" Ryann-slash-Lux eyed the forcefield.

"Where do you think?" I replied, still grumpy.

"One of your mother's?"

I flashed a sarcastic smile. "Pat yourself on the back."

"It is good to see you thinking outside the box. You might have had a much harder time lighting that fire, had the bag become damp. Yes, very sharp intuition." Lux nodded proudly. It burned me up inside—who did she think she was? My *actual* mother?

"Actually, it was Ryann's idea. I just put up the magical heft. What can I say, we make a great team." I left the shallows and walked right up to the cliff face. I didn't have the energy to traipse across the island after dark, with all its dense forests and creepy hidden critters. Nope, this called for a quick trip through a chalk door. I sketched the outline on stone and whispered the *Aperi Si Ostium* spell. Honestly, I had no idea why everyone whispered it. It'd probably have worked just as well if I screamed at the doorway, which was exactly what I wanted to do. A much-needed vent. But hey, I wasn't one to break tradition.

Lux moved to pass through the chalk door first, but she turned on the threshold. "You have pleased me, Finch, despite your obvious attempt at sabotage. But if you try to thwart me again, you *will* force my hand. Ryann will suffer for your transgressions."

"Yeah, I get it!" This time, I did scream.

Lux strode through the doorway, leaving me huffing and puffing like the proverbial big bad wolf. Oh, I'd blow that piggy's house down a million times over, and kick her out of her shiny-ass other-world, given half a chance.

Cool your engines, Finch. My brain kicked in with some common sense. Ryann's safety was on the line. I couldn't let my anger get the better of me. There'd be time for retribution later, perhaps, after Lux made good on her promise.

Taking a deep breath, I followed Lux through the chalk door and slammed it behind me. One of those bone-shaking slams adored by teenagers the world over. It felt so good, a small defiance to keep me from losing it.

"Easy there. You trying to break that thing off its hinges?" Nash offered a nervous smile.

"Sorry," I mumbled. My eyes darted straight to Melody, willing her to sense the weird emotions in Ryann-Lux's head. But I got nada back. Just her usual sweet face, apparently sensing nothing amiss. Lux had clearly covered her bases.

We stood outside the island Bestiary, all the new Muppet Babies back together. The trouble was, I didn't see their body-gargoyles anywhere, and I'd taken great pains to threaten them into protecting my pals. I mean, there was no way Joker would've left Nash for anything, even if he'd gotten bored or distracted by a plump swamp goblin. That one had a little crush going on. So, where were they?

"No gargoyles?" I asked, looking around in case they were hiding from Erebus. Or Lux. Purge beasts were more perceptive than us "mere mortals." Maybe they'd cut their losses at two Children of Chaos.

Luke shook his head. "They disappeared after we lit the spell bags."

Hmm... This island vacay was getting weirder by the second.

THIRTY-THREE

Ryann

Sitting in the backseat of your own body wasn't comfortable. My consciousness had been squeezed into a corner of my sentient mind, though I could see and hear everything happening in the real world. Like an old, blurry movie playing out on the big screen, only I couldn't turn to the person next to me to talk about it. I couldn't speak at all. I kept trying, but Lux held the reins now. Even my vision had been covered by a haze of light, warping everything as though it had an intense filter on it.

You need to cease your attempts to regain control. Lux's voice echoed in my head. *You offered anything I asked in return for wiping that poor handsome young man's mind. Be obedient and diligent, and this will all be over before you know it.*

That's easy for you to say, I replied. I hoped she could hear me. *You're not the one trapped in your own body, unable to speak. When you made that deal with me, you never, for one second, suggested it might be something like this. What sort of person refuses to give the terms and condi-tions before making someone sign on the dotted line? That's bad business.*

Lux chuckled in my mind. *What sort of person accepts a deal without demanding the terms and conditions? I helped you in a moment of despera-tion. That should suffice as reason for why I have chosen you as my vessel. I have acolytes who would give their right leg to be in your position.*

Then why didn't you choose one of them? I retorted. Having her point out the unfairness of our deal didn't soothe my fury. Yes, I'd been desperate, and she'd milked that for all it was worth. True manipulation, kicking someone while they were down.

They are touched by my Light, having served me for so long. Atlantis may have noticed and cast them out. But you—you have not been under my influence long enough for the threshold to sense my presence. Lux sounded smug. I could picture her swirling vortex of a face, in her true form, basking in glory. *Besides, you are adored by Finch, and I must ensure he remains on his mission. Having your form increases the chance of that happening.*

That's sick, Lux. You can't just threaten people to make them do what you want. Have you considered—oh, I don't know—asking nicely? Maybe if you'd explained more to Finch about what you were doing, he'd have gone along with your ideas willingly. Plus, when has he ever given any indica-tion that he won't continue his mission? This is the last stage in getting to Atlantis, right? And he's still here! He's doing everything Erebus tells him to. If that's not showing dedication, then I don't know what you want. You don't need to force him into things by using me as leverage.

Lux sighed. *Your voice is so grating. I will put it to you simply: I am on a mission of my own, and I will see it through to the end. You can either struggle and suffer in vain or go along with it. I suggest you choose the easy path, for both our sakes. I'd hate to have to push you farther into your subconscious mind. Call this a gift—that you get to see and hear. I do not have to allow you that courtesy.*

Well, that shut me right up. I didn't want to be pushed any farther back. No way. I wanted to stay as close to Finch and the others as I could, even if I wasn't the one in control.

Excellent choice. Lux laughed and left me to my secondhand view of the world.

Erebus had wrenched open the doors to the Bestiary and led Nash, Luke, and Finch inside. They filtered out as a quartet, carrying long pythons of cable with a strange, cylindrical glass bulb at the very end. The python's head, so to speak. Erebus set it tentatively on the remains of one of the crumbled statues Finch had brought down when he unraveled the hexes. He stood before the bulb with his arms raised, ready to... do something. I'd heard Erebus mention more power being needed, but I had no clue how they would make that happen.

Melody sidled up to me. "Hey, are you okay? I know I keep promising not to delve into people's emotions without permission, but there are so many flying out of you that I couldn't help it. I didn't want to show that I sensed something, in case it worried Finch—you know how he gets—but I need to make sure you're all right. Did something happen with Finch? Is it Adam?"

Lux spoke on my behalf, though I was desperate to send some kind of SOS to Melody. "I'm fine, just a lot going on, you know? All this Adam stuff, and then the Finch stuff, and being thrown into Erebus's business... it's driving me crazy, to be honest, but I'll be okay. You know me."

Gah, she nailed me... That sounded exactly like something I'd say.

"Oh... of course. Anyone would be," Melody replied, her tone flat. She looked skeptical.

Don't you believe her! I'm in here! I tried to send out some feelings of panic, but I had no way to know if they'd reached Melody.

Enough of that, Lux cut in. *Another whimper from you, and I will bury you. And when that happens, there are no assurances that you will return to your mortal mind as you were. There may be pieces missing— valued memories, skills, the knowledge of loved ones... You wouldn't want to risk waking up and not remembering Finch, would you?*

Lux had played us like a pair of fiddles. She was using me to keep Finch in line and using Finch to keep me in line. But I held on to every scrap of determination I had left. I felt a sudden flurry of sensation that didn't belong to me. A feeling of worry, directly from Lux. Clearly, she'd sensed that Melody had grown wary of her.

"Will this be enough power?" Nash distracted me from my hopes. "There weren't many critters locked away in there."

Erebus shot him a warning look. "This will be plenty. Katherine possessed some very rare Purge beasts. Their Chaos energy is worth far more than, say, a handful of Sylphs." He grinned to himself as if it was a private joke. I felt Lux bristle with annoyance. Understandable, considering the Sylphs were her... I didn't know what to call them. Pets? Creations? Servants?

"Wait... you're not going to kill them, are you?" Melody ran from my side, her eyes wide with horror.

"The weak may perish, but the strong will survive. As is always the case," Erebus replied matter-of-factly. "Now, stand aside, unless you want to be the first casualty."

"No! You can't kill innocent creatures. They haven't done

anything wrong!" Melody protested. The pain in her voice stung me, and even Lux seemed somewhat moved by her display of bravery.

Erebus turned to face her. "Their deaths are necessary, but not all will die. That sounds more than fair to me. At least they will be useful, instead of fading away in glass cages."

"Is everything just a tool to you—something to be used?" Melody wrung her hands, despairing. "They're living things. The least you can do is show them some respect!"

Luke hurried to Melody. "Melody, this isn't the time. I know it's sad and unfair, but you've said it yourself, time and time again... he is a Child of Chaos. Don't get on his bad side, I'm begging you."

"Listen to your pet," Erebus hissed. "Time, and my patience, are rapidly running out. If I do not succeed in this because of your mortal qualms about evaporating what is, essentially, energy bundled into a random shape, then perhaps I will use *you* as my power source instead."

"Please, Melody." Luke stared at her in desperation.

"But..." Melody's lip trembled.

"I know." He put his arms around her, and she buried her face in his chest to avoid seeing the next step.

He's right there, Melody... My heart went out to them.

Mortals rarely see what is right in front of them until it is too late, Lux chimed in. *Though it is somewhat baffling that she hasn't noticed his adoration for her. She's an Empath, and he is not exactly subtle. Even Finch looks like a master of discretion compared to that one.*

Before I could retort, Erebus lifted his hands to the heavens, seizing the entirety of my focus. He began to recite Latin that boomed across the island, sending a shudder up my spine. Melody must've given him the necessary spell earlier, and he seemed to be a quick learner. It rolled off his tongue as though it had always been there.

"*Terra. Ventus. Aqua. Ignis. Septentrionalis. Meridionalis. Orientem. Occidentem. Audi me. Ego sum vocant. Mutationes fiunt. Lavamini mundi estote auferte clypeus. Redire ad priorem locum. Audi me. Ego sum vocant. Audite vocem meam. Senex mundum ire necesse est. Ad illud reponere. Cor meum non quaerit.*"

As he started the second recital, he drew a hand back. A stream of black mist spiraled out, straight to the weird Bestiary bulb in the center of the clearing. The first coiled tendrils touched the bulb, and the entire thing lit up with blinding light. I wanted to close my eyes to protect my retinas, but Lux didn't seem fazed. She kept staring as vivid bronze energy poured from the bulb and traveled back up the stream of black. It disappeared into Erebus's body, cracks of light slithering up his jet-black arms, a few shining on the bare skin at his throat.

More and more energy built inside him as he repeated his chant, five times in total. As he finished the fifth recital, he lifted his head skyward, and all that pent-up light exploded out of him. All I could see was a pillar of pure radiance, piercing straight through the gauzy filter of the interdimensional bubble.

Four more pillars shot up—north, south, east, west. The four pillars arched and met with Erebus's pillar in the center, forming one giant ball of pulsating light where the five streams connected.

A moment later, all that gathered energy pounded downward, using Erebus as a lightning rod. It flowed through him into the ground, followed by an earth-shattering blast that knocked us all to the ground, Lux included.

There are safer ways to do this, Lux grumbled, dragging my body back to its feet. She rose first. Another sign that I wasn't me. A blow like that would've knocked a human into the middle of next week. And it definitely would've left me unconscious. Unfortunately, Melody hadn't seen the feat, as she was being helped up by Luke.

However, it seemed the blast had some effect on Lux. Not at all what I'd expected. She'd just regained our feet when a wave of memories crashed into my skull. Memories that didn't belong to me. They were more like flashbacks, ignited by the detonation.

I saw a strange city with towering silver spires as far as the eye could see and buildings made of shimmering white stone that reminded me of mother-of-pearl. Above my head, the unmistakable shift of dark water flowed over an interdimensional dome. No sunlight penetrated the shield, the city illuminated by huge orbs that hung at even intervals.

Atlantis. I didn't know how I knew, but the name traveled through my mind alongside the visions.

The image in my mind shifted to a Grecian courtyard surrounded by bronze statues of gods and goddesses—some of them a little too familiar. I had a strange, subconscious sense that one of them had Erebus's face, and the slender female form beside him had to be Lux. Back then, they'd been regarded as deities, so it made sense that they'd appeared in the architecture of this bizarre realm. Then again, why had Atlantis prohibited their entry if they'd been worshipped?

I jumped as Erebus appeared before me in somewhat solid form. Not quite human, not quite cosmic. I realized I must've been seeing these flashbacks through Lux's eyes. Erebus's face twisted in a sour look, his mouth moving vehemently. I couldn't hear what he was saying. Hands gestured in my vision—Lux's hands. And they weren't happy. Waggling like this always spelled an argument, and Erebus's increasingly furious features only cemented my assumption. They'd had a mud-slinging match in the middle of Atlantis; I just didn't know why.

The scene shifted again. I stood at the end of a cavernous hall with a throne directly before me. Well, before Lux. The back of the throne emulated the silver spires of the city, inlaid with blue and green pods of blown glass that resembled bubbles. An older man with silvering hair and a blue streak across his cheek glowered at me from the impressive seat. He wore a crown of silver, each spike designed to look like a waving frond of seaweed, though they glittered with about a hundred precious gemstones, with one enormous gem front and center.

Is that the rare jewel Erebus is after? Or is it the whole crown?

Ear-splitting sound finally accompanied the memories, coming from the Atlantean king. He raised his hands, and blue light burst from them, carried on a wave of tangible fury.

"For as long as we exist, you shall never return!" the king bellowed. The blue light careened into me as Lux's head turned to look beside her, where Erebus was also struck by that powerful energy. The hallway spun, as if Erebus and Lux had been physically cast from Atlantis by that solitary, defiant king.

So, that's why they can't enter Atlantis. Perhaps that spell, cast by the king, had outlasted the city itself. A last-ditch attempt to prevent the Children of Chaos from claiming that drowned world for themselves.

The images vanished. I found myself back in the clearing, watching Erebus emerge from the ashes of the spell, miraculously intact. From within the nearby Bestiary, the most heartbreaking sounds rose. Howls and cries of bestial loss. As Erebus had said, not all those creatures would survive, and it sounded like others barely had. In the magical world, Purge beasts were often thought of as byproducts. But hearing those harrowing sounds made me realize they were so much more. They were creatures capable of feeling and loving and caring, the way Murray and Selma did.

There was nothing I could do, though, so I tried not to think about it. Instead, I focused on what I'd seen. Lux and Erebus had visited Atlantis before, but it must have been long ago, and it involved an incident that had seen them cast out altogether. I had to be onto something here, and I needed to keep digging, for all our sakes. If I could somehow find a loophole, maybe I could stop Erebus, or get us some leverage… something that might save Finch. Anything. I kept these intentions abstract, not forming thoughts in case Lux picked up on them.

"Look sharp, guys." Nash dusted himself off and checked Huntress over.

"What do you mean?" Luke was similarly evaluating Melody for injuries.

"That spell will bring Davin down on us at any moment. He's been following this mission from the get-go; he's not going to miss this, even if he's still missing parts." Nash glanced around as though he genuinely expected Davin to arrive that very second. It certainly made me nervous, though Lux didn't seem to care.

Finch turned to me, about to speak, when his eyes widened. I'd seen that same look a few times since we'd set foot on this island. Lux glanced over my shoulder to follow his gaze, and my heart lurched. A woman stepped from the woodland behind us. But who was she? A spy of Davin's? A leftover cultist who'd been waiting for her moment to strike? She had large, violet eyes and a short, blunt cut of black hair.

Nash whipped out a knife. "Who are you?"

Finch gestured for him to lower his weapon. "It's okay. I know her."

"You do?" Nash frowned.

You do? I tried to echo Nash's sentiments, but Lux didn't allow it.

He nodded. "It's her... Adley."

Finch hadn't been going crazy at all, though he'd had me worried for a minute back at the library. Mental health was a journey, with troughs and peaks, and though Nash had given him a potion to keep his delusions at bay, there was no such thing as a cure-all for conditions like Finch's. I was glad to be wrong, at least when it came to him seeing things.

Adley de la Barthe was real. And she was here. But why?

THIRTY-FOUR

Finch

"You see her, right?" I whispered to Nash.

"'Course I see her," he replied. "I'd have thrown this knife at her if you hadn't stopped me."

My heart strained. "It wouldn't have done you any good."

Adley's form phased in and out, a momentary glitch showing the corpse beneath. Not her corpse, which duly gave me the shivers, but the body being used to hold her returned spirit. Nash's eyes widened in understanding.

"She's dead?"

I nodded, tears welling. "Because of me."

Adley stood at the forest's edge, waiting. Bowing my head, conscious of everyone's eyes on me, I walked toward her. I couldn't keep her waiting any longer. How long had she been waiting? Since her death? What if her spirit had never made it to her home coven with her body?

What if Katherine had made one last cruel jab and trapped her here after she passed? After all, she'd promised to resurrect Adley if I rejoined her. How could she have made that offer without knowing where Adley's spirit was? I'd thought it was a lie, given my mother's penchant for those... but now I wasn't so sure.

"Finch..." Her voice drifted over me in a faraway lilt.

"You're actually here." I gazed into her eyes, feeling every emotion under the sun: grief, joy, bitterness, anger. "But... why?"

"I've missed you." Her lip trembled as she reached out to me. I jumped as her fingertips made contact and sent a chill through me. It reminded me of when Davin Dingleweed and Alton had brought back Hester and Hiram. My first and last moment with my dad.

I lowered my gaze. "You're here because you missed me? That doesn't make sense."

"In part. And no, I suppose not." She gripped my arm tighter. Whether it made sense or not, I couldn't give up the opportunity to say everything I should've when she was alive.

"I'm so sorry for everything I did, Adley. And everything I didn't do. I should've been there for you. I wasn't good to you, and I can't change that. If I could go back, I'd have done more to save you. I'd have hidden you away where Katherine could never have tracked you down," I rambled, trying to get it all out.

Adley smiled sadly. "There is no use dwelling on the past. I chose to stand by you, no matter what. Love made me stay, and love made me certain that you would find out, one day, that you could be so much more. You always had good in you. Of course, I wish I could still be with you, to share in what you've become."

"I'm so sorry." The tears fell, and the ugly sobs came in force.

She touched me again, and a jarring shiver spread down my arm. "No, I'm the one who should be sorry." Her eyes glinted with her own tears. "I'm not here by choice…"

"You aren't?" My Katherine theory started to disintegrate, since there was no way anyone could've known we'd return here. Aside from two people—Davin and Erebus.

She wiped her eyes. "I'm here to kill you, and there's nothing I can do about it."

I stepped back involuntarily, my eyes bulging. "What?!"

"I'm sorry… it's not what I want."

"It's Davin, isn't it?" I asked, recovering from the initial shock. "He's got you like a puppet on a string, doesn't he?"

She nodded. "Davin dragged me from the afterlife a few weeks ago and sent me here with instructions to wait for you."

I seethed with rage. The woman I'd loved stood in front of me, alive for all intents and purposes, only to put an end to me. And through no fault of her own.

"We figured he'd be coming for the Gateway after he put himself back together again." I balled my hands into fists. "I didn't think he'd stoop this low, bringing you back to get me out of the way."

If Davin had brought Adley back weeks ago, then this had been his endgame all along. A way to stop me if I managed to get ahead of him. Cerberus at the gates of Hades, only more beautiful and way more painful.

"He's coming now, isn't he?" I held on to her peaceful image a while longer, trying to freeze time before she became my assassin.

Her face crumpled. "He's already here."

Chalk doors opened around us. Adley had been the prologue;

now the main act was beginning. Davin stepped through a door of his own while cultists filtered through the rest—some of the ones who'd scampered off in Maine and locked themselves in the bar. But he'd brought reserves, too, from the island's spook pantry. Shimmering specters appeared out of nowhere, their eyes tinged purple. The ghosts of cultists who'd died right here on this island. Though it didn't stop at spiritual theft—their edges solidified, implying they each had a temporary physical body.

Davin had clearly been stepping up his Necromancy game. I had no idea how he'd pulled this off. It shouldn't have been possible, but here I was, staring at the impossible. I imagined some rare spell or sketchy artifact had come into play. The guy had raised a literal army of zombies to bring us down. It was flattering, in a way.

Erebus nodded slowly, somewhere between impressed and livid. In his human body, he had limits. Could he take on an undead army singlehandedly? I doubted it; not without tearing a few holes in his precious meatsuit.

I glanced at Lux and lowered my voice to a whisper so the others wouldn't hear. "You going to help out here?"

She gave a barely perceptible shrug and replied in an equally conspiratorial whisper. "You're on your own, Finch. I am pretending to be human, remember? I highly doubt it would go unnoticed if I suddenly obliterated these people. Besides, it is not in my nature to enter conflict."

"Only when it suits you, huh? You'll get splinters in your ass, sitting on the fence like that," I replied dryly. "Silly me, to think you might want to make yourself useful. Anyway, it's not like we didn't expect Davin to show up again... albeit not with a zombie horde. That's a surprising little treat for us to deal with."

Nash had a fan of knives ready. Luke, meanwhile, had his palms up and was drawing metal from everywhere possible. Fortunately, the Bestiary had plenty to supply him. It was just a shame there weren't many beasts left to join the fight. And we didn't have Harley to persuade them to help out. Those who were left were more likely to rip our throats out than attack this horde.

Melody caught my eye. She crouched over her bag, pulling out bits and pieces and forming a ball of random things shoved together. Evidently, she had an idea. She clutched the ball in her hands, whispering to it. The whole thing ignited. Melody skimmed the ball across the ground like she was ten points down at the local bowling alley.

It exploded at the feet of a confused zombie, enveloping a few more who'd foolishly stood nearby. Their solid forms disintegrated in a powdery cloud of ash that turned my stomach, rendering them inert spirits who could look but not touch. A few even attempted to touch their own arms, only for their hands to pass straight through.

Yes, Melody! Transformative spells for the win! The trouble was, I didn't know how much of that stuff she had in her bag. But it would slow them down, if nothing else.

Erebus, on the other hand, was doing absolutely jack squat. He just stood there, staring at Davin like a long-lost boyfriend, equal parts admiration and loathing. The most beautiful of all bromances. Frenemy on frenemy. Davin stared back with a little more triumph on his slimy face.

I didn't know where to turn. Adley had been resurrected to kill me, but the murderous intent didn't seem to have kicked in just yet. Did I try and get her to safety, at the expense of Lux-occupied

Ryann? I wasn't sure I could protect both, not with the enemy surrounding us.

A chalk door might've worked, but what if Adley couldn't get through? I didn't know the spiritual limitations of chalk doors. Adley might make it, only to get separated from the animated corpse. I couldn't have handled that, even if Adley *was* here to kill me. My heart was a mess, the old and new colliding at the worst moment.

"Shall we get this show on the road?" Davin declared. He lifted his hands and released a wave of energy into the center of the island, no doubt giving it the new coordinates to open the Gateway. After all, we'd done the hard part, unpicking Katherine's work. All he had to do was sign the dotted line and get this place where it needed to go.

The moment to make a decision whizzed by as the island began to thrum. The trees shook violently, knocking a few ambling zombies off their feet with the intensity. Panicking, I grabbed Adley and wrapped my free hand around the nearest tree, clinging for dear life. Guilt twisted in my stomach. I'd left Ryann behind, praying Lux would protect her. Honestly, she probably had a better chance of surviving with Lux holding the reins, but I still felt like crap that I'd chosen Adley over her.

"You shouldn't protect me, Finch," Adley whispered miserably. "I can't fight Davin's will forever. The moment he pushes the destruct button, I will try to kill you. I won't have a choice."

"Well, that's not happening yet, is it?" I clutched her tight as the island twisted, the very atoms of it fragmenting into puffs of bronze dust. Glancing down, I saw that my own body had started to disintegrate. It was like being sucked through a djinn portal but on a massive scale. Everything got drawn in, until I no longer had any sense of being. The molecules of me jangled together with everyone else's, my mind vaguely conscious of the island spiraling up into a single, enormous globe of energy that would've made the sun envious, dragging everything into it like a not-so-black hole.

The next moment, a resounding *snap* echoed, like thunder. And everything, including me, disappeared.

THIRTY-FIVE

Finch

The island and everything on it reappeared, though not quite the way I'd expected. I'd figured we'd pop right up wherever we were supposed to go, and everything would look normal. Instead, the island sped across open expanses of ocean, the starlight flashing past.

Though the earthquake still rumbled through the island, everyone seemed to have gained their sea legs. The zombies' eyes glowed violet—Davin using Necromancy to give commands.

My head whipped around to look at Adley, who was still in my arms. Her hands reached for my throat, the strain showing in her face. She was trying to fight the impulse with everything she had. I saw the veins bulge in her arms. I let go of her as though she were made of piranhas, staggering back.

"I'm sorry," she whimpered. "Get away from me. As far as you can!"

I did as she asked, though it tore me up to leave her to fend off

Davin's influence alone. Running full pelt, I joined the rest of the new Muppet Babies. Out of the corner of my eye, I noticed Lux slinking behind an old hut.

Still not entering the conflict, huh? How noble of you. It pissed me off to know we had a power player on our team, but she'd decided to bench herself. Then again, it meant Ryann was out of harm's way. That was worth losing one of our most valuable assets, however selfish I might've sounded. And if Erebus found out wifey darling was here, he'd flip. Maybe he'd even hurt Ryann, just to ruin Lux's chance of following us to Atlantis.

"Luke, duck!" Melody shouted. He'd decided to use himself as her human shield.

"What?" Luke glanced back and quickly ducked as a ball of mangled ingredients sailed over his head. It ignited on the ground, taking down another cluster of zombies. They stared in blank surprise as they poofed into dust, returning to their spirit forms.

Huntress charged forward and flung herself at a zombie. I should've looked away to prevent any ensuing nightmares, but I couldn't. Huntress tore out the ambling flesh puppet's throat. But that didn't stop its advance. Huntress then ripped off its forearm, and it still kept walking toward our group.

Well... that's new.

I realized I had merely been spectating this creepy battle. Turning to make sure Adley wasn't encroaching, I lifted my palms and sent out a combination of Fire and Telekinesis. One to hold the zombies in place, one to toast them. The first zombie sparked like a firecracker, the temporary skin and bone crumbling to ash. But the Fire sputtered out before it reached any more of the grisly assailants.

Another of Melody's bombs went off, flattening me to the

ground, face first. I jumped up straightaway once I spotted Erebus standing on the sidelines.

"You might want to help!" I yelled at him. My voice seemed to jolt him out of his private reverie. Davin was actively trying to screw up his plan, and he wasn't doing a damn thing. Lights on, no one home kind of vibe. I had no idea why he'd hesitated, but he needed to get his ass in gear.

Erebus hunched his shoulders and clasped his hands together. Black smoke billowed from between them and cascaded down in a dark waterfall, drifting over the ground. The strands slithered up the zombies' legs and wrapped around them, crushing them with sheer Child of Chaos power.

Davin had a semicircle of cultists defending him, shooting every Elemental ability out there, including a few rare ones—a Glacier, a Geode, and a Terra. The latter I vaguely knew, since there'd been only one in Katherine's ranks. She possessed the ability to bring temporary sentience to anything natural around her. And, right now, she had the trees around us coming to life, their branches ready to swipe us into oblivion.

I realized why Davin needed the cultist taskforce when he poured purple magic from his hands, recharging the groaning zombies with another temporary burst of life. That seemed to be taking up most of his energy, which meant the army he'd brought— the living and the undead—needed to pick up the slack. Whether that would work to our advantage or not, I had no clue. But at least with him distracted by Necromancy, we weren't on the receiving end of his crippling pain spells.

"Finch, watch out!" Melody spun and hurled a bomb in my direction. I twisted away, catching a glimpse of Adley about to plunge a knife in my neck. Tears streamed down her cheeks, and her knuckles whitened on the hilt.

"I'm sorry, Finch. I don't want to… I don't want to do this. I still care about you with all my heart. I don't want to end your life." Her hand shook as she tried to pull the blade back. The bomb had done nothing to affect her, since she'd been resurrected properly, unlike these other stumbling, braindead biters.

"Fight it, Adley!" I backed away only to end up face-to-jaws with a zombie. I slammed a blast of Fire in its face, and it went up in flames, blasting my skin with heat. Where its temporary body had been, ash drifted down in bleak, gray snow.

"I'm trying," she murmured desperately. "I'm trying so hard, but he's in control. I can't stop!"

My heart broke for her. "What can I do?"

"You can't do anything. Just stay away from me." She shook her head vehemently. "I don't know how to stop myself from killing you."

I wanted to hold her. I wanted to take her pain away. But that would've ended with a blade in my throat. Davin had tricked me and deceived me at every step of this mission, but he'd never made me feel so utterly broken. I guessed that was the point, to drive me to the brink of submission, knowing I'd never lift a finger to hurt Adley. I'd rather have let her kill me than inflict pain on her again.

"I can't bear it, Finch. Make it stop!" Adley crumpled to the ground, the knife clenched in her hands. All around me, knives tore through the air, bombs exploded, and random shards of metal flew. And we were caught in the center of it all—two lost souls who'd loved one another, once upon a time, now facing the prospect that one of us had to die.

I knew I deserved to die with Adley tonight, as payment for the pain I'd caused her. But Ryann kept my desire to survive flickering brightly. I'd done wrong, and I wanted to make amends... but I wanted Ryann more.

"Adley... you can fight him. He's busy with the zombies. You can push him out, I know you can." I risked rushing to her, kneeling on the ground. With one hand, laced with Telekinesis, I grabbed the knife and pressed it flush against my chest, where the pointy end wouldn't be able to sink into me. With the other, I held her. She sobbed on my shoulder, her arms looping around my neck. A little unsettling, considering they were corpse arms, but I ignored that for her sake.

"I missed you so much," she whispered into my ear. "I thought about you when the cultist killed me. My very last thought... it belonged to you, just like my heart."

I had flashbacks to Remington and Odette, and how her last thoughts had been of him. But Adley's and my love story had ended. I hated that it had, but my heart didn't belong to her anymore. A part of it, yes, but not the whole thing. If anything, that made it worse. Adley had given everything to me, and I'd given her nothing but misery. Even after she'd reached the afterlife. Davin had yanked her from that peaceful world just to punish me. She'd have been better off if she'd never met me. And, so help me, I didn't know how to fix any of it.

"I'm sorry, Adley." I pulled her closer. "I wish I was what you wanted me to be."

"You are." Her arms closed tighter around my neck. Too tight.

"Adley, don't!" I choked, as my air was cut off.

"I'm sorry." Adley's fingers grasped tighter, until my eyes started to bulge.

Panic hit me. Thoughts of my near kiss with Ryann. Waking up this morning in each others' arms. I wanted more. I wanted to see if I was worthy of happiness. And I couldn't do that if I was dead. My brain was in tatters, wracked with guilt over my new love while my old one was suffering so much. But I couldn't help it. I sent tendrils of Telekinesis slithering up her arms and yanked, pulling them away with an almighty wrench.

Adley collapsed, her expression one of crushing devastation.

"It's worse when I'm close to you," she sobbed. "Why did he do this, Finch? Didn't that evil witch do enough to me while I was alive —why did he have to come in and continue what she started, making me suffer? Why couldn't he have left me alone?"

I scanned the battlefield, watching the cultists clash with my friends. Melody had apparently run out of bombs and turned to ordinary transformative spells instead. One of the cultists protecting Davin suddenly sprouted multicolored wings and took off into the air, hitting the slipstream overhead and disappearing. Huntress had gone full wolf, tearing pieces from every zombie she came across and terrifying the living cultists while she was at it. Nash and Luke were working together, Luke dragging bits of metal from wherever he could find them and putting them into Nash's hands. Our resident Marine had excellent precision, lashing the metal pieces out with deadly accuracy.

I heard wet thuds as the shards pierced the zombies and living cultists, though only the living ones paused to assess the damage. The zombies kept right on coming, as did the sentient trees crashing through the clearing.

"He's doing it to get to me. You can't let him." I turned back to Adley, loathing Davin to my core.

Her eyes widened. "I love you, Finch. I never stopped."

"I..." I hesitated. It wasn't fair for me to tell her I loved her, but how could I leave her hanging? I had to say something, so I let what I felt leave my mouth. "A part of me will always love you. You changed me. Every time I think of how far I've come, I remember you and how much I adore you still."

"You won't forget me after this? You won't hate me?"

I shook my head. "I couldn't if I tried. I don't blame you for this. This is all Davin."

"Then... forgive me for this, too." Quick as a flash, she turned the knife on herself, using the last of her strength to plunge it into the heart of the body Davin had used to resurrect her. My heart lurched violently.

"Adley!" I reached for her, but it was too late. Thick, congealed blood oozed from the wound in her chest. She stared up at me with a strange smile on her lips, as though she could see that sweet light waiting for her. "Adley..." I clutched her, rocking her gently. No... this couldn't be happening again. *No... please, no.* I hadn't expected her to go on living in a borrowed body, and Davin wouldn't have allowed it anyway, but I didn't want her second death to happen this way. Why couldn't she have had a peaceful way out this time? Why did it have to be brutal again?

"I didn't want... to hurt you. Davin... wouldn't have... let me live, even if I... killed you. It's better this way." She gazed at me. "But kill him, Finch. For what he's done... and what your mother did."

"Adley... no. This isn't fair! Davin releasing you would've been the better way. At least then it would've been... I don't know." I buried my face in her shoulder, though her skin had already begun to chill. She was slipping away from me.

"It was never going to be fair. This was Davin's doing. At least, this way, I leave on my terms. Don't you see? I'm doing this because… I love you, silly. You never… did listen, did you?" She gave a soft chuckle and then lifted her hand to my cheek. She brushed away the tears that poured down, and then, as suddenly as she'd appeared back in my life… she was gone. Her eyes turned milky, and her face changed to that of the body she'd used. She lay in my arms blue-tinged and waxy, yet I still couldn't let go. As if holding her tightly enough might bring her spirit back.

A cold rush washed over me as her spirit phased out of her vessel and drifted upward. Turning upright, she came to rest beside me for a moment. The time had come for me to let go, for the last time. I dropped the limp body that didn't belong to her anymore and looked up at her lingering specter with tear-blurred vision.

"I'm sorry. I'm sorry for everything. I'm so, so sorry," I said.

Adley smiled. "I love you, Finch. And I always will. And what's more… I forgive you. Please, be happy now. Let's both find peace."

She departed in a haze of glowing light. I'd exchanged my last words with her, but it still didn't feel like enough. As I looked over the battlefield, the island still tearing through the oceans toward its final destination, my heart pounded with rage.

The zombies fought through Erebus's smoke. Luke was drenched in sweat, and Nash was on his last leg, with Huntress a mess of pink fur and panting, foaming mouth. Melody leaned on Luke as she continued to pummel the zombies with transformation spells, but her face had gone damp and pale.

I strode toward Davin and his squad of goons. He didn't seem to be in the best shape, either, after keeping all these zombies moving for so long.

Good... let's see how you fight back when you're weak, shall we?

I lashed out with every Elemental ability I possessed. Every zombie near me went up in a whirl of dust and flames. I didn't even feel remorse as I sent cultist after cultist spinning into the air, where they were dragged away from the fast-moving island. They'd made their choice. I had no fricks left to give.

Cutting a swathe through the army, singeing a few lurching trees for good measure, I approached Davin like a vengeful god about to do some smiting. With a yank of Telekinesis, I grabbed the Terra around the waist and flung her into the air. The slipstream took her, and the woodland cavalry came to a standstill, granting my friends a brief reprieve.

The cultists jittered nervously, whispering among themselves.

"That's him, right?" one said.

"Katherine's son. Look at him! He's like her, incarnate!" a second squeaked.

Well, I wasn't having that. "No, I'm Hiram Merlin's son."

I grabbed two more cultists with my Telekinesis and launched them sky high. Davin's eyes narrowed as I plowed toward him. I needed to keep his focus on me. Just behind him, I saw a figure dart through the trees, having somehow managed to sneak behind enemy lines. Lux-slash-Ryann, finally entering the fray.

I grasped another cultist and threw him into the air. This time, I let go just before he hit the rapid current overhead. He plummeted to the ground and hit the earth in front of the other cultists with a sickening thud. The rest of the cowards screamed, backing away from the crumpled figure as though they hadn't seen worse at their own hands.

My remorse would hit later, I knew, but right now I was working on pure adrenaline. That left no room for human feeling. Hey, maybe I'd taken a page from Erebus's book after all.

"You're outnumbered, Finch," Davin said.

"And you're tired, old man," I shot back. "You think I don't see that sweat on your forehead? Your designer suit must stink right now."

Davin scowled. "My undead won't falter. They'll keep going, no matter how many limbs you tear off. That pooch of yours has already proven that."

"I'm guessing they *will* stop if I cut you to pieces. Sure, you'll only put yourself together again and spoil my fun, but I'll drag that amulet out of wherever you've hidden it, with every spell I have. Even if I have to ransack my mother's library twice over and kill you a hundred times more, I'll find something to take that amulet away from you. And then I'll be the one standing there all smug."

Davin paled. "Your mother's library wouldn't have that sort of information."

"Your face tells me otherwise." I flung two violent blasts of Fire at encroaching zombies, turning them back into spirits.

"Don't pretend to know my expression, Finch. You're the only one dying today. I will not die again at your hand." He clearly had a chip on his shoulder about that. Hell, he probably had an actual chip, after what Murray had done to him.

"Aww, is that why you're so tired? Did your meat puzzle take a lot out of you?" I resisted looking behind him, in case it tipped him off.

"You little—"

He didn't get to finish what would likely have been a less-than-witty retort. Ryann-Lux snuck up behind him at that exact moment and clubbed his head with a massive rock. Keeping it human but hitting him where it'd have the most effect.

Davin collapsed, and a gasp went up from his remaining posse of gaping idiots. A moment later, the zombies disintegrated into dust, sending a veritable snowstorm of ash floating down. In the grim flurry, the cultists ran into the woods, cutting their losses. I made no move to follow. They wouldn't be back anytime soon.

"Nice aim," I said sarcastically, as Ryann-Lux stepped toward me. She'd even gone so far as to tremble, as though she'd been the least bit scared about whacking Davin into oblivion.

"Thanks," she replied softly.

Oh, you're good...

Erebus emerged from a pile of fallen trees and baffled spirits, plus a few cultist bodies. He looked stunned, glancing from Ryann to Davin and back again. A deep belly laugh echoed from the back of his throat.

"My, my, turns out the human isn't useless, after all." He held his chest as he fell into hysterics.

"I told you," I retorted. *And, by the way, your wife has turned her into a condo, and she isn't paying rent.*

"That you did." His laughter halted abruptly. "Everyone, gather here!" He gestured to the center of the clearing.

Atlantis beckoned. And there was no turning this boat around.

THIRTY-SIX

Ryann

I might have hated Lux for taking over my body, but it had felt so good to smack Davin over the head with that rock. I had to give her kudos for that slick move. But I couldn't enjoy the victory too much. Through Lux's vision, I'd seen Adley and Finch, and what she'd done to stop herself from hurting him. That had taken guts. I wished I could've spoken to her, alone, to thank her for everything she'd done for Finch.

Her second death had lit a fire under him. I'd never seen Finch like that before, tearing through an army like it was nothing. It was strangely exhilarating to see him use the full force of his powers.

The earthquake intensified as we huddled in the center of the clearing. Above our heads, the flashing starlight seemed to slow.

Hold his hand, I urged Lux.

He might pull away, she warned.

Do it anyway.

I heard her sigh inside my head before reaching for Finch's hand.

My fingers interlaced with his, and I could almost feel that solid, comforting touch. I needed it, sensing that we were about to step into a whole world of insanity. This island was on a one-way trajectory to Atlantis. Actual Atlantis. The stuff of stories and legend. A small part of me felt excited to find out what that fabled city had become after the ocean had swallowed it. The rest of me wanted to run.

With a jolt that made everyone topple into each other, the island came to a stop. We'd reached our destination. At least, I hoped so. Could an island malfunction? It wasn't really my area of expertise. But if this island was meant to be the Gateway to Atlantis, then it looked like we might have reached the point of connection.

"What happened?" Nash asked. "Are we there?"

Erebus grinned. "Indeed we are."

The sound of his voice made my head feel funny. One moment I was staring up at the sky, wondering if we'd landed in Antarctica—where Finch had marked the position of Atlantis. The next, I was staring up at an eerie, dark blue, suggesting I was underneath very deep water.

Those silver spires glinted—I'd jumped into Lux's memories again. I saw Atlantis in its prime, Atlanteans strolling casually around the elegant city. Each had one or more blue streaks on their face, though the streaks had different shapes. I wondered if that meant something—a diamond indicating Glaciers, a circle for Air Elementals. I didn't know why those ideas came to me. Maybe they were a part of this memory and the knowledge attached to it.

The memory slipped away.

They wore their abilities for everyone to see. An honest, open race of people, I thought to myself. I supposed that was one way to keep everything transparent among the populace. Then, there'd be no confusion or suspicion between them. Perhaps those streaks were even charmed, to prevent Shapeshifters from using them to their advantage, or stopping folks from simply painting whatever they wanted on their faces. Another speculation that didn't seem to belong to me.

"Erebus?" Melody asked shakily. "Why is the ground crumbling?!"

"The Gateway is opening. Stay where you are, unless you wish to be left behind," Erebus replied. "Finch, don't even think about it. Where I go, you go."

Finch flashed a cheeky grin. My favorite, though it didn't reach his eyes. "Can you blame a guy for trying?"

"Very amusing." Erebus cast him a sharp look.

Sure enough, the ground around us began to crack. The forest fell away as the earth beneath it crumbled, revealing a gaping hole filled to the brim with swirling blue light that looked remarkably like water. Some sort of magical whirlpool about to devour us whole. And we stood in the center of it all, on a worryingly small scrap of land that diminished with every passing second.

The full moon glowed overhead in all its glory, reflecting in the whirlpool that surrounded us. We were a few meager yards from getting soggy. The final part of the Atlantis spell was underway. But what came next? Did we have to jump into the pool? Would this piece of land fall away, too?

"Something's coming!" Luke shouted, pointing at the sky. Threads of smoke twisted through the atmosphere before tumbling to the ground and snaking across it. At the edge of the bizarre whirlpool, the smoke stopped. Limbs stretched out, a cluster of beastly forms emerging.

"It's the gargoyles!" Melody shrieked delightedly. "Our gargoyles! They came back!"

I'd wondered where they went. They'd just disappeared after the leather bags caught fire, and we hadn't seen hide nor hair nor slobbery tongue of them since. But here they were, flapping their leathery wings to fly to our aid.

We were so focused on the arrival of the gargoyles that we didn't notice the figure on the farthest tip of the remaining scrap of land. Not until a barrage of purple-tinged smog careened into us.

Davin!

Erebus unleashed a whorl of black wind that dispersed the smog. And sure enough, through the fading haze, Davin stalked toward us with venomous eyes. Purple energy crackled between his fingertips.

"Look who decided to join us." Davin gave the gargoyles a savage look. "I thought my cultists had kept those vile creatures distracted. I have quite the headache now, thanks to you, Miss Smith."

I hope it's the worst migraine of your life. Lux didn't humor me by saying that, so I had to be satisfied with thinking it.

"As if you could beat me, Davin." Erebus snorted.

"Oh, I am far from done with you, Erebus." Davin broke into a sprint and tackled Erebus with his full weight. Lux screamed unexpectedly, as Davin almost knocked Erebus over the edge of the tiny island.

What are you so worried about? I thought you wanted him to go through the Gateway. Isn't that why you're here? I said.

It took me by surprise, that is all, she replied defensively.

That blew my mind. Was Lux still concerned about Erebus? She didn't give off loving vibes, but that one outburst made me think otherwise. That had been the shriek of someone who cared, not someone riddled with loathing for a person.

It was all the rest of us could do to keep away from Erebus and Davin as they descended into an all-out physical brawl. No magic, no Chaos, just hand-to-hand combat. And they couldn't have picked a more precarious boxing ring. I didn't understand why they weren't using their power to beat one another into submission. Maybe it had something to do with the whirlpool.

"You keep thinking you can kill me, and I keep making you look like a fool!" Davin roared as he pummeled Erebus's face.

"*You* are the fool, thinking I cannot kill you!" Erebus snarled back as he served a swift kick between Davin's legs. Not very sportsman-like, but I guessed there weren't any rules in this game.

Davin grunted. "You're not winning this time!"

"I already have," Erebus shot back, delivering a gut-wrenching punch to Davin's stomach. Although, for a Child of Chaos, he wasn't as impressive at boxing as I expected. This had to be his first human fight, I supposed. He was still learning the ropes.

"You think so, do you? You're in a human body now, Erebus. You're weak!" Davin lunged, dragging Erebus to the ground. They tangled in a turbulent mass of limbs. All I could hear were the thuds of blunt punches and the groans that followed, plus Lux's inwardly anxious *oofs* and *ahs* as her beloved took some brutal knocks.

"Call me weak again, I dare you." Erebus headbutted Davin, making his nose pour blood.

"You're weak!" Davin repeated, jabbing his fingers at Erebus's eyes. If we hadn't been teetering on the edge of a precipice above a magical whirlpool, I would've found this fascinating. A cross-species example of fragile masculinity and the desire to batter the living daylights out of one another out of a sense of pride. Even Children of Chaos weren't immune, apparently. In this case, Davin had an obvious grudge, and Erebus didn't want to be beaten.

They continued to tussle, rolling around on the ground like complete idiots. I'd seen enough scenes like this on Saturday nights in San Diego. Surely, such esteemed magical entities could've found a more elegant way to resolve their differences. The fascination quickly wore off, turning into a sort of pitying disdain. They really did look pathetic. Even Lux had stopped making noises.

Erebus had just landed a punch on Davin's chest when the ground beneath us rattled violently. It didn't look like they had time to establish a winner. The shudder spread across our small island, the solid rock crumbling at the edges. Then, with one enormous crack that splintered the air, the entire thing fell away. And it took us with it, straight into the swirling whirlpool.

THIRTY-SEVEN

Finch

Eris Island sat directly above Atlantis now. I recognized the location from my Casper time in the skies over Antarctica. The spell was complete. The Gateway had opened, and now we were falling through a miasma of blue and white sparks, screaming and flailing like Alices who'd gone down the wrong rabbit hole.

Melody appeared beside me. Somehow, she'd managed a flying-squirrel skydiver position, looking a lot cooler and calmer than the rest of us. Not even Nash could style this one out.

"Remind me to talk to you about what's going on with Ryann, if we survive this!" she shouted.

Ryann-Lux shot me a warning look, but I ignored it. I couldn't stop the Librarian from casting aspersions, even if they revealed Lux. Anyway, maybe we wouldn't survive this, so I wouldn't have to worry about protecting Melody from any repercussions. Could a Child even do anything to a Librarian? That seemed like breaking some fairly massive Chaos rules, to me.

I gaped at Melody. "You need to work on your timing, Winchester!"

Her sudden revelation begged a few questions. Did she mean the Adam stuff? Or the unwanted joyrider who'd taken the wheel in Ryann's body? I'd been so sure she'd figure out something was up, considering she was an Empath, but I hadn't seen much to suggest she had.

At least plummeting to my potential death gave me a moment to stop thinking about Adley. I'd tried to be Finch about it in the aftermath, wisecracking with Davin and Erebus. But I'd see her ghost in my dreams for a long time to come, remembering everything we had said. Hell, maybe I'd see her spirit again in about five minutes, when I got smooshed into a human pancake. We had to hit ground sometime, right? And I guessed it wouldn't be a soft landing.

"Brace! Brace! Brace!" Luke barked, reminding me of a frantic flight attendant.

Tumbling through the air, I managed to awkwardly twist my head to follow Luke's line of sight. There she was—solid ground, rushing up to meet us.

This is going to hurt.

And it did, but not the way I'd anticipated. A few moments shy of slamming into it, my body came to a sudden, crushing halt. The air turned thick and heavy as some kind of… magnetic force engulfed us. Judging by the sheer pressure that squeezed the breath from my lungs and hammered my bones until they felt like they might break, we were deep underwater now.

Strained groans and pained cries echoed around me. My face contorted under the spine-bending atmosphere, agony charging through my body. I managed to steal a glance at Erebus. He was suffering the same as the rest of us, his teeth gritted and every visible vein bulging. That made me feel slightly better, dulling the searing agony ever so slightly.

Then... we hit the ground. The magnetic force had slowed us enough to prevent visceral explosion, but it still stung when I slammed into the solid expanse. It was enough to knock me out for a few minutes. In that momentary darkness, I heard rushing water and the eerie song of a whale. Though that might have been my exhausted brain filling in the gaps.

"Finch..."

My eyes flew open at the sound of my name. A quick recovery spurred by the person crawling toward me. Ryann. Actual Ryann. She and I had landed slightly away from the others, who were starting to come around. I could tell it was her from the look in her eyes. Even though every bone in my body ached like it belonged to an octogenarian with chronic arthritis, I turned to meet her. The others lay on the ground, coming around slowly.

"Ryann." I put my hand out and grasped hers. "Are you okay?"

"I was about to ask you the same," she replied, giving my hand a weak squeeze.

"Sore," I wheezed.

She nodded. "Same."

"How come you're... out?" I wondered if the fall had somehow removed Lux.

"When we hit the ground, I saw an opportunity. I fought to the front so we could have a minute together." Her eyes turned sad. "Although, I wouldn't have survived that landing without her."

"And she hasn't hurt you or squashed you into submission?"

Ryann shook her head. "No. As long as I mostly obey, I'll be fine. I hope."

"I'll kiss you so hard when she's gone." I leaned forward and planted a smaller kiss on her hand. Kissing her on the lips would've been too weird, knowing Lux was playing voyeur inside her.

"I'll hold you to that." She smiled, and everything seemed less awful.

"No, I'll hold you to that. Right against this strapping chest of mine."

She chuckled. "Smooth, Finch."

"I'm working on it." I kissed her hand again, wishing Lux would go away. But I was thankful she'd used her Child strength to keep Ryann safe.

Her eyes suddenly lit with that cold, shining white. Lux had taken over again. "What have I told you about touching?"

I yanked my hand away. "Sorry." Still, that brief moment with Ryann had given me comfort. She was in there, fighting tooth and nail, struggling for control over her own body.

Don't ever change, Ryann. Ever.

"I'll make sure your sweetheart is well compensated for this temporary use of her form, I promise." Lux leveled a cool grin at me. "Despite her recalcitrance."

"What did you expect from a scrappy mortal?" I replied. "We never back down from a fight."

She laughed. "I'm starting to realize that."

Now that Ryann had been forced under, I pulled myself to my feet. It took a solid couple of groans and grunts and some bending and stretching, but I managed.

Blinking slowly, I took in my surroundings. The others were

slowly coming to, with the usual pairings seeking one another out. Luke shuffled toward Melody. Huntress had her paws on Nash's chest, urging him awake. She seemed to have fared the best out of all of us, with all that canine flexibility. Or was that cats? And Erebus and Davin had landed near each other, their hands almost touching. *Bless them...*

I turned my eyes skyward, satisfied that everyone had survived the fall. Gargoyles included. A gasp escaped my throat. Above us, the Gateway had closed, leaving us stuck in a gigantic bubble of glass. On the other side, pitch-black water loomed. Bioluminescent creatures floated along, creating a neon lightshow that stole my breath. No whales, so no idea where that sound had come from, but a haunting melody under the unsettling creak of the bubble made me wonder if the ocean itself was singing. I turned in a circle, taking in every angle.

I stood corrected; we weren't entirely surrounded by water. Through a long glass tunnel—locked shut, of course—I saw the place we'd come to visit. In the snow-globe setup of an interdimensional bubble, a vast city rose in this underwater realm. It was unlike any city I'd ever seen. Silver spires and glinting turrets shone as far as the eye could see, every building glimmering in the light as though crafted from pearl.

The place had a Grecian quality to it, the roofs painted in shades of blue and green, the shuttered windows overlooking the cobbled streets made from that same shining material. It glowed, taking its ambient radiance from swollen orbs of light hanging from the curved dome. They'd built their own *suns*.

And what was more, the city had green expanses of grass and flowers on every corner, curious blooms I'd never seen before.

Handcrafted windchimes and sea glass ornaments decorated the doorframes. And beyond the residential streets, towering monoliths glinted in the fake sunlight—ornate structures that would've put the world's greatest palaces to shame, with fifty minarets apiece. They reminded me of coral but were built from pure silver.

But the most surprising part... none of it was in ruin or submerged, aside from being in a bubble, and *people* were walking the streets. Real, living people, dressed in flowing dresses and silky suits.

The city of Atlantis had never been lost. It had simply been hiding all this time, cut off from the world above.

THIRTY-EIGHT

Finch

E rebus lurched to his feet and gazed at the city like the cat who'd gotten the cream. Even Davin's presence didn't seem to dampen his enthusiasm. Speaking of that stuck-up turkey, he'd dragged himself to his feet and was taking in Atlantis for the first time. His eyes bugged out of his stupid head, though typically, he couldn't resist getting in the last word.

"Looks like we both made it, you wretched blighter."

"But I landed first, ergo I reached Atlantis first." Erebus had turned into a child, determined to be king of the castle.

Davin huffed. "Details, Erebus. Details."

"The devil is in them," Erebus shot back. If these two kept going, they'd spend every moment down here sniping at each other across the proverbial playground.

I realized Lux had been right about those two. Their brawl could've been nastier, but neither had resorted to Chaos despite being very powerful wielders of the stuff. Instead, they'd grappled it out magic-less, suggesting they hadn't intended to kill one another. Each simply wanted the other to wave the white flag, so he could name himself the victor. The kind of fight that frenemies would have, not adversaries.

That can't be good for me. Lux had warned me they might turn their focus on me if I pissed them off. I hadn't believed it then, but I was more inclined to now, listening to their almost-brotherly slinging match.

Harley, I hope you've found that djinn. I was determined to get out of this mess before the Frenemy Gang strung me up and hung me out to dry. And I couldn't exactly trust Lux to make good on her promise of help.

I checked my phone, but there were no bars whatsoever. I was at the bottom of the friggin' ocean; of course there wouldn't be any bars. But the sight of *No Signal* made me bristle with nerves. I was completely isolated from the OG Muppet Babies. I couldn't reach out to them, and even if they found what I needed, how would they get it to me? I was locked in a literal bubble, staring at a city that should've been about a foot thick with ocean sludge. A city that, as it turned out, had carried on bustling with life, tricking the world into believing the greatest lie ever told.

I copied the rest of the group, staring at the beautiful underwater city. The people had facial markings and walked with a regal air. The fake orbs of sunlight and the way their glow shone down on the fluid architecture, all metal and fine sculptures, had a hypnotic effect on me. Somehow, the effect escaped being ostentatious. I could've stood here all day, and I still wouldn't have been satisfied that I'd seen everything.

But the peace and tranquility didn't last. My heart jolted as smaller bubbles emerged from the astonishing city and made straight for us—ten in total. Erebus frowned at their approach, which worried me even more. The bubbles docked under the glass floor where we stood. The next moment, holes appeared in the floor, and silver-caped soldiers in full armor leapt out.

A thick-set guy who made Luke look like a sapling shouted something at us in a language I couldn't understand, until he jabbed the sharp end of a spear at Erebus. Now *that* I understood. We weren't welcome here. The spear crackled slightly, and I realized it must be the soldier's Esprit. The men and women who'd come with him pointed their Esprits at us, too. We were surrounded.

A sudden thought dawned on me. *If this city has been inhabited continuously, then these must be... holy crap... the direct, pure-blood descendants of the original Primus Anglicus.*

Another bubble docked, and a strange young woman emerged from the glass floor. Her beauty was unlike anything I'd ever seen. Paler than pearl, with five blue markings on her left cheek, her dark eyes matched the ocean above and her strong features wouldn't have looked amiss on some ancient statue. Dressed in robes of Hawaiian-beach blue, with a silver circlet adorning her pure white hair, she moved through the soldiers without a hint of fear. They bowed reverently as they let her pass.

Erebus's mouth dropped open, his eyes twinkling in an unsettling way.

She gave an order to her soldiers in that same odd language. It didn't match any of the languages I vaguely knew. But they sure understood her. The armored unit surged forward and seized us, Erebus included. My arms were wrenched behind my back as two sharp kicks behind my knees sent me crashing to the ground. Luke tried to reach for Melody, only to end up with a sword brandished in his face. We fell like dominoes.

Next thing I knew, the soldiers grabbed our throats and tugged our heads up. Each one pulled an eerie, glowing handful of algae from their pocket and rather rudely forced the damn substance down our throats. I had a choice: choke or swallow. Struggling, my throat made the decision for me and gulped that slimy mass down as if it were seaweed at a sushi bar.

A sour taste filled my mouth, making me gag. What the hell was that stuff? Was it going to poison us? My eyes darted toward Ryann-Lux. She seemed to be obeying, as was Erebus. Maybe they knew something I didn't, but neither looked afraid.

"Do you understand me?" the warrior woman asked.

I gasped. "Yes... yes, I do."

The others gave similar replies, in awe of this curious creature. But none more than Erebus, who still hadn't dragged his jaw off the floor. He couldn't take his eyes off her.

"Good." She opened her arms. "My name is Princess Kaya, the daughter of the King of Atlantis."

"Kaya..." Erebus whispered.

The princess frowned. "How dare you speak to me so informally!"

"You don't recognize me?" Erebus sighed like a lovesick teenager. "It is me, Kaya. Erebus."

The stoic expression on her face morphed into obvious conflict, with a touch of panic. "Erebus? How can it be you?"

"I took human form so I could see you again," he replied.

She cleared her throat. "That was foolish of you. You should not have done that."

"I had to." He clasped his hands, but she rallied, donning that fearsome expression again.

"I will contend with you later, Erebus."

So, they obviously knew each other, and she clearly wasn't all that impressed to see him.

Davin snorted. "All this rigmarole, failure after failure, just to woo the Atlantean princess. It is woeful, even for you." He nodded politely to Kaya. "I am Davin Doncaster, and I am here in pursuit of your hand in marriage. I have traversed continents, crossed oceans, and delved into the darkest depths of magic to come here. My heart is honest and open, and it is yours, if you will consider me."

What in the name of Bruce Springsteen is going on here? A marriage proposal? From Davin? To the princess of Atlantis? I'd clearly landed in some alternate universe. This didn't make any sense. Or maybe it did, which was even more baffling. Plus, there was the bit about an honest and open heart. Pfft, as if. His heart was as closed and rotten as they came. I made an involuntary snort that earned me a slightly amused look from the princess and a death stare from Davin. Although, it got the old gray matter whirring, mostly from sheer shock. Erebus had come here for... this woman? And so had Davin? Did she have the rare jewel, or... oh, for the love of Chaos, I was genuinely going to hurl at the corniness of it all... was *she* the rare jewel he'd spoken of?

"Your purpose for being here does not interest me, Mr. Doncaster," the princess replied. "In fact, the fact that you have managed to gain entry to this realm, with a contingent of secondary magicals, leaves me feeling less than amorous."

Who're you calling secondary? Blood of a Shipton and a Merlin, right here! I kept my mouth shut on that, at least for now. Instead, I flipped the embarrassing tables on the E-man.

"Tell me she's not the rare jewel, Erebus." I shot a snide look at him.

He scowled back. "Be silent, Finch, if you know what is good for you. That goes for all of you—be compliant. The Atlanteans are not to be toyed with, especially not the princess."

"These are Primus Anglicus," Melody said softly. Magicals were like helpless infants compared to Primus Anglicus. But…

I gaped at Kaya. "That's not possible. You can't be *the* Primus Anglicus who escaped all those years ago. Their descendants, sure, but not the real deal."

She smiled coldly. "There are many mysteries in these waters. None of them ought to be understood or discovered by inferior magicals."

"Hey, I'm a—"

Before I could finish, Kaya interrupted.

"Soldiers, arrest them and put them in the dungeons. I will speak with them later. Do not, under any circumstances, answer their questions. I must decide what to do with them after they have been interrogated, and any knowledge they pry from you will not work in their favor. Think on that."

Erebus wrestled free of his guard. "Kaya. My sweet Kaya. Don't throw me into the same category as these wastrels. You know me. And I have finally come for you, as I swore I would, to ask for your hand in marriage."

A hint of a smile tugged at Kaya's lips before a stern frown replaced it. "As I said, I will contend with you later." Maybe she thought nobody had seen that short-lived smile, but I had. And it suggested a smorgasbord of conflicted emotions over this shiny human-shaped Child of Chaos. Someone she evidently knew better than she dared let on.

Ryann-Lux pinched the bridge of her nose and muttered under her breath. "Very displeasing. Oh yes, displeasing indeed." As the closest to her, I was the only one who heard. Another outburst that could well have exposed Lux, and she didn't seem to realize. Then again, she could've gone way bigger, considering what was going on —aka, Erebus trying to marry someone else. Her restraint was actually pretty impressive.

Oh dear... It looked like wedding bells were the last thing Erebus needed. He'd annoyed his missus, and now he could look forward to spending the rest of eternity locked in the center of the earth. But not right at this exact moment, right? Lux had said she wanted to see how far Erebus would go. Maybe he hadn't gone far enough yet.

The soldiers took out a variation of my old favorite, the Atomic Cuff. A single manacle clamped around my neck, rendering my abilities inert with a single turn of a key in the lock. I felt the instant dulling of my powers course through me, the magic on these puppies far more powerful than anything I'd encountered before. And I'd lost count of the number of times I'd wound up in cuffs.

I kept expecting one of the new Muppet Babies to say something. Nash, at least. But they crouched in stunned silence. The presence of royalty could have that effect, I guessed. Even Huntress had gone quiet, though the soldiers were having some trouble shackling her. Every time they approached, she snapped at them, until Kaya herself clamped the neck cuff on the pooch. That time, Huntress didn't bite back. She could evidently sense the Atlantean power bristling off Kaya and didn't want to leave any marks that got Nash in trouble.

Hauled to our feet, the armed guard dragged us through the glass tunnel connecting this bubble to Atlantis itself. I hadn't expected to be marched into the city. But then, I hadn't expected a living, breathing city to be here. And being arrested was fairly low on my list of concerns. Lux hadn't made her Jules Verne move yet, but that didn't mean she wouldn't. Plus, we had no idea whether the Atlanteans were the good guys or the bad guys, or in-between guys. Kaya gave little away. Her expression was unreadable.

I eyed the princess, who marched on ahead. On the surface, royalty were no more than figureheads, but I didn't sense that was the case here. We'd made a bad first impression on a very influential woman, by the looks of it.

Harley didn't know where I was. We were alone down here, and Erebus and Lux had their own agendas, which meant they wouldn't lift a finger for us "secondary magicals." So, once again, we would have to dig ourselves out of this mess. The trouble was, I had no idea where to begin. How did one dig themselves out of a city that shouldn't exist, under miles of ocean, with the actual Primus Anglicus and their shining princess taking us away to a prison that probably had better defenses than anything I'd ever seen, if this neck cuff was anything to go by?

"Kaya, please," Erebus murmured.

She shot him a dark look. "I don't want to hear anything from you at present."

"But you will speak to me soon?" What had *happened* to him? In the presence of Kaya, he'd transformed into a completely different person.

"We shall see. Perhaps you will catch me in a generous mood." Reaching the end of the glass tunnel, Kaya turned to address us all.

Her tone came out sarcastic, which made sense, given how we were entering this city. "You have come so far. What sort of princess would I be if I did not say something?" She paused and gestured to the silver spires. "Welcome to Atlantis."

Good one... We were about as welcome as a rectal examination.

HARLEY MERLIN 14: Finch Merlin and the Forgotten Kingdom

Dear Reader,

Harley Merlin 14: **Finch Merlin and the Forgotten Kingdom** releases **December 11th, 2019**.

It's going to be a wild ride!

Visit www.bellaforrest.net for details.

See you there.

Bella x

P.S. Sign up to my VIP email list and you'll be the first to know when my books release:

www.morebellaforrest.com

(Your email will be kept 100% private and you can unsubscribe at any time.)

P.P.S. Feel free to come say hi on **Twitter** @ashadeofvampire;

Facebook BellaForrestAuthor;

or **Instagram** @ashadeofvampire

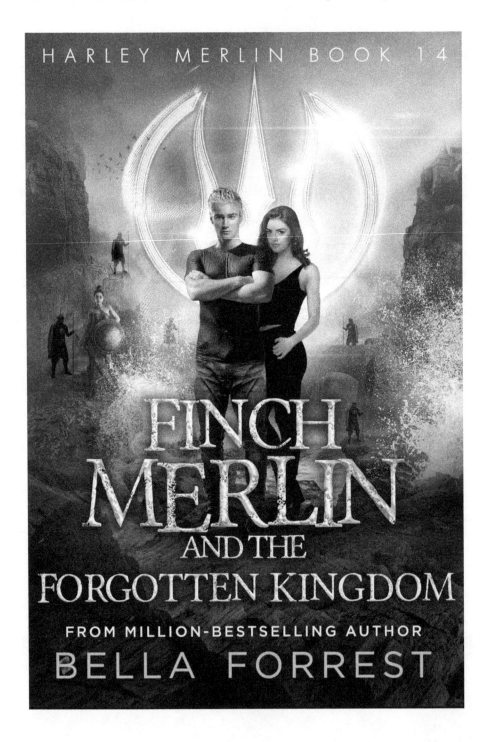

Read more by Bella Forrest

DARKLIGHT

(NEW! Fantasy)

Darklight (Book 1)

Darkthirst (Book 2)

Darkworld (Book 3)

HARLEY MERLIN

Harley Merlin and the Secret Coven (Book 1)

Harley Merlin and the Mystery Twins (Book 2)

Harley Merlin and the Stolen Magicals (Book 3)

Harley Merlin and the First Ritual (Book 4)

Harley Merlin and the Broken Spell (Book 5)

Harley Merlin and the Cult of Eris (Book 6)

Harley Merlin and the Detector Fix (Book 7)

Harley Merlin and the Challenge of Chaos (Book 8)

Harley Merlin and the Mortal Pact (Book 9)

Finch Merlin and the Fount of Youth (Book 10)

Finch Merlin and the Lost Map (Book 11)

Finch Merlin and the Djinn's Curse (Book 12)

Finch Merlin and the Locked Gateway (Book 13)

Finch Merlin and the Forgotten Kingdom (Book 14)

THE GENDER GAME

(Action-adventure/romance. Completed series.)

The Gender Game (Book 1)

The Gender Secret (Book 2)

The Gender Lie (Book 3)

The Gender War (Book 4)

The Gender Fall (Book 5)

The Gender Plan (Book 6)

The Gender End (Book 7)

THE GIRL WHO DARED TO THINK

(Action-adventure/romance. Completed series.)

The Girl Who Dared to Think (Book 1)

The Girl Who Dared to Stand (Book 2)

The Girl Who Dared to Descend (Book 3)

The Girl Who Dared to Rise (Book 4)

The Girl Who Dared to Lead (Book 5)

The Girl Who Dared to Endure (Book 6)

The Girl Who Dared to Fight (Book 7)

THE CHILD THIEF

(Action-adventure/romance. Completed series.)

The Child Thief (Book 1)

Deep Shadows (Book 2)

Thin Lines (Book 3)

Little Lies (Book 4)

Ghost Towns (Book 5)

Zero Hour (Book 6)

HOTBLOODS

(Supernatural adventure/romance. Completed series.)

Hotbloods (Book 1)

Coldbloods (Book 2)

Renegades (Book 3)

Venturers (Book 4)

Traitors (Book 5)

Allies (Book 6)

Invaders (Book 7)

Stargazers (Book 8)

A SHADE OF VAMPIRE SERIES

(Supernatural romance/adventure)

Series 1: Derek & Sofia's story

A Shade of Vampire (Book 1)

A Shade of Blood (Book 2)

A Castle of Sand (Book 3)

A Shadow of Light (Book 4)

A Blaze of Sun (Book 5)

A Gate of Night (Book 6)

A Break of Day (Book 7)

Series 2: Rose & Caleb's story

A Shade of Novak (Book 8)

A Bond of Blood (Book 9)

A Spell of Time (Book 10)

A Chase of Prey (Book 11)

A Shade of Doubt (Book 12)

A Turn of Tides (Book 13)

A Dawn of Strength (Book 14)

A Fall of Secrets (Book 15)

An End of Night (Book 16)

Series 3: The Shade continues with a new hero...

A Wind of Change (Book 17)

A Trail of Echoes (Book 18)

A Soldier of Shadows (Book 19)

A Hero of Realms (Book 20)

A Vial of Life (Book 21)

A Fork of Paths (Book 22)

A Flight of Souls (Book 23)

A Bridge of Stars (Book 24)

Series 4: A Clan of Novaks

A Clan of Novaks (Book 25)

A World of New (Book 26)

A Web of Lies (Book 27)

A Touch of Truth (Book 28)

An Hour of Need (Book 29)

A Game of Risk (Book 30)

A Twist of Fates (Book 31)

A Day of Glory (Book 32)

Series 5: A Dawn of Guardians

A Dawn of Guardians (Book 33)

A Sword of Chance (Book 34)

A Race of Trials (Book 35)

A King of Shadow (Book 36)

An Empire of Stones (Book 37)

A Power of Old (Book 38)

A Rip of Realms (Book 39)

A Throne of Fire (Book 40)

A Tide of War (Book 41)

Series 6: A Gift of Three

A Gift of Three (Book 42)

A House of Mysteries (Book 43)

A Tangle of Hearts (Book 44)

A Meet of Tribes (Book 45)

A Ride of Peril (Book 46)

A Passage of Threats (Book 47)

A Tip of Balance (Book 48)

A Shield of Glass (Book 49)

A Clash of Storms (Book 50)

A Love that Endures 2

A Love that Endures 3

THE SECRET OF SPELLSHADOW MANOR

(Supernatural/Magic YA. Completed series)

The Secret of Spellshadow Manor (Book 1)

The Breaker (Book 2)

The Chain (Book 3)

The Keep (Book 4)

The Test (Book 5)

The Spell (Book 6)

BEAUTIFUL MONSTER DUOLOGY

(Supernatural romance)

Beautiful Monster 1

Beautiful Monster 2

DETECTIVE ERIN BOND

(Adult thriller/mystery)

Lights, Camera, GONE

Write, Edit, KILL

For an updated list of Bella's books, please visit her website: www. bellaforrest.net

Join Bella's VIP email list and you'll be the first to know when new books release. Visit to sign up: www.morebellaforrest.com